# A Day Out of Time

## KELSEY CLIFTON

Original cover art by Miranda Moorhead
http://mirandamoorhead.com

ISBN-13: 978-1-7181-6118-4

*For those who always get back up for more.*

# FOREWORD

I hope that I don't have to tell you guys that this is a work of fiction. I mean, it involves dinosaurs, for God's sake. In New York. That being said, I did try to be as accurate as possible. I put a lot of research and thought into both the history and the theoretical science that's about to blow your mind, and I bothered the hell out of my friends who actually sorta knew what they were talking about. Where possible, I included historical figures and tried to portray them as accurately as possible; where not possible, I just made a bunch of shit up. That's my prerogative. So please, *please* believe me when I say that if I screwed something up, I'm sorry. But dammit Reader, I'm a writer, not a historian/linguist/physicist/zoologist/neurologist/ registered nurse/engineer/biologist/temporal expert/ doctor.

Please be nice to me.

# PROLOGUE
## In Which Gamma Team's Day Gets Complicated

In Cat's professional opinion, things were already going to shit by the time the pteranodon attacked. In theory, the addition of a reptile the same size as a four-year-old child would mean it was time to panic; in reality, it was just another Day at the office.

So when the aforementioned reptile swooped over her head with a soft *whomp* of displaced air, she immediately drew a bead on it with the Peacekeeper and tapped her ear.

"Darwin, what the *hell* is that thing?" Cat asked, watching as the creature wheeled over the shallow water of Azalea Pond, giving everyone a view of its pale, wrinkly underside.

The zoologist's voice, when it came through the bud in her ear, wheezed and sputtered with exertion. "What the hell is *what*, Ca—JESUS FUCK, IS THAT A PTERANODON?"

"I DON'T KNOW, DARWIN," Cat hollered back, "IS IT A *FUCKING* PTERANODON?"

"Commander," the New Kid called, fumbling for the clip to his sidearm. "Um. I think Captain Renault might be getting ready to charge after all."

Cat relaxed from her defensive stance and pushed a thumb against one caffeine-deprived temple. "Specs, what the hell is a pteranodon doing in my city?"

The big man in tactical gear standing beside her wiped sweat from his lips and swallowed. "I don't know, Cat. There's never been any historical evidence for them this far north."

Cat eyed the reptile suspiciously as it landed on a low-hanging branch, panting. "Try telling it that."

"Maybe she's lost," Helix offered, looking over the data on her tablet. She tapped her own ear and said, "Darwin, what period do they come from?"

"How the hell should I know?" Darwin's voice chirped from the open channel. "Where in my job description does it say *paleontologist*? I guess right below where it says *babysitter*, and *trail guide*, and—"

With a tap of her finger, Cat ended the transmission. "Tell your brother that if we survive, he's fired."

"Mm-hm," Helix said, eyes flicking over the screen. "Fired. Got it."

Turning to the man in gleaming greyscale armor behind her, Cat holstered her weapon and said, "Grunt, I want two Dogs on this thing at all times until we can send it home. Everybody else, get ready to move out."

"Yes ma'am," Grunt replied.

"Specs, you're on point with me," Cat said, finger-combing her short blonde hair out of her face. "Let's go talk Captain Renault down before they head north and find Belvedere."

"Cat—Cat, just wait—"

She spun around. "Wait for *what*, Specs? There's a regiment of very confused 18th century Frenchmen holed up in the Ramble, and last time I checked, you're still the only one here who speaks French."

"Cat," he said, holding up his hands, "do you really think they're going to listen to a black man? Or a woman?"

Cat stared at him, taking in the obvious dark walnut tone of his skin, and then with a mini scream of frustration she drew the Peacekeeper again and fired a single round into a nearby rock. Half of it melted into a glowing puddle that blackened the grass like Cajun fried fish. As the silence lengthened, Cat holstered the gun and drummed her fingers on her leg with a sigh.

"Feel better?" Specs asked, raising both eyebrows.

"You know what, I really do." Looking back over her shoulder, she barked, "New Kid, with us. We're going to play a game of Telephone."

"Telephone?" he asked, following the closest of his team members as though tugged along by the very end of a short rope.

Cat glanced back at him as they trekked towards the rougher high ground of the Ramble, where their new friends were headed. "What, they don't have sleepovers wherever you're from? Telephone. I tell Specs, he tells you, you tell Captain Renault. But in French."

"French? Commander, I—I can't speak French."

"*Really?* You *can't?* Oh, well, there goes the whole day. We might as well pack it in now. Specs, tell the twins we're done here, Beta can come deal with the pteranodon. I'm sure they've got a dinosaur expert."

"What the commander means," Specs told the scrambling man, "is that she's going to tell me what to say, I'm going to translate it into French, and then you're going to repeat it to Captain Renault."

"Why me?"

Cat threw a glance over her shoulder. "I'm not touching this one."

Snorting softly, Specs said, "From far enough away, you pass."

"Pass—oh. But wouldn't—wouldn't the others be better?" the New Kid asked, looking at the group of Watchdogs fanned out around him.

"Maybe so," Cat said. "But I want their focus on our surroundings."

"O-okay." Swallowing gamely, the New Kid began following Specs better than the bigger man's own shadow.

Cat didn't blame the kid a bit. Given the choice between

herself and Specs, she would have done the same thing; the historian was twice his commander's size, and a good deal more pleasant.

They came around a copse of trees and there, huddled around a pool at the base of an anemic waterfall, was a pack of animals that didn't require Darwin for identification. A three-quarters blind octogenarian wouldn't have mistaken them.

More dinosaurs. People-sized dinosaurs.

Cat sighed and closed her eyes. "Oh. Fuck. Me."

# TWO DAYS EARLIER

## Cat

The forty-eight-hour countdown to the Day Out of Time had begun approximately thirteen and a half hours earlier, at midnight. Like all seasoned agents, Cat Fiyero could swear that there was some kind of demonic game show clock in the back of her mind, slowly ticking its way towards utter chaos. The resulting tension along her shoulders and jaw made her disinclined to pet-sit, but that was exactly what was about to happen anyway.

The New Kid was cute in a wide-eyed, Labrador puppy kind of way. He glanced around the lobby of the Cirius Trading Company twice, as if to reassure himself that the only other people were the two agents in black, the single security guard hunched over in a misleading slump, and the double row of imposing portraits on the wall behind him. The snarling black dog on his new badge gleamed in the fluorescent lighting like the toy Sheriff stars Cat's brothers had worn in the seventies.

Stepping away from the front desk, he walked blindly past a marble wall chiseled with dozens of names, tucking the badge into his back pocket as he did so. Before it disappeared, Cat could just make out the metallic circle and upside-down L at the bottom of the badge that marked him as hers.

"I have scars older than this kid," Cat grumbled under her breath. Out of the corner of her eye she saw Specs smile, but it could just as easily have been for the benefit of the man-puppy heading their way.

"Commander," the New Kid said, offering Specs his hand. "Kevin Harrison, reporting for duty."

"Christ, I don't have time for this," Cat said, rolling her eyes. "Give him to Hill."

Specs put one hand on her shoulder. Still smiling down at the New Kid, he said, "I'm Lieutenant Forrester, actually. You can call me Specs. This is Commander Fiyero."

The New Kid's brown eyes went wide as he looked at the middle-aged woman in front of him. "Oh—sorry, ma'am."

"*Ha*, not yet. Give it two days and you'll be real sorry." As she led the way through the corridors, Cat glanced back at him and asked, "So are you a chipper or a natural?"

"A—a what?"

"Do you remember the Days naturally, or did they recruit you from some other agency and give you a chip?" Specs clarified.

The New Kid swallowed. "I've always remembered."

Something about his voice worked like water on Cat's tough old hide, and her steps might have slowed down just a bit.

"Did you have anyone to help you?" Specs asked as they came up to the first security checkpoint.

"Uh, no," he told the floor. "I didn't have anyone. It was just me."

"Rough time," Cat admitted. "Hold your badge against the screen, right in the middle of the box." She waited for the New Kid to follow her instructions, and when the screen turned yellow she nudged him aside and pressed her own badge in the same space. Specs copied her, and the screen softened into green.

"Did I do it right?" the New Kid asked as the door opened with a soft beep.

"You did fine," Cat said, leading the way over the pressure pads concealed beneath the tiles. The little group was halfway down the next dull grey corridor before she spoke again. "What did they tell you before punting you down here to me?"

"Um—well they, they sort of explained it, but then my—I guess he's my handler, or my recruiter, I dunno—he started talking about some old calendar made by, by what's his face—"

"The Gregorian calendar," Specs supplied, eyes sparkling as he warmed up to the topic. "The last of the old solar calendars. Introduced to the Western world by Pope Gregory XIII in 1582 and eventually superseded by the Georgian calendar in—"

"Give it a rest, Specs, he can read the Damn Handbook*," Cat said.

The historian *harrumph*-ed. "In 1745," he finished primly, clasping his hands behind his back.

They reached the end of the hall, where a slim panel waited. Cat and Specs showed the New Kid how to peel back the lid over his right eye so the retina scanner could do its job; when this screen flashed its yellow warning, they leaned in as well. The door swooshed open, revealing a circular elevator into which everyone stepped. Cat scanned her badge on a new panel and the elevator began to descend.

"It's all got something to do with—with the extra day, doesn't it?" the New Kid asked, rubbing his eye.

"It has everything to do with it," Specs said. "Basically, when the West transitioned from twelve solar months to thirteen lunar ones, there was a single day left over."

"A day out of time," the New Kid offered. "Yeah, I remember that from school."

"Exactly. This 'day out of time' didn't really fit in anywhere, so the reformers decided to plop it down right in the middle of the year and collectively shrug their shoulders."

"A healthy attitude if I ever saw one," Cat added.

At that moment the elevator finished its descent and began to move laterally. When it stopped at last and the doors opened, the New Kid's mouth fell to somewhere near his knees.

The New York City Doghouse was an impressive one-point-two miles, nearly half the length of the park under which it was buried. A long bank of computers stretched out before them, and a full-sized hospital took up the right side for as far as the eye could see. Men and women in various forms of dress—from jeans and suits to lab coats and tactical uniforms—passed in front of them, generating a soothing level of chatter that made the massive space feel strangely intimate.

Cat tapped the tragus of her right ear, waking up the bud burrowed behind it. "Cat to Gamma officers. Come meet your new playmate."

"Rodger-dodger," Darwin said. "Affirmative. Over and—"

"Out," Cat interrupted. "Helix?"

The younger woman's voice was tense over the connection. "Can't right now, Cat. Playing with the building blocks of life."

"You're officially excused. Millennia?"

"On the way, Captain my Captain!" Millennia said a beat later. "I'm downstairs though, so it's gonna be a minute. What's the four-one-one Cat, is the new guy a babe? He doesn't have a bud yet, does he?"

Cat sighed. "No, but this is still an official channel, Millennia. Which reminds me: If anyone is passing near the Bog, pick him up a seedling, will you?"

"On it," Darwin answered, and Cat cut off the transmission.

"Gamma," the New Kid repeated, rolling the words around in his mouth like a cherry pit with a stubborn bit of fruit still clinging to it. "That's Greek, right?"

Specs eyed the back of his commander's head and coughed. "It's the, ah, third letter of the Greek alphabet."

Technicians twenty yards away and with their backs to the elevator banks shuddered in the sudden basilisk-cold glare emanating from Cat's eyes. The New Kid opened his mouth, looked Cat over, and abruptly came to a decision.

"So what's the Bog?" he asked.

"Botanical Studies," Specs said. "The New York Doghouse has over a dozen sectors in all, each with their own specialists. For example, you can usually find me down in the Historical Archives—fondly called the Sticks by everyone *except* the historians, ahem—"

"Oh come on, Specs, don't be such a *stick* in the mud," Cat said, and the frigid halo around her thawed a bit as she cracked a grin.

The big man cleared his throat. "You're not as funny as you think you are." To the New Kid he added, "A lot of the agents like their little nicknames."

Nodding, the New Kid said, "I noticed. Cat, Specs, Millennia—does anyone go by their real name here?"

"As far as you're concerned, that is my real name," Cat replied, waving a lanky young Indian man over. He had warm brown skin and a shock of black hair that stood straight up from his head, and there was a specimen jar cradled carefully in his left hand.

"This is our animal whisperer, Darwin," Cat said as he approached. "His twin sister Helix is our specialist in really tiny things. Darwin, this is the New Kid. He's not important enough for a real name yet."

"Well, put me down as 'pleased as punch' to meet you," Darwin said, shaking the New Kid's hand with his free one. "And I'm a zoologist, you barbaric gunslinger."

"My bad, Captain Planet," Cat said. "You got the bud?"

Darwin handed the specimen jar over. "Picked it off some new Bravo twat in the elevator. Idiot didn't even feel me."

"I thought you got here a little too fast. Good man." Cat untwisted the lid, revealing a green seedpod no bigger than a pinky nail. It quivered as she picked it up.

"What's that?" the New Kid asked, peering in for a closer look.

Cat let him have a peek, and then held the seedpod against her ear. "Your bud."

"My—my what? What are you doing?"

"Tuning it to the Gamma frequency." Holding it out to him, she said, "Come 'ere."

The New Kid backed away from the innocuous little pod. "Uh, no?"

"It doesn't hurt," she insisted. "Just hold still."

"What the commander means," Darwin explained, "is that we're going to insert this little pod into your ear canal, where it will take root and link you to the Gamma hive mind."

"What *Darwin* means," Specs said, frowning down at the zoologist, "is that they're like plastic ear buds, but organic. We use them to communicate."

"How?" the New Kid asked, looking only slightly less worried. "It's a plant."

"Darwin, you want to take this?" Cat asked. "And that was only a request in the barest sense of the word."

He sighed. "It's a waste of my talent, but fine." To the New Kid he said, "The buds in each group are linked by psychic wavelengths as a defense mechanism. That's what Cat was doing before; she was adjusting your bud so that it can pick up the Gamma signals. We all have them, see?" Darwin turned his head, proving that there was indeed something that looked like a tiny green nodule tucked inside of his right ear. It was only about half the size of the seedpod. "It's really not a big deal, so quit freaking out."

"And they just—they just transmit, right?" the New Kid asked. "They can't, like—make you do stuff."

"Oh, for fuck's sake," Darwin said, rolling his eyes, "this isn't the SyFy channel. We aren't plant people. There is no hive mind. If you're so damn worried about it, there's a whole chapter on Arcturus orbitonia in the Damn Handbook*."

The New Kid inhaled and blew the air out in a slow stream, puffing his cheeks out as he did so. "Okay. Okay, let's do it."

"Remember, don't fidget," Cat warned as she positioned the pod at the opening of his right ear. "It'll tickle, but that's just the bud trying to find her way."

"Right," the New Kid said. His nose wrinkled when the seedpod cracked open and a thin green shoot tentatively poked its way out. It felt around the inside of the New Kid's ear, tripping the sensitive nerves like burglar alarms, until it finally nestled just behind his tragus.

"They prefer dark places," Darwin explained as he took the

empty pod away from Cat. "No, don't rub! Let the poor thing settle in before you go abusing her like that. Now she's dormant at the moment, but all you have to do is tap the skin over her— yeah, right there—once to talk, and once to close the line. This part is important, okay?" Darwin paused until he was sure of the New Kid's undivided attention. "That line will stay open until you tap it again, so unless you just have no personal boundaries—cherish them if you do, 'cause they won't last—for *fuck's sake*, don't forget to turn the bud off. Two taps in a row shuts her down completely so you can't hear or talk to anyone, which is exactly what Cat will do to your skull if we ever have to hear you getting *intimate* with anyone."

"Amazing," the New Kid breathed, his hand unconsciously drifting up again. Cat smacked it away.

"Any more pressing questions?" she asked.

The New Kid turned in a slow circle. "So many."

"Well, Millennia can answer some of them, and Helix can take care of the rest. They're the only ones you haven't met yet." Snapping her fingers, she added, "Oh, and Grunt. Specs, later on, would you take him by the training roo—"

"I'll do it!"

The excited offer came from a red streak that suddenly appeared on the outer rim, bouncing in excitement. In the professional background of white lab coats and black tactical gear, the newest addition was a breath of acrylic-scented air. One side of her head was shaved, exposing olive skin underneath a coat of dark baby down. The rest of her hair had been left shoulder-length and dyed a violent shade of chili-pepper red. Her exposed ear was lined with silver hoops and studs, and a single tiny diamond graced her elegant nose. The grinning mouth underneath it was a soft shade of Washington apple red. Something with long claws was tattooed on the arch of one shoulder, peeking out as if waving hello.

"Speak of the surplus-clad devil," Cat said, clapping the shorter woman on the shoulder. "He's all yours, Millennia. Play nice with your new toy, or they won't send us another one."

"Before you drag him off to your bower, he really does need to meet Grunt," Specs said. "And he'll need to see Helix for his vaccines."

"Got it, *mon muffin petit chaud*," Millennia said.

The smile on the historian's face widened. "It's *petit muffin chaud*. A few more lessons wouldn't kill you."

"Any time, babe." Millennia blew him a kiss and took the New Kid—who still looked a little alarmed by the word "bower"—by the hand. "Come on, handsome. Let's go meet Captain Blue Eyes."

# AN EASTERLY WIND

## The New Kid

By the time Millennia took charge of him, the New Kid had figured out that if he followed along and nodded, he would get answers to most of his immediate questions—including a few that he'd just as soon forget.

Pointing to a line of glass-fronted offices, Millennia said, "The Pound is where you'd usually end up for general training until a department and-or team adopted you, but with the Day so close we could use every pair of hands. It's the building on the left, not to be confused with the Hatbox on the right. That's Tactical and Command, and if anyone catches you trying to bust in by mistake, they'll hang you up by your toes." Shrugging one petite shoulder, she added, "It's all pretty standard procedure; just read the Damn Handbook and you'll be fine."

"Could—everyone keeps talking about this, this handbook," the New Kid said, "but I don't have one."

"Shoot!" Millennia said, slapping her forehead. "We'll dig one up for you, don't worry."

The manic punk continued dragging him past the rows of computer banks— "That's the Hive, bunch 'a *nerds*," she hissed at a young woman sitting in front of a screen full of code, who calmly flipped her the bird in response—and through a large open area full of tables and chairs. Through the decorative wall of various potted plants, the New Kid could make out a ring of innocuous chain restaurants, including a shiny new Starbucks and something with glowing noodles.

They stopped in front of an enormous glass wall that split the space in two. Several pairs of doors appeared every hundred feet, and one enormous set nearly half the height of the wall itself stood unused. Beyond the glass, the New Kid could see rows of sweat-soaked figures in grey sweatpants and tank tops moving silently on thick blue mats. In the distance a massive oval running track hung in mid-air, complete with tiny dots moving along it at a steady pace.

Pointing at the wall, Millennia said, "Alright *bizcochito*, we've got the training area dead ahead and a weapons range behind it. There's a gym in the middle, and that entire right wall is the barracks." She winked at him. "Every Dog gets their own little bed, but you're welcome to bunk with me any time."

When the New Kid just swallowed loudly in response, Millennia shrugged and continued narrating. "These lead to the rest of the Doghouse," she explained, pointing to a second bank of elevators on their left. "There are two levels below us, mostly science departments and storage, but right now we're concerned with the training room. Captain Blue Eyes should still be putting the newbies through their paces."

"Newbies?" the New Kid asked as Millennia led the way through the glass doors. They opened with a smooth *swoosh*, and the air suddenly filled with the sounds of bodies taking and giving hits, accented by the nearly visible smell of sweat. The group to their left stood around a pair of sparing partners, while a row of men and women behind them worked their way through a set of push-ups.

Millennia winked at him. "What, you thought you were Gamma's special new snowflake?"

"No, no I mean—Commander Fiyero said that Captain Blue—that Grunt, Helix, and you were the only ones I hadn't met."

"Grunt and Helix may be the only officers you haven't met,"

Millennia said, leading him further into the room, "but Gamma Team is a lot bigger than just the eight of us. Come on, he likes to hide in the corner like a spider."

The two of them found a white man in his late twenties calling out basic taekwondo forms to a group of ten in the front corner of the training room. His back was to the concrete, and his gaze flicked occasionally to the space beyond the glass wall. He had a solid, athletic build and dirty blond hair an inch or so past military length. Just as Millennia had promised, his steady eyes were quite blue indeed. When a woman near the end fumbled a step, he immediately showed her a better way to place her feet and then continued on with the drills as if nothing had happened.

"Hi lovebug!" Millennia called, waving both hands over her head. When Grunt looked up at her and nodded, she blew him a loud kiss. "I have been trying to make that man blush for four years," she confided to the New Kid. "He's completely immune. I think I could dance naked in front of him, and he would just blink and give me his jacket."

"So you're not, um—you and he don't—" Flushing, the New Kid lapsed into helpless silence rather than continue.

"Oh you are *precious*," Millennia said, clapping her hands in delight. "No, my pet, Grunt and I have never had *the sex*. He does look delicious, but I take the word 'lover' very seriously." Punching him lightly on the shoulder, she said, "So will you quit looking scared? I'm not going to take you to my room and devour you."

The New Kid wilted. "Oh! Okay. Okay, good. I mean, you, you're nice, but I-I-I—"

"Jesus Christ, take a deep breath, okay?" Nodding at the elevators, she said, "Come on, let's go down to the labs. It's much quieter there."

As they crossed through the glass wall, the New Kid cleared his throat and said, "I still don't really understand how, how the Days work. Specs was telling me the history, but he didn't really...explain them."

"That's a better question for me anyway," Millennia said, using her badge on the panel beside the elevator. "I'm the team physicist and temporal expert. Plus I dabble in computer science a bit, but that's more of a hobby. After seven years here, the best explanation I can give you is that time is fucking weird, man."

"That's—that's it?" the New Kid asked as the elevator began its descent. "'Time is weird'?"

"Not just weird, *fucking* weird. You know how the Panama Canal works?"

"Yeah, sure. Kinda."

"Well, think of time like that," Millennia explained. "For humans, our concept of time is a line: One day leads to the next, and each day is separated by locks. No way to go but forward, in sequential order. With me so far?"

"Uh-huh."

"So on one of the Days," she said as the elevator slowed and then stopped, "the locks disappear."

The New Kid followed her out into a small lobby and then towards a clinical corridor. "They disappear?"

"Yup. And it gets weirder." Millennia pulled a Sharpie out of her back pocket and began drawing along her forearm, making the molecule chain tattooed across her knuckles sway. "Okay, picture this kinda crazy, meandering river, right? It switches back and forth, yadda-yadda, but it's still mostly going in one direction. You have to go all the way through it to get from Point A to Point B."

"Right."

She pointed to a thin gap at the bottom of a large loop. "But let's say that there's been a lot of foot traffic right here. People stamping all around it like a bunch 'a cows, ground's gonna get weak, right? So what happens is that a canal forms, linking these two parts that otherwise don't touch." She drew a line across the gap, connecting them. "And *bam!* Instead of it taking a hundred years to get from the Civil War to the swingin' sixties, it only takes seconds."

"And the canal runs both ways," the New Kid said, finally catching on to her roundabout reasoning. "So with no locks keeping the Days apart, and canals popping up all over the place—"

"Exactly!" Millennia said, capping the Sharpie with a triumphant flourish. "Not bad, New Kid."

"But how? Why do the locks disappear?"

"As near as we can tell?" Millennia shrugged and turned right at an intersecting hall. "Because humans think they should."

Frowning, the New Kid said, "Okay, you lost me again."

"Never, ever underestimate the power of human thought, *bizcochito*." She pointed to a glass-paned door, through which the New Kid could see giant computer screens the size of obnoxious TVs. "Prepare to be amazed."

Inside, half a dozen men and women in lab coats or wrinkled plaid shirts sat staring intently at the screens. Each one showed a meteorology map overlaying streets and buildings. Most of the screens were covered in shifting patterns of blue and green, but every now and then the New Kid saw an arc of deep, unsettling purple flash across one part or another.

"Welcome to the Wormhole!" Millennia said proudly.

"The Wormhole?"

She grinned. "Temporal Monitoring. Home of legends."

"Surf Avenue, near the boardwalk," an older African-American man with a short Afro called over his shoulder. He was slowly swirling a pair of smooth green stress balls in one hand.

"Got it," a sandstone-skinned young woman with dark braids replied, marking a tally on a big whiteboard. "Brooklyn Bombers lead with twenty-one."

"Goddamn Coney Island," someone muttered.

The New Kid leaned in. "Wait, are those the boroughs? Why isn't Jersey lit up?"

The man with the Afro snorted. "Not my circus, not my monkeys. They got their own teams."

"What's with the purple lightning?"

"Possible trouble spots," Millennia said. "We started watching them yesterday. In less than two days, some of them will turn into tiny white hurricanes. The Wormhole can radio problems to whichever team has jurisdiction. How many so far for Gamma?"

"Twelve, but one peeks into the Barrio a bit," the young woman with the braids answered. "You and Ramos can fight over that one if you want."

"And deprive Cat of the chance to shoot someone?" Millennia grinned. "Not on your life." Crooking her finger at the New Kid, she led the way to a suite of private offices and ushered him in.

"Wow," he said, turning in a circle so he could see the whole room. Every inch of wall space was covered in canvases: Cityscapes, abstracts, even portraits. They were vibrant and almost alive with a fragile, Impressionistic beauty, though he didn't have the words to explain that this was why he liked them. "These are amazing."

"Thanks," Millennia said, flopping onto a sheet of soft balls that had been pushed up into the loose form of a chair. "If you want, I can make something for you."

"Are you sure?" the New Kid asked, leaning in to take a closer look at one in particular. It showed a dark-haired woman in a red dress, captured in the act of turning her head. "These are really, really good."

"You sound surprised."

Looking around at the paintings, the New Kid rubbed his neck and said, "I just never pictured a scientist being so...you know. Into artsy stuff."

"Don't pigeonhole me," Millennia objected. "I am in love with the whole *universe*, man. And science and art are a lot more connected than you'd think." She patted the space beside her. "Shit, when you get down to a quantum level everything's fucking connected." When the New Kid sat down, she pulled her hair back into a ponytail and said, "Speaking of, we still need to cover the mechanics of the Days. Ready to have your mind blown a little more?"

"I guess?"

"Cool. This is where shit gets crazy, so pay attention." Millennia inhaled dramatically and then said, "So for about a hundred years after they changed the calendar up, everything was fine. People got used to having an extra month, and a random day that didn't have a date. Because they didn't pay too much attention to the days, the days didn't pay too much attention to them. Then in the early 1850's—check the Damn Handbook*, I don't remember the date—a sort of cultural shift started happening, and this semi-religious holiday got turned into a party celebrating the strange and spectacular. And they did it again and again, year after year. They celebrated the day out of time, and after about ten years of the parties growing and spreading, it slowly turned into the first *Day*."

The New Kid frowned. "Okay, but—how? I don't get how parties changed anything."

"Good question," Millennia said. "Let me ask you this: Do cats ever worry about being late?"

Taken aback, the New Kid shook his head and said, "No, I guess not."

"Right. What about birds? Do birds celebrate birthdays? Does a frog know what day of the week it is?"

"No."

Millennia smiled. "When you think about it, the only things that really exist are years and days, and maybe seasons— basically, the motion of the Earth. Hours, weeks, seconds, they're all human inventions. Earth did just fine for billions of years without the concept of time."

"So—you're saying time isn't real?"

"Time is a lie we tell ourselves in order to make sense of the world," the physicist said simply. "And we believe that lie. We believe it with every cell in our bodies, without ever being conscious of it. That level of focus and belief is fucking powerful, man. So when all those people started thinking that this new Day was special and not subject to the normal laws of

19

time, that belief was so strong and repetitive that after a decade of it pounding up against the great Panama Canal of time—a structure that *we* built in the first place—the first lock cracked. Pretty much every weird story or picture you've ever seen can be traced to canal activity."

"Like that guy from Canada? The Time-Traveling Hipster?"

Millennia snorted. "Yeah. Phil. He jumped the wrong rift and was stupid enough to get caught on film, though thank God he wasn't in uniform. Vancouver transferred him right after that, I think. Somewhere nice and low-risk. Not that Canada's really high-risk in the first place."

"He was a Time Dog? What was he doing going into a rift?"

"What, you think rift-jumping just works one way?" Millennia asked with a smirk. "People from our time get caught up too. That's why every sector has a home team and an away team. Gamma defends our turf and coordinates removal slash cleanup, and the away guys—Charlie team—they track schmucks who fall in, because once the Day is over, the locks fall back into place for another year."

The New Kid gulped. "So—so people can get *trapped?*"

"Yup. People *and* things. Where'd you think Nessie came from?"

Just as the New Kid's eyes were about to pop out of his head like overheated grapes, a melodic voice in his ear said, "Helix to the New Kid. Can you hear me?"

The young man jumped and cupped a hand over his ear. "Y—Jesus, yeah. Loud and clear, Helix."

"New Kid? This is Helix, are you there?"

"Tap your ear," Millennia reminded him, not bothering to hide her smile.

"Oh." The New Kid did as he was told, and then said, "Sorry, Helix—this is Kevin. The New Kid."

"Hey there. Cat says you're with Millennia?"

"Yeah, we're in—um—"

"Temporal Monitoring, probably. If you're free, we should really update some of your vaccines before tomorrow. I'm down in the Lamp. That's Molecular Biology and Biochemistry."

"Uh, yeah—I mean I guess, if that's what the commander wants."

"Okay, I'll see you in ten."

As the New Kid ended the transmission, Millennia stood up and stretched as far as her body would go. "You're headed down to the Lamp, right? Come on, I'll walk you out."

"But—Millennia, wait—" The New Kid fumbled his way off the strange seat and into a standing position. "A minute ago we were talking about Nessie. *The* Nessie?"

Millennia's office and the hall outside echoed with her giggling as she opened the door and leaned against the frame for a moment. "You should have seen your face!" she said, wiping at her eyes and gesturing for him to follow her down the hall. "Yeah, as far as we can tell, she's an apex predator from, like, half a million years in the future. Loch Ness is so freaking big we just can't find all the rifts that open, but it's not big enough to hide her all the time and we don't have the tech to deal with her. Most years she gets back alright, but every few Days she gets her scaly ass stuck. Seriously, I wouldn't join the Highland Time Dogs for fuckin' *anything*, man."

Easily matching stride with the petite physicist, the New Kid raised his hand. "Hold up. I have a question. All these people who've seen her, all the stories—do that many people really remember the Days?"

"Nah," Millennia said, shaking her head. "Only point zero-zero-zero-zero-two percent of the world population can remember the days naturally. That's, what, a hundred and forty thousand people? Add in another two hundred and sixty thousand or so chippers like me culled from various agencies and fields, and you've got around four hundred thousand people who remember the Days. That's globally, mind you."

They reached the elevator banks, but the New Kid hesitated. "So why—"

"Will you let me finish? No, most people who see her don't remember, as long as she makes it back home. That's the rule:

Anything that leaves the way it came before the Day is over goes *poof* and disappears like a magic trick. But if it stays?" Millennia tapped a finger on her mouth. "Then it becomes trapped in our part of the Panama Canal. It joins the main timeline for a whole year. That's how you get people who know about the Days, even if they don't remember them."

With that unsettling thought—and with a large, wet lipstick print still gleaming on his tanned cheek—the New Kid found himself released into the elevator, bemused and wondering how in the world he had ended up in this ridiculous place with a plant in his ear.

The panel in front of him dinged, and the doors opened to reveal a woman in a lab coat. She was of medium height, with Indian features, slim glasses perched on a hooked nose, and thick black hair pulled back in a ponytail.

"You must be the New Kid!" she said, offering him her hand. It was rough with new calluses. "I'm Helix. Genetics and molecular biology." Smiling warmly, she dug in the pockets of her lab coat and offered him a package of wipes. "I guess Millennia liked you."

When the New Kid stared at her blankly, she tapped her cheek. "Oh," he said, wiping the lipstick off. "Better?"

"Much. Come on, I'll give you the tour."

Without waiting for his response she turned and began walking, the low *click-click* of her heels echoing across the tiles. "You'll find the biological science departments down here," she said. "Plus storage facilities, archival sectors, and Med Bay C1 and C2."

They took a few short turns down a white-paneled hallway and came out into a great open space. The New Kid blinked up at the massive wall of green in front of him, and muttered, "Whoa."

Helix smiled. "Welcome to the Bog."

The fantastic structure that had entranced the young agent was an eighty-foot-tall tropical snow globe. A wide platform spiraled up from the bottom of the glass dome to the top, and each level was filled with a riot of green occasionally speckled with brighter jewel tones. In the center stood a grove of trees with thick, gnarled roots and branches that nearly brushed the peak of the dome. As he stepped closer in wonder, the New Kid became aware of a light buzzing in his ear. He swatted the air absentmindedly.

"It's the bud," Helix offered. "The mother *Arcturus* is inside. They're calling to each other."

"It's beautiful," the New Kid breathed, trying to look everywhere at once.

"None of the teams have an official botanist—in this part of the world, there usually isn't a need for one—but there are always a dozen or so in the dome. Once this is all over, you should ask for a look around."

Helix took him by the arm and guided him away. As they passed a sterile white building covered in equilateral red crosses, she said, "That's one of the medical bays on this level. There's another one on the opposite side of the Bog, near the Live Storage Unit."

"The Savannah, right?" the New Kid asked. "Could—could I see it too?"

"Darwin should take you through it at some point."

They approached a single door set in a huge blank building, and Helix scanned her badge on the panel beside it. "Lotta security checks," the New Kid joked, but the geneticist just shrugged.

"Due to the sensitive nature of our work, the council insists on several redundant security protocols," she said, pushing the door open when it flashed green. "You'll find panels like this in front of each department, and every agent has a different access pattern. Your badge, for example, would barely get an intruder in the front door."

The New Kid looked down at his badge, which suddenly seemed a lot less important. "Oh."

"Don't worry," she said, turning her head to smile at him as they walked. "Once you're settled in a department, your clearance level will increase. And there are still plenty of places in the Doghouse that I can't get into."

At her gesture, the New Kid turned with her down a hallway. "The Hatbox has one of the highest clearance levels in the Doghouse," she continued, "but even it doesn't beat the inner parts of the Archives."

"The Archives?" he asked, hesitating between steps. "Why would that be at a higher level?"

She glanced over her shoulder. "Because information is the most dangerous thing that passes through here." Gesturing at a stretch of large windows, she said, "This is my lab. Unfortunately, I can't actually take you in, but I can answer any questions you might have."

The New Kid watched two people in lab coats make mysterious circuits of the gleaming room. A woman in a bright purple hijab with large goggles strapped to the top was in the process of unrolling an ornate green and white prayer rug. On the wall in front of her, the New Kid could see a framed child's sketch of a star and a crescent moon. A tall white man with long brown hair was carrying a tray of clean test tubes across the lab.

"I just really—I wanna know one thing," the New Kid said softly. "Why? Can you tell me why this happens? Why me?"

Helix tilted her head and pushed her glasses up the bridge of her nose. "You mean why do naturals like you and me remember the Days when no one else does?"

The New Kid swallowed and nodded. "Yeah."

Opening one of the doors in the row behind her, Helix said, "Why don't we go into my office?"

The New Kid stepped past her into a pristine workspace. Half of the room had been left as a combination office and library, and the other half had been turned into a miniature lab. Out of all the instruments and tools, the only thing the New Kid could identify was a mini-fridge.

"Have a seat," Helix said, pulling a stool out from underneath the workspace. "I thought you might be more comfortable doing this in private. The med bays get pretty crazy this time of year."

"Thanks," he mumbled, settling down on the stool. He placed his hands on his knees and began to turn himself back and forth gently.

"Alright, let's see what we've got here." She withdrew a paperback-sized tablet from the pocket of her lab coat and began scrolling. "Good on tetanus, good on MMR. Looks like you've never had HPV, thank you rural healthcare—but otherwise you're pretty up to date. Let's focus on smallpox, yellow fever, and cholera. If you don't immediately keel over, you can have the 1918 Spanish flu and polio."

"Uh, thanks."

"Any time." She drew a pair of blue gloves out of a box and pulled them on with a faint *snap* of latex. "We'll get you on a regimen for the rest; trust me, you do *not* want to deal with swine flu and space plague side effects at the same time."

He swung himself around just as she opened the mini-fridge. "Hold up, space *plague?*"

"Relax, we haven't seen a case come through in almost a decade," she said, withdrawing a tray of capped tubes. She set the tray down and began picking up tubes and pipettes. "So. You wanted to know why you and I are the way we are."

The New Kid swallowed and swung away. "Yeah."

"Honestly, we still have a lot of work to do on the subject," Helix said with a sigh, "but what we know so far is that it's caused by a dormant mutation in an extremely low percentage of the population."

"A mutation?"

Smiling, she said, "Most of our progress as a species has been based on beneficial mutations, so don't get sized up for that super-suit yet."

"Oh."

"The human brain has a lot of complex ways of handling different types of memories," she continued. "Basically, the memories that are formed on a Day are more dense than normal. We're not completely sure why, but there are a couple of theories bouncing around. You'll find a whole section on it in the Damn Handbook*. I actually co-authored the new edition with a geneticist in Istanbul," she said, winking at him. "Whatever the cause, there don't seem to be enough neural pathways to support the transfer of these denser memories from short-term to long-term storage."

"So what happens to them?" the New Kid asked.

Helix shrugged. "The same thing that happens to everything else that we forget. They just get...lost. But people like us—the naturals—we have, on average, fifty-three percent more neural pathways in our hippocampi. They allow the heavier memories to actually make the transfer."

The New Kid began pushing himself back and forth again. "What about people with chips?"

"The chips do the same thing as the additional pathways," Helix explained, setting the tray beside him. "They act like bridges, so a norm can retain all of his or her memories. Our numbers almost tripled when we started recruiting people like Grunt and Millennia. Before that technology..."

The New Kid winced. "How did they do it all themselves?"

"It was rough." She motioned for him to roll up his sleeve, and then cracked open an alcohol Q-tip and rubbed it across the bare skin of his arm. "You're not gonna pass out on me, are you?"

"No, no," the New Kid said. "I'll be okay."

"Alright, first shot in three—two—one."

The prick of the needle barely registered. Heat flushed along his arm, and Helix withdrew the needle and capped it with a satisfied sound. "Nice job, tough guy. We'll wait about ten minutes before giving you the next one." She twisted the needle off of the syringe and threw it away, along with the gloves. The rest of the tray went back into the fridge.

"Thank you for telling me," the New Kid murmured into the silence, swallowing. "I've wondered about this my whole life. Why I was—why I was different."

"Genetics," Helix said. She opened a purple bandage and

smoothed it along his arm. "It's passed down from parents to offspring, just like any other recessive trait." Grabbing a second stool, she sat down beside him and clasped her hands together. "Does it make you feel better, knowing that it wasn't an act of God?"

The New Kid nodded. "When I was a kid, I thought I was being punished."

"For what?"

He chewed on the inside of his cheek and looked down. "I don't know," he said at last. "For being bad, I guess."

Helix clasped his hand, and when he looked up at her she smiled. "You're in good company then," she said. "We're all a little bad here."

# TINY VALKYRIE 1, EVIL OVERLORD 0

## Cat

Two levels up and five hundred and forty-two feet to the west, Cat was composing a truly spectacular rebuttal to Director Tamiko's proposal. Specs had often told her that she was the only person in the world who could have made pirates blush.

"And *another* thing, you horse-fucking thundertwat," she raged from one end of the conference table. "My team members are not fucking baseball cards for you to trade around."

"Alpha has priority when it comes to resources," Director Tamiko reminded her.

"I don't give a flying *fuck* how many times Haverty's lips are tattooed on your ass," Cat hissed. "He can have Millennia the day she puts in the transfer request herself."

"Commander Fiyero is right," Specs remarked. He was the dark, steady ground to Cat's blonde hurricane. "Barring a demotion, interpersonal issue, or medical recommendation, agents can't be transferred without their consent."

"Thank you, Lieutenant Forrester, I'm aware of the rules." The director sighed and folded his long, elegant fingers under his chin. "I was hoping that you would be more reasonable about this, Cat."

"*Reasonable?*" Cat demanded, slapping her open hand on the conference table. "Those rules are in place just so bullshit like this can't happen. There is no way in hell I'm gonna let Haverty drag my people into his fucking political coups. You and that dancing ass-monkey can go plunder somewhere else."

One of Director Tamiko's perfect black eyebrows lifted. "Another outburst like that, Commander Fiyero, and you will be the one looking for a new team to lead."

Slowly, Cat came to her feet. "Oh, do it. I dare you. I double-fucking-dog-*dare* you to do it. Bump me. Send me to the Bronx, or Astoria, or fucking *Iceland* less than forty-eight hours from a Day."

Director Tamiko pressed his lips together and didn't respond.

"Let's be real here," Cat continued. "You need me right where I am. No one else could manage that incredible, crazy-as-balls herd of cats you created."

"Again, she's right," Specs added delicately. "They would eat another commander alive within hours. I might be able to keep them together for a few weeks, but a lot of my authority—especially over the twins—is rooted in their feelings for Cat."

Glancing over the Gamma commander's shoulder at her silent shadow, Director Tamiko said, "Captain Walker. What are your feelings on the matter?"

"I go where she goes," Grunt replied.

"And that's what you'd be facing if you reassigned her," Specs added. "Mass transfer requests, especially from the officers and Rottie. You'd be lucky to keep half the team intact."

Cat nodded. "As much as it kills you, you know that if you tried to get rid of me, a third of the New York Doghouse and a good portion of the council would come to blows over it."

"Would they, now?"

"Oh, you'd have the fight of your career on your hands. Especially when word got around that you tried to steal my temporal expert and pass her to Alpha like a spoil of war," Cat said, smirking. "So no, Tamiko, you're not going to transfer me away from Gamma. You're not going to bully me until I fall in line. And this next part is especially important, so pay attention."

The director's gaze was steady. "I'm listening."

Bracing her hands on the table, Cat leaned forward. Black ice dripped from her lips with every word. "Millennia is not a resource. She is not a reward for a job well done. She is a person, and she's happy, and I'm ready to go to war with you if it means keeping her that way. Do we understand each other?"

"Completely. That will be all, Commander Fiyero."

With a curt nod, Cat turned and stormed out of the Hatbox with Specs and Grunt at her heels. "I need to hit something," she growled as the other Dogs in the training barracks miraculously moved away. Most of the ones who survived their first year had the sort of fine-tuned instincts that encouraged them to get out of Cat's warpath. "Grunt? Would you oblige a lady?"

"Yes ma'am," the younger officer said in his easy way.

"Excellent. Specs, unless you'd like to team up, you're free to go."

The historian nodded. "Not on your life. I'll see you at dinner." He broke away as his teammates found an empty section of blue mat and began stripping down to tank tops and bare feet.

"How's your Muay Thai?" Cat asked as she stretched. Despite being able to see forty-two if she squinted hard enough, Cat's body was stronger than that of a woman half her age. She bent over in a deep toe touch, reveling in the pull of muscle along bone.

Grunt shrugged and rolled his shoulders. "Good enough. No gloves, though."

"I'll risk it if you will." Raising both of her hands into the basic guard position, Cat grinned at the younger man. "Just be careful of my pretty face."

Another agent might have seen the twitch of Grunt's lips as a sign of amusement, but Cat knew the motion for what it really was. She slid back just as he threw the first of two punches, and interrupted the second one with a swift sidekick to his ribs.

The solid *thunk* of her foot and her sparring partner's accompanying grunt lit up the pleasure centers of Cat's brain faster than sex or food ever could. It was spoiled a bit when he grabbed just under her knee and lifted, sweeping his longer leg against the back of her suddenly off-balance ankle.

Cat hit the mat with an undignified squawk. She immediately sat up, swinging her fist behind Grunt's leg and hitting the knot of muscle at the back of his knee, causing it to buckle. He too fell to the mat, and both officers rolled sideways and came to their feet.

Grunt feinted to one side. When Cat fell for it he kicked the inside of her thigh, and she staggered back with a wince. While she was on the retreat he switched legs and kicked the back of her other thigh once, and then a second time in the same spot. With a snarl Cat turned and slammed a back kick southwest of his solar plexus, causing him to gasp and stumble away.

Panting now, the agents circled each on trembling legs. Cat executed a near-perfect hook kick, but Grunt blocked it and closed in, clasping his bare hands behind her head and trapping her between his powerful forearms. Before she could free herself he aimed three alternating knee strikes just under her ribs, causing starbursts of pain and a worrisome lack of oxygen each time he connected. In the space between the second and third strike Cat thrust her hands up and jabbed at the base of Grunt's throat. He gagged and let her go, blocking about half of the elbow and knife hand strikes intended for his diaphragm.

Cat barely avoided the reverse roundhouse kick that had been meant for her face, ducking at the last moment and sliding in to kick the back of Grunt's thigh and then his side. One fluid motion followed the other, and before he could stop it she turned and hit him with a roundhouse of her own. It landed true, snapping his jaw sideways and planting him quite firmly on the mat.

31

He sagged, admitting defeat, and with a pained moan Cat fell down on her back beside him. "You're a bastard," she wheezed, pressing a hand against her aching sides. "Three? Really? Was that—" A coughing fit interrupted her. "Was that necessary?"

To her pain-fevered brain, Grunt chuckled and mumbled something like "Didn't start it," but that was impossible. Grunt didn't chuckle, and he certainly did not *sass* her. Cat shook her head, and the inconceivable sounds resolved into moaning and groaning much like her own.

"Thought you said—Muay Thai," he panted.

"Changed my mind." Patting his shoulder, Cat said, "Thanks for letting me take my misplaced anger out on you, Grunt. You're still my favorite punching bag."

Grunt slowly pushed himself up on all fours and then to his feet, still breathing hard. He looked down at his commanding officer, the picture of the dutiful soldier once more. "Better me than the director, ma'am."

"*Ha*. You've got that right. Just once though—" Cat sighed and let the young tactical officer pull her up. "Maybe for Christmas this year."

"Maybe." Rolling his shoulders, Grunt said, "Your hook kicks have been too low the last few weeks."

Cat searched her memory. "Son of a bitch. *That's* how you've been blocking them. God, I'm getting old."

Choosing not to reply, Grunt picked up his discarded clothes and nodded to Cat before heading for the barracks, perhaps walking a little more gingerly than usual. Cat accepted a towel from a member of Gamma's tactical squad and mopped the sweat off of her face before collecting her own shirt and shoes. She was surprised to see Specs among the gathered crowd, and even more surprised to see the sand-colored pup at his side.

The New Kid was staring at her with something like incandescent awe. "That—I mean, that was—"

"Even after all these years, I never get tired of watching that," Specs remarked, grinning down at his friend. "What's the score, thirty-two to twenty-seven this year alone?"

"Forty to thirty-two, actually," Cat corrected. "His favor. There was that vacation you took to Normandy in the spring."

Specs's smile widened. "Ah. Let me guess: You celebrated my absence by throwing a two-week temper tantrum, and poor Grunt had to suffer for it."

"Who's suffering? Didn't you see how much fun he was having?" Snorting, Cat reached up and lightly slugged Specs on his well-muscled chest. "And don't talk to your elders like that. I thought you weren't going to stick around?"

Specs glanced down at the New Kid. "Change of plans. I thought I'd see if our newest member needed anything else explained to him."

Cat shrugged. "No skin off my nose. Now, if you gentlemen will excuse me, I smell like the underside of a water buffalo. Pasha at 19:00?"

"See you there," Specs said.

"*Hasta la vista*," she said, putting two fingers against her head and tipping them in his direction. As she walked away, she saw a trim figure waiting for her at the end of the row of mats.

Daniel McNab, Cat's ginger-haired Charlie counterpart, grinned down at her. "You're so darn cute, Cat, I just want to pick you up and put you in my pocket sometimes."

"Don't you have better things to do than asking to be punched in the dick?" Cat asked, turning her nose up at him as she passed. "Like, I don't know, working on your left sidekicks? Or grooming your face-weasel?"

McNab smoothed his mustache. "Has anyone had a talk with you about flies and honey?"

"My work-ordered therapist tried once. If you find him, you can ask him how well that conversation went."

The Charlie commander barked out a laugh and called after her, "Don't ever change, Cat. Not for Tamiko, not for *anybody*."

"Please," she replied, glancing over her shoulder. "If my own mother couldn't get me to behave, what chance do you think Tamiko has?"

# THE BELLY OF THE BEAST

## The New Kid

As Cat walked away, the New Kid finally shook the bedazzlement out of his eyes. "She's amazing."

"They both are," Specs agreed. "Five years ago, Grunt was taking part in a mission with the Navy over in the Middle East when a Day hit. Their influence isn't as strong over there, but the sheer amount of bloody history makes up for it. One minute his Humvee is cruising through open desert, and the next it's surrounded by well over a hundred Persian warriors on the march for Greece."

"No shit?"

"No shit. Everyone around him panicked, but Grunt kept his head and got his unit up into high ground. They were hunkered down on a ridge for six hours before the Baghdad Doghouse could get to them." He motioned towards the glass wall, and the New Kid followed him through a set of doors. "According to their report, the ground was covered in dead Persians, but without any eyewitness accounts it's hard to know how much damage he did on his own."

Glancing around, Specs leaned in closer and said, "I will say this, though: Xerxes's legendary Immortals were more terrified of Grunt than the Humvee or the tanks. The Baghdad Dogs claimed that whenever he walked into sight, they would fall to the ground and call him Verethragna—that's an old name for the Persian god of victory. Even the Dogs were afraid of him, and they've seen some things."

The New Kid swallowed loudly and mirrored the older man's cautious glance around.

"That's what really convinced the council that we needed him on our side," Specs continued at a normal pitch. "With all of the paperwork it took about a month to sort everything out—especially since they had a hard time convincing him how he got all those injuries—but by the end of it, Grunt had a chip in his head and a forever home here in New York."

"As the—the tactical officer?"

"That's his official title, yes, but he also has the rank of captain." Nodding at the grey-clad men and women around them, Specs continued, "The security units that he and the other tactical officers lead are called Watchdogs. There's one unit of about ninety agents assigned to each home and away team, broken up into smaller groups of eight to ten. They're primarily responsible for the physical side of our job."

"Watchdogs," the New Kid mumbled under his breath, raising an eyebrow. "Is that what I'm supposed to be?"

Specs chuckled. "That's up to you. Gamma is fostering you until the Day is over. After that, you'll get to do things properly." Clasping the younger man on the shoulder, Specs said, "Just remember that this isn't a conscription, Kevin. You can join the Watchdogs, or one of the science departments, or the Hive. Or you can walk out that door and never come back. The choice is yours."

"That's not—" Clearing his throat, the New Kid kept his eyes on the ground and tried again. "That's not what it felt like when there was a man in a suit at my door."

Specs's gaze softened even more. "Let's get some food in you, maybe give you some time to relax. You'll need to do a weapons evaluation with Grunt before the end of the day—just so we know that you won't shoot someone in the foot," he soothed when the New Kid looked panicked. "Your file said that you have a license, right?"

"Yeah, but I haven't renewed it in a while," the New Kid said. "My brother—I've got a lot of, of trophies back home. I'm a good shot."

"Then what's the problem?"

The New Kid swallowed. "Just—just Grunt."

His smile turned gentle, and Specs said, "I trust him with my life, if that helps."

The New Kid felt a bit of his tension leak out, thankfully not in the form of urine, and he let Specs lead him forward into the sprawling food court.

"So," he said as they joined a line at the restaurant with the glowing noodle bar. "Helix said that the Archives have the highest clearance level. In the Doghouse, I mean."

Specs sighed in a long-suffering way. "They do. Not for the outer levels; almost any agent can access those. They contain information about the past. The inner levels—Angela, could I get two *ta'kichik* specials and some *pong* juice? Oh, and a water, please," he said to the young woman with cornrows behind the counter, tapping his tragus.

The teenager smiled, showing a gleaming set of braces in her teak face. She gave him a thumbs-up and lifted a small plastic container questioningly.

"Yes, please." He nodded and rubbed his chest in a clockwise motion.

She rang them up without comment. Down the line, an older man with skin like raw chicken dished up a steaming pile of pearlescent blue noodles. There were other trays further down, each filled with a different type or color of noodle. The New Kid saw several varieties of meat and vegetables that he sincerely hoped were only unidentifiable because of the mixed glows. The server made up a second dish and set the tray where the New Kid could reach it.

After dispensing some thick purple drink in a cup and grabbing a plain bottle of water, the teenager reached under the counter and brought out a paper bag. Her hands danced through the air, and she winked at Specs.

"She says it's the last *yama-yama* bun," the older man told them easily. "The next shipment doesn't get in until after the rifts open tomorrow night."

Specs's face lit up with delight, and he touched his chin with both hands, gesturing away twice. "Angela, you are as luminous as the moon."

Shrugging broadly, she grinned and tapped the center of her chest, followed by her right temple. "I know," she told them loudly.

Specs led the way towards an empty table, glancing over his shoulder several times so he could continue talking to the New Kid. "Like I was saying, the inner levels of the Archives contain intel about the future. Everyone picks up a little general knowledge, especially the away teams. It's just a hazard of the job. But the inner Archives consolidate that information."

"What kind of information?" the New Kid asked, setting the tray down carefully. He eyed the noodle bowl, on the lookout for any tentacles that might suddenly reach up and grab him.

"Technology, major world events, that sort of thing," Specs said. "There's some knowledge that we use to benefit our agents, but for the most part, we lock it away until the time is right to release it. Too much foreknowledge risks damaging the timeline, and its preservation is one of our core missions." He glanced down for several seconds, focusing on his food. "Besides. There are some things that you don't want to know about."

"That makes sense, I guess." Taking a deep breath, the New Kid finally screwed up his courage enough to twirl a single glowing strand around his fork. He found, to his absolute shock, that it was delicious. The flavor was close to strong garlic, but that was the end of his ability to compare. It was deep and rich without being overpowering, and he tucked into it with abandon.

"So you like it," Specs said, the heavy pall that had been gathering around him dispelling. "They just use regular udon or soba noodles. It's the spices that make them glow. We import them every Day."

"From where?"

Eying him, Specs said, "From a race of aliens who will one day set up trade with the Fourth Cosmic Empire, of which the Earth is a minor facet."

Chewing slowly, the New Kid lifted a fresh forkful of glowing noodles. "So this—this is really from another planet?"

"It is. Under the light of their resident star, the bacteria of the homeworld evolved with these phosphorescent qualities. Every species, from the tiniest plant to the largest beast, gives off its own light." Specs's eyes went introspective, and his fork slowed down as he spoke. "If I ever make it to retirement, I'm going to see it for myself. They say the whole planet is like being inside a living rainbow."

"What?" the New Kid asked, his fork pausing for the first time. "You can go places?"

"Only after a lifetime of active duty," Specs clarified. "The away teams obviously travel through the rifts to rescue people, but they always have to come back before the Day is over. When an agent retires, they can apply for a year-long sojourn through one of the stable rifts."

"Isn't going through the rifts—dangerous?" the New Kid asked delicately.

"Depending on where you go, it can be very dangerous." The lieutenant cleared his throat and asked, "Are you going to finish that?"

The New Kid, stuffed beyond all good sense, shook his head and pushed the last quarter of his meal towards the much larger man. "So how long have you been with the Dogs?"

"Since I graduated high school," Specs replied, twirling a strand of noodles around his fork. "Well, even before that, I guess; I started working here when I was sixteen, just like Angela. But I've been an agent for eighteen years. CIRIUS prefers to wait until new agents are twenty, but they make exceptions for talented individuals like Millennia or Legacies like

Cat and myself."

"Legacies?"

Wiping the last of the glowing blue sauce off of his plate, Specs said, "Agents who are second generation or beyond. Cat's grandmother and uncle were both Dogs, so that made remembering much easier on her growing up."

"What about you?"

"My ancestor was one of the founders, back in 1874. If you want, there's a whole section about the agency's start in the Damn Handbook."

"So you grew up with this, I guess," the New Kid said.

"It's always run strong in my family. I have two siblings, a mother, and an impossible number of cousins and second cousins spread across the world. My mother is the director of the Paris Doghouse."

"Wow. That's—wow."

Smiling through teeth stained green by the *pong* juice, Specs said, "It's less 'wow' than you'd think. We moved around a lot growing up. If there was an opening for a higher position, no matter where it was in the world, she would apply. And she usually got the job. She's still the youngest person to be made full director of a Doghouse in the agency's history." Tearing the *yama-yama* bun in half, he handed one part to the New Kid and said, "Even after all this time, my mother still has a will like iron."

"Like the commander," the New Kid offered, taking a bite of the soft dough. It tasted like strawberries and pistachios.

"Yes and no," Specs said. "Cat is a fine team leader, probably one of the best in the States, but she's not director material. She doesn't have the political finesse that it takes to run an entire Doghouse and liaise with the rest of the agency. And she has no idea how to back down from a confrontation. She'd rather die swinging."

"Even with Grunt? She didn't look like she was gonna give up."

Specs shook his head and bit into his own half of the bun.

"They're more evenly matched than you'd think. If Grunt had her experience and training, she'd rarely beat him. He's bigger than she is, plain and simple, and he's almost as fast." Chewing thoughtfully for a moment, he swallowed and said, "I take that back. If it ever gets to the point where his experience starts catching up, she'll change the game. Right now she plays by the rules because it suits her, but old age and treachery will overcome youth and skill any day."

The New Kid choked a bit on his bun and took a drink of water, coughing the whole time. "She'll—she'll cheat?"

The look that Specs gave him was infinitely weary. "A lot of the situations we face are life-or-death. Wouldn't you want to cheat too?"

¤ ¤ ¤ ¤ ¤ ¤

Gamma's head Watchdog might not have been a god of victory, but as far as the New Kid was concerned, he was definitely a ghost.

"Ease up on the pull," Grunt said, suddenly looming at the New Kid's side like magic. "It's a hair trigger."

"S-sorry," the New Kid said, trying to calm his racing heart. "My—my family only had old rifles."

Grunt's face moved not an inch from its previous expression. "It's okay. Do it again, and be gentle." His voice carried the remnants of a soft Southern burr, and it played over the New Kid's nerves like a razor over piano wire. He might have gotten over his initial fear quickly, but it still resurfaced every time Grunt appeared near him without warning.

After another half hour of target practice, Grunt cleared him to carry a handgun from Stocks the next day. The New Kid breathed a sigh of relief; it had been good to stand on familiar ground, and even better to prove that he wasn't completely useless. As Grunt led him down the concrete stairs to the ground level, the New Kid felt that strange human compulsion to fill the tactical officer's silence.

"We went on, uh, hunting trips with my grandpa when I was a kid," he said. "Deer mostly, but uh, sometimes turkey or dove. Actually, I never shot anything other than paper. I just liked being outside."

Grunt nodded politely and held the door open so the New Kid could exit first. They walked back into the main training area and maneuvered their way around sweating, lurching bodies to where the Gamma newbies practiced sparring drills.

Leading him a bit to the side, Grunt turned and asked, "Do you know any fighting styles?"

The New Kid shrugged, resigned to uselessness again. "I did wrestling and, and football in high school, but that's it. And that was—four years ago."

"Okay." Grunt lifted his hands in a basic guard and said, "Punch me."

"What?" the New Kid asked, taking a step back. "I can't—I can't do that."

"It's okay. It's part of my job."

The New Kid blew out a breath. "This—this feels like a trap. I can't just *hit* you."

"Yes, you can. I promise you, it's not a trap; I have to make sure you can defend yourself if you get in trouble out there."

The New Kid swallowed. "Okay." He took a deep breath, stepped forward and swung with all his strength at Grunt's face.

With a bare flick, the Watchdog swatted the fist aside, sending the New Kid stumbling forward. When he recovered his balance and turned around, Grunt was facing him as if they hadn't moved at all. "Again," he said. "Don't commit your whole body yet."

The New Kid tried to do as he said, and this time when he threw a punch Grunt grabbed his arm and turned, stopping when the New Kid's body was cradled against his back and the captured limb was immobilized. "In a real fight, I would finish this by throwing you. Got it?"

"Yeah, I got it," the New Kid mumbled, flushing.

Grunt let him go and turned around, crossing his arms in the process. "You've got decent strength going for you, but everything else is sloppy. Those hits might work in a bar fight, but not here."

Heat washed over the New Kid, and he hung his head like a scolded puppy. "Sorry."

Grunt's feet stepped closer, and when the New Kid looked up he didn't see scorn on the officer's face. It looked just the same as it always did. "Nothing to be ashamed of, it's just the truth. We'll work on it. Hit me again."

And so it went. Grunt worked with the New Kid for nearly an hour, patiently explaining moves and breaking them down until he could throw and block a decent punch.

"Very neat," Grunt said finally. "You would've hit a norm with that last one."

"A norm?" the New Kid asked, panting and rotating his sore right arm.

Untouched by sweat, Grunt began walking back to the other Gammas. "It's their word for a regular person. Someone who doesn't remember the Days."

"Like you. I mean, I mean like you used to be. Before— before everything." After a few seconds of silence he carefully asked, "Do you miss it?"

There was the tiniest hitch in Grunt's step. "No."

"But you do miss something."

When the answer came, it was so quiet that the New Kid had to struggle to hear. "There are over two dozen days of my life missing. I want them back."

After a couple of minutes of silence, the New Kid glanced at Grunt again and said, "Sorry. I always thought we—I mean naturals, I guess—I always thought we had it worse, because we had to deal with, with things only we knew. I thought it didn't really matter to other people, because they wouldn't remember anyway. But it—it has to suck. Not knowing what happened, or what you did. I'm sorry for asking about it."

For the first time, Grunt looked over at him as they walked. "It's okay. And thanks."

As they came up on the circle of Watchdogs, the New Kid's steps slowed a fraction. The officer glanced between him and the array of sparring Gammas and added in an undertone, "Most of them joined the agency within the last ten months, and a few are transplants from other teams. Don't put too much pressure on yourself. "

"Oh!" the New Kid exhaled. "Oh good."

A beautiful dark-haired woman smiled at him as he approached and shifted over to make room. He wasn't an expert, but it looked to him like she was wearing full makeup and sporting a ponytail that had been artificially curled. The smell of hairspray flashed past his nose as she turned to face him.

"Ramirez," she said, offering a hand to shake. "Comma Melanie."

"New K—uh, Kevin," the New Kid said. "I'm new."

She smirked. "Yeah, I could see that. You'll get better, don't worry."

"How—how long have you been here?"

"I joined the Dogs three years ago, but I've only been in Gamma a few days. Tell you the truth, I didn't think the transfer would go through in time. I've been requesting Manhattan for *ages*."

In the middle of the circle, Grunt stepped up beside Cat and a tall white man with red-gold hair and a ginger mustache. The blonde commander eyed them all once before speaking.

"I'd like to take this opportunity to officially welcome all of you to Gamma," Cat said. "And to offer my condolences."

A round of nervous chuckles fluttered around the ring in a wave. "This is Daniel McNab, Charlie Team's commander and my less-attractive counterpart," she continued, thumbing over her shoulder at the redheaded man. "You'll be working closely with Charlie from here on out. If Commander McNab gives you an order, I want you to obey him almost half as well as if he were me."

McNab crossed his arms and grinned at them. "And for

once, you'll be able to hear my orders without bending over."

"Congratulations, you have officially reached the end of your usefulness," Cat said, turning to the new recruits and drifting along the inside of the ring. "If you're new to the Watchdogs, there's something I want to make crystal clear about this job: We are not in the Middle Ages. What you've got in your pants is irrelevant to me, unless it's a fifth of tequila. Ramirez, have you got a fifth of tequila in your pants?"

"No ma'am," the new Gamma said, straightening.

"What about you, Hoffsky, any tequila?"

A thick-necked bruiser shook his head. "No ma'am."

"Then it is certainly a shame, but it's not relevant," Cat enunciated. "You will not be given a free pass because of your gender, and I don't want you to give them out. We are Time Dogs, and Time Dogs hit girls. We also hit boys, and mammoths, and World War IV mech-tanks. If there is a crazy woman in a dress coming at you, I expect you to knock her goddamn lights out. The point, kiddos—" Without warning, Cat aimed a blow at Grunt's middle that he used to smoothly flip her over his shoulder. She landed on the mat with a soft *thunk* and craned her head to look back at the stunned audience. "The point," she continued, "is that Time Dogs play for keeps."

Ever the gentleman, Grunt offered Cat his hand. She let him pull her up and clapped him on the back with a smile. "Nice throw. Make sure they practice it." Meeting Melanie's eyes, Cat said, "Ramirez, come show 'em how it's done."

"Yes ma'am," the younger woman replied, taking up a ready position directly in front of the tactical officer. In the seconds before he struck, Melanie couldn't quite stop the edges of her mouth from curling into a smile. She flipped Grunt just as easily as he had done Cat, and he hit the mat with an exaggerated *smack*.

"Nice work," Cat said. "Grunt, you have the floor."

"Pair up," the tactical officer said, accepting Melanie's hand.

Once everyone had practiced on each other until Grunt was satisfied, he called a halt. "We're done for today. I'll see Group

A tomorrow morning at oh-nine-hundred and B at eleven-hundred. You should get your final team assignments at that point. Dismissed."

Everyone else broke away, leaving the New Kid alone with Grunt. "I'll show you to your room," he said, leading the way towards the barracks. "You're welcome to stay here tonight if you want, but once you report to the commander in the morning, you'll be required to stay in the Doghouse or under her direct command until the end of the Day. Do you understand?"

The New Kid nodded. "Yes sir."

"You'll be okay, Agent Harrison," Grunt offered, glancing back at him. "You'll adjust."

"Yeah, sure," the New Kid said. "If I make it out alive."

Grunt nodded. "If you make it out alive."

# HONEYBEE

## Cat

"I like him," Specs announced the moment he sat down. "Well he does fill out those pants in a nice way, but I didn't think you'd notice," Cat remarked, leaning sideways to eye their waiter as he left another table and passed into the kitchen. She hadn't even bothered to open her menu; in fact, the handsome waiter had come ten minutes before and taken her order for both of them, drinks and all.

With any other attitude, she would have looked very out of place in the sumptuously decorated Turkish restaurant full of WASPs. In defiance of CIRIUS policy, she wore the snarling black dog from an old badge on a necklace, and under her black tank top and leggings, the bruises from her match with Grunt were just starting to color. Her second-in-command, on the other hand, was the picture of respectability in his three-piece charcoal suit.

"Kevin," Specs patiently corrected, sipping his wine. "I like Kevin. I think he'll be good for us."

"The New Kid?" Cat asked. When Specs made an affirmative noise through his mouthful of Tempranillo, she shrugged. "I hate putting them in the field so green. I'd rather plant him in the Bog and let him grow for a few months."

"He's not David, Cat."

"David Krevitz was my fault," Cat mumbled, fingers curling around her fork until the metal dug into her palms. "I should've told Tamiko to fuck off. He wasn't ready."

"It wasn't your call," Specs reminded her, "and you've still got your rose-colored glasses on. David got himself killed. He was overconfident—"

"He was a stuck-up little dickhead, and I spent two months wanting to punch him in the throat," Cat said with a sad smile. "See? No glasses here."

"It was still six years ago, Cat. Before Edwin and Marisol, before Jamal, before *Grunt*. Jesus Christ, that man was the best thing to happen to Gamma since you."

Cat rolled her eyes, but Specs pointed a finger at her. "Don't give me that look, Alexa Clementine Fiyero—"

"Jesus *fuck*, I wish I could shoot you for knowing that name," she said, sipping her mojito. "Fucking librarians with your *fucking* records access."

"I remember this team from when I was a kid," Specs continued, as if she hadn't spoken. "It was a madhouse. The Dogs have used it as their dumping ground for years. After the accident, do you really think it surprised me to find myself transferred out of Charlie and into Gamma?"

At that moment their food arrived, and the tense atmosphere dissolved a bit. Cat gratefully dug into her *tavuk adana*, savoring the tastes of coriander and cumin as they bloomed on her tongue.

After a minute or so of flavorful silence, Cat put her fork down and sighed. "I'm sorry. I didn't want to talk about this."

Specs shrugged and cut a thin slice of lamb kebab, taking the time to gently dip it in a puddle of homemade yogurt. "The Days make us introspective. We don't know what's waiting for us, or if we'll make it to the other side."

"You got that right." She took another bite and chewed for a moment. "How's Grace?"

"Unstoppable, like always. It's a national holiday, and she's still going to try to get some work in."

"Henry'll take care of her. He's got the—what's it called again?"

Specs smirked. "Helix calls it Faux-ver. Faux fever."

"That's a terrible name."

"I know," the historian said, laughing. "It's awful. But the thing's damn effective. He's gonna have a bad day if he takes it."

"He'll only use it if she tries to leave. Give him some credit." She gestured around the restaurant. "I don't know if I envy or pity these bastards more."

"Don't tell me you're getting philosophical," Specs said.

"Maybe I am a bit, in my old age."

Specs raised his eyebrows. "Here's a day I never thought I'd see. Does that mean you're ready to be put out to pasture, then?"

Snorting into her glass, Cat said, "Just as soon as you can catch me, hot shot." She observed him in silence for a moment. "You're my better half. You know that, right?"

"I do." Offering his glass in a toast, Specs said, "Here's to Gamma, long may we reign."

Cat clinked her mojito against his wineglass. "Here's to surviving the madness just one more time."

"One day," he said, "that toast is going to retroactively come true."

Shrugging, Cat sipped her drink and said, "I try not to ask too much of the Universe at once."

¤  ¤  ¤  ¤  ¤  ¤

The New Kid was leaning against a wall with a blue duffel bag at his side, watching the people who crossed his path and occasionally shaking a fine tremor out of his hands. He was so focused that he didn't immediately register Cat and Specs's presence until the former snapped her fingers by his ear, causing him to jump.

"Morning, newbie," she said, toweling off her short blonde hair.

Specs shifted his weight, and Cat saw the New Kid's eyes dart down. Like his commander, the historian was dressed in black shorts and a tank top, and though the front of his prosthetic leg was patterned to match his skin tone perfectly, the knee winked up at the world with a large silver eye.

Glancing carefully between the two of them and *not* at the prosthesis, the New Kid swallowed and said, "Good, uh—good workout?"

"Sit-up race," Cat said, twisting the towel and flicking it at Specs's arm. "Monthly tradition. Someone's a sore loser."

"Not as bad as the sore winner," Specs said with a grin. "The sore winner neglects to mention that the sore loser is a foot taller than herself and a hundred pounds heavier."

"With stomach muscles the size of her head," Cat quipped. "Quit whining. New Kid, drop that off and get down to the Savannah; you'll be with Darwin until lunch. He's going to go over contact protocols."

"Okay. Yes ma'am."

The New Kid scurried off, duffel thrown over one shoulder, and as they watched him go Cat shook her head. "Little shit didn't even have the balls to ask."

"You're too sensitive."

"And you're not sensitive enough," Cat argued, slicking her sweat-darkened hair back. "It's a metal leg, not a fucking anaconda. It's not gonna bite him if he looks too closely."

"Cat—" Specs began, but the commander had already turned away. "Come on, Cat. Give the kid a break. He's trying to be polite."

Instead of using her words, Cat grumbled in his general direction and made her way to the Hatbox alone. On the eve of a Day, it was packed with all fifty commanders as well as the director, and the tension inside was like wading through peanut butter. Cat was the last one to enter, and as the automatic doors swooshed open the closest heads turned her way.

Completely unconcerned with the attention, Cat took the open place beside McNab. The Charlie commander bent down to exchange a good-natured shoulder bump with her. "You know you're dripping on the carpet, right?" he asked, scratching the itchy new growth on his mustache as he straightened.

Cat eyed the perfectly groomed Alpha commander directly across from her. "Sorry. Didn't have time to powder my nose."

Seconds later, Director Tamiko looked up from the folder in front of him and made a quick visual circuit of the room. "Is everyone here? Who has eyes on Cat?"

Half the commanders chuckled, including Cat and McNab. "Back here, Tamiko," she called.

"It's no' her fault," Fergus said over the fresh outbreak of laughter. Grinning at Cat through his thick black beard, the Echo commander continued, "Ye lose the wee thing in a closet; dinnae what she does in a crowd."

Cat grinned back. "We've all heard about that wee thing that *you* tend to lose, Fergus. Or so your lady friends tell us."

This was met with a rumble of laughter from most of the room, and nobody laughed harder than Fergus Calhoun. A lot of the cancerous tension bled away like a lanced sore. "Ah, lass," the Scotsman said, wiping his streaming eyes. "If on'y ye were a bit taller, an' a bit softer. Aye, then!"

"You can't handle me right now, Fergus; what makes you think you could handle more of me?"

As Fergus continued to hoot with laughter, Director Tamiko cleared his throat and said, "Enough. We're behind schedule as it is. Hill, what's the status of the Bronx?"

"Light activity," the Epsilon commander reported with a flick of her long brown hair. "Two or three major holes, but nothing we can't handle. Commander Franklin and myself are very confident."

"Yeah, because none of the big holes are in your sectors," an older Korean-American man grumbled.

"Should we be concerned about Zeta, Commander Kim?" Tamiko asked.

Kim's mouth turned down at the corners. "No sir. We'll be okay."

"Good. How does Manhattan stand?"

"Drunkenly, with her high heels in one hand," Cat murmured, and McNab snorted.

"Heavy activity as always, but we don't expect any problems," the Alpha commander reported smoothly. Light from overhead illuminated his coldly aristocratic face as he turned to look directly at Cat. "That is, as long as everyone is feeling up to the challenge."

"Feeling bad because you didn't get a cookie in your lunch today, Haverty?" Cat asked with an exaggerated nod. "I'm sure someone'll trade with you if you ask nicely. Or maybe Mommy could bring you one."

Haverty's hands clenched into fists. "You're a fucking cunt, Cat."

The room, which had been buzzing with low conversation, went grave-quiet. Rather than interfere, Tamiko sat back and looked between the two commanders with impenetrable black eyes.

Cat leaned forward intently, eyes alight. "And you're a childish little shitstain with cow balls where your brains should be." A slow, dangerous smile spread across her face, and in spite of the table and dozens of people between them, Haverty suddenly seemed extraordinarily uncomfortable. "The next time you wanna question Gamma's capabilities, you do it directly to me, in private. Is that understood?"

In the fresh silence that followed, Haverty found himself at the center of everyone's attention. Some of the commanders shifted closer to him, but the rest of the Hatbox seethed.

"Commander Fiyero asked you a question," McNab prompted, crossing his deeply freckled arms.

"Aye," Fergus added softly. "Ye'd best be careful how ye answer, lad."

Haverty's eyes went bright with gagged rage. "I understand," he said at last, bowing to the pressure around him.

"Good," Director Tamiko said. "Now that the question of Gamma's competence has once again been addressed, we can return to our real problems. And Commander Haverty—see me after the meeting."

The rest of the briefing went as smoothly as could be expected with fifty Type A personalities crammed into a too-small room. As everyone except Haverty and the director exited the Hatbox, Cat couldn't resist turning her head and watching the scene that was playing out through the soundproof glass. The dark-haired Alpha commander had come to his feet, and while he didn't seem to be shouting at the director, he was definitely gesturing quite dramatically. Tamiko, as always, was as neutral as his portrait in the lobby upstairs.

"Look at him," Cat muttered. "Cool as a fucking cucumber."

"And why do you think that is, Cat?" McNab asked. "Maybe because all you cowboys come charging in every day, yelling at him. The best way for him to do his job is to let you tire yourselves out until you're ready to be reasonable. Like putting toddlers to bed."

"You know you're one of those toddlers, right?"

McNab grinned. "Unlike you and Haverty, I throw my tantrums in private."

Snorting, Cat said, "Yeah, you'd think he'd know better by now. But I'm more than happy to thrash him any way he wants to take it." She glared up at McNab. "Speaking of thrashing—"

"Cat," he said, the way one might fondly say the name of a cranky tiger, "remember the flies and the honey?"

She raised an eyebrow. "Sorry, let me try again. Gosh, I am so lucky to have such big, strong men like you and Fergus here to defend my honor."

"Well, you just make it so much fun." McNab started cackling as they turned and walked through the Hive. "The look on his face when you mentioned his Mommy—"

Cat grinned. "For fuck's sake, Daniel, he's almost as young as Grunt. He makes it so easy. And what is he going to say about me? That I'm a mean old bitch? Stop the presses."

"That's why he picks on Gamma," McNab said. "You might be invulnerable, Cat, but most of them aren't."

"Jesus Christ, don't I know it. The last few years—" She broke off with a shake of her head. "It doesn't matter. They're my people, and I protect what's mine."

"Easy," McNab soothed. "You know that I'll always have your back. If you ever really go toe-to-toe with Haverty, you'll have most of the Doghouse behind you, no matter who his Mommy is."

The bud in her ear chirped as a channel opened. "Grunt to Cat, what's going on?"

Cat held up her hand and pointed at her ear, and McNab nodded. "Nothing," she said. "Haverty took a shot and I fed him his kneecaps. Daniel and Fergus helped. Kind of."

"No ma'am, not that—something's wrong with the New Kid. I got a message from him, and he was panicking. Is he with you?"

The ground suddenly trembled, and there was a faint sound of impact from far below. Cat froze, and then sprinted for the elevator banks. "He's in the Savannah with Darwin."

"Cat?" McNab asked, following behind.

"*Move!*" she barked at the few agents too slow to clear a path. Slamming her badge on a panel, she typed in the emergency override code. "Grunt, I need you down there *now*."

"Roger that," the Watchdog replied. "I'm in the Batcave. ETA's less than five minutes."

The elevator to her right dinged, and when the door opened Cat leapt inside and shoved a very confused botanist out. She paused long enough to let McNab in, and then ordered the elevator to descend. "Goddammit," she muttered, "please be safe."

# HERE THERE BE MONSTERS

## The New Kid

When Darwin's gangly form appeared in the doorway of the Savannah, the New Kid lifted his hand in greeting. "Morning."

Scowling, the zoologist said, "It's too early for babysitting duty. Come back in an hour with donuts."

"I don't—that's not what the commander said to do."

"*Fine.*" He reached forward and snagged the front of the New Kid's shirt, dragging him in and shutting the door behind them. "So. Newbie. Ever studied biodiversity?"

"Um," the New Kid said. "I mean, I took bio in high school and college."

Darwin rubbed his face. "Let me guess: Business major."

"Um, psychology."

"Typical. Be ready to shit bricks, then."

They stepped all the way inside, and the New Kid caught his first glimpse of the Savannah. If you were to build a reptile house with five levels of double glass enclosures, each twenty feet tall and forty feet long, then you might have something similar to the Savannah. It was almost like being in a great, open warehouse. A little over half of the enclosures were dark, and one entire column had been converted into aquarium tanks. At the base of each column was a pair of railed walkways, one for each stack of enclosures.

Darwin reached over and closed the New Kid's loose jaw. "Welcome to Live Storage. Don't drool on my floor."

"I—I mean—"

"Yeah, yeah, it's fucking incredible. I hope it doesn't need to be said, but don't touch anything." He led the way while the New Kid trailed behind like an obedient puppy. "I'm supposed to go over the *rules of contact* with you, but they basically boil down to one thing: Don't have any goddamn contact. Yeah, most of our territory is in Central Park, so a bit of wildlife is to be expected. But if you find a crocodile the size of a minivan walking around the Lawn, for the love of Christ, tell someone and don't touch it. It's not supposed to be there."

The New Kid nodded, trying to look everywhere at once. "Got it. No touching."

Darwin stopped in front of a double enclosure with a huge marsh built into it, complete with a pool along the closest side. Ripples appeared across both ends of the murky water, and the New Kid leaned in. "What's in here?"

"Wait for it."

Ripples spread out again, and a scaly tail flashed behind the glass. Then the water lurched, and a massive crocodilian heaved itself out of the pool and onto land.

Jumping back, the New Kid covered his mouth and hissed, "Jesus, is that—"

Darwin crossed his arms. "Yep. That is the aforementioned giant crocodile, *tyrannosuchus diabolikós*. We call him the tyracroc."

"Is he—he's not—they're not common, are they?"

"Not since the end of the Cretaceous period, " Darwin said. "In all honesty, we don't get that many prehistoric creatures. The rifts are a human problem, so only a few open up before the 1600s every year. And we could have it a hell of a lot worse."

"Worse—worse how?"

"Worse as in dinosaurs. Go to the New Mexico Doghouse

sometime, you'll shit yourself."

The New Kid watched the tyracroc test the air, his green-and grey-pebbled snout swinging back and forth. "Can—can he see us?"

"That depends on the controller's mood," Darwin said, pointing down the aisle to a squat control booth. "They can change the opacity at will, but they mostly leave it dark. No need to freak the residents out."

A panel opened in the back wall, and a haunch of meat the size of a deer slid out with a bloody flop. The enormous reptile immediately turned his great body and seized the meal with gusto, thrashing his wedge-shaped tail back and forth in excitement.

"So, just to clarify," Darwin said, tapping the glass, "this is one of those things that should make you call someone in a blind panic. Preferably Grunt, and preferably from atop the closest tree."

"I should call Grunt?" the New Kid asked. "Not you?"

Darwin snorted. "I mean, by all means, call me too," he said. "But I'm not going in before Grunt. He's a fucking maniac."

A little gratefully, the New Kid turned away from the raw spectacle and frowned. "He was—I mean, he seemed—"

"Nice? He is, normally. Well, actually he just sorta stands there, but whatever. Point is, you've never seen him fight."

"Yeah I have. He and the commander were fighting yesterday."

Darwin shook his head. "Not like that. He'll kick Cat's ass ten ways to Sunday, but he's not trying to kill her—or keep her from killing him" Pointing at the reptile in front of them, he said, "See that scar on the tyracroc's back?"

Squeamish as he was about the animal's meal, the New Kid obediently leaned forward. After a moment of searching, he spotted a raised lump of flesh a foot long behind the tyracroc's head, nearly camouflaged against the thick slabs of beaded muscle.

"I see it," he said, moving sideways to get a better look.

"What happened?"

"Grunt tried to cut its head off with a goddamn Bowie knife."

The New Kid's eyes widened as he took in the thirty-foot tyracroc, which stood as high as his waist. "Grunt tried to kill *that?*"

"Damn near did it too. The bastard came outta the water and went for Millennia, and Cat jumped in front of her and started firing, but her bullets just sorta imbedded in its hide and pissed it off." Eyes lighting up, Darwin began to pantomime the story. "Then all of a sudden Grunt comes flying in outta nowhere and lands on its back, and he stabs in and jerks to one side, trying to sever the spine, but this thing's got vertebrae the size of small plates. It jerks around and throws him off, and Cat comes running in to save him, but this nasty motherfucker just *wham*—whaps her with its tail. She goes flying through the air, damn near into the water. Broke her arm in two places, she was all scraped up, it was a mess. I thought they were both done for sure, but Grunt must've hit *something* important, because after a few steps it collapsed from blood loss."

By the end of the story, the New Kid's eyes were like saucers. "They—they did that by themselves?"

"Yeah. Grunt wanted to finish the job too, but I wouldn't let him. I mean, look at this thing; when am I ever gonna get a chance to study one of these again? We didn't even know they existed until two years ago. I know he's a brute, but right now he's a *unique* brute." Darwin stared at the tyracroc in absolute rapture for a moment as it worked its way deeper into the gory carcass. Finally tearing his gaze away, he began walking again without looking back. "So yeah, Grunt's a great guy, but he's also bugfuck crazy. Don't ever give him a reason to kill you."

The New Kid's mental threshold for the weird was sorely tested at the next enclosure, which looked for all the world like the Broadway version of a stage apartment. There were even photos of the Manhattan skyline taped behind fake windows.

A paunchy white man in his forties with a receding hairline

and an unassuming face sat in a comfortable armchair on one side, reading the newspaper. He glanced up, gave the New Kid an appraising look, and then raised an eyebrow at the zoologist.

"Mr. Ramachandra, what a pleasure," he said. His voice was wispy, like a particularly delicate librarian, and his eyes were the faded blue of very old denim. "Have you brought me a present to celebrate my imminent release into the wild?"

Darwin made a *tut* sound and put his hands in the pockets of his long khaki shorts. "Come on, Harold. If we let you have your pick of the newbies, eventually they'd stop signing up. Besides, this one's Gamma."

"Ahh, and therefore under the protection of the incomparable Captain Walker," the older man sighed, shrugging. "It's just as well. There's something of a Negro look to this one. I find it distasteful."

Harold set the newspaper on the table beside him and picked up a pack of cigarettes. Shaking one free, he lit it and inhaled slowly. Blowing the smoke out, he watched it dissipate for a moment and then murmured, "I dream about Captain Walker sometimes, you know. Of the things I would do to him."

The hair on the back of the New Kid's neck stood up, but Darwin just shrugged. "That is one hundred percent your funeral, Harold. And frankly, I'm a little hurt. You've only seen Grunt once, and you see me at least a few times a week."

"Ah, but you are entirely too...*exotic* for my tastes, Mr. Ramachandra."

"Your loss. And it's still Dr. Ramachandra."

Exhaling again, Harold asked, "Will you miss me, when they take me away tomorrow?"

"Not even remotely," Darwin said. "I'm hoping they'll turn your tank into a culture chamber for slime molds. Keep with the theme and all."

"Very clever, Mr. Ramachandra. Very clever, and very cutting." He flicked ash into the glass dish on the table beside him. "In spite of your remarks, I believe that I will miss you." His gaze moved back to the New Kid for the first time. "Would you like me to tell 1957 that you said hello, little Negro boy?"

Darwin clapped the New Kid on the shoulder and steered him away. "Always good talking to you, Harold. Rot in hell."

Harold laughed and took another drag from his cigarette. "With pleasure, my boy. With pleasure."

As they walked, the New Kid was mortified to discover that his hands were trembling. When they were beyond the view of the apartment, Darwin pulled him aside and peered into his eyes. "You doin' okay?"

"Yeah. Yeah, I—" He swallowed. "Who was that?"

"Harold Vance Junior. Serial killer from the late fifties with a particular taste for Caucasian men below the age of thirty, hence his really inadvisable fixation on Grunt. Personally, I'm all for letting him have his shot, but Cat said no."

"You keep...*people* in the Savannah too?"

"Only badly behaved ones like Harold." Crossing his arms, the zoologist looked the New Kid in the eye and said, "The most important thing to remember in this place is that there are no rules when it comes to appearance. Not everything with fangs and claws is a monster...and not all the monsters have fangs and claws."

The New Kid nodded slowly. "I'll remember."

"Good. Hey, wanna see some mermaids?"

"I'm sorry, *what?*"

But Darwin had already scampered around the corner towards an entirely new row of enclosures. He stepped onto the railed walkway in front of the second column and waited for the New Kid to catch up before pushing a button on a nearby panel, causing the walkway to ascend. Three levels up, one of the glass tanks had been converted into an aquarium that spilled watery light across the New Kid's awed face.

It had been one thing to be confronted with serial killers from the fifties and ridiculously huge killer crocodiles, but this was in a class all by itself.

There were five mermaids in all, and though none of them had red hair or a seashell bra, there was no mistaking them for anything else. They had light blue skin rather than scales, and storm cloud-colored rosettes that ran from their temples all the way down their sides before spreading out across their lower backs. The human halves blended seamlessly into elongated tails that started thick where their hips should be, grew slender for several feet, and then suddenly flared out into a fin, like bubble gum that had been stretched too thin.

Though they were nipple-less, there was a definite outline of small but firm breasts above taut stomachs and below elegant necks fletched with thick gills. Their hair, which floated gracefully behind them in undulating waves, turned out to be seaweed-like protrusions like those of leafy sea dragons. Flat black eyes contrasted sharply with their otherwise alluring faces.

"How...how?" the New Kid stammered, staring at the closest mermaid with the same terrified fascination that one would give a great white shark circling a diving cage. "What are they?"

"I told you, they're fucking mermaids, though I like the word 'sirens' better. They're the origin of the Greek myth. I mean, not these exact ones, but others like them."

The New Kid swallowed. "So are—are they from another world?"

"Nah, I wish, man." For the first time since they had entered the Savannah, Darwin looked less than excited. "They're from our future. This is something that *we* do."

"I don't understand."

"Genetic engineering. Helix can explain it better, but basically in a few hundred years a bunch of fuckwads decide to play around with Mother Nature. What they come up with, among other things, is a sex slave for the wealthy."

The New Kid's head whipped around. "A *sex slave?*"

"Yeah man, it's fucked up. Their DNA is capable of shifting, and it's triggered by saltwater. As long as they stay submerged they're locked in this form, but as soon as they're on dry land, *bam*—legs and toes and, ah, other bits." Shuddering, he continued, "The idea was to build massive resorts featuring the sirens, so wealthy clients could admire them in the tanks and then choose their favorite for some personal time. Problem was, the scientists in charge got a bit too cheeky, and Mother Nature gave 'em a little love tap to put 'em in their place. They got the cocktail mix wrong and added way too much shark, and nobody noticed until it was too late." Darwin grimaced. "Or...they're *going* to get the cocktail wrong and add too much shark. Fuck tenses, man."

Absolutely sure that he didn't actually want an answer to the question, the New Kid asked, "What happened?"

The zoologist shook his head. "Poor bastards thought the sirens were harmless, if a bit bigger than they expected, so they decided to take 'em for a test run—you know, professional curiosity and all—and found out that most sharks look pretty fucking harmless too, until you're close enough to count the teeth."

"They didn't—they didn't really—"

"Eat anybody? Nah, but they did kill pretty much everybody they could reach. And Jesus *fuck*, they're smart. No voice box, so they don't have a language the way we do, but they're on par with a really conniving ten-year-old psychopath." Darwin framed the sirens with his hands, like they were letters on *Wheel of Fortune*. "So picture a super intelligent great white shark that can grow legs and actually does want to murder you, and you'll have the sirens."

"Shit," the New Kid breathed, staring at the sirens as they spun through the water, sliding around rocky outcroppings and beds of kelp. Well-loved puzzles and games lay scattered across the sandy floor of the enclosure. "How...how long have they been here?

"Almost three years." The zoologist scratched his neck and watched the nearest siren meander closer and closer. "Honestly, we could send them back, but we don't really want to. They're fully mature adults, so at best they've only got two more years left before their DNA becomes unstable, and at least here they're looked after. The Doghouse from their time would probably just get rid of them."

"Get rid of them?"

"Destroy them. Humanely, of course, but still."

The sirens began to play a game of tag, and within minutes the water was a confusing swirl of bubbles and sand. The New Kid swayed slightly, entranced by the sharp flash of fin and the lithe twist of their bodies as they spun and dove, but something nagged at him. With a tightening in his stomach he did a quick head count and realized what it was.

"Hey, Darwin?"

"Yeah?"

"Aren't there supposed to be five?"

"What?" The zoologist's eyes roved around the tank, and he muttered, "Fuck, where's Bernadette?"

The missing siren rose up suddenly from her hiding place behind a cluster of rocks, carrying something long and sharp in her webbed hands.

The New Kid edged closer. "She's not trying to bust out, is she?"

"It's okay," Darwin said, putting one hand on his chest. "The glass is over three feet thick. They'd need a spear made of diamond to even chip it."

The siren's weapon was a large chunk of sharpened rock, not a diamond spear. The problem was that she wasn't heading for the walls at all. She was heading down, towards one corner.

"*Fuck-shit*," Darwin hissed, lifting a gleaming black watch to his mouth and turning the dial. "Dr. Ramachandra to Control, we've got a *big fucking problem* at tank 15-23. Repeat, tank 15-23. The sirens are trying to bust out. Bernadette's got a rock and she's going for the lower left corner."

The watch spit static for a few seconds, and then a woman's voice said, "Copy that, we've got security en route—"

While they were talking, the sirens had split into two teams. A second rock knife had been produced, and they were taking turns hacking at the lower seams of the tank. One siren lifted a bigger rock and then rammed it against the broad base of the first rock, the corded muscles of her arms standing out sharply with every strike.

"They're trying to break the seal and tear the whole wall down," Darwin said, going for the control panel before pausing and speaking into the watch again. "Control, can you raise the walkway one tank down up to our level?"

"Copy that, it's headed your way."

"Bless that unflappable woman, I could kiss her," Darwin muttered as the walkway to their left started to rise. "She's got nerves like solid spider silk. Right, get ready to jump."

"But—but—" the New Kid stammered.

"Look, do you really wanna be on the ground if that thing goes?"

Gulping, the New Kid shook his head.

"Alright, then let's blow this popsicle stand." The zoologist waited until the walkway was on the third level and then backed up. "It's only six feet. You'll be fine."

Unsure if the older man was talking to himself or not, the New Kid watched in mute horror as he took a running leap and landed well on the walkway. Darwin turned and gestured frantically.

*"Come on!"*

The New Kid took a deep breath and ran before he could talk himself out of it. As he leapt there was a temporary sensation of flying, and he yelped in mingled fear and excitement. Fear overrode everything else as he landed far short of the lanky zoologist, pin-wheeling his arms. For one heart-stopping moment his balance faltered—and then a long brown arm shot out and grabbed him by the shirtfront, hauling him to safety.

Breathing raggedly, the New Kid clutched the rail and looked back at the tank for the first time. The sound of the sirens hammering away at their respective corners could be heard even from outside the tank. "I don't—I don't get it," he panted. "Won't it take—take them a while? To cut everything?"

Darwin's dark eyes narrowed as he stared at the sirens. "They don't *need* to cut everything. That glass is twenty-three by forty-two by three. All they have to do is cut enough sealant away on the bottom so that it puts strain on the top, and then let gravity do its thing. That clever, clever bitch," he said, and there was rough admiration in his voice. "A hundred and fifteen *thousand* gallons of water suddenly pressing on the weak point will take care of the rest."

At that moment, the glass enclosure in front of them gave a great groan, and four of the sirens immediately dropped their rocks and dove for cover. Only Bernadette, the largest of them, continued resolutely chipping away at the seams along the bottom.

Bitten by sudden panic, the New Kid reached for his bud and said, "Grunt, Grunt—we're screwed, the wall's gonna go any—"

*CRAAAAAAAAACK.*

When the wall went, it went with gusto. The bottom half creaked loose from its mooring, and water began spewing out. Bernadette turned and swam against the sudden current in short, powerful strokes, and the other sirens were quick to reach out and pull her to safety. Within seconds the wall began to tear up its sides, and the rush turned into a waterfall as the tank emptied. It cascaded over the walkway and crashed down onto the tile below, raising an awful racket.

Darwin went the same sickly shade as stressed coral. "Holy. Fucking. *Shit.*"

The New Kid had covered his ears when the wall tore, inadvertently cutting off the transmission. Now, with his eardrums somewhat cushioned by the muffled filter of muscle and blood and skin, he felt his world shrink down to Darwin's image floating in front of him. The zoologist was in the middle of saying something when his face went slack. The New Kid turned in time to see the entire wall rip free.

As if in slow motion, the massive panel of glass came loose and rode the resulting wave down. It clipped the walkway as it passed, causing the outer railing to crumple and shear away. The New Kid pressed his ears even harder, but he knew before the wall hit that it wouldn't be enough.

**BOOM.**

The whole level trembled, and the rest of the Savannah became a riot of movement as the other occupants proceeded to panic in their enclosures. The New Kid's ears rang like a struck gong. The glass panel forty feet below had cracked apart into a dozen or so huge chunks on impact, and the tiles beneath it were completely shattered. Sand and loops of kelp were strewn everywhere, along with most of the sirens' algae-encrusted puzzles. The smell of saltwater was like a living thing clawing at the back of his throat and nose.

Both Gamma men had stopped breathing. For nearly a minute, the only sound was the slowing trickle of water. Then, just as they heard faint shouting below, the first of the sirens appeared.

Even with fear filling his veins like snowmelt, the New Kid couldn't help his small gasp of awe. It was Bernadette, of course, and her human shape was no less powerful than her aquatic one. She had packed more muscle onto her eight-foot frame, and the same dark rosettes patterned her striking blue skin.

Though shaky on her new legs, she stepped to the edge of the tank and peered out at her suddenly expanded world. There were holes where her ears should have been, and her gills had been slicked shut with some sort of shimmery mucus. The curtain of seaweed-like hair fell in thick ropes down her back, and she pushed it out of the way with web-less fingers in a curiously human gesture. One thing that had stayed the same was the emptiness in her shiny black eyes.

"Fuck me," Darwin whispered. And then, a little louder, "*Fuck me.*" He scrambled for the control panel as Bernadette turned that terrifying gaze on the two men, and with a sharp motion he raised the walkway up to the next level.

The siren's eyes narrowed, and she opened her mouth in a long hiss, revealing a double row of shark's teeth nearly as long as the New Kid's pinkie finger. She might have been more wild than not, but no shark had ever regarded another creature with so much malice.

"Shit," Darwin breathed, visibly shaking as they traveled outside of her range. "Remember when I called them conniving, psychopathic ten year-olds?"

"Uh, yeah?" the New Kid said.

"Let's add vindictive to that list too."

Bernadette watched them ascend, and then looked back inside the enclosure and made a high-pitched clicking sound. Slowly, the remaining sirens made their careful way forward in pairs, one of them stumbling while the steadier partner supported her. When all five were gathered together at the edge, they stepped over the railing and huddled on the walkway.

Leaning down, Bernadette examined the control panel. She cocked her head this way and that, like an inquisitive bird, and then confidently pushed the button beside the downward-facing arrow. The walkway gave a brief lurch and then stilled, so she pressed again and held it.

For the first time, the New Kid looked past the sirens and saw the security team gathered below. Eight men and women in tactical black had their guns trained up at the descending walkway, forming a half-circle in the wreckage of the tank. Glass and sand crunched under their boots, though the largest part of the wall was well behind them.

Bernadette shifted until she was in front of the others, turning her head and clicking at them as the walkway came within twenty feet of the ground.

"What is that shifty bitch up to?" Darwin muttered, running the controls on their own walkway so that it followed the sirens down. To the New Kid's immeasurable relief, Darwin took his finger off the button when they reached the second level, while the sirens continued all the way to the bottom.

As a pack, they shuffled forward and picked their way through the debris of their old life. The closest Dog lifted his pistol a little higher and yelled, "*Get down!*"

Darwin's mouth popped open as all five sirens immediately

obeyed. Bernadette stepped forward and went down on one knee in the sand, and the others followed her lead. As a final show of subjugation, they bowed their heads.

"What are you up to?" the zoologist asked again, frowning furiously.

Though there was still a faint ringing in his ears from when the wall had crashed down, the New Kid was now faintly aware of a second sound: The unmistakable snarl of his new commanding officer.

"*God-fucking-dammit, you two, what the fuck is going on?*"

Shaking his head, Darwin said, "Cat? Cat, where are you?"

When it came again, her voice was strained with hard labor. "About fucking time. Grunt and I are in the Savannah, column thirteen. We see you. *Stay put.*"

"You better hurry, Cat, because I don't like this. It's too easy." He peered down at the sirens, taking note of their splayed hands buried in the watery sand. "Is it my imagination," he muttered, "or—"

"Hey, are their fingers webbed again?" the New Kid asked.

"Holy fuck," Darwin breathed as two things happened almost simultaneously. The three tactical officers in the center of the half-circle took two steps forward, and Bernadette's hands clenched. "Holy fuck *the sand!*" he screamed.

He was too late by far. As the Gammas watched in horror, the sirens scooped up sand and flung it at the faces of the security team in one lightning-fast movement. The line collapsed as they all cried out and rubbed furiously at their faces, and in the chaos the sirens struck.

Bernadette took down the middle Dog like a linebacker and clamped down on his shoulder, biting through the Kevlar and crushing the bone underneath. Blood soaked into the sand beneath him as he screamed and thrashed against her superior weight, trying to reach his gun.

The other agents fared better. Though much larger than any human, the sirens were unsteady on their feet and uncoordinated in their attack. By comparison, the members of the security team worked together with the ease of long practice. Two or three of them stood in front, yelling and blindly waving their arms in an attempt to keep the sirens at bay while the others huddled behind them and desperately tried to clear their eyes.

"Oh my God," the New Kid said, frozen except for the litany that poured out of him as fervently as the water had fallen from the shattered tank. "Oh my God, oh my God, oh my God. We have to do something."

"Like *what?*" Darwin demanded, hands fisted uselessly in his hair as he looked back and forth between the Dogs.

The New Kid looked down at himself and reached down for the laces of his sneakers. He fumbled at them for a subjective decade, finally yanking the first off. He leaned over the side and flung it at Bernadette, missing her by a good two feet.

"H-hey," he called, kneeling again. The second shoe came off easier, and thumped solidly against the siren's broad back. "*Hey!*"

She whirled around and hissed up at him, eyes like empty pits. He began to tremble as she slowly rose to her feet and approached the raised walkway. "Oh fuck."

"Nice job, hero," Darwin muttered, kicking his own shoes off and flinging them at her. She dodged both with ease and offered them a slow smile in return.

Then Grunt and Cat came tearing into view, and the whole game changed.

"*Hit the deck!*" Cat bellowed, and the Dogs obeyed instantly.

Silver streaked through the air as Grunt hurled two stilettos at the closest siren. The first caught in the thick mass of her hair, but the second buried itself hilt-deep in her throat. Jerking back, she let out a choked shriek and clutched at the blade. Her companion turned to the new threat in a turbulent rage, mouth open and jagged teeth gleaming in the light.

She only had time to take a single step before Grunt hit the sand in a smooth roll and Cat appeared behind him, gun drawn. Two shots rang out, and two perfect holes appeared in the siren's forehead, stopping her short. Blood poured out, black against the blue of her skin. Her face went slack as she fell to her knees and then pitched forward. By the time she landed, Cat was already moving on. Grunt finished off the first siren with one quick slash.

The furious pair had bought the agents in back enough time to recover their sight. They came up to their knees and took down two of the remaining sirens through their reddened and blurry vision while their teammates stayed flat on the marshy tile. This just left Bernadette, who had turned towards Grunt with a whistling shriek. Trading the gun for a corded blade around her neck, Cat grabbed the siren by the hair and yanked back, baring and slitting her throat in almost the same instant. Blood sprayed out in a gruesome arc, and Cat shoved her aside.

Bernadette landed on her back, gasping and clawing at the cut on her neck even as Cat tore off her shirt and knelt to press it against the fallen agent's gushing wounds. The siren never took her eyes off the commander, whom she could have cradled in her arms like an older child.

Grunt did a quick visual circuit of the room, letting his eyes trace up to where Darwin and the New Kid were perched. "They're safe," he told Cat.

"Thank God. Where's that fucking med team?"

The med team in question arrived a few seconds later, guarded by Daniel McNab. Cat stood aside as most of them gathered around the injured agent, injecting him with all manner of things. From his improvised crow's nest, the New Kid could see the shallow rise and fall of the agent's breathing and the sickly white shade of his skin, not to mention the glistening hamburger meat where his shoulder should have been.

While the rest of the med team was occupied, the two remaining technicians tended to the others, rinsing out eyes with saline solution and bandaging wounds. There had been injuries, but only bruises, cuts, and one missing finger. Though both Cat and Grunt were covered in blood-encrusted sand, neither of them had been injured in the slightest.

The New Kid swallowed. "Darwin. Darwin, I think we can go down now."

The zoologist continued staring—not at the injured agents, but at the still blue bodies of the sirens. Even Bernadette's chest had long since stopped moving.

"Alright, get him outta here," the lead nurse said from below, coming to her feet. The team had lifted the agent onto a lightweight stretcher, and now that he was stable they picked him up and carried him towards the closest exit. "You, you, *definitely* you—screw it, all of you report to a med bay within an hour. If I check your files and don't find notes and a clean bill of health, heads will roll. That means you too, Commander," she ordered fiercely. "I will lock you out of duty so fast it'll make your head spin. That is, if it's still attached."

Cracking a weak smile, Cat nodded at the matronly woman and said, "Wouldn't dream of it, Greta."

"You'd better not." Without looking back, she herded the injured security team out like a dog with lost sheep.

Swallowing, the New Kid reached past Darwin and pressed the down button. Cat's head turned at the sound of the walkway's motor, and she met them at the bottom, retrieving their shoes on the way. Though she clasped the New Kid's shoulder warmly, she left the zoologist alone. He still hadn't looked away from the vibrant carnage.

"I'm sorry it had to be this way," she murmured. "There wasn't time."

"I know," Darwin said, blinking furiously. "I know, it's just—" He broke off and swallowed a few times before bending over and stepping into his untied shoes. "It's just such a waste. They were safe, and now they're—"

"*Jai!*"

The cry came from behind Cat, and when she moved the New Kid saw Helix running through the Savannah, her heels left behind.

"Helix, don't—" Cat began, but Darwin ran out over the sand and glass and met his twin before she could cut her bare feet. She slipped a bit on the wet tile, and they crashed together in a tangle of limbs, knocking her glasses askew. Darwin lifted her up in a bear hug and then set her back down, burying his face in the crook of her neck while she clutched his back with hard fingers.

Cat nodded and looked back at the New Kid. He tried to focus on his commander, but like Darwin, his eyes were drawn instead to Bernadette. She was captivating even in death, and he felt the loss of her and her sisters as an acute ache in his gut.

"Talk to me, New Kid," Cat said, turning his chin to look at her. "Let me know you're okay."

He took a deep breath and let it out. "I'm—I'm okay. Sad and scared, but okay." His eyes cut back to the siren, and he sighed. "It's not fair. They just—they wanted to be free, and I know why they couldn't be, and, and I know why we had to stop them. I know it, but..."

"But it still hurts. Bit of advice?" Cat asked. "Let it hurt. The day you stop hurting is the day you stop being human." Tapping her ear, she said, "Cat to Gamma officers. Team meeting in Camelot, half an hour. No exceptions." She cut off the transmission before anyone could chime in with questions or complaints.

Grunt stepped up beside her. "Commander, I should get back down to the Batcave as soon as possible."

"Of course," Cat said with a wave of her hand. "Of course you're excused. They're doing the final fitting for the new gear, right?

"Yes ma'am."

Smiling up at her tactical officer, Cat said, "Go on, I'll see you tonight. Oh, here—" She took the gun that had been used to kill the second siren out of the back of her shorts and passed it over, along with the sheathed knife on its cord. "Thanks for the loans."

"No problem, ma'am. Do you want my shirt?"

Cat glanced down and seemed to register the fact that she was standing around in nothing but blood-soaked gym shorts and a formerly white sports bra. Shrugging, she said, "Thanks, but they've seen me like this before. I'll clean up at the decon showers and borrow some scrubs before the meeting." She pointed at the New Kid and said, "Camelot, twenty-eight minutes. Don't forget your shoes."

"Camelot?" he asked.

"The food court," she called over one shoulder, gingerly picking her way through the wreckage.

"Ah." For the first time since the wall had come down, the New Kid really took the time to look around and assess the damage. Water had pooled inside little dips in the churned and bloody sand, creating a chain of lakes among barren black mountains and seaweed forests. Beyond the reach of the sandbar, the water spread in a gleaming mirror in every direction. Clean-up crews had already begun to arrive, assessing the edges of the disaster zone in resigned despair.

In the sudden absence of adrenaline, exhaustion rolled over the New Kid like a riptide, and he rubbed his eyes. "Thanks, Grunt."

The officer nodded, blue eyes as steady as ever.

"See you later, I guess," the New Kid said, carefully following in Cat's footsteps. It was the silliest thing, but he tried not to get his feet wet.

◘　◘　◘　◘　◘　◘

"—and then Cat and Grunt came in and saved everyone's bacon," Darwin finished, tearing his second soft taco to pieces. The first was already a shredded pile of tortilla, beans, and cheese, and his fingers were a slick mess. His face and napkin, by comparison, were spotless.

Cat snorted at the description, but didn't elaborate. "You two bought us time."

"Yeah," Darwin muttered. "Captain Sneaker and Shoe Man. The great heroes of the Savannah."

"Well, I personally saw Sneaks over here save Peterson's

life," Cat pointed out. "Word from Greta is that he's gonna pull through. He's missing a huge chunk of his shoulder, but it's better than a memorial and a grieving fiancé."

"They'll retire him and Marcus to some nice, quiet island with a lot of coconuts," Millennia said, shifting closer and laying her head on Darwin's shoulder. "I'm glad you two are okay."

Helix was silent, but her hand hadn't left the crook of her brother's arm. The mood of the table was one of subdued relief, flavored subtly with melancholy and bone-deep exhaustion. The New Kid had nearly fallen asleep in his shower, and even now his head bobbed on his neck like a drunken ostrich.

Cat slurped up the last of her pad thai and set the empty carton down on the table with a sigh. "Christ, I needed that. Are we good on prep for tomorrow?"

There was a chorus of affirmatives, and Helix stirred from her quiet stupor. "I—" Her voice croaked, and she took a sip of her water before trying again. "I still need to requisition a few things from medical. And I want to give everyone's files one more look, make sure I didn't miss anything. I was going through Travis's old entries when...when I got the call."

Nodding, Cat said, "Okay. Everybody take the next couple of hours to unwind. Get a massage, go for a run, get laid. Heads on pillows no later than 14:00. I want you all gathered at the meet point by 22:00. I'll get grumpy if you make me hunt you down."

Everyone nodded their agreement except for Helix. She had pulled a tablet out of her bag and was flicking through it, occasionally mumbling to herself and making notes.

Millennia tipped her head towards a curly-haired Adonis with tan, sculpted shoulders who was hovering too casually by a nearby potted tree. "Incoming Alpha attack," she muttered with a grimace.

Sure enough, the Adonis strolled up to the Gammas, hands tucked in his pockets and a smirk on his brutish, too-handsome face. "Yo Gamma-Gammas! How goes it on the Island of Misfit Toys?" he asked, leaning his hip comfortably against the table.

"I have a question, Oscar Wilde," Helix said without looking up from her tablet. "Did you practice that line all the way over here—"

"Or did it just occur to you naturally, like your Cro-Magnon forehead?" her twin finished, perking up and actually scooping a bite of taco into his mouth.

"This isn't a good time," Specs advised in his gentle way. "You should probably move on."

"Come back if you grow a personality," Millennia said, wiggling her fingers at him in a flippant wave. "Bye now."

They all looked at the New Kid expectantly, and he shrugged with utterly unfeigned nonchalance. "I almost got eaten by killer mermaids today," he said. "This is kittens and rainbows compared to that. But yeah, fuck off anyway."

Cat stole a Snickers from the pile of candy in front of Specs and looked up at the reddening Alpha matter-of-factly. "You heard them. Get the fuck out of my sight before I kick your balls up into your windpipe."

He opened his mouth to retort, and then closed it. Choosing instead to shrug his shoulders as if it didn't matter to him either way, the Alpha beat a hasty retreat with his tail hung low in defeat.

"God, I hate them," Darwin said, shoving cold taco pieces into his mouth. "If I could just lock them all in a room with a stick of dynamite, that'd be great."

"Tara and Neriah aren't so bad," Helix said. "You just have to catch them away from the others."

Her brother snorted. "Give them a few years. They'll have gone native by then."

"Neriah," Millennia mused. "That's the cute one with the lip piercing, right?"

The New Kid's head began drifting downward again, and he felt a firm poke in his shoulder. "Go to bed, kid," Cat told him. "Set your alarm for 9:00 p.m. and get ready to work."

"Mm-hm. Work. 9:00." Blinking sleepily, the New Kid got to

his feet and stretched with a jaw-cracking yawn. "Night everybody."

Their farewells trailed behind him as he left the food court and headed in what he thought was the direction of the barracks. After several minutes of wandering, however, it became clear to the New Kid that he'd gotten turned around somehow. He was about to pick a new direction and try again when he heard the sounds of a mat being struck over and over with distinctive speed and viciousness. Curious, he followed the sound and found a door that had not been closed as effectively as it could have been. Peering in through an opening as wide as his head, the New Kid stared in awe at the scene within.

Grunt was in shorts and a thin tank top, the scarred muscles of his back pulled taut with each hard breath. He stood in a guard position, surrounded by a trio of training bags secured to the floor and ceiling with heavy chains. As the New Kid watched, Grunt released his breath in a long, slow exhalation, and then exploded into movement.

Bags swung from side to side as he thrashed them, delivering kicks and punches that would have sent opponents to the floor. For that matter, they might have taken down mammoths or mech-tanks as well. The chains clanked ominously, but Grunt seemed completely deaf to the sound as he moved from one punch to another with animalistic grace. One bag in particular seemed to spur his aggression, and he fell on it with relentless energy that left the New Kid gulping back amazement and not a little fear.

Grunt arched into a high spinning kick, striking the offending bag one more time. When he landed, he paused long enough to wipe the sweat from his eyes before asking, "Can I help you with something, Agent Harrison?"

Until that moment, the New Kid hadn't known that he'd been made, and to his exhaustion-and-weird overloaded brain, Grunt was like a superhero. "Um, I was just watching," he managed to slur, straightening and daring to step a little further into the room. "Sorry. Got lost. You're really good."

Grunt turned to face the New Kid, his careful breathing the only sound. "Thank you."

The New Kid opened his mouth, closed it, and then opened it again when the last of his inhibitions caved. "You're mad about something. Wanna talk?"

The Watchdog cocked his head, and the New Kid hurried to say, "I figure, if you just wanted to practice, you'd go out with the others so you could help if they needed it, 'cause that's just how you are. But you didn't." Gesturing around, he continued, "You came in here, alone. And I think you did it because you're upset about something, and you didn't want them to see you like this."

During his speech, Grunt's wrapped hands had tightened reflexively, making the tape creak. He forced them to relax now. "It's nothing."

"You sure? I swear, whatever it is, secret dies with me." Ice settled in his gut, and he added, "Please don't kill me though, I can keep it on my own."

Grunt's nostrils flared, but he just picked up a towel from a pile of workout gear and used it to wipe himself off. "I get why you'd be worried. But I hope one day I can show you that as long as you do right by my team, you never have to be afraid of me." Hooking the towel around his shoulders, he added, "Have a good evening, Agent Harrison."

The New Kid knew his exit line when he heard it. With a sloppy salute, he eased the door closed and released the breath that had been locked inside of his chest, right around his thundering heart.

# A WORLD OF DIFFERENCE

## Cat

Elsewhere in the Doghouse, agents from all divisions and teams were either frantically finishing one last project or settling down comfortably, depending on their years of experience. Slowly, the Hive and the Hatbox petered down to nothing but a skeleton crew, and the gym emptied except for one senior Dog. Sweat had molded her short hair into a sleek cap, and she was rhythmically punching a training dummy with the sort of deep, meditative focus normally reserved for a Siddha of the highest order. In fact, she had long since passed the need for active thought at all.

As she paused to drink from a sports bottle, a deep voice from behind her said, "Want me to hold that for you?"

Cat turned and raised her eyebrows at Chris Haverty. He stood with his arms crossed in front of his impressive chest, as handsome and unreadable as ever.

"Shouldn't you be entertaining Hill?" Cat asked, taking another drink. "She's gonna get awfully lonely without you."

"Robin's perfectly capable of entertaining herself for a while," Haverty said. He stepped behind the training dummy and braced himself against it. "When you're ready."

Cat wiped her forehead and settled back. She whipped her leg around in the same roundhouse kick that had taken Grunt down the day before. "Is this your way of—making nice?"

"Yeah," he said. "Tamiko and I had a talk earlier about my loyalties. He wants this feud to end."

"He's not—the only one." She switched sides and started again. "So why don't—you tell me—what's bothering you?"

A faint smile tugged at his mouth. "Get it all out in the open, you mean? Fine. I think your team is reckless. I think they're an unprofessional disgrace, and I think they're gonna get themselves or someone else hurt. My people maybe, or a bunch of unsuspecting norms." Shrugging, he added, "You and I both know it's just a matter of time."

Cat closed her eyes and took a deep breath, drawing energy in. "They're doing the best they can," she said.

"They're unstable. The only one who's salvageable—other than Walker—is Millennia. All she needs is a bit of reining in."

"Ahh," Cat said, drawing the sound out with her exhale. Her eyes opened, and she began striking the bag with the blade of her hand. "So that's why you want her."

"She's brilliant, Cat," Haverty said, his hazel eyes completely sincere. "If she had been born fifty years ago, she might have pioneered her entire field. She belongs in Alpha, where she can do the most good."

The tempo of Cat's strikes never faltered. "You have a temporal expert."

"Veronique is good," he admitted. "Millennia's better."

"And only the best for a councilor's son, right?"

Haverty's face pinched in slightly. "My mother has nothing to do with this. And I'd appreciate it if you'd stop bringing her up every time you want to win an argument."

Cat shook the sweat from her face and reached for the sports bottle. "Funny. I'd appreciate it if you'd stop taking potshots at my team."

"Cat, I'm trying to be an adult about this," Haverty said, coming out from around the bag. "That's more than you're doing."

"You're being a little weasel," Cat corrected. "Going behind everyone's back to get Millennia transferred. She's *happy*, Chris. You know that brilliance you admire so much? What do you think's gonna happen to it if you stuff her into a little eight-by-eight box? How's she gonna react?" Shaking her head, Cat capped the water again. "She'll dry up faster than an old maid's cooch."

In spite of himself, Haverty snorted. "Colorful yet effective. Personally, I think she's more adaptable than you give her credit for."

"Oh, she's highly adaptable. You just have to give her room to breathe." Leaning down in a deep toe-touch, Cat exhaled slowly. "That's the trick with all of them, Chris. Enough freedom so they can shine, but not so much that they'll get in trouble."

Crossing his arms, Haverty said, "They need discipline. I'd expect someone with your experience to know that."

Slowly, Cat rolled up. She braced her legs and leaned to the left, stretching the muscles along her side. "They need to be beaten into submission, is what you're saying."

"If that's what it takes to guarantee loyalty and obedience, then yes."

Cat leaned to the right for a moment, and then came to a standing position again. She looked up at Haverty with something like pity. "There's a world of difference between someone following you because they trust you, and because you've broken them."

"I haven't *broken* my team," the Alpha commander said, heat toasting his words from the inside. "They just know how to obey orders. They know what's at stake if they fuck up." He came closer, stopping only a foot from her. "People's lives, Cat. That's what we're talking about."

"Is this supposed to be news to me?" Cat asked.

"You act like it is." Haverty rubbed his eyes and sighed. "Look, I'm just trying to do what's best for my team and my city."

"Then stay out of Gamma's business," Cat said, slinging the

towel around her neck. "And keep your hands to yourself." She picked up her gym bag and left him in the workout area, with only the dummy for company. At the edge, she turned her head and said over one shoulder, "Thanks for the help. And good luck."

His laugh was short and brutal, like the downswing of a hammer. "Anytime, Cat. Good luck."

# CALL SIGNS

## The New Kid

When the pleasant chime of the New Kid's phone alarm began to ring, he rolled over groggily and turned it off without giving the time much thought. 9:00 was later than he usually got up, but if he showered immediately and caught the N train, he could still make it to Tia Dora's before they ran out of *crema* cakes—

The sudden memory of a waterfall made of glass, sand, and saltwater rushed through his mind, and the New Kid bolted up, double-checking the time and date. It was indeed 9:02 p.m., with two hours and fifty-eight minutes left until the Day Out of Time. He should have been preparing, not sleeping in a strange bed.

Stumbling to his feet, he used the bathroom attached to his bunk to shower until the cobwebs in his brain were all washed down the drain. Knotting a towel firmly around his waist, the New Kid dug through his duffel bag until he came up with a set of thin cotton sweatpants and a dark t-shirt of some indeterminate color. Once he was dressed, he tentatively activated the bud in his ear.

"Um, New Kid to Commander Fiyero?"

After a second, Cat's voice answered. "Hey there, sunshine. Had your Wheaties yet?"

"Oh, uh—"

"It's a joke, kid. Relax. You ready to move out?"

The New Kid swallowed and stepped into his sneakers. "Yeah, yeah, I just have to—"

"That one was a trick question, precious. You still have to gear up in the Batcave. That's R&D, second level. Get down there and grab your new toys, then scoot back up to the weapons lockers. Did Grunt show them to you?"

Trying to tie his shoes in midair was a mistake, which the New Kid discovered when he lost his balance and nearly toppled back into bed. "Uh—yeah. Yeah. Top level of the range?"

"Bingo. Be there by 22:00."

The New Kid started to agree, but Cat was already gone. He finished lacing up his shoes properly and tucked his badge in a pocket, flicking his eyes around the sparse room the entire time.

The ride down to the second level was so cramped that he found himself squished between the wall and a rather buxom older black woman. When the doors opened, he squeezed past and looked around the new floor in confusion. "Um, the Batcave?" he asked, turning back to the older agent.

"That way," she said, pointing to the left at a white building that easily took up half of the level. Most of the men and women that he saw seemed to either originate from the building or be destined for it.

The New Kid tried to thank the agent, but the elevator door had already closed. When he approached the door to the Batcave and scanned his badge, there was a faint chime as the screen turned yellow.

*WARNING*, it read, *PLEASE WAIT FOR ESCORT.*

After a few minutes, a portly dwarf with awful sideburns and only half of one eyebrow opened the door and peered out. "Agent Harrison?" he asked.

The New Kid nodded and nervously flashed his badge.

"Come on in," he said, holding the door open. "Mind the rocket launcher."

"Mind the—oh," the New Kid said, hopping sideways to avoid the gleaming black weapon propped up by the door. He fell against the inner doorframe and froze in awe.

The Batcave was like an airport hangar, if they ever housed rows of mini-Transformers and precision robotic arms and what looked like a pair of fighter jets at the far end. He couldn't even begin to fathom what he was seeing, only that it all looked like something that belonged in a super villain's lair.

"You'll want Sia," the dwarf said, pointing to one side. "She's in charge of newbies." Without any further directions, he hefted the oversized launcher over one thick shoulder and waddled off.

Following the man's finger, the New Kid turned to the left and saw a slender woman sitting behind a long table stacked with black clothing and assorted pieces of Kevlar and Nylon. She looked to be in her early thirties, with doll-like eyes, a medium-sized Afro held back by a pink elastic headband, and skin the color of leaves at autumn's end. She glanced up as the New Kid approached and reached into the pocket of her lab coat for a tablet like Helix's. Scrolling through it, she looked him over and asked, "Agent Harrison?"

"Yes—yes ma'am," the New Kid said, shifting uneasily. The stark white of the facility was a bit hard on the eyes, and the mysterious technology hovering at the edge of his vision compounded his anxiety.

"I'm Agent Hounsou. Here's your first layer," she said brusquely, thrusting a thin pair of black pants and a matching short-sleeved shirt into his hands.

"First—wait, first layer?" he asked, looking down at the black and thinking of a New York day in the dead of Benedictus.

"Relax. The material is made to wick off excess body heat. And—" She took the shirt back and put it on her lap before pressing a button on the armrest of her chair. She glided backwards, revealing the rest of her motorized wheelchair.

Approaching a dummy at the other end of the table, she hefted it off its stand and pulled the shirt on over its burn marks. Then the delicate engineer picked up a short knife from the table and thrust it up into the dummy's ribcage. To the New Kid's shock, the blade didn't even puncture the cloth.

"It's rachneweave," she explained, setting the knife aside and giving his new shirt back. "It won't stop bullets, and you'll still be bruised as hell, but at normal speeds it would take something thinner than paper and as strong as steel to actually pierce it."

A vivid memory rose up, and he swallowed. "Does...everyone have it?"

"Every active member of the Doghouse is *given* it," Sia said, sighing, "but not everyone chooses to wear it. You're talking about Agent Peterson, aren't you?"

When the New Kid nodded silently, Sia rolled to one side of the table and began snatching up gear. "Arrogant asshole," she muttered. "I can only do so much, you know." Turning back around, she thrust everything up into the New Kid's arms and said, "Do me a favor, and actually *wear* the gear, alright? Every bit of it, even if it looks redundant or unnecessary. I promise that I'm giving it to you for a reason."

"Um—okay, but I—"

"You've got a standard-issue flak jacket, weapons belt with adjustable holsters for primary and secondary blades or pistols, ammo storage here-here-and-here, padded gloves, Nylon backpack with a 200 pound limit, steel-toed boots, two boot sheaths, two *calf* sheaths, LBD, tablet, a second belt pouch for whatever random bits you wanna fill it with, and a walkie watch. Those are all the toys you've been cleared for."

Juggling approximately a hundred different things, the New Kid blinked and said, "Sorry, a Wookie watch?"

"A *walkie* watch," Sia corrected, holding up the black device on its sleek band. It was indeed shaped like a watch, but there were buttons and a small display screen where the face would typically go. "It's for communicating outside of your team. Big button opens a channel, little button underneath closes it. These are your dials; if you need a cheat sheet for the different channels, the major ones are engraved on the band. For today, I recommend memorizing the main comms channel and Med Bay

A."

"Okay. Yes ma'am. And the LBD?"

The engineer fished a plastic rectangle the size of a deck of cards out of the second pouch. "Stands for 'little black device.' They're what we use to close rifts. All you gotta do is hold down the big red button for five seconds."

"Okay. Got it."

Sia's demeanor softened. "Look, I know you didn't mean anything nasty before. But when the tech fails—well, it's never the agent's mistake, is it? Always the geek's fault. Peterson was stupid, and I'm sorry that he got hurt, but *my* gear was not to blame." Shaking herself, the engineer gave him a wide smile and said, "I'm turning you over to your tactical officer now. He'll get you where you're going. Good luck, Agent Harrison."

"Thank—" he began, but she was already zooming away. The New Kid felt a tap on his shoulder, and when he turned around his eyes widened.

He had overheard Cat's earlier comment about new gear for Grunt, but the only word for what the Watchdog in front of him was wearing was *armor*. It was made of overlapping black and gunmetal grey panels that flowed seamlessly down his body like high-tech geometric scales. On top of it, he was layered with so many pouches and sheaths that it was a wonder he hadn't requisitioned a utility belt.

Against all of that black and grey, Grunt's eyes looked even bluer than before. He nodded at the New Kid, who was doing his best not to swoon, and said, "Agent Harrison. Are you ready?"

The New Kid's throat clicked when he tried to speak, so he swallowed and nodded instead.

"Okay. Follow me." Without waiting for confirmation, Grunt turned and escorted the New Kid to the front of the Batcave, proving that in spite of the weaponry and battle armor weighing him down, he could move just fine.

Upstairs, almost every active agent was gathered in or near their weapons locker, including Gamma and Charlie. They tossed insults back and forth like a ball, and more than a few of them eyed the approaching tactical officer with approval. No one voiced their opinion quite like Millennia, who wolf-whistled better than a cartoon character.

"Show some respect," Cat ordered, quieting everyone down with a look. "And don't get your hopes up; that shiny new armor is worth three of your yearly paychecks, and it's going on its maiden voyage. Grunt has graciously volunteered to be the Batcave's guinea pig."

Millennia looked him over again, this time with an analytical eye. Her face, though devoid of its piercings, was just as bright and curious as before. "He's the perfect candidate for it."

"On the one hand, I'm glad that Grunt gets to play with the new toys first," Cat said, leaning into one hip, "but on the other, I'd rather have someone like Haverty wearing it if it's going to explode."

"Plus then we could help him test it by firing ballistae rounds into his back," Millennia added.

Cat grinned at that and put two fingers between her lips, whistling sharply. "Gammas, move out!"

As a group, the Gamma officers approached their private weapons locker, a gleaming black storage unit embedded deep in a concrete wall. The screen on the door was more elaborate than usual, and much larger. One by one, the officers lined up with Cat at the head. She placed her hand on the screen and leaned forward.

"Initiate unlock sequence. Alexa Fiyero, call sign: Bellona."

As she spoke, a red speech pattern appeared on the screen and a red light ran down the length of her palm. Both lights turned green, and she stepped aside. Specs took her place and mimicked her actions.

"Damani Forrester, call sign: Blackbeard."

He gallantly stepped aside and let Helix have her turn. "Devi Ramachandra, call sign: Kali."

Her twin practically shoved her aside in his excitement and slapped his hand down. "Jai Ramachandra, call sign: Karma

Chameleon."

Millennia shooed him away and removed both of her rings. "Eleadora Mendes, call sign: Oracle."

The quietest officer approached the panel without fanfare. "Aaron Walker, call sign: Dreadnought."

Finally, it was the New Kid's turn. "I haven't—what do I do?" he asked.

"Just place your hand on the screen, and then say your full name and call sign," Specs said. "We use them like passwords. Yours will be a recording, authenticated by myself and Cat."

"So make it good," Darwin added. "But no pressure."

"Okay. No pressure." He did as the others had before him and placed his hand on the now-warm panel, juggling the pile of black clothing and matching boots in one arm. "Um—um—" His eyes went to the floor automatically, and in a minor panic he said, "Kevin Harrison, call sign: Sneaks."

Helix clapped her hand over her twin's mouth.

"Ver—*mgh*, verified by Commander Alexa Fiyero, Bellona-1527." Cat barely finished speaking before turning away to choke back her own laughter.

Though more composed than his teammates, Specs couldn't hide a smile as he too spoke into the panel for a final time. "Verified by Lieutenant Damani Forrester, Blackbeard-2633. Terminate unlock sequence."

The panel accepted all the codes and call signs that had been given to it and unlocked the door with a heavy *clunk*. "That went well," Cat commented as she pulled the door open. "Other than the fact that your verification now starts with *um-um*."

The New Kid flushed and followed the group of excited officers inside. Tall black lockers lined the walls, and a quartet of benches had been arranged in the shape of a square. Through a second door, he could see private changing rooms.

Cat immediately darted for the fourth locker, which was so large that Specs could have stood comfortably inside of it. Reaching into its depths, she first pulled out a sleek holster and threaded it through the belt loops of her pants and around her right thigh. Then she removed the largest gun that the New Kid had ever seen, a gleaming blue-and-chrome monstrosity that looked more fiction than science.

"This is the Peacekeeper," Cat crooned, gently caressing its side. It had a traditional shape, but the gun was taller near the barrel, and strange tubes wove in and out of the thick casing. She flicked a button, and sky-blue lights appeared along the sides. "Remember the phasers from *Star Trek*?"

"Uh—yeah," the New Kid said. "It's like that?"

"Sure, if those phasers could knock a comet out of the sky."

"Cat's exaggerating," Millennia said, "but not by much. I'm pretty sure it could at least bat a passenger jet around."

"Like Ali in his prime." Cat spun the Peacekeeper and holstered it in one buttery move. "Suit up, kids," she said with a grin. "It's showtime."

"You are entirely too cheerful," Darwin informed her, "since we could all end up mauled to death. Or vaporized, there's always that option. I'm not in the mood to be vaporized this year, Cat."

"Next year for sure," Helix said, heaving a massive black backpack out of her locker. It was half as tall as she was and lined with bulging pockets. "Personally, I think there are worse ways to go."

"Immolation, for example," her twin agreed. "Poison—"

"Prion build-up—"

"Suffocation—"

"Brain tumors—"

"Being eaten alive—"

"Will you two cut it out?" Millennia asked, running mysterious algorithms on her tablet with one hand and pulling on her flak jacket with the other. "We're obviously gonna die doing something extra stupid, like falling off a building."

"Not if Grunt's hiding a jet pack," Darwin said, eying the Watchdog's sleek new battle armor. "What kinda toys you got in there, man?"

Cat loaded rounds onto her belt and grinned. "I dare you to frisk him and find out."

"There's a way we never thought of," the zoologist told his twin. "Death by Grunt."

As always, the tactical officer accepted the change in conversation without even a twitch. "You should change," he told the New Kid.

"Oh! Yeah, yeah."

While the others continued bickering, he set his boots, flak jacket, and holsters on one of the benches and took the rest of the clothes into a dressing room. Though it had a proper door, he could still hear the Gammas outside. It was oddly comforting, like the familiar hum of the space heater in his Chinatown loft during winter.

Two layers of official black later, the New Kid came back into the main room and received a nod of approval from Grunt. He shrugged into a flak jacket and began buckling it up until it swaddled him tighter than a newborn's first blanket. He relaxed a bit at the pressure, not even flinching when Grunt handed him a bundle of Nylon.

"Here," he said, pointing to the outside of the New Kid's thigh. "It's a leg holster. Puts your main weapon in easy reach."

While the New Kid secured the sturdy Nylon around his hips and leg, Grunt pushed a flat rectangular section of wall. It slid open with a *hiss*, revealing rows of sleek black and silver weaponry. Grunt selected a Glock, checked its weight, and then passed it over to the New Kid.

"How does that feel?" he asked.

The New Kid curled his fingers around the butt of the unfamiliar weapon. "It's alright," he said, carefully checking the safety before holstering it.

Grunt handed him several cartridges, most of which he stuffed in his pack. "Those are bio-sensitive stun rounds," the officer told him. "Don't waste them."

"Each one comes equipped with a microchip," Helix explained. She had changed out of her black glasses and into contacts. "On impact, they take tiny tissue samples and calculate a non-fatal dose of electricity that will overload the target's neurological functions."

"Like—like a stun gun."

Cat snorted. "Yeah, if a stun gun was over $200 per discharge. Like Grunt said: Don't fucking waste them."

Shifting his suddenly expensive pack more carefully, the New Kid said, "Uh, how long does all that take?"

"Three to five seconds," Darwin said, "so if you're feeling funny about something, don't wait to shoot it. At least they stick like goddamn burrs."

"Static cling," Helix said, pulling a round out and holding it up to the light. It was like a tiny hypodermic needle attached to a clear bullet. "This pretty lady needs time to do her work, so the silicon prongs on either side emit a tiny initial charge. Not much, just enough to mess with the electron discharge between the silicon and your skin. That helps her cling until she figures out how to knock you on your ass."

"Sounds like my ex-girlfriends," Darwin said.

"When exactly did you have one of those?" Helix quipped back.

He stuck his tongue out at her. "Ha-aha. You're a fucking riot."

"Every time my mother asks why I don't settle down and have kids," Cat remarked, "I laugh until I go hoarse."

"If she just wants grandkids to spoil, I could use some new ink," Millennia said, holding out her relatively blank forearm.

Helix raised her hand. "I'd really like an RNA analyzer."

"Are we making a Christmas list?" Darwin asked. "Because I want a grey-banded kingsnake for my lab."

"I'll be sure to pass all of those along."

As the others continued to add things to the list, the New Kid peered at Helix's stuffed backpack. It looked like the type that hardcore travelers took across Europe or Asia. "Is all that—medical stuff?"

She nodded. "I'm the team field medic. We had an official

one, but—"

"She suffered from a sudden acute onset of nerves," Millennia said delicately, "and had to be removed from active duty."

"That means we broke her, and they won't send us another one," Cat said.

"We?" Darwin asked, sharing a pointed look with Helix.

She rolled her eyes. "Apparently latex suits can trigger latent claustrophobia. Who could've seen that coming? And she knew exactly what she was getting into." Turning back to the New Kid, she said, "Anyway, she quit a couple years ago and I've been covering ever since. It's actually a lot of fun, and let's be honest: There's usually not much use for me in the field. But it means—" She got to her feet and heaved the backpack up with a grunt of effort. "I get to carry this monstrosity around all Day."

Cat laced up her boots with practiced ease. "Military medics carry all that and more every day."

Helix made a face at the older woman. "Military medics don't usually have to deal with tyracroc bites."

"Point." Standing up, Cat adjusted her flak jacket and said, "Alright, other than Grunt, who's ready?"

Specs and Millennia lifted their hands, the latter without even looking up from her tablet. Less than a minute later, Helix triumphantly attached the last buckle on her backpack and raised her hand. Meanwhile, Darwin was busy dumping out the main part of his pack and rearranging the materials inside while Grunt loaded the New Kid up with more mundane toys.

"MagLite with seventy-two hours of light," he said, passing a black cylinder over. "Emergency wallet with cash and credit cards. Extra rachneweave. Canvas. Basic first aid kit."

"Don't forget your copy of the Damn Handbook," Darwin said, passing a floppy black book over to the New Kid. "It's secondhand, but the info's still good. Just pinch the spine and it should stay together."

The yellowed book had been released sometime in the

seventies. There was hardly an intact chapter, and something with an alarming bite radius had taken a chunk out of the top corner.

"Secondhand?" the New Kid asked, eying it. "What—what happened to the last owner?"

"Don't worry about it," Darwin said with a wave of his hand. "I hear they totally replaced his fingers. And don't mind the brown stains in Chapter Twelve."

The New Kid held the book away with the lightest grip that he could manage. "O-okay. No problem," he muttered to himself between deep breaths. "Yeah, no, that's fine, that's totally—totally fine—"

"Oh for fuck's sake," Cat said, snatching the book away and tossing it on a bench. "Knock it off before you give him a panic attack."

Darwin and Millennia, meanwhile, had lost their composure. They leaned against their respective lockers, laughing to the point of oxygen deprivation.

"Couple of assholes," Cat said, though her lips twitched. "Kid, they were just fucking with you. There's a digital copy on your tablet."

The New Kid wilted onto a bench and braced his hands on his knees. "Oh, thank God."

From his place near the door, Specs spoke up for the first time. "That wasn't necessary, you two."

"Relax," Millennia said, coming to her feet. "He's probably a giant ball of stress like, twenty-four-seven. Think of all the cortisol being flushed out of his system right now. It was good for him."

"I just did it because it was funny," Darwin said.

"If you're done horsing around," Cat said, checking her watch, "we're heading topside in ten minutes. Grab the last of your shit and head to the hatch."

"Hatch?" the New Kid asked Specs, snatching up his remaining gear in trembling hands.

"Most of the teams drive to their sectors, but Central Park

takes up a good part of Gamma and Charlie's territory," the historian explained. "We have our own entrance that leads directly up into the park, and it's much faster for teams like Mastiff or Rottie."

"Mastiff and Rottie? Like—like the dog breeds?"

Specs nodded. "Exactly. Each Gamma Watchdog team is named after a dog breed. You'll be dealing mostly with the Command team, Rottie."

As a group, the officers left the weapons locker and met up with their Watchdogs outside. They gathered in front of a mysterious black elevator that looked like something straight out of *Star Trek*. It was only large enough to accommodate three people at a time, so they queued up in a nervous line.

"See the woman with the blonde ponytail?" Specs asked, pointing at a slim figure in black who was chatting with a taller, broad-shouldered white man. "That's Sasha. For all intents and purposes, she's the team leader for Rottie, even though they're officially under Grunt's direct command. If she gives you an order, you follow it."

Sasha tucked a strand of hair behind her ear, flashing a tattoo of a black willow tree on the inside of her left wrist. She and the unnamed man entered the elevator behind a smaller biracial woman with curly brown hair and faint freckles, and the trio disappeared with a soft *whoosh*. Darwin hopped in next and held the door open for Helix, but she glanced back at the New Kid and shook her head. Frowning, the zoologist let a muscular Arabic man and a sturdy black woman with cornrows in instead.

"You're up, New Kid," Helix said, coming to stand beside him. "I'll go with you."

"Mind if I join you?" Specs asked. "Bit of a squeeze, but we'll make it work."

It was indeed a squeeze with Specs at the back and the two smaller Gammas crowded in front of him, but as the elevator began to rise and everything became a shade more real to the New Kid, he was suddenly very glad to be so close to the others. When the elevator slowed and his breathing came a little quicker, Specs was right there with a hand on his shoulder.

"It's going to be fine," he said. "We'll keep you safe."

"Yeah. Yeah, I know," the New Kid said, breathing out in a long stream. "Old habits, you know?"

The elevator came to a stop and the doors opened, spilling light into the gloom. The room was large, with a hard-packed dirt floor ringed by deep ruts. At the center, a spiral staircase led up to a hole in the ceiling. Strange shapes covered in tarp lined the walls, and the New Kid swore that he could see a hoof sticking out from under one.

"The others are already upstairs," Specs said as everyone stepped out of the elevator. When it closed behind them, he pulled a flashlight from the pocket of his flak jacket. "Come on."

The historian led the way up. There was a thin wooden door at the top of the stairs that led to a smaller room. Specs's flashlight caught the edge of a control panel with two small screens, and then another door that had been painted white.

"Go on out," Specs said. "I want to look for something."

Nodding, the New Kid opened the door onto darkness. The space felt larger than the room below. His footsteps echoed off of some slick surface, almost like a ballroom floor, and as his eyes adjusted he sensed a shape directly in front of him. Trembling just a little, he reached for his own flashlight and turned it on, illuminating the lacquered face of a lunging horse.

The New Kid managed to slap a hand over his mouth in time, so the only sound that came out was a faint whine. He swept his flashlight around, taking in dozens of downsized creatures in mid-leap. Just to double-check his theory, he looked up at the thin red beams and then back at the elaborately decorated blue door that Helix was currently closing.

"Are we in the *Carousel?*" he asked.

"Yup!"

This time the New Kid did gasp and whirl around to find Millennia looming uncomfortably close. Grinning, she pinched his cheek and said, "You're adorable, New Kid. Come! Meet the children." She led him to a black horse bedecked in blue ribbons. "This is Oppenheimer. Then you've got Herschel, Curie, Newton, uh—shit, is that Meitner or Einstein? Whatever. And *this* baby—" She proudly patted the side of a majestic wooden palomino. "This is Tesla."

Still struggling to calm his heart rate, the New Kid reached out to numbly pet Tesla's side. "Why? Why are we in the Carousel?"

"There was already an underground room," Helix said, stepping up beside him. "That's where they worked the horses who ran the original carousel. They use it for storage nowadays. Making it our access point meant less digging."

"Damn," Specs said, finally coming out of the control booth at the same time as a group of Watchdogs. "The last guy who worked here kept a package of Oreos in one drawer. Since he also kept his weed in there, I'm going to assume he's been fired."

"Specs, didn't we repurpose most of the tunnels under the park when the Doghouse was built?" Helix asked.

"Decades ago," he confirmed. "You know, Gamma's entrance used to be the old Indian Cave until they sealed it up. Where's Cat?"

"Outside," Millennia said, taking the New Kid by the arm. "Come on, handsome. It's almost time to rock n' roll."

Gulping, he followed the physicist around the carousel until they reached the building's entrance. The rolling metal door had been half raised, and plastic sheeting covered the opening. The New Kid lifted the sheeting for Millennia, who blew him a kiss before heading out into the thick New York night. Plastic sheeting crackled softly as a team of Watchdogs finished winding it around the outside of the brick building.

"Where are we going?" the New Kid asked.

"Wagner Cove."

"I—I don't think I've been there."

"It's below Cherry Hill, by the water. Nice and isolated, but with easy access to the rest of the park. Now hush and cuddle me closer, like we're lovers in the nighttime."

The New Kid swallowed but did as Millennia said. They marched at the head of a pack of Watchdogs, the physicist's chili-pepper hair glowing like a beacon every time they passed under a streetlight.

They crossed 65th and continued north, past the open expanse of the Sheep Meadow and the heavy scent of the Lilac Walk. Millennia waved cheerfully at the memorial busts of Victor Herbert and Beethoven as they passed. Finally, they crossed Terrace Drive and began walking along the outside curve of Cherry Hill, eventually taking a slender stone path. The greenery closed around them in a wall, enveloping them in quiet and the scent of growing things.

"Here we go," Millennia said as they came in sight of the small wooden pavilion at the end of the path. "Home sweet home."

The rectangular pavilion backed up right to the shadowy water. There were no lights in that part of the park, but the Gammas had come prepared: Three halogens the size of hubcaps had been erected on stands, and a table had been placed in the center of the pavilion. Cat was currently bent over a large and detailed map of Manhattan from 59th up to 110th Street, which covered the entire length of the park. She conferred with Grunt in quiet murmurs and finger points.

"One team down at Umpire," she said, "and another near the Lawn. Tell Marco I want him in the Upper West Side, north of 86th. Jamal and Paolo get to slum it down here with us." She made slash marks on the map as Grunt relayed the instructions through his bud, consulting a second map covered in purple swirls as she went. "One team to Roosevelt Island. Edwin can have the Upper East Side and Yorkville up to 85th, and I want Marisol in the bottom of the Barrio. Are we forgetting anything?"

"New data's showing a lot of pre-rift buildup by the Warrior's Gate," Millennia said, consulting her tablet. "Could be a big one."

Lifting her watch, Cat adjusted the frequency and said, "Lover's Lane to Troll Bridge. You guys got anybody up in the Meer?"

There was a spat of static, and then Daniel McNab said, "Negative, Cat."

"Sending you some playmates. They're only partially house-trained though, so mind the rugs."

"Roger that, Lover's Lane. Troll Bridge out."

"What do you think?" Cat asked Grunt.

"Ramirez," he said immediately. "I can put her in charge of Malinois."

"Good call." She checked her watch and then opened a channel on her bud. "Cat to all Gamma teams, t-minus twenty minutes. That means you've got negative ten minutes to get your asses in place." She made eye contact with Specs, and licked her lips. "Stay safe, everyone."

Grunt picked up the communication, relaying instructions to his Watchdogs. The rest of the officers had scattered to the winds, leaving the New Kid hovering by himself at the edge of the artificial pool of light. He felt the old anxiety creeping up, and as the minutes ticked by and everyone around him fell into their own habitual preparations, he was torn between relief at the presence of other people and frustration with himself for ending up closer to the things that were trying to kill him.

So absorbed was the New Kid in his thoughts that the sudden beeping of his watch caught him by surprise. Though they all knew what it meant, the Dogs around him simultaneously checked their own wrists, which displayed the same message:

## 00:00

A cold sweat broke out all across the New Kid's body, only to be soaked up by the cool fabric pressed against his skin.

Ten feet away, Cat looked up from her watch and grinned at her tactical officer. "Lift-off."

# GRUDGES

## Cat
### (7:27)

"Team Viszla to Command, we got more ammonites on the Lawn."

"Great," Cat said, picking her head up from the map. "We can have a cookout. Grunt, you know how to boil crawfish, right?"

"Not four-foot-long crawfish," he said.

"Actually," Darwin piped in through the open channel, "they're more like cuttlefish or octo—"

Cat casually switched it off and curled back up on one of the pavilion's benches. "Wake me up when something interesting happens."

Specs set his notes down in exasperation. "Why would you say that? Do you *want* mayhem and—I'm sorry. Of course you do."

It had been over seven hours since their clocks simultaneously struck midnight, and the most action that Gamma had seen was a liquor- and cocaine-fueled bachelor party from 1972 stumbling home somewhere in the West Side. They had turned back around with easy cheer, even inviting some of the more attractive members of Team Pit Bull (of all genders and persuasions) to join them. Now the sky was lightening from dusty black velvet to pool-blue, and other than an unusual deluge of prehistoric sea creatures (all of whom were *quite* surprised to find themselves suddenly out of the water), everything had been quiet on the Western front.

"Hey," the New Kid asked suddenly, "what happens if, you know, a rift full of ammonites opens in the Reservoir, or—or something? And one escapes?"

"If it survives the difference in water quality long enough for someone to find it and post pictures—" Specs began.

"Doubtful," Cat interjected.

"—then we'll have some of the ruder members of the Hive spam them with debunk posts until the sample can be collected," he finished calmly. "That's what happened the one time a siren washed up on someone's private beach."

"I remember that," the New Kid said. "You mean it was—"

"The realest," Specs said.

Cat rolled to her feet with a groan and stood in front of the map with her back to the water. "None of our problem children have shown up?" she asked, rubbing her face. "Not even Max?"

Grunt shook his head. "Not even Max."

"Jesus Christ, I never thought I'd see the day when I missed Max."

Leaning towards the historian, the New Kid asked, "So...who's Max?"

Specs sighed. "Max is a certain...admirer of Cat's."

"He's a goddamn pain in the ass," she corrected.

"He's a carpenter from the late 1910s," Specs continued, as if she hadn't interrupted. "He knows about the Days and the rifts, so he used to wander around New York looking for one that would take him to Cat. They're impossible to navigate or even spot unless you have the right tech—though if you actually touch one, it's cold enough to make you take notice—so his aim wasn't great."

"What happened to him?" the New Kid asked.

Cat smiled at the memory. "I told him if he ever came near me again, I'd push him into the Lake and laugh while the ducks ate him. He's been pretty scarce ever since."

"Oh." The New Kid furrowed his eyebrows. "Why are the rifts cold?"

"Read the Damn Handbook*," Cat said. "That's what it's there for." She lifted her arms and stretched until the ache of inactivity quieted down. "I swear to God, if something doesn't happen in the next five minutes, I'm gonna go looking for trouble myself. Is that bachelor party still around? I'm gonna—"

She was interrupted by a dark green tentacle as thick as a baseball bat shooting out of the water. It wrapped around her calf, and Cat yelped in surprise as the tentacle yanked back, nearly pulling her through the gap and into the murky water. Had she not instinctively grabbed onto a pillar, she would have disappeared.

The Command center went from nearly catatonic with boredom to a frantic hive of activity. Specs pulled the table away and wrapped his arm around Cat's much smaller body. Grunt unsheathed an impossibly large knife from around his thigh and hacked at the tentacle, holding onto the same pillar. The wood groaned under the weight of all three Dogs.

Cat glanced behind her at the boiling patch of water, which had disgorged a second tentacle. This one wrapped around her other leg, followed by a third flailing tentacle that latched onto the pillar and pulled.

Her center of gravity shifted suddenly, and there was a terrible cracking sound. "*Fuck*," she hissed as the assaulted half of the pavilion began to tear along its foundations.

Specs bucked instinctively, every muscle in his body fighting back as the additional weight hit him.

The Watchdogs exploded into action, two of the bigger agents pushing the bench down to counter the pressure. Though the groaning continued, the pavilion reached a tenuous equilibrium.

Cat barely had time to catch her breath before she saw the New Kid raise his Glock and sight along the barrel.

"*Don't!*" a Watchdog named Mia cried, shoving the New

Kid's gun up. "That's a stun round!"

The New Kid paled and holstered his gun. He glanced around, and then tapped his tragus. Cat saw his lips move, but her concentration was spotty at best. Something in her knee had popped with agonizing heat, and her arms were trembling against the impossible strength of the creature below.

Grunt had finally cut his way through the slippery, muscular limb gripping Cat's calf, but there were still two others in play. Inexplicably, Grunt sheathed his blade and began smacking the tentacle currently wrapped around the base of the pillar until it switched to his outstretched arm. The creature had no problem holding on to the battle armor.

"What the *hell* are you doing?" Cat gasped.

He heaved backwards, face turning bright red. After a moment of confusion, Specs reached down for the tentacle that was still lashed to Cat's leg.

"Help!" Specs called.

Several of the remaining Watchdogs grabbed the pavilion, freeing the bigger agents to lunge forward and grab onto the two officers. Together, they slowly dragged the creature forward.

"You're all *fucking morons*," Cat hissed, her face bloodless with exhaustion and pain and just a hint of excitement. "A little more!"

With one big heave, they pulled the creature up onto the concrete, where it lay in a glistening, flailing pile. It was like a forest green Pacific octopus, if they grew to be ten feet long from mantle to tentacle tip and had heads covered in rubbery spikes the size of a human forearm. A jet of warm water from its siphon soaked the entire team, especially Cat. She gasped and flung water out of her eyes, overwhelmed by the smell of stagnant plant growth.

"*Don't hurt her!*" a voice yelled, and Darwin emerged from the greenery. "Who's got chocolate?"

"Pack," Specs grunted, leaning against the devastating pull of the creature.

Darwin lunged for the historian's back and unzipped a few pockets before finding a candy bar. He unwrapped it and waved it in the air. "Here girl. That's a good girl."

Incredibly, the creature stopped struggling. She picked her green and gold-flecked head up, peering at them with one rectangular pupil. To everyone's amazement, she willingly heaved herself forward and reached delicately for the chocolate bar with the same limb that had previously held on to Grunt.

"Nobody move," Darwin gasped in the sudden silence, pulling an entire stash of candy bars out of Specs's pack and unwrapping them. "Come 'ere, gorgeous."

The cephalopod disengaged all of her remaining tentacles and reached for the bars, plucking them out of Darwin's hands like a child picking wildflowers. Cat sat panting on the stone path, staying upright only by sheer willpower. The severed tentacle still clung to her leg with tenacious fervor, leaking blue fluid.

"It's a Caledonian devilfish," Darwin said, continuing to lead her out of the pavilion. "She's not a maneater, she's just curious. Everybody take it easy." While the devilfish devoured the candy bars one at a time, Darwin opened his own pack and dug through it until he found a vial with pink liquid and a sterile syringe. Opening the syringe, he uncapped it and inserted it into the top of the vial, turning both upside down and drawing ten milliliters out. "Grunt, get her in the closest arm," he said, offering the syringe plunger-first.

Though the tactical officer moved to carefully do what he was told, Cat threw her hand out and glared at Darwin, managing to look threatening even when she was soaking wet and trembling with fatigue. "Why the fuck does Grunt have to do it? You're the goddamn animal expert."

"Because cephalopods hold *grudges*," Darwin explained, "and I want the chance to study her later."

Cat narrowed her eyes, but reluctantly nodded at Grunt. "You are *not* keeping this thing," she ordered, picking up a stick and using it to tickle the rogue arm. It thrashed angrily, latching onto the new source of entertainment so that she could unwind it from her leg and fling it into the water. "If you want a pet so bad, I'll buy you the fucking kingsnake myself."

"Yeah, yeah," Darwin said, waving the comment off. He reached forward and stroked one of the arms. The devilfish responded by laying her suckers on his bare hand and squeezing in a tender manner, eagerly exploring the texture of his skin. Her coloring had already lightened to a pleasant spring green, and it was turning whiter by the second.

Stepping with great caution, Grunt inserted the syringe into an arm and pressed the plunger. She immediately darkened again and tried to strike out, but the response was sluggish. Swaying from side to side, she melted into a gelatinous puddle.

Darwin adjusted his watch with a sigh of relief. "Dr. Ramachandra to the Savannah, I need a level eleven aquatic enclosure prepped for immediate habitation. Temperature should be between fifty and fifty-five degrees Fahrenheit, salinity at three point four percent."

"Copy that, sir, but—level eleven?" a male voice replied.

"I've got a Caledonian devilfish topside, by Gamma Command," he said.

"*Oh.* Copy Gamma, we'll get things ready and send a collection team up to you. Subject's condition?"

"Missing part of an anterior arm, but otherwise intact. I'm a bit worried about the condition of her slime coat though. Put everyone on germ alert."

"Copy that, Dr. Ramachandra," his watch replied after several seconds. "Think she'll be any trouble? I mean, more than usual."

"Well, she's certainly feisty, but she's been sedated with enough chocolate and GH-687 to hold her for at least two hours. Oh, and you tell Kennedy that I've got *dibs.*"

"Dibs, sir. Roger that. Savannah out."

Cat became aware of a low groaning sound. The crack in the pavilion's foundation widened, and then split neatly in half with a crash. One corner of the pavilion rose more than a foot, while the diagonal sank into the soupy water of the Lake.

The Gamma commander took in the new angle of the beloved pavilion's roof. "Fantastic," she sighed.

"Gets better," Specs said, pointing.

Across the water, Cat spotted a pair of amazed joggers holding out their phones. "Grunt, get a camo panel on this thing," she said, wringing her hair out and smoothing it back. "Who's got a wiper?"

The same curly-haired brunette who had prevented the New Kid from shooting a stun round into open water stepped forward. "I do, Commander," Mia said.

"Use it. Two hundred foot radius."

"Yes ma'am." She pulled three poles from a bag and plunged them into the ground in a rough line in front of the Command center. Once all three were primed, she took out a remote and entered a few numbers. There was a strange shiver in the air, and the people across the water started shouting.

Snorting, Cat gestured up to Specs and said, "Help me up, would you?"

The big historian reached under her arms and lifted, supporting her until she could put weight on her good leg. Meanwhile, Grunt had reached into the same bag of gear and removed a square piece of silvery material. He unfolded it and laid it across the sleeping devilfish, and with a faint crackle the material took on the appearance of a small grassy hummock.

"Good job," Cat said, brushing the dirt from her hands as well as she could. "Injuries?"

Specs mirrored her actions. "Some bruises from the suckers, but not bad. I'll be okay."

The trio of Watchdogs who had helped pull the devilfish out chimed in with similar complaints.

"What about you?" the historian asked.

Gingerly, Cat took a step and winced. "Might've strained a ligament in my knee, but I'll get it up and iced until Helix gets here. Grunt?"

"I'm fine," he said.

"Let her look at you anyway. All of you." Grinning, Cat clapped the tactical officer lightly on his armored arm. "Now *that* was more like it." Her smile died when she caught sight of the New Kid. She looked him up and down once, and then said, "New Kid! Take a walk. Make it short."

He looked down at his shaking hands in surprise, and tried to hide them behind his back.

"You're no good to me until you calm down," Cat said, her tone somewhat more gentle than before.

The New Kid nodded slowly and began walking down the stone path, head bowed in thought. He made it a dozen steps before breaking into a light jog.

"He didn't do half-bad," Darwin said. His eyes flickered periodically to the disguised devilfish. "I mean, he's the one who called me in. None of you seasoned motherfuckers bothered, so. All things considered, he did pretty good."

"All things considered," Cat said, sitting on a grey slab of rock by the path. "Anybody got an ETA on Helix?"

Specs checked his watch. "Probably two minutes or so."

"Good. Can you hand me my pack?"

Specs reached into the pile, expertly extracting Cat's pack. She thanked him and dug through it until she found the first aid kit. Using the elastic bandage, she secured an activated ice pack to the side of her knee.

"Alright, let's get the table set back up," she said, surveying her domain. "We've still got work to do."

# THE CLAWS AT THE END OF THE PAUSE

## The New Kid
### (7:42)

The New Kid headed across the Bow Bridge towards the runner's trails, pausing only for a quick stretch. As he entered the shady embrace of the trees, he felt the adrenaline slowly leaking out of him with every light step. One foot at a time, he got control of his breathing.

A rustling sound came from his left. The New Kid whirled around so hard that he lost his balance and nearly stumbled into a tree. A shape pushed its way through the brush and reached the path, resolving into a young white woman in her late teens or very early twenties. This event wouldn't have been worth noting, except that she was wearing a pale green-striped dress in the distinctive Victorian style, complete with pleats and lace at her throat and sleeves. Her light brown hair had been curled and piled high on her head.

Dusting her hands off, the young woman placed them on her hips and smiled at the New Kid. "Well hello there! This is a strange place, isn't it? I could swear that just a moment ago I was on an open lawn. Don't know how I got all turned about, but what's life without a little adventure, eh? What's your name?" Her accent dripped pure English sophistication.

"New—uh, Kevin," the New Kid stammered, glancing back

and forth down the empty stretch of trail. "I'm Kevin."

"Wonderful to meet you, Kevin! What a strange, wonderful name. I'm Miss Penrose, but I suppose you may call me Elaine. That's a funny style of dress you've got there."

"That's, um—oh no." Finally giving up, the New Kid touched his bud and said, "Commander? I've got a—um—I've got a girl."

"Well, kid, that's one way to blow off steam," Cat said, "but send her home 'til tomorrow."

"Whomever are you talking to?" Elaine asked, looking behind her.

"No, no—Commander, she's not from here," the New Kid said.

"Ah. That's a different story. Is she hostile?"

"No, I don't—I don't think so."

Elaine turned back and crossed her arms. "Really now, it's not funny. Who on Earth are you talking to?"

The New Kid swallowed. "Commander, what—what do I do?"

"Bring her down to camp—*goddammit Darwin, stop petting that thing*—bring her down and we'll deal with her later. I gotta go." Without any further advice she disconnected, leaving the New Kid alone with an increasingly wary Victorian girl.

"Poor thing," she said, her face pinching with sudden concern. "You're a bit...confused, aren't you?"

The New Kid nodded miserably.

Bouncing over, she took him by the arm and said, "Don't worry, pet. I'll see you home safe. Now, where do you live?"

His thoughts rebounded like struck billiard balls. "Uh, across. Across the water. Wagner Cove."

She tilted her head with a faint frown. "You live in Wagner Cove?"

"No, um—that's where my brother is. I went for a walk, and I got lost."

"As did I," she said, leading him down the paved path. "Mattie—that's my nurse, she's a dear but so dull you just want to scream—Mattie said that we may go for an early morning walk, but she was being entirely too proper. These open parks are made for running about, and she wouldn't let me do what's only good and natural. So I ran away!" Smiling up at the overhanging trees, she continued, "I suppose I'll go back later, but not without a good adventure first. I rather think adventure's good for the digestion, don't you?"

"Could—could be, yeah," the New Kid stammered.

"That's why I talked Father into letting me muck about the Colonies for a while," she said, eyes glowing. "I've never been, and I'd heard such wonderful things about New York and Philadelphia and—"

They came around the last curve then, and as they stepped up onto the Bow Bridge, Miss Elaine Penrose looked up and caught sight of the modern skyline rising above the distant trees. She froze, and her grip on the New Kid's arm was suddenly a vice. "What—why I've never—I don't—"

"Elaine," the New Kid said, gently leading her forward, "I'm going to tell you something kind of crazy. You're still in New York, just...not in the 1800's."

"God's mercy," she breathed, staring out over the emerald waters of the Lake in rapture. "It's beautiful. It's radiant. I haven't—I haven't the words." Shaking herself awake, she looked at the New Kid, taking in his appearance. "Why, you're a half-caste boy, aren't you? I couldn't see you properly before."

"Half—you mean mixed?" the New Kid asked, feeling the familiar heat creep up the back of his neck. "Yeah. My mom's black."

She leaned closer to him. "How intriguing. I've never spoken to anyone who's half-caste before." Without warning, she reached up and ran her fingers across the top of his head. "You have simply the curliest hair I have ever seen."

"Please don't do that," he said, stepping away.

"I was only curious, there's no need to be afraid." Turning back to the view, she began drifting along the bridge again. "What year is it?"

The New Kid told her. She paused in the middle of the bridge, first staring out at the couples already exploring the hillside, and then up to the gleaming skyscrapers. "In all my books—but no! It's just like 'The Clock That Went Backward,' except that I haven't gone backwards at all, I've gone *forward*. And I don't remember a clock."

"There isn't a clock, it's, um—well, there are these locks and canals and—and—well, somebody will explain it. Somebody else."

"Incredible," she said, leaning over the rail and gazing up at the skyline in wonder. "It's like something out of a dream." She whirled back around and clapped her hands together. "I have so many questions! What are the new serials like? Can everyone travel in time? Are there airships that can take you from London to New York in the time it takes to have afternoon tea? Can we—"

"Whoa, whoa!" the New Kid said, raising his hands in a panic. "Um, yes there are airships, but, but they're not that fast, and um, no, no time travel except today. And ah—cereal's pretty good, there are all kinds."

Elaine practically vibrated off the bridge in excitement. "When I wanted an adventure, I never thought...well, I never imagined it would be like this." Squinting at him in sudden suspicion, she said, "You're not really lost at all, are you?"

The New Kid looked down sheepishly. "No. I didn't think you'd believe me if I told you the truth."

"Oh I most certainly wouldn't have," she admitted cheerfully. "I would have made my excuses and escaped at the soonest opportunity. So were you really talking to someone, then?"

"Yeah," the New Kid said, his hand automatically straying to the bud in his ear. "My commander."

"Are you in the military?"

"No, no, it's like—"

"Are you a *mercenary* then?" she asked. "Oh, how perfectly exciting!"

"No!" he said. "I'm an agent. Like, like a policeman."

"Odd," she said, walking around him. "You don't look like one of the constabulary."

"I'm—I'm auxiliary. Time Division. Can we—" He looked around nervously. Standing in the middle of the Bow Bridge with a woman running around in Victorian dress, even so early in the morning, was attracting a bit of attention. "Can we go now?"

"Oh, of course! I want to see everything."

"Okay." The New Kid let her take his arm again, and they began walking down the Bow Bridge. The sun was just coming over the treetops, gilding the water and reflecting off the faces of the skyscrapers, and the sky had the sort of cloudless clarity that would prove brutal during the heat of the day.

If Elaine had been born with two heads that spun like an owl's, she couldn't have looked at everything, but that didn't stop her from trying. "Oh dear," she said, looking down at her dress as they left the bridge and began walking along a concrete path towards the cove. "I'm dressed all wrong, aren't I?"

"No—well yeah, but it's not your fault. You look nice."

She smiled up at him. "You're very sweet, Kevin. But won't it be a problem?"

"Oh. No, they'll just think you're an actress or—" The word weirdo died on his tongue. "Or something."

Elaine flushed and cleared her throat. "Well, I should hope not."

Inept as he was with women and their cues, the New Kid was still aware that he had blundered. "That's not—that's not a bad thing. Not anymore, I guess."

"Oh! Well, that's alright then."

They passed a weeping willow clinging to the bank and turned off onto a dirt path. As they came in sight of the Dogs' camp at Wagner Cove, Elaine hesitated. "These are—your associates?"

The New Kid nodded. "They're nice." Thinking suddenly of Cat, he swallowed and added, "Most of the time."

At that moment, the commander in question raised her head from the map of Gamma territory and caught sight of the strange pair. She waved them over and straightened, no longer favoring her right leg. Grunt hovered behind Cat's shoulder, eyes constantly roving over the landscape, and Specs was in the middle of explaining something to the younger white man who had been talking to Sasha in the elevator. The "hummock" was lying calmly in the same spot, and the pavilion was still canted at a drunken angle.

"Commander," the New Kid said as they approached, "this is Elaine Penrose. Elaine, this is Commander Cat Fiyero."

Nodding, Cat said, "Miss Penrose. Has he explained things to you?"

"Some things," she said, nodding brightly. "I know where I am. Or rather, *when* I am. He tried to explain how all this is possible, but I'm afraid the poor dear was a little confused on the finer points."

"Our historian can explain, if you really want to know," Cat said, pointing to Specs and the Watchdog. "Then we'll have an agent escort you back home. You came through north of here, right?"

"Back home?" Elaine asked, clutching at the New Kid. "Oh no, please don't! I haven't seen anything yet."

Though still polite, Cat's voice was definitely tighter as she said, "Miss Penrose, the rift that you came through is going to close in less than sixteen hours, and frankly, I don't have the resources or the inclination to babysit you. So you can either take a quick lesson from my historian and a cordial escort home, or you can be dragged there by your hair in a far less cordial way. Do I make myself clear?"

Elaine stepped back from the no-nonsense look. "But…you really are in charge then? Even with all of these men present?"

Cat's answering smile was exponentially less polite. "Isn't there a queen where you come from?"

"Well of course—"

"Then there's your answer. These men can have command of

my team when they wrestle it from my cold, dead fingers."
Leaning around her, Cat called, "Specs! Give Miss Penrose the
rundown and then the boot."

Specs finished his conversation and turned around
expectantly. Elaine gasped and covered her mouth. "But he's—
he's a teapot!" she told the New Kid in a whisper that was not a
whisper at all. "Shouldn't he be, well—busy elsewhere? Out of
sight?"

The tall lieutenant's mouth tightened, but his commander
whirled on the Victorian woman. "Listen to me, you prissy little
flower," she hissed, all attempts at goodwill going up in smoke.
"That *teapot* is a human being, so you will shut your goddamn
mouth and show him some respect."

Elaine turned pale and clung to the New Kid even harder.
"I—I think I should like to go home after all," she said at last.

"Thank God for that," Cat said, already turning away.
"Specs, make it quick."

"Oh, but—" Elaine swallowed. "Alright. Yes, please, Master
Specs."

"Just Specs, or Lieutenant Forrester," he said, approaching
her slowly. Even with his care, she still tensed at the sheer size
of him. "What would you like to know?"

Elaine's grip on the New Kid's arm relaxed a little at a time.
"Oh! Yes, that is, I'd like to know—well, everything."

He smiled. "That could take a while. Do you mind if I
abbreviate?"

"Of course not. At your convenience." Glancing suddenly at
the mix of races and genders and ranks around her, Elaine's
whole demeanor changed. Moving with a firm purpose (and not
a little effort), she let go of the New Kid's arm and stood
resolutely on her own. Looking Specs in the eye, she said,
"Leftenant Forrester, please forgive me. Those things that I
said—well, they were wrong. I spoke out of ignorance, not
malice, but I am sorry all the same."

Specs's eyebrows lifted. "Apology accepted, Miss Penrose. I
appreciate it."

"That's good, then," she said. "Kevin, I wish to apologize to you as well. I see now that my earlier comments were callous,."

"It's okay," the New Kid said.

Elaine nodded firmly. "If you'll both excuse me for just a moment? There's one more thing I must do to clear my conscience."

Then she turned and took a deep breath before doing what no Dog would ever dare: She approached Cat Fiyero after she had been dismissed. The other Gammas froze where they stood, exchanging wild looks. For her part, the commander didn't even acknowledge the younger woman's presence as she bent over the map again, marking possible weak points.

"Cat," Elaine said tentatively, sensing the unsteady ground on which she stood. "Short for Catherine?"

Cat made a slash across the part of the map marked *Zoo*. "No."

"Oh." Swallowing, Elaine clasped her hands and said, "Miss Fiyero—"

"Commander Fiyero," Cat corrected.

"Commander Fiyero," Elaine amended immediately. "I would like to apologize for my behavior. You were right; I am the subject of a most gracious queen in my own country, and I should know better. It must take unbelievable strength of character to retain such a position of power, and I respect that strength. I also respect the courtesy that you showed me before I acted so abominably. Please accept my most sincere regrets."

Cat's pen paused, and for the first time she looked up at the young woman. They stared for a long time, each taking the measure of the other. Finally, Cat looked back down at the map and said, "New Kid. Miss Penrose doesn't have to go back immediately, but she's your responsibility, understand? Don't let her out of your sight."

Elaine's entire body lit up. "Oh, thank you Commander! I'll be so quiet, you won't even notice me."

Cat snorted. "I doubt that."

The young woman practically sprinted back to Specs. "Please

begin, Leftenant," she implored, clasping her hands together. "And spare no detail!"

◻   ◻   ◻   ◻   ◻   ◻

"My word," Elaine said more than half an hour later. "That is quite a lot of detail. I feel as if my head weighs as much as an elephant!" She looked out over the tranquil green waters of the Lake and sighed, as if it were the Caribbean Sea and she a sunburnt tourist watching it from the top deck of a cruise ship. "Oh, I do wish I could see more of this new city."

"What a coincidence," Cat said without looking up from her map. "The New Kid was just about to go get me coffee. You can go with him."

"Can I really?" Elaine asked, gathering herself up in rapturous joy. "Thank you, Commander Fiyero!"

"Mm-hm."

"Uh, okay," the New Kid said. "I guess we're getting coffee." He listened carefully as everyone recited their orders, typing them down in his tablet before tucking it back into its pouch. "Um, about—about money—"

"Use the black credit card in your emergency wallet," Specs said, patting his own chest. "All expenses incurred on a Day are covered by the agency."

"And caffeine is more of a necessity than an expense," Cat added as she opened an update from Team Doberman. "Off you fuck."

"Yes ma'am," he said, leading the way down the path while Elaine trailed happily behind him.

"This is excellent!" she said. "Do you think we'll see anything wondrous and strange?"

The New Kid smiled. "I think there's a good chance."

"There is one thing that concerns me about the leftenant's explanation," she said as they reached the edge of Cherry Hill and passed the fountain. "He said that very few people remember the Days once they're over. I take it to mean that I'll forget all of this tomorrow?"

"I don't know," the New Kid admitted. "Do you—do you normally remember them?"

"I'm not sure. I feel as if I do, but it's hard to tell. We've always stayed at my family's country estate during the summer, and Father would have us spend the Day in prayer. To be perfectly honest, that's why I really escaped Mattie this morning; I thought she would insist, and I just couldn't stand it another year! I thought without Father, I had a better chance at freedom. What is it that makes people like you special?" She clapped her hand over her mouth and said, "That came out all wrong, didn't it? I just meant—what's different about you? Maybe the same thing is different about me."

The New Kid shrugged. "It's just the way I was born."

Elaine smiled and took his arm as if they were a couple out for a morning stroll. "Are you the only one in your family who is different?"

Watching the ground ahead of him, the New Kid said, "No one's ever said anything about it."

"It's no fun being alone," Elaine observed. "I'm glad that you've found people to trust, even if they are exceptionally odd."

They spoke of little things as they walked, like the changes in clothing between their two centuries and what life in London had been like. When they reached the edge of the park and encountered New York traffic, Elaine's grip on his arm nearly cut off the circulation.

"Easy," he said in a low voice. "They're cars. Like, ah, horseless carriages. They're just machines."

"Astounding," she said, daring to step closer to a parked one. "What powers them? Steam or clockwork?"

"Neither? Maybe a little of both?" As he debated the merits of trying to explain the internal combustion engine (which he barely understood himself), there came the *clop-clop-clop* of shod hooves on concrete. A rose-bedecked white carriage plodded past, pulled by a medium-sized brown horse and driven by a man in a top hat and tails.

Elaine stifled a smile. "Why on Earth do you still have carriages," she asked, "if these metal monstrosities are so readily available?"

"They're more romantic?" the New Kid guessed.

The pair of them crossed the street, drawing stares and not a few hoisted phones. As they headed towards the closest coffee shop, Elaine pulled away from him, her attention caught by the colorful window of a tattoo parlor. "What is this place?"

The New Kid spared a glance back, did a double take, and then came back for the curious Victorian girl. "It's—um—"

But she had already been captivated by the large bare-chested man lying in the artist's chair, a half-finished skull etched onto his stomach. She watched in absolute fascination as the pierced and inked artist carefully brought the skull to life on the other man's skin. "It's a *tattoo shop*," she whispered, so close to the glass that it fogged under her breath. "I've heard about them, but I never thought to see one out in the open like this! Everyone says that Missy Cunningham has a tattoo on her rather ample backside, but I've certainly never seen it, and they never do say exactly what it's supposed to be."

"Um—"

Elaine switched her attention to the artist himself, and she tugged on the New Kid's sleeve. "That man, the tattooist—he has them on his neck! And all down his arms! And look, those women in the photos—they have them as well!"

It was hard to believe that anyone had ever been as excited about tattoos as Elaine Penrose; she was practically vibrating off the concrete. "Goodness, look at the variety. Are they more popular these days? Well, more than one hundred years later, I should hope so." Glancing at him, she asked, "And tattoos are...acceptable now?"

The New Kid shrugged. "Well, more or less."

"So it would not be strange to have one, then."

"Well, no. I mean, not—not really."

Someone as observant as the New Kid should have

anticipated what happened next, but he could only watch in helpless panic as Elaine squared her shoulders, opened the glass door, and marched inside.

"I should like a tattoo," she announced, holding her chin up.

The artist paused and glanced over his glasses at the girl in the green and white Victorian dress with her head piled high with curls. "Okay," he said with a shrug. "Carla! Customer."

The woman who came out of the back of the tattoo shop a few seconds later was even more fascinating than the two men. She had black hair pulled back in a rockabilly style, gauged and quadruple-pierced ears, and piercings in her nose, eyebrows, and lips. The black tank top that she wore revealed a large purple and red bat tattooed across her chest, a brightly colored sleeve, and a floral half-sleeve.

Grinning at them, she said, "Hey! What can I do for you?"

For once, Elaine had been rendered speechless. She stared at Carla for several seconds, eyes wide as silver dollars, before taking a step forward and lifting one hand. "May I—may I see them?"

"These? Yeah, go for it." Carla lifted her own arm up for inspection, and Elaine eagerly came closer.

With almost religious reverence, the young woman gently ran her fingers over the lovingly rendered cartoon images of Carla's full sleeve, which the New Kid recognized from A Nightmare Before Christmas. A lovestruck Jack Skellington was in the process of dipping Sally backwards on their special hill, with a full moon behind them and the rest of the characters arranged underneath.

"They are so strange," Elaine murmured, "but so beautiful."

"Thanks. Paul did that one." She nodded at the artist who was still working on the skull tattoo. "And my best friend did the poppies."

She turned and offered her other arm up for inspection, and Elaine gasped. It had been hard to see before, but the flowers were just simple outlines with bright splashes of crimson across them, like paint.

"These are *glorious*," Elaine whispered. "I love that they are unbound and wild, unhindered by lines and rules. Truly, this is freedom."

Carla cocked her head with a small smile. "You got it. So what were you thinking?"

With obvious effort, Elaine tore her eyes away from the half sleeve. "For myself? A crocus. Crocuses represent cheerfulness."

Carla walked over to her station and picked up a sketchbook. "That's Victorian flower language, right? What kinda style?"

"Well, to be perfectly honest, I wasn't sure but—but there is something about these poppies that I adore."

"Works for me." Carla opened a laptop at the station and searched for pictures of crocuses. "What color?"

"Purple, if you please."

"Alright." She made a note and then asked, "Where and how big?"

Elaine cocked her head and thought about it. "Somewhere that I can conceal easily, but still see. What is your recommendation?"

"Your upper thigh," Carla said, laying a hand on her own. "That's a spot you've gotta put some effort into showing."

"Perfect! And perhaps—" She paused and looked down at her palm. "Perhaps half again as long as my hand?"

"I can do that." Carla smiled to herself and glanced at the clock. "I'm free for the next three hours if you want to get it done right now."

Elaine nodded. "I think that would be best."

"Cool. Go out and grab a coffee or something, and come back in like half an hour. I should be ready by then."

"Perfect!" Elaine said. "We are already going for coffee."

The tattoo artist glanced at the New Kid. "Did you want to get something done too?"

"Oh—no, no thanks," he stammered. "I'm okay."

"Alright, I'll see you in a bit."

Elaine practically bounced out of the shop with the New Kid

trailing miserably behind her. "The Prince of Wales has a tattoo," she informed him, "as does the tsar, and the king of Sweden, and loads of other people. I've always thought them fascinating, but Mattie says they're for sailors and whores and other rough folk. For once, I'm going to do just as I please without worrying about what Mattie will say!"

The New Kid ran a hand through his hair anxiously. "Elaine, you—you can't just get a tattoo."

Turning to face him, she said, "Whyever not? It's my body, and this is the 21st century. I'll thank you to be supportive, or shush."

Properly chastised on that front, the New Kid decided to switch tactics. "Okay, but what about money?"

"I have some pocket money with me. Tattoos are cheap things that even common sailors can afford."

"Maybe they used to be, but they're more expensive now. I mean, everything is expensive, but especially tattoos. Like, several hundred dollars, I think."

That amount brought her up short. "How much is that in pounds?"

"No idea, but it's a lot. Way more than what you've got in pocket money."

"Bollocks," she muttered, knotting her skirt in her hands and looking away in frustration. "This is ridiculous. I finally have the freedom that I've longed for all my life, and I'm stopped by something as plebeian as money." With a sudden gasp, Elaine lifted a hand to the earrings that glittered in her lobes. Quick as a wink she plucked them out and offered them to the New Kid. "Will these suffice?"

The New Kid knew next to nothing about tattoos, and even less about jewelry, but he gamely looked down at the simple drop diamonds. "Maybe, but you can't just hand them over to Carla in trade."

"But what if I gave them to you?" she asked, staring at him intently. "If you could give Miss Carla the money, I could let you keep the earrings to sell later. Surely they are worth more than a tattoo."

The New Kid stared at the diamonds glittering in her outstretched palm, and thought about the black credit card burning a hole in the bottom of his pack. "Keep your earrings," he said, folding her fingers over them. "We got it covered."

# IN WHICH WE CATCH UP

## Cat
### (10:02)

Cat narrowed her eyes at the man in front of her, who was cringing so hard that he was practically bent in half. "What do you mean, 'He won't come out'?" she demanded.

"He won't, Cat," the voice on the other end of her bud repeated. "He wants to finish the movie."

"Then drag him out by his collar," she hissed, her shoulders bunching. "There are two of you, and you have stun rounds. Use your fucking imagination."

A scant five feet away, Darwin winced and tried to make himself even smaller. Helix was winding an ace bandage around a stocky agent's ankle a few feet away, but like everyone else, her attention was squarely on Cat.

"He's huge," the Watchdog said over the bud. "Like, schoolyard-bully huge."

Cat put a thumb in the middle of her pulsing forehead. "Fine. *Fine*. But the minute those credits roll, you get him out of there and back home."

"Got it. Cole and Heather out."

Ending the transmission, Cat took a deep cleansing breath before turning her gaze on Darwin. "You took Boss-*fucking*-Tweed into a Best Buy and let him watch *Frozen*?"

"It seemed like a good idea at the time?" Darwin squeaked out. "It was playing on one of the TVs, and I didn't want to blow his mind with an action movie."

"Why the *hell* was he in there in the first place?"

In the midst of the argument, the New Kid arrived bearing stacked trays of coffee. He set one down on an open part of the table, but as the eager agents divided up the cups they jostled him just enough to shift the balance of the other tray. It tumbled to the ground, spilling drinks—including iced lattes, frappes, and Cat's precious double shot on ice—in a frothy arc.

Because Cat Fiyero was made entirely out of caffeine and sarcasm rather than the standard composition of oxygen, hydrogen, carbon, and other trace elements, this was really a much larger problem than it seemed to be on the surface. The Gammas held their collective breaths, waiting for the eruption. Only Grunt remained, as always, unperturbed; without missing a beat, he offered his drip coffee to Cat and let the smell work its soothing magic.

Appropriately pacified, Cat accepted the steaming cup and took a sip. "The fuck is everyone looking at?"

"We're just appreciating this beautiful morning," Darwin said, eying his sister.

"It's very nice," Helix agreed carefully.

"A fine morning to be alive and un-maimed."

Cat took a second sip. "I'll let this go for now, Darwin, but you need to clear a stunt like that with me or the closest team leader." Her gaze flickered to the New Kid, and she frowned. "Aren't there supposed to be two of you?"

He swallowed. "Elaine, um—wanted to read some of the new books. So I left her at, at Javanaut. She promised not to leave." Seeing Cat's face pinching inward even further, he hurried to say, "She wouldn't—she wouldn't come with me."

"It's not like he could've knocked her out," Specs added, sparing a mournful look for his lost caramel frappe. "Besides, Elaine's technically an adult, and she's smart enough to find her way back before it's too late."

Cat looked back and forth between them. "Far be it from me to argue with you two. Who's got the latest numbers?"

"I do," Helix said, standing up and digging her tablet out of the bag at Darwin's side. She took a moment to flick through the screens. "A handful of petty casualties, no deaths or major injuries. The Wormhole estimates somewhere between twenty and thirty currently active rifts in Gamma territory."

"Estimates?" the New Kid asked.

Cat blew on her coffee and took a much larger gulp. Sighing in satisfaction, she said, "They do the best they can. And just because a rift is active doesn't necessarily mean it's being used."

"Millennia to Command, we've got something nasty brewing north of you," Millennia said over the bud. "It's somewhere in the Ramble, but I can't peg the exact location."

"This is Command," Cat said, setting her coffee down. "We're on our way."

Millennia's voice was tight. "Cat, you'd better get up there quick, because whatever it is—it ain't good."

"Got it," Cat acknowledged, cutting the transmission. "Grunt, I want a skeleton crew left behind to coordinate."

"Yes ma'am." He pointed at two Watchdogs, and they both took up positions in the Command center.

"We're going light and fast," Cat said, tossing her pen down on the table. "Move out."

As a group, they headed across Bow Bridge and into the running trails that preceded the lower edges of the Ramble, where the New Kid had come across Elaine.

"Millennia, we're here," Cat said as they turned down one of the rougher trails. "No sign of trouble yet."

"It's definitely open," she panted. "There's one! Cat, I can't talk—"

"Go," Cat said. "Eyes open, people."

The New Kid pointed to an excited crowd just visible through the trees. They had gathered in a semi-circle near the edge of Azalea Pond. "Uh, Commander—"

"Darwin, stay on this trail with Elias and Mia and keep

looking. Everybody else, with me!" she said, leading the charge. They jogged forward in a loose formation with Cat at the head and Grunt protecting the rear. The shouts of the onlookers grew louder, and as they broke through the edge of the ring Cat saw a tall feathered hat trembling in agitation.

"This can't be good," she muttered, elbowing people out of the way.

"Watch it," someone with onion breath said. "You're blocking the show."

Ignoring the rising complaints, the Dogs bullied their way through mercilessly. When she had a clear view of the situation, Cat sighed. As she and Millennia had both estimated, it was definitely *not good.*

There were twenty men on and around the tiny Azalea Pond Bridge, each dressed in a ridiculous white coat and old-fashioned trousers. The man in the center of the formation stood out for a few different reasons: One, his uniform was royal blue instead of white; two, he was wearing the aforementioned agitated feather hat; three, he was clearly the one issuing commands in a language that Cat couldn't understand; and four, he was wielding a gleaming military rapier that, in spite of the audience's belief, was obviously quite real. The muskets currently aimed at the heart of the crowd were also more than likely real.

"*Où est le commandant?*" the officer screamed, face purpling under his wig.

"He's asking for the commander," Specs said into Cat's ear. "They're 18th century French militia, so I'm assuming he's asking for either Rochambeau or Washington."

"Excellent," Cat said. "I always wanted to get shot with two-hundred-year-old technology."

"Actually, the musket was designed—you know what, it doesn't matter." Specs frowned and turned his head slightly, listening to the officer's chatter. "'My name is Captain Jean-Paul Renault with His Majesty's—' bourbon-something, I don't know that word. 'And I have claimed this place for the—the glory of

the French Empire? You must clear the way immediately, or—'
Cat, he's ordering the men to fire on the crowd if they haven't
dispersed within a minute."

"*Shit*," Cat hissed, turning on the closest spectators and
shoving them away. "Get back! *Get the fuck back!*"

The people in the back who weren't being shoved began
applauding. "This is awesome," a bearded white guy in skinny
jeans and a trendy plaid shirt said. "I really appreciate your
commitment to the role."

In one of those glorious moments that proved she really
wasn't director material at all, Cat drew the Peacekeeper and
said, "Then you're gonna love this." She took his messenger
cap, flung it straight up, and fired a laser round right through
the middle. It fell between them with a quiet *plop*, the edges of
the hole still glowing cherry red.

"Get the *fuck* back," she repeated crisply.

His hip complexion turned china white, and he scrambled
downhill as fast as his thrift-store Oxfords would take him.
There was a general commotion as most of the stunned crowd
came to life and followed him, shoving and screaming. Cat
turned back and regarded the stressed French captain.

"Abandon your post—" she began, but Captain Renault spit
on the ground at her feet and screamed "*Vive la France!*" The
company began a mad retreat across the bridge and along the
Gill.

"Fuck, they're going for higher ground," Cat said. "Grunt, I
want Watchdogs clearing out the trails. There's no way they're
gonna be that patient a second time, not when they're scared
shitless. We'll send Darwin and—"

There was a great cry from overhead, and the steady beating
of leathery wings. Cat looked up in confusion.

"What the fuck was that?"

# PACK BEHAVIOR

## Command
### Present Time (10:32)

"**N**obody move," Cat whispered, lowering herself into a tense crouch and assessing the pack of dinosaurs. Six of them peered back at her. They were like smaller, more slender versions of the raptors from *Jurassic Park*, with elongated necks, whiplike tails, and—feathers?

She definitely wasn't imagining it: The dinosaurs were covered almost from skull to tail tip in short white and brown feathers. *That* hadn't been in the movies.

Whatever else they were, it wasn't herbivorous. Rows of vicious teeth became visible as they chattered to each other, obviously unnerved by the strange new creatures that had invaded their space.

"Stun rounds out, *slowly*," Cat said. She unclipped her secondary piece, a small Ruger, and raised it. "Call it, Grunt."

"Tamika, furthest left. Commander, little one up front. I'll get the alpha behind it. Kerry, middle. Oz, next over. Sasha, furthest right," he said methodically. "On three. One—"

The alpha of the pack screeched, and they made a break for it. Three agents fired anyway, including Cat. Only she and Oz hit their targets. Kerry, unfortunately, followed his target's trajectory and hit Oz instead. The unlucky Dog yelped and jumped back.

"Motherfucker, that hurt," he said, promptly followed by, "Oh *fuck*," when the stun round latched onto his lower bicep, past the protective reach of his rachneweave underclothes. He brushed at it instinctively.

"*Move*," Cat snarled, pulling out her knife. Quick as a blink, she leveraged it between the prongs of the round and popped it out like a tick. The round released its charge in midair, crackling uselessly as it spun and hit the ground.

There was no time for gratitude. Two dinosaurs were currently twitching on the ground, but the other four had scattered in the direction of the Great Lawn, where countless New Yorkers and tourists would be gathered to celebrate the Day Out of Time. "Grunt, take them down," Cat said. "Radio Darwin as soon as you do. Specs, New Kid, with me! We'll get Renault."

"Fetch," Grunt told his Watchdogs immediately. "Kerry, guard."

As a unit, Team Rottie took off at a controlled run down the trails of the Ramble rather than fighting their way uphill through the bush. Though the dinosaurs were much faster, they were easy to track due to the screams that followed in their wake.

The Watchdogs mentally thanked all the hours of training that they had put in over the year. Without it, they would have been unable to continue by the time they crossed Transverse Drive. It did seem that the dinosaurs were having trouble, as they had slowed down enough to be within sight. They tore into the Shakespeare Garden, seeking its shelter, but came out just as quickly through the other side when they found it inhabited by its fair share of tourists.

As Grunt and Cat had feared, the dinosaur pack made a beeline for the Great Lawn, where their long bodies would have plenty of room to run. The Watchdogs were keeping up, but only just.

"Free hunt," Grunt called as they came to the edge of the trees. "Do *not* shoot unless you have it."

They emerged into a world of chaos. Unlike with the French militia, almost everyone who saw the dinosaur pack was smart enough to realize that they were not part of some elaborate show. They tore through picnic baskets and smashed acoustic guitars, skidding and rolling through the wreckage in their mad attempt to flee.

The middle of the Great Lawn had been given over to the festival celebrating the Day Out of Time. Booths selling strange goods and crafts were crammed in beside even stranger carnival games. The festival wasn't as busy as it would be a little later in the day, but it was certainly busy enough to be a headache. The one benefit to the crowd was the resulting noise; the dinosaurs turned in useless circles, giving the Watchdogs plenty of time to catch up and regroup.

One pair of extraordinarily stoned teenagers watched the crazed dinosaurs approach, far too high to get out of the way. Instead, they started laughing hysterically.

"Dude," the teen with blond dreadlocks said, picking up one of the blunts littering the grass around them. "What the fuck did you put in this?"

His best friend giggled. "Shit, man, it's pure, it's fucking *pure*, I swear!" Squinting through the tears in his eyes, he said, "Dude, why's that dinosaur coming at us?"

"I don't know, man. Why's it being chased by Captain America?"

The brief moment of clarity was ruined by a new giggle fit. They were still rolling around when one of the dinosaurs crashed through their little spot, placing one sharply-taloned foot right where the dreadlocked teen's stomach had been.

His friend's luck ran a little drier when a second dinosaur heading their way was pegged by a shot from one of the Watchdogs. The electricity hit its system ten feet from the boys, causing it to spasm and collapse on the one without dreads. Though less than thirty-five pounds, it still hit with enough force to knock the wind out of him.

What had been hilarious just seconds before was now slowly

crushing the teen's lungs. He flailed around uselessly, too stoned and confused to do anything even remotely smart, until an angel in black descended directly from Heaven to save him. She had corn silk hair pulled back in a ponytail and the bluest eyes he had ever seen. A fiery halo around her blinded him, but he couldn't stop staring. Being smooshed by an imaginary dinosaur had definitely been worth it for a glimpse of her.

The angel (whose name was Sasha) easily heaved the limp reptile off of the teenager and put her hands on his face. "Breathe," she said. Her voice was low and reassuring. "Are you hurt?"

His diaphragm stopped spasming, and as he took a deep breath the first words out of his mouth were, "I think I love you."

Sasha rolled her eyes. "Uh-huh. You'll be fine. Can you stand?"

"I—" He tried, only to wince and lay back down. "Hurts."

"Where?"

When he laid a hand on his side, she lifted his shirt and gently palpated the area, stopping when he hissed in pain. "Damage to the seventh rib. Definitely cracked, but I don't think it's broken all the way. Stay put, okay?" Standing up, Sasha opened a channel on her bud. "Sasha to Helix. If you're near the festival grounds, I've got a kid here with a fractured rib."

"I'm at the southern edge of the Great Lawn," Helix panted. "Keep him still."

"We really need hoverboards," Sasha grumbled, ending the transmission.

At the same time that the currently paralyzed dinosaur had been landing on the teenager, Grunt was in pursuit of the stockier alpha. It outweighed its pack mates by about ten pounds, making it more intimidating, but just a smidge slower. This also put more pressure on its respiratory system, and the higher oxygen levels of the present era finally caught up to it near the balancing booth. Dizzy with an abundance of air, it stumbled and knocked over the delicately crafted pyramid of eggs with its long tail, sending them flying in a wide arc. As an evolved primate of the highest order, Grunt felt no such limits on his breathing and easily caught up to the dinosaur, pegging it in the meat of its hind limb with a stun round.

He looked around and allowed himself a small smile of satisfaction at the efficiency of his team. Sasha, Oz, and Tamika had each bagged a dinosaur of their own, officially accounting for all of them.

Tapping his tragus, Grunt opened a channel and said, "Darwin, we've got four unidentified dinosaurs on the Great Lawn and two more back in the Ramble with Kerry. All subjects neutralized."

"Whoa-whoa-whoa, *what?*" the zoologist demanded. "Grunt, are you telling me there are *more fucking dinosaurs?*"

"Confirmed. Six of them. I need you, Elias, and Mia to rendezvous with Kerry and gather them all here."

"Of all the—" What followed was a stream of four-letter words that would have made Cat fluff up with pride. Eventually he ran out of steam and just said, "Alright, fuck. We'll be there ASAP."

The tactical officer closed the channel and opened a new one. "Grunt to Team Viszla, I need you on guard duty."

They radioed in their acknowledgements as Oz, Sasha, and Tamika gathered around him with their targets, looking winded but otherwise no worse for the wear. "Viszla's on the way," Grunt said, holstering his weapon and wiping the sweat from his forehead. "When they relieve you, head back to Command unless you hear from me."

Without waiting for confirmation he took off back down the Great Lawn, hoping that for once, Cat had chosen the path of diplomacy.

# ALL UPHILL FROM HERE

## Cat
### (10:37)

C at cursed Gamma's luck to herself as she led Specs and the New Kid up into the depths of the Ramble, where Captain Renault and his men had taken the flat, open ground behind Bonfire Rock.

"Not one dinosaur, but *seven* where they aren't supposed to be," she muttered in Specs's direction as they fought their way uphill. "What's that you were saying about 'no historical evidence'?"

"One set of footprints near Blauvelt!" Specs insisted, climbing up a rocky patch. "That's all they've ever found."

"*Blauvelt?* That's less than thirty miles from here!" Cat hissed.

"Well I'm *sorry* that I never imagined that the one pack of dinosaurs that made it this far north would ever end up in our territory," Specs said, stress sharpening his normally dull temper. "And I'm sorry that some random pteranodon got lost and is currently dive-bombing tourists, but none of that is *my fault.*"

Cat stopped walking and turned to face her lieutenant, panting with effort. He pulled up short, eye-to-eye with her for once due to her uphill position. They stared at each other for several seconds before Cat ducked her head in acknowledgement.

"You're right, Specs," she said, looking back up at him with far less hostility in her eyes. "Fuck, I'm sorry. I know it's not your fault, okay?"

"Okay," he said, letting out a great breath of air. "Yeah, okay. Thank you."

"A-Game, yeah? We've got a pack of rabid Frenchmen to talk down."

"'Rabid' is a harsh word," Specs said as they began to climb again.

"Don't make me kick you downhill."

Near the top, they received a furious warning in French, and Specs immediately pulled everyone short. "We're not supposed to take another step."

"Get back," Cat said, shoving the New Kid behind an oak tree. Out of habit (and practicality), she went to one knee under the cover of the surrounding bushes and let Specs loom behind their new pup like a brick wall.

Ahead of them, the angry boulders were quiet but for the occasional whisper of shifting bodies. Cat took a breath and let it out slowly, wishing for the cigarettes that she hadn't smoked in close to ten years.

"Okay guys," she said, "this is where it gets complicated. Specs, tell them that we know they're confused, but we're friends and we want to help. New Kid, repeat what he says."

The New Kid swallowed, looking like sour milk. "Okay."

"*Bonjour. Nous savons que vous êtes confus,*" Specs said.

"Bonjour!" the younger man called. "New—new sav-on kay voos et con-foo."

"*Mais nous sommes amis et nous voulons vous aider.*"

"Uh—my new some a-mees aye new voo-lon voos—what's the last one again?"

"*Aider.*"

"A-ider!"

Cat buried her face in one hand. "Oh my God."

The white curls of Captain Renault's wig appeared above the rocks as he peered down cautiously. "*Quel est votre régiment?*" he demanded.

"He wants to know what regiment we're in," Specs translated.

"Tell him that we work directly under the commander."

"*Nous sommes—*"

"Fuck's sake," Cat hissed, "just tell him yourself and don't let them see you."

Specs nodded and called, "*Nous sommes avec le général Washington! Nous sommes son régiment personnel.*"

Captain Renault narrowed his eyes suspiciously. "*Je demande à parler avec le commandant.*"

"Oh damn," Specs said, wiping his forehead. "They want to talk to Washington."

"Fuck me," Cat muttered. "Okay. Okay, tell him that we'll go get Washington, but he's a very busy man and it might take a long time. Hours, even. Ask them to stay here, *without shooting anyone*, and we'll be back later."

As Specs relayed this request, Cat lifted her watch and tuned it to the main comms channel. "Commander Fiyero to the Hive, do you copy?"

"Copy that Cat, we've got you loud and clear," an older female voice said.

"We're up shit creek, Mariska, and I need you to find me a paddle. Can you put out a mass bulletin to every active team, requesting that anyone who comes across either General George Washington or Rochambeau needs to call me ASAP?"

"Of course. Did you lose them?"

Cat laughed. "I wish. No, I've got a stubborn French captain camped up in the Ramble and he won't come down without talking to one of those two. This is more of a desperate longshot than an actual plan."

"Roger that, Cat," Mariska said. "Do you need a security team?"

"If you've got it to spare. Otherwise, I'll put half a team on guard duty."

There was the faint sound of keys clicking. "Go ahead and

do that, and I'll send someone to relieve them as soon as I can."

"I owe you pie, Mariska. With crumbly things on top."

The older woman laughed. "You know you don't owe me anything, dear, but I'm always a fan of pie. Hive out."

"It's settled," Specs said as Cat closed the channel. "Captain Renault has agreed to wait for Washington."

Glancing uphill, Cat bit her lip. "What do you think the odds are?"

"That one of them will show up?" Specs asked, crossing his arms. "I'd say low, but not impossible. It was a crazy time, with a lot of turmoil. That kind of environment breeds rifts like the plague."

Cat sighed and rubbed her face. "It'll have to do. Per usual, it's a ridiculous plan."

"What's Plan B?"

"We put McNab in a white wig and uproot that glorious red weasel currently camped above his lip. Oh, and we drop a team with stun rounds in the middle of them as Plan C. Call it the Alpha Plan." Tapping the bud in her ear, she said, "Cat to Grunt, status report."

The tactical officer answered immediately. "All six subjects tagged and under guard. Do you need support?"

"Negative. We've stalled for now, but I want the first free team up here establishing a perimeter. Security will relieve them eventually."

"I'll call it in. Viszla should be up any minute."

Cat grinned. "Excellent work, as always. Call in backup from Rottie too; I'll get ahold of Darwin myself. The dinos are his responsibility, and I want them out of the way until Millennia can send them home. Does anybody have eyes on that goddamn pteranodon?"

"Rex and Camilla are still watching it."

"Grunt," she sighed, "have I told you that you're my favorite person?"

"Always nice to hear, Commander. Grunt out."

As they turned to go, the New Kid opened his mouth, closed

it, and tried again. "I'm sorry, Commander."

Leading the way back down the forested hillside, Cat glanced back and asked, "Sorry for what?"

"For, you know—messing it up."

"What, the French? Relax, kid. I can't speak it either."

"She really can't," Specs said. "She's terrible."

Cat winked at her lieutenant. "Come on, boys. Once more into the breach."

# RIVER-DANCING DINOS

## Darwin
### (11:03)

Darwin whistled in appreciation as he picked up the edge of the camo sheet. "Well, if this isn't the nicest present that anyone's ever gotten me," he said. "But what the fuck am I supposed to do with six dinosaurs?"

"Start a basketball team," Helix suggested, cleaning the tiny spot on Oz's forearm where the stun round had collected its sample.

"Cat to Darwin," the commander's voice said from inside his ear. "I'm sending the New Kid your way. Get those dinos out of sight until Millennia gets back. Somewhere they won't get too much attention."

"Aye-aye, Captain my Captain. Out of sight," Darwin said, a cheerful smile on his face. When he closed the connection, the smile took a nosedive. "Seriously? What the hell am I supposed to do with these guys?"

Oz thanked Helix and turned his arm back and forth, admiring the Princess Jasmine BandAid. "Say the word and we'll take 'em wherever you want."

"Some of us, anyway," Sasha corrected. "The commander will probably want us to split up."

"Grunt to Rottweiler and Viszla. Darwin too, if you're listening," everyone's buds said. "Listen up. I need half of Rottie to escort Darwin wherever he's going, and half of Viszla establishing a perimeter around Captain Renault and his men until security can get there. Keep it nice and calm: Nobody in, nobody out. Team leaders, make your picks. Everybody else, get back on patrol."

"Yes sir," Sasha said, closing the channel and immediately opening a new one. "Sasha to Rottie, I need Burke, Kader, Francis—"

"She's eight pounds of dynamite in a two pound bag, isn't she?" Darwin asked when Sasha walked out of earshot.

Oz shook his head. "Wasting your time, bro. She'll stomp your heart under her pretty pink combat boots."

"Among other things," Helix added. "I should get back to Command with the rest of Rottie. I'll see you later." She kissed her brother on the cheek and walked off, massive backpack bobbing with each step.

"Alright, let's see what we're dealing with," Darwin said, taking a peak under the camo sheet again and scanning the unconscious dinosaur with his tablet. It completed the visual analysis and beeped triumphantly. "Bingo. It's a kind of coelophysis, from the Triassic period. Damn, the Southwest? These boys are a long way from home." Reading a bit more data, he corrected himself. "These girls, actually. Wasn't there a bigger one?"

"Over here," Oz said, waving the zoologist over and lifting the sheet for his inspection.

"Yeah, that one's definitely a male. Not sure if this is his harem or if he was the only bastard unlucky enough to get sucked into the rift."

"What do you want us to do with them?" Oz asked.

Running his fingers through his thick hair until it stood up in an Elvis pompadour, Darwin turned in a slow circle. The Lawn was still full of people enjoying the festival; in typical fashion, everybody seemed to have forgotten the dinosaurs that had crashed through their picnics less than an hour before. A couple not fifteen feet away from him was arguing over the woman's guidebook. As she slapped it against her boyfriend's chest, Darwin recognized the building on the cover.

"Now there's an idea," he muttered, rubbing his hands together in a vaguely maniacal fashion. "Hey, Tamika!"

The stocky, handsome woman with chestnut skin and short cornrows hollered back, "Yeah?"

"You packing any perimeter tape?"

Tamika's hand went to her leg pouch and she nodded. "Yeah, I got some. Why?"

Grinning, Darwin said, "Because the Museum of Natural History has some exhibit space we need."

"Need for what?" Oz asked suspiciously. "Need for *what*, Darwin?"

"River dancing," he retorted, "what the fuck do you think we need it for?"

"Aw no, man," Oz sighed, pushing longish brown hair out of his eyes. "Come on, that's just wrong. We can't hide six dinosaurs in the *Natural History Museum*."

"We can if we get them out before midnight," Darwin said. "We'll just say they're part of an upcoming exhibit. Super-advanced animatronics, and all that. 'Dinosaurs Alive'!"

"You're fucking nuts, bro."

"Hey, Cat said, 'out of sight.' She said, 'not too much attention.'"

"Alright, let me clear it with Sasha." Oz opened a channel on his bud and said, "Oz to Sasha, we're stashing the dinos— somewhere safe. You aren't gonna like it." He listened to the reply, then glanced at the zoologist. "The-Natural-History-Museum-and-it-was-Darwin's-idea," he said, as if the statement was one word.

Darwin chucked a nearby stick at him. "You're an asshole."

Oz held up his hand and nodded along with something Sasha was saying. "She thinks it'll probably work," he admitted.

"Thank you, Sasha," Darwin said, leaning over to speak into the Watchdog's ear.

Oz shoved him away and said, "Right, we're heading to the

museum. Oz out." Brushing his hair back, he said, "Jesus Christ, dinosaurs in Central Park. At least there's no mammoths this year."

"You think we got it bad?" Tamika said. "Ribbit says Tokyo has a megalodon circling the whole island of Hokkaidō."

"Shit, for real?"

"Yeah, and Cairo has some idiots firing blasters in a mini-mall." Shaking her head, Tamika muttered, "Whole damn world needs a little divine intervention, ya feel me?"

"Alright, who've we got?" Darwin asked, putting his hands on his hips and surveying his minions. He spotted the New Kid some sixty feet away, slowly trudging his way across the Lawn. "Right, everybody grab a lizard. I need my hands free."

"What happens if something else attacks us?" Oz asked. He knelt down to help Elias wrap the closest coelophysis in black canvas.

"That thing weighs, what—thirty pounds? Big guy like you, I'm sure you can hold it in one hand and shoot with the other."

Oz sighed, and it was as long-suffering as an exhalation of air could possibly be. "I hate you so much sometimes."

"It's that 'sometimes' that still gives me hope for the future," Darwin said. Waving the New Kid over, he called, "Join the party, newbie! We're going on an adventure."

Like Oz, the New Kid sighed and looked up. "Oh good. I was getting bored."

Hefting a coelophysis over one shoulder, Tamika asked, "Any chance a cab'll take us with these things?"

"Any chance we can call a transport van?" Elias piped up.

"Oh my God, you *weenies*," Mia said, mimicking Tamika's fireman carry. Since she was about the size of a twelve-year-old, the move lost a little of its dramatic effect along the way. "It's not even half a mile."

"In the middle of Benedictus," Elias grumbled.

"Aren't you Jamaican or something?" Darwin asked, drawing a small amount of bright pink GH out of a vial and injecting it into each coelophysis's leg.

Proving that he for one could hold a dinosaur up with one hand, Elias flipped Darwin the bird. "I'm Haitian, motherfucker, and I don't wanna hear anything about it from *you*. You bitch louder than anybody else in the whole Doghouse."

"That's because I'm a delicate Punjabi flower. Make sure they can all breathe," Darwin said. "Everybody ready? Alright, single file. The Hunter's Gate is pretty secluded, so that's our exit. It'll come out right at 81st, and it's just a hop over to the parking garage and museum side entrance."

"How—how long are they out for?" the New Kid asked, shifting his burden nervously.

Darwin checked his watch. "Forty minutes, tops. We better scoot."

The Dogs fell in behind him and began trudging towards the bottom of the Great Lawn. Though this part of the park was full to bursting with people, no one paid the Dogs any attention. They all possessed a sort of vacant complacency, as if each moment existed in a vacuum and was gone from memory as soon as it passed, like steam wiped from glass.

It was disconcerting to finally break free of the tree cover and emerge into the modern world again. Even native New Yorkers like Darwin and Mia sometimes had trouble adjusting to the vastness and isolation of Central Park. Cars inched past, honking petulantly, and bicycles whizzed between them with reckless abandon. The thick green smell of trees was replaced with exhaust, dirty human, and a nearby Korean barbecue van. Diagonally to the pack of Watchdogs sat the famous cream pillars and pale russet walls of the American Museum of Natural History, with the gleaming glass cube of the Rose Center behind its facade.

"What's the plan again?" Oz asked.

Darwin sniffed the air, sorting through the smells with practiced ease before grinning. "Anybody else have a serious craving for some melted cheese?"

Mixed in amongst the various food trucks was a petite red

van that sold a truly astounding variety of grilled cheese sandwiches. The taller of the two workers, a big-boned woman of mixed Filipino and Samoan heritage, was putting together a gruyère and tomato sandwich for a businessman in a three-piece suit. Her shorter companion was busy grilling something that oozed macaroni and cheese. They were between the breakfast and lunch rushes, so when the businessman stepped aside to wait for his sandwiches, there was no one to block the tall woman's view of Darwin.

She glared down at him and reached for the window. "Sorry, we're closed."

Darwin stuck his hand into the gap, squeezing back a yelp as the glass panel slammed into it. "Yaz, I—"

The angry woman wrenched the window open again and leaned out. "Jai Ramachandra, you have three seconds to move your hand before I break it. Here's your order, honey."

This last part was directed at the businessman, who accepted the wax-wrapped sandwiches with a meek nod of thanks and a quick exit. The woman called Yaz turned her glare back on Darwin, who was, for once, completely serious.

"Yaz, I need your help," he said. "I know you're pissed—"

"*Pissed?*" she repeated, dark curls dancing as she shook her head. "Pissed is what I was three months ago. Nobody reneges on my tables. You turn that perky ass right around and go on home, because I don't want nothin' to do with you."

"Yasmin runs the best mahjong tables in the city," Darwin explained before turning back to the furious woman, who was currently clicking her pointed red nails on the window ledge. "And I apologized when—"

"I want you to apologize with my money."

Patting his pockets helplessly, Darwin looked back at the Dogs and said, "Does anybody have $850?"

Oz hefted the unconscious coelophysis higher on his shoulder and raised an eyebrow. "Seriously, dude?"

For the first time, Yasmin took a really good look at the group in front of her. "What's going on?"

"We need your help," Darwin said. "We've gotta sneak something into the museum, and we need you to watch our gear."

"Do what?" Elias asked.

"Come on, man, they're not gonna let us in there with full SWAT gear. We need somewhere safe to leave everything but our clothes."

The New Kid lifted his dinosaur burrito higher. "Everything?"

"Not *everything*, you moron."

Yasmin held up one hand. "Let me get this straight. You want me to let a pack a' Dogs stash their collars and tags in my van—collars that can get me arrested about twenty times over, mind—in exchange for, what? A look at your pretty face?"

"My debt covered and then some," Darwin promised. "Five."

"Twelve," Yasmin countered immediately. "Do I look like I was born with my ass and my brain switched like you?"

"Seven."

"Ten, and you'll kiss my feet and call me your sweet island princess."

Slumping, Darwin winced and said, "Eight and a half? Just for an hour?"

Yasmin cocked her head. "Deal. But for every ten minutes you go over, my fee doubles, so I'd get to steppin'." Closing the window, she opened the back of the van and gestured everybody forward. "Hurry up, I don't got all day."

Starting with Darwin, the Dogs lined up and begrudgingly divested themselves of their tactical gear and weapons, all of which Yasmin and her silent assistant hid in secret compartments under the van's seats. They kept a careful list of everything, and at the top Yasmin wrote a very brief explanation of the deal, which she and Darwin both signed. At the end of everything, the Dogs were left standing in plain black like catering staff.

"Much better," Darwin said, nodding. "I owe you, Yaz."

"Yeah, like I'm even gonna remember that," she grumbled, folding the makeshift contract up and tucking it deep in her apron pocket. "Don't make me regret this, Jai, or I swear to God I'll come after you."

"Love you!" he called, hopping out of the van. "Okay everyone, here's the plan. We'll go in through the Rose Center, up to the temporary exhibition hall on the fourth floor—"

"The *fourth?*" Mia squeaked.

"That's where they keep the fossils," Darwin said, shrugging helplessly. "It wouldn't make any sense to put them somewhere else."

"How're we supposed to get in?" Kerry asked. "Do you have museum credentials?"

Darwin grinned. "Not yet, but I will by the time we get there."

As he led the rest of them across the street and towards the entrance under the Rose Center, the New Kid caught up to Kerry and said, "Uh, do I want to know?"

"Probably not," the Watchdog advised.

The answer became obvious once they reached the main area in front of the entrance. It was packed with people, including a few black-clad workers and one extremely harassed-looking man with a clipboard near the parking garage. Pulling out his phone and fiddling with it, Darwin gestured for the others to hang back.

"Do you think he has the *Mission: Impossible* theme playing in his head?" Tamika asked.

"Nah, *Pink Panther*," Oz said. "Cousteau is his hero."

"He's an overlooked genius," Darwin agreed over his shoulder. "Watch and learn."

Apparently absorbed in whatever was on the screen in front of him, Darwin walked straight into the man with the clipboard, causing everything to tumble to the ground.

"Oh my God, I'm so—I am so sorry!" Darwin said, his actions an eerie mirror of the New Kid's.

The man's face shifted from irritated to neutrally pleasant in a second, and he got down on his hands and knees to pick up the scattered papers.

Darwin went to his knees as well. "Here, please let me help, I'm so sorry."

"Sir, it's really okay—"

"No, no, it was my fault. That's what I get for trading on the go. My wife says I'm always in the office, even when I'm home. Even when I'm asleep!"

When everything was in order he helped the older man stand up and tried to brush him off. After a few begrudging seconds the museum worker said, "Thank you, sir, but I actually have to get back to work."

"Yeah, of course. Sorry again." The zoologist nodded and casually made his way back to the group, pocketing his phone and pulling out the laminated badge that his long fingers had brushed from the other man's shirtfront. "And that is why my hands need to be free.

Oz shook his head. "One of these days, man."

"I wouldn't bet on it." Swinging his arm, Darwin said, "Come on kids, chop-chop. Be sure to look extra busy."

"I'm gonna punch him," Tamika promised.

"Get in line," Mia and Kerry muttered together.

The Dogs carried their bundles to the entrance, following Darwin's lead when he rushed up to the ticket counters. He waved the badge with his knuckle carefully positioned over the picture. "Paneling for four," he said. "Jay's been waiting for it."

The dark-haired woman in front of him couldn't have been older than twenty. She just gave him a mystified look and said, "Sorry?"

"Jay!" Darwin insisted, tucking the badge away and motioning the rest of the Gammas through. "Don't tell me you don't know Jay?"

"You mean James?" she asked. "Mr. Buchanan?"

Offering up his own confused look, Darwin raised his hands and said, "Who the hell else would I be talking about?" Flicking through his phone, he continued, "Shit, he's already upstairs.

See you later, Jules!"

"Oh—okay," she called, obviously frightened enough of disappointing Mr. James Buchanan that she didn't want to keep him waiting.

"How'd you know her name?" the New Kid asked as they walked away.

"Nametag," the zoologist replied, tapping his own chest.

The New Kid glanced back just before they rounded the corner. The shiny nametag on the woman's chest read *Julia*. She'd gone back to her computer, brow puckered slightly.

"Who the hell is Jay?" Oz asked as the Gammas followed Darwin down the crowded white hall towards a pair of elevators.

"Fuck if I know. Too many J-names in the world. Straight up to four," Darwin said, shooing Oz inside with Mia and Kerry. Tamika and Elias took the second elevator, leaving Darwin and the New Kid to wait anxiously for it to come back down.

"Relax," Darwin said. "I mean, don't relax too much, but you're about to stomp a hole through the floor."

The New Kid's foot stilled. "Sorry."

"Hey, you're doing pretty alright. I would've pissed myself if my second day on the job was an actual *Day*," Darwin said, whistling. "Talk about a fiery fucking baptism."

Glancing at a clock on the wall, the New Kid groaned. "How is it not even noon yet?"

One of the elevators returned and belched out three passengers, including a little boy about waist-high. As he walked past the two men carrying large black bundles, he got a good look up at a slack reptilian face and inhaled sharply.

Darwin gave the kid a cheeky wink and put his finger to his lips. You could have used the boy's eyes for ping-pong balls.

"Sometimes," the Dog admitted as the elevator doors closed, "I love this job so much it hurts."

¤　¤　¤　¤　¤　¤

145

The male coelophysis was just beginning to stir when the last of the perimeter tape was laid down. All six dinosaurs had been placed at the feet of the museum's interpretation of a juvenile *Barosaurus*, which stood guard outside the theater in its own partitioned display area. A group of tourists sat inside the theater itself, listening to an introductory video while a pack of live dinosaurs groggily came to their feet less than sixty feet away.

"This is insane," Oz muttered, nervously fingering the place where his gun normally sat. He watched the alpha totter drunkenly over to the waist-high barrier, which had been outlined with live perimeter tape. "I hope you're happy with yourself, Darwin. One of these days, your stupid fucking plans are gonna get us all killed."

"Or worse, expelled," Mia muttered, causing Tamika to crack up.

The coelyphysis's long nose poked over the barrier and came into contact with the invisible wall of vibrating air. It shrieked and fell back in a confused whirl of feathers, triggering a similar reaction in its harem.

Oz relaxed and stretched his sore arms over his head. "Gotta love our tech department though."

"What *is* this stuff?" the New Kid asked, eying the innocuous-looking tape.

"Perimeter tape," Tamika answered. "Uses ultra strong subsonic vibrations so ya can't get past. I mean, somethin' big that really, *really* wanted to get through could do it, but it wouldn't be any fun. These oversized chickens? They ain't goin' anywhere."

"Think of them like coked-up tuning forks," Darwin said. "It takes mass and determination to get through. A really pissed-off elephant wouldn't have much trouble, but a calm one would touch it once and probably back the hell off."

"People work the same way," Mia added. "We're smaller, but usually a lot more stubborn. It'll cost you a bloody nose and a massive headache, but you could break through the barrier in

146

less than a minute. The chickens are too light; the barrier'll bounce them around like a basketball."

Oz chuckled and put his hand on top of Mia's head, which was just level with his shoulder. "Kinda like you, short stuff?"

Mia used the opening to punch Oz in the base of his ribcage, and he doubled over. "I'll bounce *you* like a basketball, McAfee."

"Easy, kids," Tamika said, holding up both hands with a grin. "Oz, we both know little bit here can get through perimeter tape quicker than you, so don't go startin' shit."

"That was *one time*," the tall Watchdog wheezed, holding his aching side gingerly. "Ah-ha, you got me right in the floating ribs. That was uncalled for."

"Who's gonna stay behind and play guard dog?" Tamika asked.

"Kerry," Darwin said, passing the other Dog a spare magazine of stun rounds. "Wish I had a gun for you, man, but that's all I could get past the security guard."

Nodding, Kerry pocketed the rounds and crossed his arms. "I'll be fine."

Meanwhile, all six dinosaurs were awake and exploring the range of their new territory. It only took one hit on each side for them to learn the lesson. Instead, they began to circle aimlessly around the legs of the much larger model sharing their temporary home.

"Man, everybody's gonna get a kick out of this," Darwin said.

"Don't get too pleased with yourself," Oz warned. "It's still batshit crazy."

"I hope you're this cheerful come Christmas time, Mr. Grinch." Sighing, the zoologist said, "A'ight kids, field trip's over. Time to quit dicking around and get back to work. After all, they aren't paying us all that money to stand around and look pretty."

"Thank God," Oz said, his face deadpan, "because some of us would be way better off than others."

# THE GHOST OF DAYS PAST

## Millennia
### (11:18)

The only person who could rival Cat for the Busiest Team Member Award on a Day Out of Time was Millennia. She had just located and sent off the last of a rogue group of day laborers when word about the coelophysis pack and the lone pteranodon came in.

"*Dinosaurs?* Are you freaking kidding me right now?" she said, running her hand through the messy front of her hair, which was slowly coming out of its well-intentioned ponytail. "I don't know whether to be stressed or piss myself from excitement. I'm like a really confused Chihuahua."

A nearby Watchdog from Pit Bull snorted and scratched his tanned neck. "If I wanted to see dinosaurs, I'd go back to Texas. You need an escort?"

"Nah, I'm good. Azalea Pond, right?"

"That's what Ribbit said."

Muttering to herself, the petite physicist took off at a jog down Fifth Avenue in the direction of the Ramble. As she passed behind the Met, she opened a channel on her bud.

"Millennia to Cat. Who has top priority, the flyer or the raptors?"

"The flyer," Cat said. "The raptors are on lockdown for now, but if you find theirs instead, tag it and let me know."

"Roger. Where did you first see them?"

"Somewhere to the east of Azalea Pond, around ten. I was a little preoccupied at the time."

"Alright, I'll start at the pond and work my way east when I'm done with the flyer. Who's guarding it?"

"Camilla and Adam."

"Roger dodger. Millennia out."

She wasn't proud of it, but the temporal expert may or may not have stolen a bike in order to complete her noble quest in a timely manner. Her reasoning was that they should have known better than to leave an unchained bike unattended, and really, dinosaurs were involved at this point. Any situation that included giant reptiles allowed for a bend in the rules.

When she reached the uphill slope, Millennia slowed the bike and swung down, walking it up to a lamppost and propping it up with an apologetic wince. "No hard feelings, dude."

Pulling out her tablet, Millennia scrolled through the programs and opened the archived data from earlier that morning. There were a few possibilities, but it was hard to pinpoint the exact rift without a better idea of the timeframe.

The physicist opened a channel and said, "Millennia to Camilla and Adam; olly-olly-oxen-free!"

A hyper-posh London accent responded a few seconds later. "Camilla here. We've relocated to where the Gill feeds into the Lake."

"I'm just north of you," Millennia said, turning to follow the narrow path that the water carved into the trees. "You got eyes on the pteranodon?"

"We're staring right at her," Adam said. "She's been fishing off and on, but she gets tired pretty quick. Doesn't really wanna leave the trees. Atmosphere changes, I bet."

Millennia stepped delicately over a fallen branch and said, "I'll be there soonest. *Ciao-ciao!*"

It wasn't hard to locate the two Dogs and their charge. The pteranodon's breathy calls echoed over the water, and as Millennia came to the edge of the Lake she could see it perched up in a large tree to the right. A small red crest crowned the animal's head, and its weight was balanced between its hind legs and the middle joints of its wings, the way a bat might sit. Unlike a bat, the pteranodon's membranous wings were thick and solid; they looked as if they could sustain it for hours under normal conditions. Millennia had been down to the Southwest before, but there was a vast difference between seeing dinosaurs in the Santa Fe Doghouse and seeing them perched in a tree in Central Park.

Adam emerged from his post, brown hair tousled where he'd run through the underbrush to keep up with the dinosaur. "*Pteranodon longiceps,*" he said, pushing his glasses back up his sweaty pink nose. "Normally found in the last ten or twelve million years of the Cretaceous period. Not sure what she's doing this far north since the rookeries were typically on the inland seas, but it's possible there was a colony established on the East Coast at some point."

Fanning herself, Millennia winked and said, "Adam, you know I can't handle it when you talk nerdy to me. Keep going."

Long-used to the physicist and her comments, Adam's cheeks only flushed a little. "Definitely a female, which is good; the males are a lot bigger and probably more territorial."

"Cool beans. I didn't know you were into dinos."

Adam shrugged. "I saw *Jurassic Park* at a tender age. And strictly speaking, pterosaurs aren't dinosaurs." Adjusting his glasses again, the Watchdog said, "But I guess that's not important. What do you need?"

"A clear shot at her. If there's an ion trail left over, I'll need to be within a few feet to trace it." Millennia cocked her head and asked, "Out of curiosity, why didn't you knock her out?"

Adam ducked his head sheepishly. "Camilla wanted me to, but she wasn't bothering anyone. And I like watching her."

"Aw, you're such a sweetheart," Millennia said, patting his cheek as she passed.

As she approached the tree, she lifted the tablet and aimed its sensor up at the pteranodon. "Good giant flying lizard," she said, lining the image up. "Hold still now."

The program gave a soft *beep*, logging the ion signature. "Gotcha," Millennia muttered. "We'll get you home in no time. Well, in some time. Probably a lot of time. *Man*, I wish I could run more than one active track at once. Think how easy my life would be."

"Do you want company?" Adam asked. "Camilla can handle the pteranodon if she causes trouble."

"Well-phrased on both counts, pumpkin," Millennia said with a grin. "Let's get to work."

¤   ¤   ¤   ¤   ¤   ¤

"*Bingo!*" Millennia whooped as the tracking program began to beep enthusiastically. She and Adam had been following the pings for almost forty minutes, and they had finally located the right rift just behind the Boathouse. "Dinner's on you, Smokey."

Adam blushed and sniffed his fingers, which reeked definitively of cigarettes. "I'm quitting soon."

"Yeah, and I'm gonna start wearing a lab coat to work. We've all got our little lies we tell ourselves." Millennia lifted her tablet and superimposed an infrared filter over the tracking program, which immediately turned the screen into a rave. To the left, a hazy smudge of dark purple shifted back and forth like psychedelic mist. Thin circles of red appeared as the program isolated traces of the pteranodon's ion signature. "We've got confirmation!"

"I'll call it in," Adam said, lifting his watch.

Before Millennia could respond, a second blotch of purple appeared a few feet to the right of the first and a black-clad figure stumbled backwards out of it. Freezing in surprise, the physicist and the Watchdog watched the dark-haired man fumble at his pockets, drop something in the grass with a curse, and kneel down to rifle around for it. With a triumphant exclamation he scrambled to his feet and aimed his prize—a little black device the size of a deck of cards—towards the rift on the left.

"*No!*" Millennia shouted, but it was too late. The stranger in tactical gear pressed the LDB's single button, firing an invisible stream of compressed energy that hit half of the rift and caused it to collapse.

Storming forward, Millennia shoved the Time Dog aside and lifted her tablet. The screen confirmed her fears: Every trace of the pteranodon's rift was gone. "Oh, you stupid mother—"

"Watch it, lady," a gruff voice behind her said. "You'll get—Millennia?"

She whirled around in a rage and froze, all the color draining from her face. "David?"

The Watchdog in front of her was short for a guy, with beefy arms and a gut that hadn't quite finished the transition to muscle yet. Furrowing his thick eyebrows, he asked, "What's with the haircut? You got that much free time?"

Millennia's hand automatically went to the buzzed side of her head. "What? Uh, yeah. Slow hour. What the hell are you doing here?"

He ruffled his hair sheepishly. "I know, I know, I'm supposed to be up on Cedar Hill, but I got bored. Thought I'd wander back down here for a while."

"The rift—" Millennia began, swallowing against the dry click of her throat.

"Yeah, it almost got me," he said, "but I shut it down. Speakin' of, why'd you yell at me?"

"I—I thought it was a different one. My bad."

"Hey, no problem. I won't tell Cat if you won't tell her I was off my post."

Millennia nodded. "Deal."

Grinning, David slugged her shoulder gently. "You're the best, Mills. See ya around."

He started to walk off, but Millennia stepped forward and caught his sleeve. "David, wait." When he looked back down at her, she swallowed again and pointed to the right. "It's faster if you go up the south side."

With a cocky salute, he winked at her and changed course. Millennia watched, trembling, as he passed confidently through his original rift and disappeared. She pulled an identical LBD out of her own pocket and fired it, locking him away for good.

Adam, who had watched the entire exchange in silence, spoke up when Millennia swiped at her eyes and came back to him. "Who was that?" he asked, following behind her.

"His name is David Krevitz." Millennia pulled her tablet out as she walked, flicking through messages and rearranging them based on priority. "He was part of Gamma."

"What happened to him?"

She was silent. Adam picked up his pace and stepped in front of her, causing her to come up short. "I saw your face, Millennia. I thought for a minute he'd stabbed you."

The physicist's soft mouth flattened. "He died, okay? He wandered away from his post and ended up in the middle of a turf war between two displaced Redeemers. Doberman came to back him up, but not before he took two Tango rounds to the chest." Millennia wiped her nose. "You know why they call them Tangos? Because no matter where you're hit, at best you'll make it eight steps."

Licking his lips, Adam asked, "When?"

"Exactly six years ago. Or, for him—" She checked her watch. "In about two hours."

Adam rocked back a bit. "And you just let him go home?" he demanded as Millennia pushed around him.

"We have to follow the rules," she said grimly. "No one goes, and no one—no one stays. Not even one of our own."

"But—"

"It just doesn't work that way, okay? Time is like—like a super advanced organism with its own defense system. Even if we managed to get David out, *something* would happen to him because he's an infection. He doesn't belong." Millennia opened her tablet again, but she couldn't remember what she had been doing before that had seemed so important. "Look, I don't know if an alternate universe exists where the past is mutable, but it's not this one."

"Then what the hell is the point?" Adam asked, struggling to keep up despite the difference in their heights. "Why do any of this if time can just fix itself?"

"For the same reason we take antibiotics and get chemo."

That drew Adam up for a second. "Okay, but if you'd let him stay, then he would have just disappeared instead of dying. Either way, he wouldn't have been in the picture. The timeline would be the same."

"In that part, maybe," Millennia muttered. Her screen filled with more and more programs. "But what about here? Do you have any idea how many people even one human affects? If time is like a body, then each one of us is cancer."

"Millennia, stop. *Stop*."

She came to a halt, clutching the tablet with shaking hands. Slowly, she looked up at Adam, her brown eyes ready to overflow. "I had to do it. I know what's going to happen to him, but I had to do it. And you know what the real bitch of it is? There's still time. For him, on his Day, it hasn't happened yet." She snorted and pulled the tablet against her chest, like a shield. "Hell, we have *ages*. I could call the Doghouse and have a team go after him. But then where does it stop? Why not go after Dr. King, or Franz Ferdinand, or Joan of Arc? Why not try to rescue everyone who's ever died before their time?"

Swallowing, she looked down and relaxed her death grip on the tablet. "We have to preserve the timeline at all costs. Everything started to crack when humans fucked with it on *accident*; can you imagine how bad things would get if we started doing it on purpose? The air would be like Swiss cheese."

Adam adjusted his glasses and shifted his weight to one leg. "You're right, I guess. I mean, I didn't even know the guy."

Wiping her eyes, Millennia took her feelings and tucked them inside a little wooden box on a high shelf. There would be time to look at them later. "Tag the flyer and get it down to the Savannah, will you? I've gotta get back to work. I'll tell

Cat...something." She wiped the screens on her tablet away and began organizing them with calm purpose.

Adam watched the physicist leave, unsure if the dull sheen of her normally peppery hair was real, or nothing more than a trick of the light.

# THE SOLAR JAGUAR STRIKES

## Cat
## (11:26)

A small security team from the Doghouse had arrived a little after midday to relieve the tense members of Viszla standing guard over Captain Renault and his men, but neither they nor their predecessors spoke more than a few scattered words of French. As a result, Specs was forced to continue haunting the bottom of the Ramble in case of an emergency.

"I'm going stir-crazy," he mumbled to Cat, who had come to bring him water. "I've been circling the same little patch for almost two hours."

"We could all use a break. Why don't you go see if our friends are hungry?" Tapping her bud, she said, "Hey New Kid, meet me at Command. We're going on a hot dog run."

"Um, okay. Both of us? I can do it, if you want."

Cat snorted. "Only an idiot gets between me and food."

"Ehe-he." The New Kid tried to laugh, but it was a bit on the anemic side.

The trip was just as much fun as he seemed to think that it would be. Cat practically dragged him along behind her as they barreled towards the edge of the park, knocking aside joggers and baby strollers alike. Finally, they escaped the grasping fingers of the park and emerged onto Central Park West.

"Smell that, New Kid?" she asked, inhaling deep. "Smells like freedom and dollar dogs."

"Peace, brother," a tall white woman with long honey-colored hair said, holding out a bright pamphlet as they passed. "Peace, sister. How goes your Day? Have you already felt the waxing pull of the Magnetic Bat Moon?"

Cat ignored the hippie completely, but the New Kid hesitated. "The—the what?"

"The Magnetic Bat Moon," the woman said, the limp daisy in her hair bobbing sagely as she nodded. "Last night we said goodbye to the Cosmic Turtle. Tomorrow it's the Bat's turn to watch over our beloved planet."

With a look that said he knew he was probably going to regret it, the New Kid asked, "What about tonight?"

"Obviously it's the Patchouli Moon," Catt muttered, rolling her eyes.

Suddenly serious, the honey-haired hippie leaned down and said, "Tonight is the end of the Day of Peace. The beginning of the New Year. There is no moon."

"For fuck's sake, it's a goddamn full moon," Cat said. She whirled around and grabbed the New Kid by the collar of his flak jacket. "And no, before you ask, he doesn't want any lavender to open his third eye, or some rose quartz to wear inside his left sock for luck while Jupiter is in Cygnus."

The beflowered hippie looked down her nose at the much shorter commander. "Lavender is used to *cleanse* the third eye," she said. "And clearly, *you* were born during the dark of the Overtone Peacock Moon. So full of yourself, and unafraid to say what's on your mind."

"Solar Jaguar, actually," Cat said, grinning up at her. "So full of sharp teeth, and not afraid to reach up and smack the shit out of you if you keep blocking the way to my hot dogs." Without further ado, she dragged the New Kid around the incensed hippie.

"What—Commander—"

"One of the many downsides to the lunar calendar," Cat said, "is that it inspired some *interesting* theories about the Universe that have never really gone away."

"The Arcturians rejected us because of carnivores like you!" the hippie called as they walked away. "They abandoned the colonies on Mars and went home rather than be around the violence and warmongering of our species!"

"Ridiculous," Cat muttered, homing in on the hot dog cart better than a bloodhound. "Arcturians won't get here for five centuries. And why the hell would they ever go to Mars? By then it'll be nothing but resorts. I swear, the day the artists move out is the day the neighborhood goes to shit." Bulldozing relentlessly past the line of outraged New Yorkers, Cat flashed her badge at the vendor. "I'm gonna need as many dogs as the kid can carry," she said, flicking a pair of mirrored sunglasses on for effect. "It's for a hostage situation."

Whether it was her tone or the shiny badge that did the trick, no one could say, but before the New Kid could blink there were five cardboard boxes full of hot dogs and condiment packets in his arms.

"Thank fuck," the Gamma commander said, opening the top box and fishing out two steaming wienie and bun combos. "One more hour and I was gonna see what that pteranodon tastes like."

"Probably a bit fishy," the New Kid offered.

Snorting, Cat led the way back into the sweltering shade of the park. The crowds inside had reached ridiculous levels by this point.

"Uh, Commander," the New Kid said after a few minutes, pointing with his chin.

Cat followed his gaze, picking out a mini parade of neon- and spandex-clad people being led by a man in a rainbow umbrella hat, like some demented Chinese dragon at a festival. As the leg warmers and baggy shirts made their way closer, she felt the overwhelming need to start humming the theme to *Footloose* under her breath.

"Wonderful," Cat sighed. "So much for a lunch break." She

marched over, prepared to turn the line around and escort them right back to their rift, but the man in the umbrella hat lit up at the sight of her.

"And *here*, cats and kittens," he said, pointing triumphantly at the suddenly confused Dog, "is an actual Time Agent! Notice the bygone technology and clear lack of a portable data core. Welcome to the 20<sup>th</sup> century! Your iLids should be displaying the relevant *current events*, a-ha-ha."

The guide's laugh grated Cat's nerves to shreds. "Who the hell are you?" she demanded.

"*Whoa* there, bodacious!" he said, laughing so loudly that his pale ginger mustache trembled. "I'm Tubular Tim, and this here's Tubular Tim's Wild Time Tours! Certified on three continents since 2148. Home of the original Day Trip!"

Looking down the line of eager tourists, Cat rubbed her forehead and said, "Let me guess: This is the 1980s edition."

"Right on!" Tubular Tim said.

"When can we meet Madonna?" a soccer-mom type with blue hair asked.

"Sorry, sport, but you're thirty years off," Cat said. "Now turn your smiley ass *back* around—"

"Hey, hey," Tubular Tim said, leaning down and speaking in a much lower voice. "Look mama, I'm tryin' to run a business, okay? I got a permit to be here."

"Show me."

"Alright, alright! No need to get scratchy. Here, it's all in the folder." He turned over a manila folder, worn at the edges and covered in stickers advertising Tubular Tim's Wild Time Tours and Buffalo Bill's Wok-a-Mole Grill: Chinese Takeout, Burritos, and More! "And hey, can you keep it down about the year? We jumped the wrong ride, and I mean, they ain't never gonna know the difference, ya get me?"

Cat ignored him and flipped through the folder, peering carefully at the bottom right corner. Though grimy with grease and coffee stains, a genuine holographic seal gleamed up at her from every page. "Unbelievable," she muttered, flattening it against his flaccid chest with a sigh of disgust. "Cock this up even a little bit, and I'll stick you in a cellar to rot and grow roots."

"Of course I can get you some radical discounts," Tubular Tim said loudly. "The next time you find yourself in the 2160s, you look me up! How does Pompeii on volcano day sound? Or Victorian England during Jack the Ripper's *reign of terror?*"

"Those sound like terrible destinations," Cat told him flatly. "New Kid, my hot dogs are getting cold."

"Hot dogs!" Tubular Tim shouted, turning his back on the Dogs entirely. "Did you hear that, folks? Honest-to-goodness vintage hot dogs, as real as the nose on your face! Well, maybe not the nose on *your* face, a-ha-ha—"

"I hate people," Cat said, leading the way towards Cherry Hill.

From just behind her right shoulder, the New Kid asked, "All people, Commander?"

"Sometimes. Well, that's not true. Let's say sometimes I hate everyone except Gamma."

"Because we're your people."

"Damn right you are."

"And nobody—nobody messes with your people."

Cat froze and looked back at the New Kid. "Nobody."

"That's why we're the only ones with nicknames," he said, nodding eagerly. "Because you want us to stick together, so you can protect us."

She chose to turn away and continue walking. "That's an interesting theory, New Kid."

"I don't—I don't think it's a theory!" he said, trailing after her carefully. "You're like a, a big, cranky mama bear—"

"*Enough,*" she hissed, rounding on him in the middle of a crowded path. Around them, kids played and teenagers made out and married couples argued, but the New Kid's world narrowed to the furious edge of Cat's finger and her coal-fire eyes. "Not another sheep-fucking word."

The New Kid swallowed thickly and nodded his head.

Her point made, Cat resumed walking. A channel opened on her bud, and a timid voice said, "Um, Commander? It's Adam. We lost the pteranodon."

"*What?*" she demanded, tapping her ear. "What the hell happened?"

"We went to catch her, and she took off. Camilla and I tracked her for a while, but then she took off towards the Hernshead and we couldn't get to her in time. I've been searching the area for twenty minutes. No luck."

"What about the ion signature?"

"I've got it logged on passive mode, and I've added it to the collective, but honestly Commander—"

"Aerial subjects are a bitch to track, I know. Especially with all this open water." Sighing, Cat rubbed her temple and said, "Grab some lunch, then you and Camilla head back to Command."

"Roger that, Commander. Adam out."

Cat spared half a glance back at the New Kid, who continued to follow silently in her wake, watching everything around him. As long as he thought himself unobserved, those eyes never stopped moving, never stopped absorbing whatever was within sight. Even, she acknowledged irritably, what had quite plainly been stowed away for no one to see.

¤ ¤ ¤ ¤ ¤ ¤

"Am I a cranky mama bear?" Cat asked some time later, taking a bite from her third hot dog. She and the New Kid had made their delivery without speaking again. Now, she and Specs were camped out on a rock near Willow Cove, where they could keep an eye on everything.

Wiping mustard from his neatly clipped beard, the historian nodded. "Absolutely. Who told you that?"

"The New Kid."

"Well, he's right. I've seen you on a rampage."

That bought him a soft chuckle. "I am pretty scary, huh?"

"Terrifying. But you know that, so what else is bothering you?'

Cat stuffed the last bite of hot dog into her mouth to buy a little time. Swallowing, she said, "He thinks that all the nicknames we give each other are a way to band us together."

Looking down at her with his gentle black eyes, Specs asked, "Aren't they?"

"Maybe. Yes. I just didn't want them to feel alone," she admitted. "They've had enough of that their whole lives. We're a family, and families bicker and have stupid nicknames and drive each other batshit crazy—"

"And they stick together," Specs finished. "They belong to each other. *That's* what you've done, Cat. You've given them a home, a safe place where they don't have to hide the things that make them look broken to the rest of the world."

"You are not broken," Cat said, a rattlesnake's polite warning in her voice.

Specs looked out across the little cove to Bethesda Fountain. "Yes I am, Cat. In more ways than one. And you know what? Most days it's okay, because I have a mama bear looking out for me." Gesturing around them, he said, "A lot of the assholes who used to torment Gamma have learned by now that if they so much as *look* at us sideways, you'll beat them to death with their own torn-off limbs. That kind of security gives us the confidence to actually deal with our problems, instead of hiding them until they get worse. In the simplest of terms: You make us feel loved."

Cat felt heat prick the backs of her eyes, as rare as a unicorn sighting. "You *are* loved," she said roughly, clearing her throat and blinking fiercely. "Every stupid, irritating one of you."

Specs opened his arms. "Come on, Cat. No one's looking."

Glaring up at him, Cat glanced around to confirm this observation and then carefully leaned in and accepted her lieutenant's hug.

"Commander Fiyero?" Cat's walkie watch asked, before the moment could really gain any momentum.

Sighing, she pulled out of Specs's arms and lifted the watch. "This is Cat."

"Captain Terrell, ma'am. We've got a young woman here, about twenty years old, brown hair, Victorian dress. Says she knows you and someone named Kevin."

"Where the hell is she?" Cat asked, coming to her feet.

"One of my agents has her by the mouth of the Gill. Apparently she's been flirting with a French soldier."

Cat rolled her eyes. "Fucking wonderful. Thanks for the call, Captain; I'm a few minutes south."

"Roger that. Terrell out."

"Do you want me to come with you or stay here?" Specs asked.

Waving her hand, Cat said, "Finish your lunch. I'll be back soon."

After an easy hike, Cat found Miss Elaine Penrose in the company of a stocky olive-skinned woman with acne scars and a shoulder-length French braid. They were at the base of a long tumble of rocks, over which a thin stream of water flowed. Perched on the metal bridge uphill was a handsome young Frenchman with light brown hair and a full mustache. In spite of the musket leaning against his hip, everyone seemed relaxed.

Cat stopped in her tracks and looked around for a moment before tapping her tragus. "Cat to Millennia, I just remembered where we saw the dino pack this morning. It's that tiny-ass waterfall up where the Gill starts."

"Aye-aye Cat, I know the one you're talking about," the physicist answered. "I'm helping Komondor clean up a cheeka bird infestation, but I'll be down there soon."

"Have you had lunch yet?"

Cat couldn't quite hear Millennia roll her eyes, but she could imagine it. "Jamal fed me kebab from his mouth like a mama bird, okay?"

"Did he chew it up for you first, just the way you like it?"

There was a brief sound of Millennia faux-retching. "And now I don't want to eat for a week. Always good talking to you,

Captain my Captain."

Cat disconnected the bud with a smile, ticking one internal worry off of her list.

The security agent and her charge were waiting patiently at the edge of the gentle flow of water. When Cat approached, Elaine stepped forward and began, "Commander Fiyero—"

"Miss Penrose, didn't you tell me just this morning that you would be so quiet I wouldn't even notice you?"

Elaine ducked her head. "Yes, Commander."

"And don't you think dragging me all the way over here to fetch you is a bit fucking *noticeable?*"

"Yes, but—I was just going for a bit of a walk, and Romain was having a drink, and we started chatting and—"

"Wait," Cat said, holding up a hand. "In what language? French?"

Puzzled, Elaine nodded. "Yes, of course. I've had French-speaking governesses for years. It's a lovely language, though the people—" She glanced behind and waved daintily at Romain, who smiled and waved back. "Well, they can't help being French, now can they? And he's an alright sort."

"Did you tell her anything about the situation?" Cat asked the stocky security agent.

"Just that it was delicate and she shouldn't interfere," the woman answered. "The soldier hasn't made any threatening moves. He just keeps throwing flowers down to us. Well, down to her."

"Oh no," Elaine said, "he was throwing them to *you.*"

The Dog blinked. "What?"

"He was throwing the flowers to you," Elaine insisted. "It's been a scraggly bunch, but the poor thing's doing the best he can. He's done nothing but ask about you since you arrived. I couldn't even tell him your name."

The other woman looked behind her, and the handsome Frenchman's smile widened into a broad grin. Turning pink, she swallowed and said, "It's Sarah."

Elaine waved at the soldier with much more enthusiasm.

"*Elle s'apple Sarah!*" she called to him.

Romain removed his black three-cornered hat, placed it over his heart, and bowed deeply to Sarah. As the Dog blushed furiously, he straightened and cupped his hands around his mouth, yelling something back in rapid French.

"Oh," Elaine breathed, putting a hand over her own heart. "Oh, that was lovely. He just misquoted Voltaire for you."

A smile stole across Sarah's face for a moment before she turned back to Cat and tried to smooth it down. "Orders, Commander Fiyero?"

"As you were, agent," Cat answered, crossing her arms. "Miss Penrose, I'm willing to let you stay longer if you'll agree to act as a translator until our situation has been resolved."

Elaine's eyes lit up. "Oh, could I? That would simply be the thing!"

"I'll bet. Come on, we don't have all day."

"Okay!" Turning back to the confused Frenchman, Elaine called out, "*Prends soin de toi, Romain!*"

He waved at her and continued making cow-eyes at Sarah. The security agent faced forward resolutely, refusing to take her eyes off of her assigned area.

"Lead the way, Commander," Elaine said, picking her way delicately over the rocky ground.

"Something happen to your leg?" Cat asked as they walked away.

Elaine froze. "What?"

"Your right leg. You're favoring it."

"Well, that is, I—"

"Just stop," Cat said, holding up a hand and continuing down the path. "Whatever you're about to say is gonna be a lie, so save it. Do you need medical attention?"

Elaine's voice was very small when she answered. "No, Commander."

"Is anybody else irrevocably damaged?"

"No, Commander."

"Then I don't give a shit what you've done to yourself."

The younger woman breathed a sigh of relief and followed meekly, forcing her gait into its normal rhythm. Cat heard the change, and allowed herself a tiny smile.

# THE PATRON SAINT OF LIMPING DOGS

## Helix
### (13:11)

There's an old American saying which goes like this: It's the squeaky wheel that gets the grease. This usually results in the other wheels being both underappreciated and overlooked. Devi Ramachandra—known to our team as Helix—was one such wheel.

"Hold still," she told the young man lying prone on the ground. "You definitely have a concussion."

"You sure?" he asked groggily, touching the back of his dark head with sticky fingers.

"Pretty sure, since this is the third time we've had this conversation."

He sighed and relaxed, closing his eyes against the bright sun. "Sorry."

"It's okay. You're going to be fine." She pulled on a pale yellow glove with bulky filaments in the lining and leaned the tablet up against her backpack. As the glove finished warming up, she gently ran it along the side of the Watchdog's head. The screen went black, and then the image of a ghostly skull appeared. Everything seemed to be in its proper place, so Helix turned his head and ran her hand along the back side. A tiny lightning bolt appeared on the left side of the new image.

To be safe, she flicked her thumb across the glove's controls and deepened the scan before moving to the top of his head. "Good news, Carlos," she said. "You get to be the Boy Who Lived."

"What happened?" Carlos asked for the fourth time.

Helix put her free hand on his chest before he could try to sit up. "Lie still." Lifting her watch, she dialed in to the Doghouse channels and said, "This is the hotter Dr. Ramachandra to Med Bay, I have a Watchdog with a linear fracture smack on his posterior parietal bone, about an inch above the lambdoid suture. Request immediate pick-up."

"Roger that Helix, I've got a med team headed to the lifts," a cool voice replied. "What's your location?"

"Central Park, lower East Green."

"Patient's condition?"

Carlos heaved. "I'm gonna be sick."

"Concussed but stable," Helix said, helping Carlos shift so he could heave into the grass. "Initial scans show no internal bleeding or swelling. He's coherent but looping."

"What happened?" Carlos gasped, right on cue.

"Hush," Helix soothed. "Med Bay, I'm going to stay with him. I'll send a ping your way."

"Roger that," the cool voice said. "I'll route it to the med team. ETA's ten minutes."

"Thanks Med Bay. Helix out." Once she activated the tablet's tracker, she turned her attention back to poor, confused Carlos.

"My head hurts," he said. "Everything's really bright."

"I know, sweetie," Helix said, entwining the fingers of one hand with his. "You took a pretty nasty hit to the back of the head. Help will be here in a few minutes."

"What happened?"

"Constance said that some strong-man from an old circus whacked you with a rubber mallet."

He winced. "Like...like in the game?"

"I think so," Helix said. "He rang your bell pretty good, but he didn't get a prize. You're too tough for that."

Noticing that they were alone, Carlos asked, "Where's

Constance?"

"Chasing bad guys with the rest of your team."

"Oh. Okay." He was silent for a moment, thinking unfathomable thoughts, and then his eyes cracked open. "Helix? What happened?"

Smiling, she rubbed his skin with her thumb. "You threw yourself in front of a runaway hot dog cart and saved a toddler."

"I did?"

"Absolutely."

Carlos digested this information. "Am I going to die?"

"No, sweetie," Helix promised him. "You're going to be just fine. Help is coming."

"Cat to Helix," her bud said. "If you're free, I want you to take a look at our Victorian friend. Name's Elaine Penrose. She's done something to her leg, but she won't tell me what."

"I'm with Carlos right now, but I'll head that way as soon as I can."

"Is he okay?"

Proving that she did indeed have the patience of a saint, Helix promised once again that Carlos was going to be just fine.

"No rush," the commander said when Helix finished. "She'll be up in the Ramble when you get a chance. Captain Terrell can point you in the right direction."

"I'll keep you updated," Helix said, ending the transmission.

"Helix?" Carlos asked, squinting up at her. "Why does my head hurt?"

The geneticist sighed, thinking that sometimes even a saint's patience could run a bit thin.

¤　¤　¤　¤　¤　¤

Miss Elaine Penrose was resting in the shade of a vibrant tree, minding her own business and completely unprepared for anything like an ambush. This was, of course, exactly how Helix would have preferred it.

"Alright, let's see it," she demanded, appearing from between two trees and slinging her massive backpack to the ground.

"*Eep*," Elaine said, nearly falling off of her rock. "Who are you?"

"Helix. I'm Gamma's medic."

"Where is Agent Donovan?" the younger woman demanded.

Helix shrugged and pulled a pair of rubber gloves from her backpack. "Chasing squirrels, for all I know. I've got a lot of people waiting on me, so let's move this along, okay?"

Instinctively, Elaine's hand went to her right thigh and she winced. "I have no idea what you mean."

Taking a deep breath, Helix softened her demeanor. "Commander Fiyero sent me. She said that you hurt your leg, and she wants me to take a look at it. Please cooperate?" When Elaine didn't respond, Helix walked up and knelt in front of her. "I'm not going to hurt you."

Cheeks burning, Elaine looked away and slowly bunched her dress in her hands before lifting it up and baring the snowy skin of her right leg. Helix frowned at the white bandage. "This tape isn't even medical grade. Someone did a pretty sloppy job of patching you up." She fetched a water bottle from her pack and used it to wet the tape enough so that it came away without a fuss.

Underneath the bandage in glorious, puffy detail was a tattoo of a purple flower. Helix stared at it for several long seconds before turning her eyes up to Elaine, who was still resolutely looking somewhere else.

Mutely, Helix cleaned the edges where dirt had snuck under the bandage and mixed with the antibiotic. She applied a fresh white square lined with self-adhesive, and then pulled a small tube of ointment from her backpack.

"They told you how to take care of it, right?" she asked Elaine, who finally looked down at her in surprise.

"Yes. Leave it alone until tonight, then anti—antibiotic cream for five days whenever it feels tight. Scent-free lotion after that until it heals."

"Don't forget to clean it. And don't scratch. If it itches, slap it, but no scratching."

Elaine snapped her fingers. "Right!" She pulled a folded piece of paper from her handbag and opened it. "Miss Carla gave me this. The shop must be wonderfully profitable if they have their own printing press!"

Helix looked the instructions over briefly. "Do you have any lotion at home?"

Nodding, Elaine said, "My mother showed me how to make Milk of Roses when I was young. I still have the recipe."

"Hmm." Helix opened a screen on her tablet and did a quick search for the lotion. "Is this it?"

Peering down curiously, Elaine nodded. "That's it exactly! How did you draw the image so quickly?"

"I didn't draw it, I summoned it." The geneticist read over the ingredient list and said, "That should work, but you'll probably need at least two batches."

"Mattie will help, I'm sure of it. She's always begging me to take better care of my skin." Elaine closed her eyes and inhaled deeply. "I have to stay inside for *hours*. What's the point in a holiday if I can't enjoy the world around me?"

"Good for you," Helix said, cleaning up her supplies. "Life is meant to be lived."

"Agent Helix?"

The Dog looked up and found Elaine staring at her from atop the rock. "Are you from India?" she asked.

"No, but my grandparents are."

"Have you ever been there?"

Helix smiled. "A few times."

Sighing, Elaine said, "I would love to go. I want to drink darjeeling from the back of an elephant and watch the sun rise over the harbor in Bombay."

Helix, who was not a fan of darjeeling, wrinkled her long nose. "You should visit Udaipur instead. I think you'd like it better."

"Thank you!" Elaine said, grinning. "I will, one day."

Helix believed her. She hefted the backpack up and waved

goodbye, already pulling out her tablet to check the list of injured waiting to be seen. *No rest for the wicked*, she thought as the names continued to appear.

# ZOOT SUIT RIOT

## The New Kid
### (13:50)

Gamma Command was enjoying a rare break from the madness. Everyone except for Darwin sat around the little table, polishing off the last of their late lunch. Even the most wayward members had managed to take a few deep breaths of clean air.

Millennia chugged an energy drink and crushed the can in her delicate, tattooed hands. "When's Med Bay gonna share their bio-caff shots?" she asked. "I know they got 'em, Helix, don't lie to me."

"Do you have any idea what those can do to your system?" Helix asked. "It takes weeks of testing before they can clear the healthiest, most mentally stable doctors and RNs for bio-caff injections. There's no way in hell you're getting one."

Millennia grabbed her tablet and plopped down on a slab of rock. "Dude, I'm so amped right now. If you gave me a bio-caff shot, I bet I could solve these decay rate algorithms that we've been stuck on for *months*."

"Or you could go into arrhythmia and die," Helix pointed out. "Or possibly launch yourself into space. You're too caffeinated as it is."

"I've always wanted to go into orbit," she replied, flicking through screens faster than the human eye should have been able to function.

"Maybe when you retire," Cat said, stretching her arms overhead. "What've we got?"

"No word yet on the raptor's rift, but..." Millennia's pixie-like face scrunched up. "Remember when I said there might be a rift at the Warrior's Gate?"

"Vaguely."

"Well, there's a rift at the Warrior's Gate, and it lit up like a Christmas tree about half an hour ago."

Cat blew a long breath out. "Who can we spare?"

"Malinois is up there," Grunt reminded her. "Ramirez would have radioed if they were in trouble."

"Unless a T-Rex came through and ate them all," Millennia supplied helpfully.

"Yesterday I would have rolled my eyes," Cat said. "Today, I'm taking no chances." Tapping her tragus, she said, "Cat to Ramirez, Millennia says there's an active rift northwest of you. I want you to check it out." Making eye contact with Specs, Cat raised an eyebrow, to which he responded with a nod. "I'm sending Lieutenant Forrester and the New Kid to back you up."

"At least I finally get to stretch my legs a little," Specs said as Cat ended the transmission. He twisted from side to side and clapped the New Kid on the shoulder. "We'll call you from the Warrior's Gate."

"Don't get eaten by anything," Millennia called as they headed out of Command.

"Ha-ha," the New Kid muttered, swallowing. "She's kidding, right?"

Rather than answer, the big historian lifted one shoulder in a helpless shrug.

About halfway up the side of the Reservoir, Specs's tablet pinged. He glanced over the message and said, "Ramirez found the rift and tagged it. Looks like she left Omar standing guard while the others investigate a crowd over by the Stranger's Gate. She doesn't think it's anything serious, but she wants us to check it out just in case."

In spite of Ramirez's words, the New Kid's heartbeat picked up when they came in sight of the stairs that led up to the Stranger's Gate. Team Malinois stood at the bottom, mixed in with the norms tapping their toes or patting their legs along with the heavenly jazz music floating by. Only Melanie Ramirez had her arms stubbornly folded.

"Lieutenant," she said, coming to attention when she spotted Specs. "We found the source of the disturbance, but—they won't come with us, sir."

"Who?"

The suddenly sheepish Watchdogs parted, revealing the quartet of musicians currently crushing a classic jazz number. The New Kid blinked and rubbed his eyes, but the humanoids in front of him still possessed abnormally large foreheads, frog-like eyes, and skin the color of a burst blue Gusher. Each of them wore a zoot suit and spats over shiny black shoes. A baseball cap overflowing with bills sat on the concrete in front of them.

"Have you had any contact?" Specs asked Melanie.

"They waved us off," she said. "And when we tried to take them into custody, the crowd almost rioted."

Specs looked around at the entranced audience. "Did you call Commander McNab?"

Melanie splayed her hands helplessly. "I haven't heard from him in over an hour. We've been handling things alright. Marco and Marisol help when they can spare it."

The combo ended their number, and the audience reacted with wild applause. A young girl with skin like brown sea glass emerged from the crowd with a stained gig bag slung over one shoulder. She walked right up to the saxophone-playing alien, who leaned down. He nodded emphatically in response to whatever she had said and gestured to the front of the group, revealing a sixth and seventh finger on each hand.

The girl grinned and gently set her gig bag down behind the band. She turned to face the curious crowd, and waited patiently for her cue. The aliens settled into place, and as the music swelled she began to sing.

The New Kid's eyebrows lifted. Each note was a bright little gem, strung together without a single gap. Clear joy shone out of her features like a sunbeam, and the crowd ate it up.

When the song finished, Specs reluctantly led him forward. The aliens were chattering to each other in squeaky clicks, and the saxophonist was going over something with the young girl. As the Gamma agents approached they fell silent and stared, unnerving the New Kid with their wide, identical features.

"Hello," Specs said. "My name is Lieutenant Forrester. I'm with CIRIUS's Gamma Team."

"A good day to you, Lieutenant," the saxophonist said, tapping a pin on their lapel. The artificial voice that came from it was melodic and gentle. This close, the New Kid could see that what passed for the alien's mouth was in fact a short trunk, perfect for placing around the mouthpiece of an instrument. "How can we be of service?"

"You've already been of great service," Specs said with a nod to their instruments, "but unless you have a permit to stay, I'm afraid I'm going to have to ask you to pack up. One of my agents can escort you back to your rift."

"As we tried to tell your agent, all of our paperwork is in order."

"Could I see it?"

The guitar player obligingly reached into their case and pulled out a folded packet of papers. Specs went through it, with the New Kid peering over his shoulder. Eventually they came across a copy in English that seemed to give the bearer permission to travel freely during the Day Out of Time for recreational or work-related reasons, on the condition that they agree to obey local laws and present themselves to the closest CIRIUS agency should they exceed their allotted time. It identified the aliens as Astijkites, and the year as 3012. Each page was signed at the bottom by Their Radiance Orion XIV, Fourth Cosmic Emperor. The holographic image at the bottom contained an alarming number of tentacles.

Handing the paperwork back, Specs smiled and said, "My apologies. I wasn't aware that the Emperor had taken to issuing permits."

"They are rare," the saxophonist said through their pin, "but we are Their Radiance's favorites. Have you enjoyed the show, Lieutenant?"

"I have." Specs spared a long glance at the portable keyboard that was currently sitting unused. "I've enjoyed it very much."

"Would you like to play?" the pianist asked, offering their seat. "Briar Jones can sing with you."

"Yes, Briar Jones," the other three chorused as enthusiastically as their pins would allow.

"That's me," the young girl said with a wave. Her sleek black hair had been pulled back in a thick bun, and a pair of guileless brown eyes sat over an impertinent nose and a mouth made for smiling. She was thin under her blue and green paisley sundress, though it was mostly the wiriness of youth.

"Maybe next time," Specs said, smiling. "Do you know where your rift is?"

The saxophonist bowed. "Of course. We will be gone before sundown."

Specs reached into one of his many pockets and fished out a simple business card. "If you need anything, give me a call."

"You are most kind." Turning to the girl, they said, "Briar Jones, will you sing again?"

"Maybe after lunch," she said, shrugging. "Will you still be here?"

"Of course. We have no need for rest or sustenance as long as the sun shines." Reaching down, the saxophone-playing alien plucked the sagging baseball cap up from the ground and handed it to Briar Jones. "We also have no need of Earth money from this era," they said. "Keep it, please."

She grinned and dumped the contents into the bright blue purse on her hip. "Dope." Putting the oversized cap on backwards, she offered her hand and said, "Catch you on the flip side, then."

The Astijkite exchanged a sideways five and fist bump with the girl. "Yes. On the flip side."

Flashing the alien band a peace sign, Briar Jones picked up her gig bag and strapped it over her shoulders like a backpack. "So. Cheeseburgers and chili fries, anyone?"

"Bit late for lunch, isn't it?" Specs observed as they turned their backs on the Astijkites.

"Yeah, but they don't really appreciate the five-finger discount on this side of town," the teenager answered, shaking her purse. She looked Specs and the New Kid over, and then glanced at the Watchdogs still gathered in the crowd. "CIRIUS, huh? Are you guys like Torchwood or MIB?"

"If we're with the Men in Black, is it smart to ask us about it?" Specs asked. "I could always have one of those memory devices in my pocket."

"See, I don't think you do," Briar Jones said, hooking her thumbs in the case's straps and walking forward. The bill of the ball cap banged into her guitar, so she turned it forward. "'Cause I don't think you need one. Nobody but me's gonna remember them anyway, and who'm I gonna tell?"

Specs exchanged a look with the New Kid. "You know what's going on?"

"No clue. But I do know that once a year, everything goes all cuckoo-for-Cocoa Puffs," she said, wiggling her head from side to side. "And then the next day, it's like nothing happened. I'm, like, ninety percent sure I'm not crazy, but if you can confirm it, that'd be great."

"You're not crazy," the New Kid murmured.

"But you *are* special," Specs added. "CIRIUS is an agency for people like us who can remember the Days."

Briar Jones grinned. "Like the sound a' that. You got summer internships or something?"

"Or something." Specs took out a second business card and handed it to her. "Have your parents give me a call next week, and we'll talk. Do they remember the Days too?"

She shrugged and pinched two fingers around the card. "Tell

you what: If you find them, we can ask. They dumped me in the foster system when I was two." Cutting her eyes at the other agents, who were now within hearing range, she muttered, "Been in...four homes since then? This one's not so bad, but a girl's gotta be independent."

Placing himself squarely between her and the curious eyes of the Watchdogs, Specs folded his arms and said, "At, what, fourteen?"

"Fifteen," she corrected. "And yeah. What happens when I turn eighteen and Miss Susan gives me the boot? She's already got two other kids to look out for, and one waiting for when Jesse graduates. She's like a charity factory." The girl chewed on her lip and dug the toe of her scuffed sandals into the ground. "So about that internship."

Specs observed the girl in silence for a moment, arms crossed and brow furrowed. The New Kid could practically see each thought suspended over his head in a speech bubble, and he saw the exact moment when the historian reached a decision.

"Why don't you come with me and Agent Harrison," Specs said at last, "and we'll consider this your working interview?"

Briar Jones brightened. "Really?"

"Really. Come on, you can meet Malinois."

The young singer wrinkled her nose up at the New Kid. "What's a Malinois?"

"No idea," he confessed, offering his hand. "Kevin. They call me New Kid."

Grinning, Briar Jones shook his hand and said, "Not for long."

The Watchdogs clapped in a subdued way as the trio approached, some even managing to quietly whistle their appreciation. Specs waved them into silence and said, "Everybody, this is Briar Jones."

"You've got a nice voice," one of the younger women said.

"You as good a picker?" someone else chimed in.

Briar Jones straightened and said, "Better. If you can hum it, I can play it."

Melanie Ramirez eyed the newcomer. "Big words for such a little thing."

"Don't you have a beauty pageant to primp for?" Briar Jones retorted, giving the Watchdog's perfect hair a once-over.

Most of Malinois eyed their new team leader, but she just cackled and relaxed her defensive pose. "Alright, fair enough." Turning to Specs, she said, "Orders, Lieutenant?"

"As you were. The Astijkites have permission to be here, and they seem like a very reasonable species."

"They're great," Briar Jones said. "They know *every* song. Like seriously, all of them."

"You'll have to ask our extraterrestrial species expert, but I think they have eidetic memories," Specs said. "That means they remember everything that they read."

"I've read a bit about them," a young man with spiked green hair and a watered-down Australian accent said. "They're wicked smart, but it's all left brain. So they can play any song you want, just don't ask for an original. They have to get all of their new music from other worlds."

Briar Jones glanced back at the blue-skinned Astijkites, who were playing a lively new song with wild abandon. "But what about the jazz solos?" she asked. "I've heard them play those."

The guy with the green hair shrugged. "Hey, I could be wrong. That's just what I read on my lunch break."

"Let's focus on getting through today, and you can tell us all about it tomorrow," Specs said, "You all have jobs to do, and I have a new recruit to educate. Off with all of you."

As the Watchdogs moved off, Briar Jones crossed her thin arms and looked up at the historian. "Now are you gonna tell me what's going on?"

Putting his hands behind his back, Specs began walking along the stone path leading away from the Stranger's Gate. "If you're sure it's what you want."

"Why do I get the feeling that you're about to say something sinister like—what's that Latin phrase that means you're taking something like it is? Dings, breaks, and all?"

"*Caveat emptor*," Specs said, winking at the New Kid. "Let the buyer beware."

# THE TROUBLE WITH THE INTERLUDE

## The Playground
(15:03)

"Wow," Briar Jones said, one long explanation (and a cheeseburger with chili fries) later. "So you guys keep the crazy at bay."

"As much as we can," Specs agreed. "Some days—"

A channel opened on his bud. "Lieutenant," Melanie Ramirez said, "we have a bunch of—actually, I have no idea what they are, but there's a lot of them."

"Those are goddamn tribbles," an unknown male voice piped in.

"You're a fucktard," a new voice added. "Tribbles aren't green."

"Real ones could be."

"Malinois," Specs said, "calm down and tell me what's going on."

"Approximately twenty-five to thirty unknown subjects in the playground," Melanie said. "They look like fuzzy green softballs. There are these weird yellow—nodes, I guess—sticking out of their bodies. I can't see any limbs or facial structures."

"Then how do you know they're alive?"

"Because they're moving, Lieutenant. They're chasing dogs and children. But for fun. They look like they're playing."

Specs glanced down at the New Kid and said, "We'll be there in five minutes. Any sign of their rift?"

"That's the good news, Lieutenant: I saw them come through myself. We've got a lock on it."

"Nice work, Ramirez. Specs out."

"Trouble?" the New Kid asked as they began walking back to where they'd left the team.

"Maybe, maybe not." Specs glanced down at Briar Jones. "I've gotta say, you're taking all of this in stride."

"My threshold for the weird is pretty high," Briar Jones said, shrugging. "And remember, I've seen the Asti—um."

"Astijkites."

"Yeah, those guys. I've seen them play up close. I know they're not wearing costumes. And it's like—" She frowned. "It's like normal people don't even notice. I guess that part makes sense now."

Specs stepped out of the path of an entire stroller brigade. "Were you ever worried about them being dangerous?"

"Nah. They were chill right from the start, and I figured that if they were bent on world domination, this was probably the slowest way to get it done." Flicking her eyes up, she said, "So if I get this internship, do I get a super secret nickname too?"

The historian laughed. "If you'd like one."

The girl bounced along thoughtfully, her guitar case thumping softly against her backside. "Let's try Supreme Overlord on for size."

"You'll have to fight our commander over that one," Specs said as they reached the quartet of Astijkites, who were currently jamming to something that sounded suspiciously like Outkast.

They followed the delighted shrieks of children to the playground area just off the Stranger's Gate, where a gaggle of squawking three-to-ten year olds were fighting over a curious pack of forest-green softballs. Team Malinois was gathered at the edges of the play area, fretting over the situation.

"I mean, they're not *doing* anything," an older Indian man named Raj said, rubbing his recent bald patch. "I say let the kids have fun."

"I'm not talking about shooting them," Melanie retorted acidly. "But we don't know anything about them. They need to at least be confined until we learn more."

"Agent Ramirez is right," Specs said, stepping into the line. "Standard containment policies. Fetch."

That was the last moment that anything went right for a good long while.

Whatever the tribbles had or lacked in terms of language, they recognized intent. The fuzzy, admittedly cute creatures suddenly began to vibrate as the agents crept closer.

"They're purring!" a little girl with dark brown pigtails shrieked. "Gimme kitty!"

An older girl with long elf-blonde hair looked uncertain. "Mikey, I don't think they're happy."

"Don't be stupid," the boy beside her said. "Cats only purr when they're happy."

In a tone that would have made Melanie Ramirez proud, the girl gave him a look and said, "Because I totally thought these were *cats* in the first place. Mrs. Watson says cats purr when they're scared too."

"Well Miss Wade says that I'm gonna use algebra one day," he retorted. "You think I believe everything teachers say?"

"I'm serious, Michael, give it here—"

"No!"

And just like that, the mostly civilized group devolved into screaming savages. Gamma, believing that the tribbles were the source of the trouble, rushed in immediately and began snatching up fuzzy softballs.

"Son of a bitch!" Raj said, flinging the creature back down and staring at his bloody fingers in shock.

"Well they have teeth *somewhere*," Melanie snapped, opening her pack and trying to use a piece of rachneweave to scoop the creatures up. She caught two, but the others rolled away, emitting high-pitched noises of derision not unlike a particularly rude raspberry. "Tac gloves on!"

"Can—can I see that?" the New Kid asked, bending down to the girl with the pigtails.

"*No!*" she shrieked, pulling the creature away. "My kitty!"

"Kid, I don't have time for this," Melanie told the little girl before swooping in and grabbing a handful of green fur. She leveraged it roughly out of the girl's hands with a few quick twists. Anyone who has ever taken something from an unwilling child knows what an extreme feat of dexterity and skill this can be, as it's commonly understood that they grow extra arms during the encounter.

The child's mother came flying over, her shiny helmet of hair practically demanding to speak to Gamma's manager (a show which the New Kid would have bought front row tickets to see). "*What* do you think you're doing?"

"We're just—it's—" he stammered.

"Sorry, public health hazard," Melanie said, stuffing the trembling creature in her pack.

"You give that back to my daughter right now, or so help me God—"

The set of her mouth told the New Kid that Melanie was sorely tempted to do just that, as the daughter in question was currently kicking her in the shins. After the third hit, Melanie reached down and swatted the backs of the little girl's legs the way you would pop a puppy. "*Stop* that."

Immediately the tiny monster's face screwed up, and she screamed like there were spikes being driven into her feet. Captain Soccer Mom puffed up with outrage and grabbed her daughter. "I am calling the police right now."

Melanie's eyelids fluttered with the strength of her eye roll. "You do that, ma'am."

Elsewhere on the playground, things were going just as well. Raj was on his hands and knees under the smallest slide where a group of creatures had hidden. He reached in tentatively with a piece of rachneweave, only to snatch his hand back as the angry balls rolled forward. Three other Gammas chased an unruly combination of children and aliens, followed closely by their confused parents and nannies.

The New Kid found himself between Briar Jones and the girl with the elf-blonde hair. She clutched the tiny creature still in her hand and began humming to herself. Her breathing immediately slowed in response to the music.

She wasn't the only one soothed by the song. Without warning, the tribble returned to its former placid state. The girl stopped in surprise, and the creature immediately began vibrating again.

The New Kid looked back and forth between the girl and the agitated alien. "Keep going," he murmured. "Briar, can you play something?"

She slowly set her gig bag down and unzipped it. "On it. Is that that *Frozen* song?"

The little girl nodded, staring down at the fuzzy green tennis ball in her hands. The yellow nodes twitched occasionally, but the tribble was otherwise quite calm.

"That's a good song," the New Kid said. "What's your name?"

The elf girl took a breath to say, "Kayleigh," and then kept humming.

"That's a pretty name, Kayleigh. I'm Kevin, and that's Briar. We're here to help, right Briar?"

"Right," the teenager said. "Gimme one second to tune her, okay Kayleigh?"

Between breaths, the girl whispered, "Okay."

True to her word, Briar Jones only took a moment to strum and tune one string on the beat-up guitar before she began to play. Kayleigh went silent, and then relaxed when the tribble in her hands stayed content.

"Well I'm glad that worked," Briar Jones said, letting out a long breath of air. "Come on." Like a pair of Pied Pipers, the teenager and the Gamma agent led their new friend over to where most of Malinois was concentrated. As they came closer, the fuzzy balls slowly fell into a trance-like state. They allowed themselves to be collected by relieved team members and placed in packs and spare pouches.

Only one continued to fight. The largest tribble, easily the size of a moldy green grapefruit, was worrying at the back of Specs's leg like a spoiled terrier. Unfortunately for the creature, it had chosen his prosthetic leg and was therefore doing very little damage. Eventually it too succumbed to the smooth chords that rose and fell like gentle waves, rolling away in blissful complacency.

The cheeky teenager winked up at Specs as she continued to play and said, "Music soothes the savage beast, right?"

He shook his head. "You two are geniuses."

"We're aware."

Specs scooped up the last creature in one large hand and said, "Someone take a picture."

A young white agent with pink streaks in her hair held her tablet up and snapped a quick shot of the tribble cradled in Specs's hands. "Got it."

"Good," he said, stuffing it into a makeshift bag that Melanie held out. "We'll get that to Darwin later. Is that all of them?"

"I think so," she said, tying the bag closed over the tribbles.

Briar Jones stopped playing, and after a few seconds the packs and pockets of Team Malinois began to thrash around. In the near silence, the New Kid glanced around at the stunned faces of the parents.

"Just the NYU Biology Department's idea of a joke," he reassured the crowd. "Have a good Day, everyone!"

Such was the power of his trustworthy presence that many guardians who had been seconds away from calling in the National Guard suddenly found themselves muttering to each other in embarrassment. Hadn't they just been hamsters painted green and yellow? Everyone knew hamsters bit. It was good that the nice man in the black vest had been there to reassure everyone.

Marching up to the New Kid, Captain Soccer Mom sniffed and said, "You might want to look at who you hire more closely. We won't press charges today, but someone else would."

Offering her a strained smile, the New Kid nodded and said, "I'm sorry about that, ma'am."

The woman *hmph*-ed and led her daughter away. The other parents followed her cue and began either herding their children off the playground or coaxing them back onto the swings and slides.

"Their rift is over here," Melanie said, leading the way to a busy ice cream stand where a short, pasty man with large glasses was doing a brisk business in spite of his outrageous prices. "It's right in front of the stand. How do you want to play this?"

Shrugging, Specs handed his fuzzball-filled packs to Melanie and said, "I guess we're getting ice cream. Tac gloves on, if you don't already have them."

Following his lead, the Watchdogs lined up in pairs. When it was his turn, Specs leaned forward and said, "Yeah, can I get, uh, a strawberry—no no, wait, you got pistachio? Alright, lemme get a pistachio in a cup, and—let's see, you wanted chocolate, right Ramirez?"

"Rocky road," she said, reaching into the pack with her thickest piece of rachneweave and feeding creatures into the front of the ice cream stand. It gave a little under her hands, like pressing down on Jell-O.

"Yeah, yeah, so that's a pistachio cup and rocky road—cup or cone, Ramirez?"

"Cup, please." She tugged on her earlobe.

"Cup it is! You got that?" Specs asked the much shorter man.

"Yeah pal, I got it," he responded in a thick Jersey accent. "You gonna pay or what?"

"Sure, sure."

The poor stand owner's trouble didn't end with Specs and Melanie. Every Gamma pair came up and gave him the same performance. Raj took nearly two full minutes to find his money, patting down his pockets over and over again and surreptitiously removing a tribble each time. The pink-haired woman started an argument with her "fiancé" that nearly had the ice cream man in tears. The non-Gamma customers soon rolled their eyes in disgust and went in search of greener pastures. When the rest of the Watchdogs finally retreated, Briar Jones and the New Kid stepped up, innocent and sweet as fresh-cut grass.

"Two hazelnuts in a cup, please," the teenager said, holding out exact change.

Nodding emphatically, the ice cream man said, "You got it, kid." While his head was buried inside the stand, the New Kid took the LBD out of his pocket and aimed it where the rift should have been. He held the button for five seconds, and a flash of heat rippled out from the end.

The ice cream man knocked his head against the inside of the stand as he jerked back. "What the hell?" When he looked up, the two of them were standing there expectantly. "My ice cream's all melted," he said.

The New Kid frowned. "Oh man, I'm sorry. I guess we'll go somewhere else. Hope your day gets better." Without looking back they turned and walked away, leaving their money behind (with a hundred dollar bill tucked in as an apology). They met the exhausted and relieved members of Malinois at the Warrior's Gate, where they were enjoying their treats.

"Mission accomplished, boss," Briar Jones said.

Specs grinned and offered his hand for a high-five. "Nice job, both of you. Ramirez, you guys earned that, but take it back to your posts."

Melanie wiped her mouth and said, "Yes sir. Malinois, move out!"

"Ramirez," Specs said, waiting for the Watchdog to turn back around. "This is your first command, right?"

Melanie nodded. "Yes sir. Omicron never offered, and I never asked."

"Shame on them for not giving you the chance to show off," the historian said. "You were wasted there."

Grinning, Melanie Ramirez gave him a pert salute and led her team away, leaving Specs and the New Kid alone with Briar

Jones again.

The teenager set her guitar down and leveraged herself up onto the wall. "What did we accomplish, exactly?"

"You made sure those little monsters can't come back," Specs said, leaning against the wall beside her.

"And how did I do that?"

"Science."

"Right. So what happened to your leg?" Briar Jones asked, swinging her own warm brown limbs against the stone wall. "If you don't mind me asking."

Specs cleared his throat. "Eight years ago, I was on a mission with my commander—"

"The Supreme Overlord?"

A tiny smile tugged at his mouth. "No, this was before I joined Gamma. I was part of an away team called Charlie. Our job was to follow people into rifts and rescue them."

Specs paused and offered Briar Jones his cup of plasmic pistachio ice cream before he continued. "We tracked a lost couple to the Eugenics Era, which is due to start in about a hundred and sixty years. It's a nasty period anyway, but this couple stumbled right into the middle of a terrorist cell's campsite. We managed to take them out, and our engineer disarmed one of their active incendiary devices, but the other malfunctioned as it powered down and took my leg with it."

The historian crossed his arms and looked up at the trees in silence. "There wasn't any pain at first. Just heat, and this long hissing noise. The device was made to dissolve the ionic bonds that hold molecules together, so everything below my left thigh just...disintegrated. Plastic, cotton, skin and bone—all of it. Like sugar in water."

"Jesus," the New Kid whispered, locking his jaw against a wave of nausea.

Briar Jones's eyes were like tiny moons. "Holy *crap*. What happened next?"

"They brought me home and rushed me to Med Bay, but it was way too late to save the leg. There was nothing *to* save. We can do some pretty miraculous things—our terrestrial medical technology is about two decades ahead of its time—but we can't regrow limbs yet." He extended the false leg out and turned it side to side. "R&D designed the prosthesis for me. It's myoelectric, so it can do this." He flexed the foot.

Briar Jones gasped. "That is so *cool*. Are you using the nerves?"

"Electrical signals from the muscles."

"You know, telling me all about how you lost a leg is really making me think twice about this whole internship thing." She looked the New Kid up and down with laser precision. "You got robot parts too?"

He squirmed away from her attention. "No."

"Most agents don't lead such adventurous lives." Specs winced and amended his statement. "Well, at least most of them have better luck than Gamma does."

"Remind me not to sign up for Gamma then," she said.

"Like it or not, Briar Jones, you're an honorary member after today. You did good out there, kid."

Grinning impishly, she said, "Does that mean I passed my interview?"

Specs threw his head back and laughed. "As far as I'm concerned, there's a spot for you at the agency the day you turn twenty. And I think we can find a few ways to keep you busy until then."

# WORLDS APART

## Grunt
(15:10)

The man known by his teammates as Grunt, and by new Watchdog recruits as the Dreadnought (and by a number of Persian Immortals as طلایی باد, or *the Golden Wind*), was perhaps the quietest wheel in the Gamma machine, though only the foolish took this as a reason to overlook him.

"Millennia to Captain Blue Eyes," the bud in his ear chirped as Grunt leaned over the map in Gamma Command.

Tapping his tragus, Grunt squared off a potential weak spot in blue and said, "Go ahead, Millennia."

"God, I could call every half hour just to hear you say my name. Anyway, I finally pegged down the coelophysis rift. It's up here in Bank Rock Bay, right by the bridge. Hella good for us, right? Darwin stashed them in the Natural History Museum."

"I heard. Has Charlie cleared it?"

"They don't have anybody nearby. I told McNab we'd take care of it."

Nodding to himself, Grunt said, "I'll get Rottie together and meet you at the bridge. Grunt out."

"What's the word?" Cat asked from the other side of the table.

Grunt capped his pen and straightened. "Millennia found the

raptor's rift. Charlie hasn't cleared it yet."

"I'd say we can take care of it," she grumbled, "except that you're the only one in Rottie who has away training."

"I'll go on my own."

Cat looked up at him. "Grunt—"

"You said it, Commander," Grunt reminded her. "No one else has the training. It's my job."

Cat maintained eye contact with him for several seconds before turning back to the map. "Take whoever else you need, but leave me Sasha. And be careful."

"Yes ma'am." Grunt had a few words with his Command team, and when he headed north over Bow Bridge he was accompanied by Oz, Tamika, Lindsay, and Fahd. Tamika was the odd-one-out at 5'6", but her height was belied by the iron in her arms. The others just kissed or exceeded six feet.

They made it to the side doors of the museum with little trouble. Darwin's friend was still working the ticket counter, and her eyes nearly fell out when Grunt pushed his way forward and held his badge against the glass partition. He hadn't bothered to ditch his weaponry, nor had he changed out of his black and grey battle armor.

"We need immediate access to the fourth floor," he said.

The young woman looked back and forth between the snarling dog emblem and the matter-of-fact Watchdog in front of her. "O-okay," she agreed.

"Thank you."

The security guard looked like he might protest as the group passed him, but one peek at Grunt's extremely professional badge changed his mind.

Within minutes they were outside the fourth floor theater. Another show was going on, so the only person in sight was Kerry, lounging easily against the far wall. Grunt and Oz drew their weapons and fired three stun rounds each, knocking out every single coelophysis within seconds. As Tamika began unwinding the perimeter tape, Lindsay and Fahd stepped over the short barrier and hefted feathery reptiles over their shoulders. They took turns handing them over to Kerry, who had already begun laying out strips of black canvas. Less than fifteen minutes from when they had entered the lobby, Rottie was ready to go.

"Darwin just had to run around here like he's some sort of secret fucking agent," Oz grumbled as they approached the door.

Lindsay's muscular legs bunched as she straightened from her crouch with a smirk. "Aren't we all technically secret agents?"

"You know what I mean. And the point is, I am never listening to him again."

"Yeah, and maybe one day flyin' monkeys'll come shootin' out my ass," Tamika said, shifting a coelophysis to one arm.

"I'm serious!"

"Yeah, right. You just keep tellin' yourself that, hon."

¤ ¤ ¤ ¤ ¤ ¤

"There's my favorite hunk-a-hunk-a-burnin' love," Millennia said, waving up at Grunt as he and the five Watchdogs made their way down the short embankment. "The rift's under here. I don't think anybody from our time crossed it."

"I'll do a sweep," Grunt said. He laid his bundle down and checked that each weapon was where it should be. "What can you tell me?"

"Not a lot, but I know someone who can." The physicist tapped her own tragus and then Grunt's. "Millennia and Grunt to Adam. We need that big, beautiful brain of yours."

"Adam here," he responded. "What do you need to know?"

"Everything you've got on the terrain and climate of Late Triassic New York."

"Um. Well, it's hard to be exact, but we were pretty close to a major mountain range back then. That means it won't be quite as hot as the surrounding desert, but it will be a lot more humid. Wherever the coelophysis pack came through, it must have been mostly flat; they're used to floodplains. Oxygen content will be lower, so you might experience something like altitude sickness. I wouldn't stay longer than half an hour if you can help it."

"Got it. Thanks, pumpkin." She ended the connection and glanced at Grunt. "So if you feel any sort of nausea or weakness, that's gonna be your first warning sign. Next comes a headache. If you feel dizzy, that's your signal to drop whatever you're doing and get the hell back here, okay?"

Grunt nodded. "Will do."

"Doesn't this thing come with a helmet or something?" Oz asked.

The physicist raised an eyebrow at him. "What does this look like, one of Iron Man's suits? The kinda tech that can fold that small and still be stable when it activates doesn't exist." Lifting a finger, she added, "Yet."

Grunt adjusted his pack and nodded at the Watchdogs. "Oz, Lindsay: If I'm not back in fifteen, shut it down."

"He means poke your heads inside to check on him, *then* shut it down," Millennia corrected.

"What she said," Grunt agreed, holding out his arms. "Give me half of them."

The Watchdogs obediently piled three unconscious dinosaurs in his arms. Grunt followed the direction of Millennia's finger and walked underneath the old wooden bridge. When he passed through the rift, every atom in his body shivered. It was definitely one part of the Day that he did not miss from his time in Bravo.

The air grew warmer and heavy with humidity. A misty forest floor surrounded him, and the background noise of New York City on a summer day had faded into silence. Towering trees covered in thick carpets of moss grew in alien shapes, and in some places the moss even crossed between branches like verdant webbing. Oversized ferns grew higher than his head, and the smell of growing things wrapped him in a gentle embrace.

Slowly, Grunt's ears became more sensitive to the sounds hidden within the misleading quiet. Far away calls penetrated the lush surroundings, and there was a faint whir of insect wings. Something landed in a tree above him, but he couldn't catch more than a quick glimpse. The soft, damp ground was free of humanoid footprints.

Even without prior knowledge of *when* he was, Grunt would have felt in his bones that he was in a different world. He had adapted to all manner of moving vehicles in his life, but less than two minutes on solid ground here had left the young tactical officer completely disoriented. Rather than risk getting turned around and losing time, he carefully set the dinosaurs down and unwrapped them like a trio of gigantic burritos. If a predator came by in the next ten minutes, it was going to get a big surprise.

Returning through the rift was even worse. His vision took on a reddish tint, and the familiar sounds of cars and construction and people laid siege to his eardrums. Grunt winced and inhaled, trying to calm the sudden tension in his muscles.

Approaching slowly, Millennia murmured, "Are you okay?"

"Fine," Grunt said. "No sign of anyone. Let's finish up."

Lindsay, Tamika, and Fahd each gently handed him a dinosaur. Without hesitation, Grunt crossed the rift a third time and began unloading his cargo. The transition was easier this time, though it was still wreaking havoc on his senses. If Tyrannosaurus had been alive at the time and prone to sneaking, one could have almost approached him undetected.

Almost.

Grunt rolled the black canvas up and tucked it under one arm. To be safe, he cupped his hands around his mouth and bellowed *"Hello!"* as loudly as he could. When no response was forthcoming, he turned around and left the Late Triassic behind without a backward glance. This time he narrowed his eyes to slits and plugged his ears, giving himself time to adjust to the abrupt changes in his modern world.

When his heart rate had slowed to acceptable levels, he tapped his bud and said, "Grunt to Cat. Mission completed. Shut it down?"

"Once you've got clearance from Charlie, yeah," she answered. "The last thing we need is more of those things coming back."

"Roger that. I'll close it and head your way."

"Good man. Cat out."

"I already got the green light from McNab," Millennia said, aiming her LBD at the invisible rift. "Did you bring me anything fun? Maybe a snow globe? Or one of those tees that says *My teammate went to the Triassic period and all I got was this lousy shirt?*"

Grunt looked at the bottom of one boot and peeled a leaf away from the dark soil. He offered it to Millennia, and she squealed in delight.

"Grunt, you shouldn't have. I knew you cared."

"He never brings us presents," Oz muttered to Lindsay.

"Aren't you glad?" she asked. "There could be all kinds of extinct microorganisms on that leaf. I don't want some weird dino-parasite."

"You're real fun at parties, aren't you?"

Lindsay shrugged and fell in formation behind the other Watchdogs, who had followed Grunt and Millennia's lead. The rolls of canvas were collected and stored in several packs, erasing all signs of the coelophysis's presence.

"One more disaster down," Grunt offered.

Snorting, Millennia said, "Yeah. Only a dozen more to go."

# BELLA MIA

## The New Kid
### (16:21)

Back at Gamma Command, Specs and the New Kid had just made their triumphant return with Briar Jones in tow. Though she wouldn't admit it outright, Cat was impressed by the fifteen-year-old.

"I'll level with you, kid," Cat told the girl. "The bad news is that until you're twenty, the Dogs won't employ you as an agent. You can intern in one of our departments for a few years or work in the main part of the Doghouse, but that's it. The good news is that unless you screw up spectacularly, I can more or less guarantee you a badge if you want it."

"I want it," Briar Jones said, her eyes fever-bright. "I didn't even know this was a thing that I could want until like an hour ago, but now I want it so bad that I'm gonna pee myself if I have to wait five years."

"At least five years," Specs said. "If you want to go into one of the science departments, for example, you'll need at least a master's."

Briar Jones swallowed, the light in her eyes dimming a bit. "I can't afford that. They're cutting funding for foster kids down to community colleges and trade schools."

"We'll send you to any university you can get into, on our bankroll," Cat said. "And we'll pay you a wage on top of it, so

198

you won't have to split your time between us and another job."

Briar Jones actually stopped breathing for several seconds. She looked between the two officers and asked, "Can I hug you?"

Pointing at Specs, Cat said, "Hug him."

At the historian's nod, Briar Jones flung her arms around his waist and buried her face in the stiff flak jacket. The action caused the oversized ball cap on her head to fall to the ground, and she left it where it was. She released him after a second and turned to where the New Kid stood leaning against a tree trunk, going up on tiptoe to hug his neck.

"Thank you," she whispered thickly, sniffing. "Thank you so much."

After a single heartbeat, he squeezed her back. "You're welcome."

"We should be thanking you," Specs said. "Naturals are hard to come by, even if you exclude temperament and skill set. I have a feeling that you've got a department head or officer position in your future."

Briar Jones laughed and stepped back. "My future. Ugh, this can't be *real*," she said, wiping her face. "I mean, I can believe in musical blue aliens and time-traveling secret agents, but I can't believe that you're handing me a brand-new future like it's nothing."

"Much as I appreciate being thanked for receiving a gift, we've got work to do," Cat said. Crossing her arms, she looked at Briar Jones, who stood at almost the same height. "And you need to go home. You have Lieutenant Forrester's card; come by that address in a week, and we'll give you the tour. If you're still interested, we'll start things rolling."

"Yes ma'am, Commander Supreme Overlord," Briar Jones said, saluting Cat with a grin.

Specs chuckled, and though her face remained mostly serious, Cat's eyes glowed. The New Kid looked down, contemplating his interlocked hands.

"Everyone has their strong suits," he reminded himself,

gently but firmly. "It's not a contest. And she probably can't do a half nelson to save her life."

"Something on your mind, precious?" Millennia asked, climbing up the nearly horizontal trunk and plopping down beside him. "Plotting the best way to send the new bundle of joy back where it came from?"

The New Kid flushed. "No."

"Mom and Dad love you too, you know. There's plenty of room for you and the new baby."

"Is that—is that what you think of them?" the New Kid asked, crossing his arms and nodding at Specs and Cat. They were standing side by side, watching Briar Jones walk away and talking quietly to each other. "Like Mama Bear and Papa Bear?"

Millennia cocked her head and then cracked a smile. "It totally is. But don't ever mention it to Cat; she likes to pretend that we're all a massive burden."

The New Kid cleared his throat. "But she doesn't really believe it?"

"For the most part, though I'm always a little surprised that she's never tried to drown Darwin in the Reservoir." Millennia stretched her arms overhead and said, "So if you're worried that she hates you, relax. Cat pretty much only hates Haverty and anyone else who picks on Gamma."

From the trees at the edge of their camp, a woman with dark amber skin and lovely brown eyes appeared. She wore a 1940s-style scarlet dress with a wide black belt, and her brown-black hair was artfully curled. The anxiety in her face smoothed out when she caught sight of the redheaded punk in the black tactical gear, who had frozen in the middle of her stretch.

"Isabella," Millennia breathed, sliding off the trunk and running forward until she could throw herself into the other woman's arms. The taller brunette stroked her hair, and they whispered to each other, but the New Kid couldn't catch what was said. Then Millennia pulled back and went up on tiptoe to kiss the woman she had called Isabella on the lips.

The New Kid didn't want to admit that he was confused for

the thousandth time in two days, but thankfully Specs chose that moment to walk over.

"That's Isabella Pannia," he said. "She and Millennia have a special relationship."

"I guess so," the New Kid said, watching the two women hold on to each other, foreheads pressed together and eyes closed. He had never seen two people stand so still, just breathing each other in. "I thought—I mean, Millennia told me—"

"You thought that she was straight."

Instead of answering, the New Kid shrugged helplessly, and Specs smiled in return.

"When you work for a time-traveling agency for nearly two decades, you learn that sexuality and gender are two very fluid, very *abstract* concepts. As far as I know, Millennia is bisexual; I think she's just more vocal about her appreciation for men."

"But it's...okay. That she is, I mean. I mean, no one—no one cares?"

"CIRIUS isn't a utopia," Specs said. "But they've always been far more accepting of others than the general population, out of necessity. That acceptance tends to rub off on people."

Patting the New Kid's shoulder in a fatherly way, Specs said, "Another thing that I've learned from working here—and from life, really—is that love is rarely convenient or considerate anyway. The truly deep kinds of love change you for good, like fire. The Millennia who is madly in love with Isabella Pannia is very different from the Millennia from five years ago who isn't."

"Where is Isabella from? She looks—older. You know what I mean?"

"She's a natural from the early half of the century," Specs said. "Not with the agency though. She and Millennia met about two years after Millennia joined the Dogs. Or rather, this Millennia met Isabella for the first time; I think Isabella was in her forties then. They take the term 'star-crossed lovers' to whole new heights. Whole new galaxies, actually."

The New Kid's mind boggled just trying to keep up. "So this

Isabella is—"

"A lot younger, I think. Early twenties maybe? From what she's told me, *she* first met Millennia when she was nineteen. Every year, Isabella jumps from rift to rift, looking for one that will bring her here to Millennia. She's seen things—" Specs shook his head. "Impossible things. Ask to read her journal sometime."

"Why doesn't she just stay?" the New Kid asked, watching the two women walk away arm-in-arm.

"For the same reason that Elaine can't stay," the historian said. "The timeline is a delicate thing, and we can't mess it up any more than it already is. We have no idea what will happen if we remove even a single person from one part of it and put them in another permanently. And remember: If *this* Isabella stays, then the Isabella who visits Millennia in twenty of her years won't exist. And then what happens?"

"Oh. *Oh.*"

"And this Isabella doesn't know it yet, but in a few years she's going to meet a waitress from Queens," Specs said, smiling. "They're going to grow old and toothless together, and be very happy. But every year, without fail, she's going to jump forward to see Millennia."

"So what about now?" the New Kid asked. "I mean, where is Isabella in our time?"

Specs held the younger man's gaze. "What I'm about to tell you is a secret that only Cat and myself know. You absolutely *cannot* tell Millennia, under any circumstances. Do you understand?"

"I understand," he said, nodding solemnly.

Looking in the direction in which the two women had disappeared, Specs murmured, "Isabella Pannia died of stage IV lung cancer in 1988, at the age of sixty-five. Her will stated that in the event of her death, a certain leather-bound journal in a locked box under her bed should be delivered, unopened, to Commander Alexa Fiyero, care of the New York City Doghouse—or the Cirius Trading Company, really. That was three years before Cat even joined the Dogs, so the agency kept both it and Isabella's letter in the Archives until the day that she was made full commander of Gamma at twenty-five. In a way, Cat knew Millennia long before Millennia knew her."

His voice became soft and faraway as he continued. "That journal is Millennia and Isabella's story, in its entirety, from Isabella's perspective. In her letter, Isabella explains who she is and entrusts the journal to Cat, to be passed on to Millennia on her fifty-seventh birthday. As far as we can tell from reading the journal, that's the furthest that Isabella has ever gone in Millennia's life." Specs cleared his throat and blinked several times. "So when she reads it for herself, she'll know that the next time she sees Isabella will be her last."

There was a sort of hollow, sympathetic ache in the New Kid's chest, and he found that his eyes were burning. "That's—" He broke off and swallowed thickly. "That's awful. That's the saddest thing I've ever heard."

"You could think of it that way," Specs said, nodding. "Or you can think of it as a love story that had no business happening, but did anyway."

From her spot by the path, Cat suddenly straightened and lifted her watch. Her face fell inward like a collapsing star, and her free hand clenched into a fist.

"Something's up," Specs murmured. "Only a handful of people merit that face."

Cat ended the communication and bowed her head, looking very much like she would punch the next person who came within reach. The New Kid's Cat senses, though not as well developed as the lieutenant's, began tingling as well. Instead of resorting to violence, she inhaled deeply and walked towards them.

"Our miracle just came through," she said as she approached. "They got a hit on Washington."

"You're kidding," Specs said.

"Nope. This nutty plan has a chance of actually working."

"Then why do you look like you just swallowed a very

enthusiastic eel?"

Cat's face puckered even more. "Because he's holed up in Fraunces Tavern."

"The Tavern? Isn't that—" Inhaling sharply, Specs put his face in one hand. "Damn. That's smack in Alpha territory."

"I'm aware," Cat said, crossing her arms. "Haverty's the one who called it in."

"Professional of him to inform you himself. What's the catch?"

"He wants Millennia to be the one who fetches Washington."

Specs looked away and muttered several words that most well-educated historians would never dream of using.

"It's a fucking power play," Cat agreed. "They don't *have* to turn Washington over to us. Technically, they're supposed to send him on his merry way with no detours."

"Just tell them that she's busy."

"I *did*," she said, running both hands through her hair until it formed a short crest. "He said that old George seemed comfy just where he was. They don't mind waiting for her."

"Meaning that they're keeping him comfy with all the cheap beer his liver can take," the historian muttered darkly. "Historically-speaking, he wasn't a big drinker, but this situation probably calls for something to smooth it over."

"And this has gone on long enough." Looking over her shoulder, Cat murmured, "Even if I didn't want to stick it to the smug bastard, there's no way I could ask Millennia to leave Isabella. Not for something like this."

Specs inhaled suddenly. "What we need is subterfuge. What we *need*—"

"Are a couple of larcenous little souls to steal us an American hero," Cat finished triumphantly, tapping her tragus. "Cat to Darwin and Helix; where are you hiding, my darlings?"

# GENERALS AND GIN

Fraunces Tavern
(16:38)

"Cat to Darwin and Helix," the twins' buds chirped pleasantly, "where are you hiding, my darlings?"

From his crouched position somewhere in the Ramble, Darwin turned unconsciously to the south, where his sister was offering a pair of painkillers to an older agent. "Oh fuck," he said, tapping his tragus. "She's never nice to us unless there's trouble."

"I have nightmares about her baking cookies and giving us a month's paid vacation," Helix added.

"Relax, you're not the ones in trouble," Cat said. "How would you two like to give Haverty a big ol' black eye?"

There was a moment of utter stillness, and then the twins asked in unison, "*Can we?*"

"We won't ask for anything ever again," Darwin said.

"Not even for our birthday."

"Or Christmas."

"Or Diwali."

"Or Hanukkah."

"Or Kwanzaa, I bet," Cat said with a laugh. "Alright, here's what you need to know."

¤   ¤   ¤   ¤   ¤   ¤

"I hate being the distraction," Helix grumbled as she unbuttoned her flak jacket and offered it to her brother.

"Don't lie to me," he said. "You like the attention."

She winked and began stripping off her top layers. "True."

"You know I'm more than happy to be the bait, but we're dealing with a Heterosexual Male out there. In this case, you're the effective one."

"I'm always the effective one. I just wish it was Elia out there; there are quite a few things I wouldn't mind doing to distract her." When she was down to just her sports bra, Helix held out her hand. "Give it over before someone walks in."

Darwin handed her the shirt that they had lifted from a tacky boutique on the way. "Or I could stand outside the door and start selling tickets."

"Perv." Helix pulled the hot pink shirt on and adjusted the bra underneath it until more of her chest was showing. "How's that? Would you follow me into a back room?"

Grimacing, Darwin said, "There's no safe way to answer that question. And no one should be following you anywhere."

"Torture devices, please." When Darwin obediently gave her the six-inch heels that matched her shirt, Helix grimaced and used his shoulder for balance while she pulled them on. "I'm going to re-gift these to you for Christmas."

"I would look stunning in them," he agreed. "Hey, at least you're finally at eye-level."

"You're hilarious." She took brown eyeshadow and began dusting it in the curves of her breasts, darkening the skin and creating the illusion of greater size. "Does the New Kid know his part?"

Her brother scoffed. "It literally has three acts. *I* still don't know why he's here at all. One little grease fire, and everyone evacuates. Problem solved."

"Because Cat said *subterfuge*, you stupid firebug."

"Yeah, but I really wanted to light something up today."

"I know," she said, giving his arm a consoling pat. "We can

go play around the Dungeon tomorrow if you want."

"That'd be nice. I feel like I barely see you some days."

Helix softened and took her brother's hand in her own, squeezing twice like a heartbeat. "Hey. I love you."

"Love you too." Handing her the bug-eyed sunglasses and rip-off designer bag that completed the look, Darwin said, "Now let's go parade you around like a prize-winning Pekingese."

"Bitch, please," Helix said, cocking one hip out and fanning her hair back. "I'm poodle-fabulous and you know it."

Darwin opened the bathroom door for her, and when they stepped out the New Kid's jaw dropped. "Wow! I didn't—I didn't even recognize you."

Helix smiled and tilted her head. "That's the idea, baby," she cooed, pitching her voice several degrees higher and a bit softer. "You don't look half bad yourself." They had nicked a blue button-up from the same boutique, and with it the New Kid looked like an eager Wall Street intern. "You ready?"

"Yup," he said, nodding a bit too enthusiastically.

In her normal tone, Helix asked, "Do you want to go over it again?"

"Nope, nope. I got it. Buy beer, break beer, be myself."

"Relax," Darwin said. "The kid's gonna do great."

Helix settled the purse in the crook of her arm and smiled again. "Showtime."

The New Kid entered the whiskey bar first, admiring the dark wood paneling and elegant, old-fashioned accoutrements. Soft but cheerful acoustic music filled the intimate space.

There were only six other people in the room: A pair of tourists happily enjoying the American Whiskey Trail; a worried banker with his tie curled up on the table beside him; the bartender, understated and bored; a black-clad Dog leaning back against the bar and occasionally sipping from the glass of water behind him; and to his right, a man in a creamy white shirt and brown waistcoat of fine make. He considered the shot glass in front of him, which was filled halfway with rosy liquid, and then downed it in one go. The forearms revealed by his rolled sleeves where brawny and pale.

When the kid in the blue shirt and black slacks entered the room, he spared a curious look for the man in the old-fashioned clothes and an apprehensive one for the Watchdog, and then approached the bar and ordered a pint without comment. The Alpha member on guard chuckled to himself; it was amazing what norms could ignore if they tried hard enough.

The initial stages of boredom started softening the Dog's posture as he continued to calmly watch over the quiet bar. He hadn't gone through a decade of training to be put on babysitting duty, but orders were orders, especially when they came from Chris Haverty. You disobeyed the son of a council member at your own risk.

The yuppie paid for his beer and took it to a table on the far side of the bar. He sipped quietly for a few minutes, and then sighed and pulled out his phone to answer a text. Distracted, he set the beer too close to the table's edge and it slipped to the floor with a glorious crash.

Every patron jumped, though the Dog was the only one to put a hand to his waist. Immediately, the bartender hurried over with a broom and dustpan.

"Oh my God, I am so—I'm so sorry," the yuppie stammered, coming to his feet. "Let me help—"

"It's okay, pal," the bartender said. "Happens all the time."

"Please, I'll do it, it's my fault—"

A clicking sound pulled the Dog's attention to the gorgeous breasts crossing his path. They were balanced flawlessly on an hourglass figure, and though he usually didn't like brown girls, he didn't see the problem in looking. His brain misfired a few times before he remembered that he needed to be watching the room, not chasing a nice pair of tits.

The woman attached to said-tits stopped at the end of the bar and peered around it, clearly looking for someone. The Alpha glanced at his silent charge and swallowed an offer to keep her company.

"I'm sorry," the yuppie said again, red-faced and stammering like a teenager with his first girl. "I'm sorry, I'll just go."

"It really ain't a problem," the bartender said. He swept up the last of the glass and lifted the dustpan clear. "Just let me grab a towel and I'll pour you ano—"

"No, no thank you." Before the bartender could protest again, the yuppie bolted from the room with his head ducked low.

This time the Alpha did chuckle out loud. He turned around for a sip of his water and noticed that the tits and their owner had vanished, presumably going after whoever had the balls to stand them up.

The atmosphere inside the bar was finally returning to normal when the Watchdog noticed that his legs were going to sleep. He twitched them, only to find that they wouldn't respond.

"What the hell?" he tried to ask, but the cottony words stuck to the inside of his mouth. Warmth spread rapidly up his legs and arms, and he had a few more seconds of clear thought before the world abruptly became opaque.

The bartender watched in confusion as the man in black slumped back against the bar, arms akimbo and legs stretched in front of him, looking for all the world like he was passed out. Unlike his oddly dressed friend—who was currently nursing his third pint in an hour—the man hadn't had anything even remotely alcoholic to drink.

"Buddy?" he asked, shaking the other man's slack shoulder. "Hey, you okay? You need me to call somebody for you?" There was no response, and though the bartender turned to the man in the old-fashioned clothes, he showed no interest in helping.

"Some men just can't hold their cyanide," a tall Indian man observed as he stepped over the unconscious man's legs.

"See if he's got a business card or something, wouldja?" the bartender asked, shaking his head and reaching for his phone. "And it's arsenic."

The Indian guy began rifling through pockets at random. "What is?"

"The line. That was from *Chicago*, right? It's 'some men just can't hold their arsenic.' My wife loves that show." The line connected, and the bartender said, "Hey Frankie, I got one for you. No idea; we're lookin' for his wallet now. Some off-duty SWAT guy or somethin', I don't know."

"Found it!" the Indian guy said, lifting a fat black square. He fished out a stack of business cards and said, "I think he works for some trading company on West 72nd. Maybe private security?"

The bartender nodded and relayed the information to Frankie. Hanging up, he said, "Good, he can go be their problem. I got a cab on the way. Thanks for the help."

"No problem," the other man said, waving the bartender's words off. He sat down beside the stranger in the waistcoat and said, "Nice to meet you, General."

Washington lifted his head and tried to focus on the younger man. "Is it, now?"

"Yes, sir. And I have some friends who'd really like to meet you too."

The sigh that escaped Washington's lips weighed a thousand pounds. "I suppose they must," he said, gently touching the side of his jaw. "Do they wish to deride me, or lift me atop my pedestal once more?"

"They need your help," the man murmured, throwing a fifty down on the gleaming bar. "I know you've been through a lot today, but you're the only one who can stop a lot of people from being hurt."

Nodding to himself, Washington took one last healthy swig of his beer and stood up. At more than six feet tall, he and the Indian man were the same height, though he easily had the advantage when it came to sheer bullheaded strength. White powder covered his shoulders, and in the overhead lighting it was possible to see silver and pale red patches in his otherwise snowy hair.

He picked up a matching frock coat from the bar stool beside him and faced the stranger, wobbling slightly as he turned. "Lead on then, sir."

¤    ¤    ¤    ¤    ¤    ¤

The dripping heat of the late afternoon hit them hard as Darwin and his new friend left the Tavern. Helix and the New Kid joined them at the Pearl Street intersection, both dressed in their original gear.

Darwin nodded at his teammates. "General Washington, I'd like you to meet my sister, Helix, and the New Kid."

"Kevin," the New Kid murmured, nearly running into a fire hydrant. "It's an honor, sir. I mean, Mr. Pres—"

"The GH worked fast," Helix observed. "Even without alcohol to speed it along."

Grinning, Darwin said, "That's because I used 685. Clear, tasteless, and faster than a scalded cheetah, though it does pack a nasty bitch of a headache."

"How unfortunate."

"I know, right?"

"Perhaps I am dead," Washington observed, not even trying to conceal the covetous looks that he shot at various women as they passed. "If so, I find myself dis—disappointed. I rather hoped Heaven would look more like Virginia." He winced and touched his jaw again. "Ah, no. This confounded pain tells me that I am still, in fact, among the living."

"Can you give him something for it?" Darwin asked Helix under his breath as he led their party down the stairs of the Whitehall street subway station. People blazed past each other like kamikaze atoms in a collider.

"I wouldn't risk it right now," she said. "Maybe when he sobers up."

"Do you believe in Heaven?" Washington asked, leaning down to blearily watch Darwin buy their subway tickets with his black card.

"If I did, I'd want mine to be a theme park run by the Rockettes," the zoologist replied.

The machine plunked out four tickets, and Washington accepted his with a grave nod. "And you, Kevin? What do you believe in?"

"I believe in Heaven, sir," the New Kid muttered, carefully avoiding his teammates' eyes. "And God."

The imposing general sighed and rubbed one temple. "I do not know if I do anymore. I will admit as much, since I am going mad and it hardly makes a difference at this juncture. We are lost, gentlemen—and Miss Helix, of course—lost and doomed, and it is all my doing."

This speech garnered a couple of strange looks as the little group pushed their way onto the appropriate platform. There was a sharp clatter, and the N train came barreling from the tunnel with a deafening *whoosh* of warm air.

Washington accepted this new development with a violent start, but he couldn't exactly stay behind when the crowd surged forward. Inside the heavily occupied subway car, the Gammas huddled together with their charge in the center. Helix leaned back a bit as Washington commandeered a pole and continued speaking.

"We are in our infancy," he said, drooping forward like melting wax. A woman in a sari glared at him as he came too close. "Still taking our first gasps of life, and I have smothered us as surely as a candle is snuffed out at day's end—*confound this pain*." This last was said with a hand pressed against his jaw

"Hold on a little bit longer, General," Darwin said, keeping one eye on the map just above the subway doors. "We'll get you something for it as soon as you sober up."

"Does beer always his strong of an effect on you?" Helix asked.

"Hardly," the man said with a great snort. "I blame that infernal wench who shot me with something that should taste like peaches, but does not."

"She shot you?" Darwin asked. "Wait, did she *give* you a

shot?"

"Yes, yes. That is what she did. She gave me a German shot."

"A German shot—schnapps? Peach schnapps?" Helix guessed.

Washington lurched a bit as the train stopped. "Delightful stuff. I had two more on my own. In fact, I rather wish for more, if you have it. It almost dulls the pain."

"Fresh out." Darwin leaned down where only his twin could hear him and muttered, "Cat's gonna love this."

"Cat will get over it." Checking her watch, Helix said, "Shit, by the time we get back it'll be after 5:30. Has Millennia found their rift?"

Her brother tapped his bud and murmured, "Darwin to Millennia."

"This is Batman, Robin; I read you loud and clear," she responded after a few seconds.

"How are you still so cheerful?"

She made a pleased sound deep in her throat. "You'd be cheerful too if you had this view. Isabella finally made it."

Darwin laughed. "Glad you're enjoying yourself. Did you ever locate the Frenchmen's rift?"

"Negatory, Robin. I was busy, and then I was...more busy."

Rolling his eyes, Darwin said, "First off: Busier. Second off: Since I'm tall and dark, and you're short and red, I get to be Batman. Third off: You'd better get a move on. We're headed your way with an eagle. A whopping *big* eagle."

"As in a thunderbird, or as in *'Murica*?" Millennia asked.

"'Murica."

"Okay. Okay, I have an idea. Where are you now?"

"On the N train, coming up on City Hall."

"Right. Call me when you get off."

Darwin grinned. "Millennia, that's not the sort of thing a gentleman calls a lady about."

The physicist hooted with mirth. "I might be a lady, but you're definitely not a gentleman. Call me, stud."

Disconnecting, Darwin glanced back at the unsteady general. "I take comfort in the knowledge," Washington said slowly, "that if I am mad, at least the rest of you are as well."

Darwin and his sister exchanged a look. "You have no idea."

# THUNDERSHOCK

## Command
### (16:39)

Nestled in the curve of East Drive and Terrace, Grunt and his team were trying to convince an actual thunderbird that the Summerstage at Rumsey Playfield was not a good place to build a nest.

"That's a lot of chicken wings, huh?" Oz asked, nudging the top of Tamika's head with his foot. He was perched on a low branch, just above the assembled members of Rottie.

The sturdy woman narrowed her brown eyes up at him. "That's two chicken wings, dumbass. And I'm a vegetarian."

"Yeah, Oz, don't be racist," Elias called over his shoulder, keeping track of the magnificent blue and black creature through the scope of his rifle. When upright, it was easily the size of a brown bear, and its wingspan nearly covered the entire length of the stage.

Oz chuckled. "Finger-lickin' good. That's all I'm sayin'."

"You touch me with that nasty foot again, chicken wings ain't the only white meat gon' be on the menu," Tamika grumbled. "That's all *I'm* sayin'."

"What do we know about them?" Sasha asked, checking that her stun rounds were loaded.

"They're solitary," Oz said, reading from his tablet. "And wicked territorial. Darwin says this one's probably a nesting female."

"Explains her behavior," Sasha said. "She probably got separated from her chicks and panicked."

"I thought the males had the cool feathers," Tamika said.

"Nah, that's just song birds and shit," Elias said, glancing over his shoulder. "Birds of prey look almost the same."

His teammates gave him looks that ranged from impassive to mildly impressed. "What?" he demanded. "Y'all act like Darwin's the only one who likes animals around here. Me and my girl go bird watchin' on the weekends."

"Everybody's full of surprises today," Oz said. He continued reading the thunderbird's file. "Jesus Christ, they've been known to hunt mountain lions. Not just survive them, but actually *hunt* the fuckers. Anybody else think this plan kinda sucks?"

"Shit. She spit lightning or anything?" Elias asked, shifting nervously.

"Nah, but—" Oz scrolled down and said, "Those slits in her beak are how she gets her name. When she's pissed, she blows air through them. According to our Southwest *compadres*, the sound is 'like rolling thunder on the plains, only loud as shit.'"

"Eloquent," Sasha remarked. "Tamika, I need you to find that rift. The Savannah isn't an option."

Tamika nodded absently, already running the tracking program and sending the thunderbird's signature to every other team in case they came across it. "Why not?"

"Because there's a good chance she can crack the glass with that call."

"Darwin's gonna be pissed," Oz remarked.

"I'll survive the disappointment."

Tamika looked up from her tablet and said, "Captain's been gone a long time."

Sasha's mouth tightened. "He knows what he's doing."

While the members of Rottie bickered and provided a fairly convincing distraction for the upset thunderbird, Grunt slowly made his way from the backstage area to where she had created an impromptu nest of cables and torn curtains. The thunderbird knew she was being watched, and she channeled the resulting restless energy into constantly rearranging her new domain.

Few things really stirred Grunt's heart anymore, but the thunderbird was one of them. She was shaped somewhat like a harpy eagle, with dusky blue plumage covered in black horizontal stripes and a white belly. Her beak was much longer than a typical raptor, almost toucan-like, and a single slit ran along it on each side. He desperately did not want to hurt her, but he was even more desperate to rescue the tiny figure currently curled up on one edge of the nest.

The little boy had light sandstone skin and tightly curled brown hair, and he was having the time of his life. The thunderbird had been so careful with him, pulling him back with one gentle foot when he wandered from the half-built nest and allowing him to cuddle up against her soft white side.

"I don't think she'd hurt him on purpose," he had told his team twenty minutes before, "but she *will* defend her nest against a direct assault, and he could get hurt on accident. Our best option is to take it slow and easy."

Now, the thunderbird came to her feet onstage and turned around to fix something on the back side of the nest. Giggling, the boy reached up and tried to grab the tail feathers that swayed hypnotically above his head.

Grunt tapped his bud and whispered, "Go."

A hoarse cry rang out from across the empty expanse of the Playfield, and the thunderbird's head bobbed up with interest. When the cry came again, louder this time, she turned to face it and fixated on a certain tree. After a third time, she hopped out and took to the sky with a thunderous whoosh of air that bowled the two-year-old over the edge of the nest. The light caught in her feathers, leaving a shadow that seemed to blanket half of the Playfield.

Grunt's mind went blank for an entire second. Shaking himself out of the stupor, he raced over to the squalling boy and scooped him up, pressing his face down to muffle the sound. From the direction of the tree, he heard Oz's unmistakable four-letter exclamation as the thunderbird descended.

The backstage area passed in a dark blur as Grunt shoved his way around control panels and a drum set before bursting through the black canvas wall. He put one hand on the edge of the stage and vaulted down, passing the little boy to a short blonde woman who burst into tears at the sight of him.

"Run," he said.

They didn't need to be told twice. The woman tucked her son against her chest and sprinted to put any running back to shame. From the Playfield, Grunt heard the sounds of furious battle. He rounded the corner of the stage and found his team fighting a creature out of legend.

The thunderbird didn't shoot lightning, but the winds created by her downstrokes were enough to knock an adult over at close range. She favored a swooping dive, claws outstretched to catch or maim. The Watchdogs crouched in a half circle and fired on her, but the biggest targets—namely, her wings— offered little for the stun rounds to sample. Thick feathers covered her belly, chest, and neck, leaving her feet as the only truly vulnerable areas.

As Grunt ran for his besieged teammates, the thunderbird landed in the half circle and fanned her great wings, knocking them off balance. Then an impossible rumbling filled the air, exactly as if a storm sat just above their heads. Every human in the immediate area, including Grunt, came to a stop and pressed their hands over their ears in pain.

The nose was incredible. One time, a freshly-recruited Grunt had ventured too close to a jet as it prepared for takeoff, and he'd missed his commanding officer's frantic signal as the engines caught. The sound had deafened him for an hour.

This was almost as bad. This was like being inside a lightning strike as it split the air, like descending too rapidly in air or water—but this sound had no end.

Grunt stumbled and hit one knee, looking up in a haze of pain. Through his blurry vision he saw the members of Rottie spread out in various recumbent positions. Slowly, Sasha picked herself up and actually crawled closer to the thunderbird, hands still clasped firmly over her ears. Though he couldn't hear anything but the giant raptor's call, he saw Sasha's face screw up into a battle cry. She took her hands away, picked up her gun, and shot two rounds at the thunderbird's feet.

One of them must have hit home, because three seconds later the thunderbird's cry cut off with a strangled choke and she collapsed, convulsing as the electricity hit her system.

The beleaguered team slowly came back to life, though their world rang. Grunt lifted his watch and put in a muted emergency request directly to Med Bay. Struggling to his feet, he stopped by each team member. Tamika and Elias were dazed and tearstained, but they seemed otherwise okay. Oz was bleeding from his nose, but he sat upright with Sasha's head cradled in his lap. She typed something weakly on Oz's tablet, and he grinned and typed right back. Grunt read the response as he turned it to face her: *Sasha used Thundershock. It's super effective.*

The injured Dog laughed weakly and looked up as Grunt appeared in front of Oz. He signed *Help on the way* and clasped her forearm. Sasha nodded and closed her eyes, relaxing against Oz. The other Watchdog held onto her hand, his thumb occasionally drifting down to rub at the willow tattooed on her wrist.

Grunt tapped his tragus. "Grunt to Cat. Half of Rottie's been incapacitated at Rumsey Playfield. Sasha, Oz, Tamika, and Elias. Medical's on the way. Eardrums are damaged, maybe blown."

"What about you?" Cat asked immediately. Her voice cut through the thick silence like cool silver.

"I'm in better shape than they are. I think we'll all be okay."

"Good. Wait for medical clearance," Cat said. "And stay safe."

A faint smile played on Grunt's lips as he closed the connection. The ringing in his ears had finally subsided, leaving everything soft and muted, as if he were hearing the world in shades of pastel. This time, when he put in a call to the Savannah for a team to help subdue the thunderbird, he could almost hear himself."

Sometime later, the medical team arrived and began working on Rottie. They declared Grunt's eardrums battered but intact, and the nurse who worked on him promised that his hearing would come back fully within the hour. Tamika and Elias were much the same, though the med team recommended that both Watchdogs be put on light duty for the rest of the Day. Oz was officially put on medical restrictions due to his perforated eardrum.

"You can be a tough guy and stay topside," a burly RN told Oz, taking off his gloves and revealing hands tattooed with intricate mandalas, "but you're off the active list. Best thing is to come down with us and get into surgery. You'll still be benched, but at least you won't be in pain anymore."

Oz subconsciously reached up and touched the outside of his bad ear. "What about Sasha?" he asked a little loudly, glancing down where the med team was strapping her to a stretcher.

"Sasha?" The RN, whose nametag read *O'Brian*, checked his tablet. "You mean Stephen? Stephen Conway?"

Oz's hand fell, and he automatically interlaced his fingers with those of the woman on the stretcher. "Her name is Sasha," he said firmly.

"Easy, man," O'Brian said, holding his own hands up. "I'm new here. I'm just telling you what my file says. Speaking of—" He clicked something on the tablet and whistled. "Jesus Christ. Both eardrums perforated, hairline fractures in his—*her* maxilla and temporal bones, and her zygomatic process on one side. No swelling, that's good. She needs a double myringoplasty and an Arcturian Cradle as soon as we can manage it."

"Will she be okay?"

"She'll be fine," O'Brian said. "We'll graft the holes closed, and the Cradle should speed the healing process by a factor of fifty. With no complications, Agent Conway will be back on active duty in a couple of weeks."

Grunt's bud chirped faintly. "Hiroto here, Captain. We got a ping on Tamika's signature near the edge of the Bird

Sanctuary."

A less professional soldier than Grunt would have rolled his eyes at the coincidence. "Acknowledged. I'll put you in contact with the Savannah team. In the meantime, call Charlie and get clearance. Grunt out."

The Watchdog walked over to where the mixed group of scientists and security officers stood watching the thunderbird, which had been trussed up as effectively as any holiday turkey. They were especially careful to neutralize the devastating vibrations from its beak.

"How did you catch her?" a mousy little ornithologist asked, bravely peering closer at the thunderbird's pinioned wings.

"We lured her in with a recording," Grunt said.

"Of what, wounded prey?"

The Watchdog shook his head. "Since she took a kid, we used a hatchling's cry from the file."

"Smart," he said. "Dangerous for whoever was playing the recording, though."

With a pang in his gut, Grunt glanced back at Oz and Sasha. "One of Gamma's teams found the thunderbird's rift. The agent in charge is Hiroto Loss. He should be on channel 127."

"Roger that. We're just about ready for transport." Eying the stunning raptor, the Dog remarked, "Shame we have to send her back. I'd love to keep her for a few years."

"I think she has chicks to care for," Grunt remarked.

The mousy scientist straightened to his full height and nodded. "Right. We'll have Agent Loss radio you when it's done."

Grunt's bud chirped as the team from the Savannah cleared out. "Millennia to Grunt; heard you got hurt. Everybody okay?"

"We'll be fine," he said. "What do you need?"

"An escort, if you're not busy. I want to borrow one of the Frenchmen so I can track his rift. Isabella's with me, and the Victorian girl will have to come."

"I'll meet you at Agent Donovan's position now," he replied. "Grunt out."

Exhaustion started tugging at his body, but Grunt ignored it. There was still a job to do. At least if Isabella came with Millennia, she would be less likely to tease him. That had to be worth quite a lot, if it worked out.

One could always hope.

# FAR ABOVE THE CLOUDS

## Millennia
### (17:15)

To the north, Millennia sighed and reached down for her discarded underwear. The bed shifted behind her, and Isabella pressed a kiss against the fractal tattoo that spiraled out across the breadth of her bare back.

Millennia hissed in a sharp breath. "You're cheating."

"I'm grieving, *amore*. You're leaving me."

"I have to," Millennia moaned, trying to force her body to move away from the burning lips that still grazed her skin. "Cut it out."

"Maybe when you mean it."

Millennia rolled over and pressed herself against the other woman, nuzzling into her neck with a contented sigh. "I need a snooze button for my life," she murmured.

Isabella's arm came around her, fingers smoothing the close-cropped hair in long strokes. "You're younger than last year," she observed softly. "Close to my age."

"Good. That means we're both fresh and limber. If you hadn't already noticed."

Isabella put a hand to her forehead and laughed, the action rippling through her body in pleasant ways. "*Amore*, you're as bad as the soldiers who come into the diner."

"Yet I," Millennia said, tracing delicate patterns on Isabella's chest, "am the one in bed with a beautiful Italian. So that makes me the winner." She pulled the taller woman's suddenly intent face down and kissed her, tasting the sigh that escaped her eager lips. Millennia guided them both to the point of losing control, and then gently backed off.

"Time's up," she whispered against Isabella's lips, stealing another kiss. With a huge effort of will, she climbed out of the hotel bed and began pulling on her clothes. Though she didn't look back at Isabella, she could feel the other woman's despair like a heavy mist.

"Is this what it's always going to be like?" she asked, sitting up. "An hour together, maybe two? And then nothing. Nothing for a year."

Millennia buttoned her rachneweave pants and pulled on the matching shirt before she responded. "*'En mi cielo al crepúsculo, eres como una nube.'*"

Puzzled, Isabella said, "In my sky of—in my twilight sky, you are like a cloud?"

"It's Neruda," Millennia said, turning enough to see Isabella's shape in the dim light. Her throat had dried up, and she couldn't quite bring herself to meet the brunette's eyes. "This is what we have. It's soft, and fleeting, and not—not quite real, I guess."

Isabella shoved the covers off, revealing a brief flash of warm skin, and wrapped her arms around the much smaller woman. "Clouds may not be real to a fish," she murmured, staring into Millennia's eyes, "but they are everything to a bird."

The physicist returned the embrace just as hard, pressing herself into Isabella's soft arms until she couldn't breathe.

"I love you," she whispered.

Isabella planted a kiss on her rumpled head. "I love you too, *amore.*"

"Come with me now," Millennia said, pulling away. "It's still early. Where did you come through?"

"The statue of the birds."

"Easy-peasy." Smacking Isabella's bare ass, Millennia said, "Get dressed. We're going on an adventure."

Though she did as she was told, the other woman took her time about it. "What kind of adventure?" she asked, wriggling into an old-fashioned bra and ridiculous panties that no self-respecting Grandma would have been caught dead in.

Millennia eyed her lasciviously as she rolled her stockings up. "Not as good as the one we're leaving, I'll tell you that."

Winking, Isabella attached her garter and clipped the stockings down with practiced hands. "Obviously, but what else?"

"Well, how do you feel about the French?"

Isabella paused in the act of putting on her slip. "I've never met one. But my grandmother used to tell me stories about the French boys who came to her village. Apparently, they're very romantic."

"I thought Italians were the romantic ones."

"We are, but the French have a bigger reputation."

"They've got a bigger something alright," Millennia muttered, clipping things into place on her belt, "but I don't know if it's their reputations."

Buttoning the top of her dress, Isabella leaned down and kissed Millennia. "You are very funny."

The physicist stretched and rubbed her stomach. "Admit it; you only like me for my body."

"Of course not. It's that beautiful mind that I love," Isabella insisted, tapping Millennia's forehead. "And to think, it will only improve with age."

"Or diminish, depending on where you end up next time," Millennia said, slinging her pack up on one shoulder. "How do you feel about older women?"

"Well, since you were thirty-four last year, and I had just as good of a time—" She smoothed the backs of her hands along Millennia's cheeks, and grinned when the other woman's pupils dilated. "I must like them well enough."

"Minx," Millennia whispered. "You saucy, saucy minx."

Laughing, Isabella took her hands away and very deliberately put them behind her back. "Then we must be clouds."

Reaching behind her back, Millennia took Isabella's hands and held them in her own. "Clouds just passing through."

"It will have to be enough," Isabella said.

Millennia's fingers tightened, and she asked, "Do you regret it?"

Isabella's laugh danced around the room again. "Not in a thousand years, *amore.*"

¤   ¤   ¤   ¤   ¤   ¤

The group that hiked through the Ramble half an hour later was perhaps one of the strangest to ever do so. It consisted of a serious man of slightly below-average height in black and grey geometric armor; a pretty, rumpled woman in a red dress that was vintage ahead of its time; a shorter woman who walked arm-in-arm with her when possible, and whose half-shorn hair was a perfect match for the dress; a lively girl in Victorian summer attire; a sturdy agent in black tactical gear who was trying very hard not to blush; and an extremely handsome mustachioed gentleman in an 18<sup>th</sup> century French cavalrymen's uniform. He was, of course, the reason that the woman in black was having such a difficult time.

"*Laissez-moi vous aider,*" he said, offering his hand to Agent Sarah Donovan as they came to a rough patch in the trail. "I help."

"No thank you," she said, choosing to navigate the jumble of rocks and dead branches on her own. She seemed clumsier than usual, however, occasionally putting a hand on the Frenchman's shoulder when her balance faltered.

Several feet behind them, Elaine struggled with her own much more voluminous clothes, grinning the whole way. "Romain is doing quite well, don't you think?" she asked the two women beside her. "He's rather sophisticated, for a French brute."

"I like him," Isabella said. "At least, I think that I like him."

"Sarah's trying so hard not to," Millennia said with a smile.

"It's very professional of her. And so boring."

Grunt appeared in their midst and gently cupped Elaine's elbow. "Do you need some help?" he asked.

"Yes, yes please," she said. "Thank you, Captain Walker."

"No problem. Is this okay?" he asked, placing one hand under her arm and the other in the small of her back.

Though the young Victorian woman colored prettily, she nodded and said, "Yes, that's very helpful, thank you." To Millennia and Isabella, who were snickering quietly to each other, she said, "Oh do shut up, the both of you."

"*Ici!*" Romain called suddenly, looking around. "*C'est là que nous avons passé au.*"

"He says that he thinks this is the place," Elaine translated.

Putting her serious face on, Millennia opened the active tracking program on her tablet and scanned the Frenchman. "He's half right," she said. "There's no open rift here, but we're close." She widened the search and zoomed in on a particular spot that caught her interest. "Gotcha. This way."

She led them to a spot a hundred feet downhill, where a great mass of underbrush had been trampled and ripped up. Millennia triumphantly marked the spot and opened a line on her bud. "Millennia to Cat, we've got your rift. Sending you the coordinates now."

"Good girl. The twins and the New Kid are about ten minutes away with Washington. The minute they get here, we'll—"

"*Stay right where you are!*" a harsh voice called from behind them.

The entire party froze except for Grunt, who turned his head to search for their aggressor. After a minute of careful attention he found a white man crouched deep within a cluster of bushes. His uniform and face had both been liberally smeared with dirt, and he had a dingy musket trained on them.

"By order of General Howe, and under the authority of His Royal Majesty King George of England, I declare you lot under arrest for trespassing," he said. "Come quietly, and no one'll get hurt. And you!" he said to Romain. "Drop your musket."

The embarrassed Frenchman did as he was told, muttering under his breath. By now, all of them had spotted the man in his hiding spot.

"Cat, I'll call you back," Millennia murmured, tapping her bud. To Isabella she said, "He thinks the rest of us are unarmed."

"Isn't Grunt a weapon himself?" she asked.

Though Millennia quirked a smile, she said, "Grunt's like a bazooka. I'd rather not bust him out if we don't have to."

The tactical officer's eyes flickered between the hidden man and their group. "Can you pretend to be nobility?" he murmured to Elaine.

"What?" she asked, clinging to his arm tightly.

"Eh now, stop that!" the man yelled. "Stop talking to each other!"

But Elaine had caught on. "Oh, for Heaven's sake," she called back in her poshest accent, "do put that thing down."

The man faltered. "Eh?"

"I said, *put that down*," Elaine demanded, taking a small step forward and bringing Grunt with her like an escort. "I am the Countess Westumberland, and you will *not* point a weapon at me as if I were some common criminal."

"I—ah, forgive me, m'lady," the man stuttered, and his heavy weapon lowered several inches. "I didn't realize—"

"Clearly," she replied, wicked delight leaking from the acidic edge of her words. "Identify yourself and your superior officer immediately."

"Private Lichberg, m'lady, under Captain Moore. M'lady, can I ask—what are you doing out here?"

Giving him her best affronted look, Elaine asked, "What does it look like I'm doing, Master Lichberg? I am taking a walk with my associates."

"But m'lady—" Private Lichberg eyed the strange dress of her companions and changed tactics. "There's a war on, m'lady. And this one—" He pointed again to Romain with a sweep of his musket. "This one's French."

"You say that as if it is news to me," Elaine scoffed, though her face turned a delicate shade of pink. "If the truth will put you at ease, Master Lichberg, then very well. Romain is my lover. The two in black are my guards, and the women—" Spots of rose bloomed on Elaine's cheeks, and she lifted her chin. "The women are our entertainment."

Happy to play her role, Millennia stepped up behind Isabella and ran her hands slowly down the other woman's arms, eying Lichberg as though inviting him to join. Isabella rotated her wrists and grabbed Millennia's hands, pulling her close.

Private Lichberg turned the same shade as his discarded coat, and completely lowered his weapon for the first time. "I-I see, m'lady. My apologies for disturbing you."

"Say nothing of what you have seen," she replied loftily, "and we will consider the matter forgotten. Now, do come out of there and be on your way. I won't have you lurking about while I am trying to relax."

"Yes, m'lady. Of course." Private Lichberg gathered his coat and musket and left the sanctity of his hidey-hole. He had barely taken four steps when Grunt seized him.

The tactical officer used one hand to grab him by the back of his neck and the other to hold the musket between them in a parody of the way he had helped Elaine along before. "This way, Private."

"My guard will escort you to an appropriate distance," Elaine said, turning towards the thoroughly confused Frenchman. "We have things to attend to."

Using Millennia's subtle hand signals as a guide, Grunt marched the dirt-smeared man to the invisible rift and gave him a hearty push the moment he felt the temperature drop. The air shivered and swallowed the British soldier whole.

The experienced group members deflated with relief, and the other two gave little starts of shock. "You were incredible," Millennia said to Elaine as she recovered from her surprise.

"Thank you, but it was Master Grunt's idea," Elaine said.

"I know, I heard," Millennia said, eying him up and down. "That was some Grade-A Gamma thinking, Grunt. The twins would be proud." Her face turned serious. "I'm sorry that I called you a bazooka. You're more like a multitool that just so happens to come with a bazooka setting."

His lips twitched up on one side. "Thanks."

Elaine put the back of one hand to her forehead and cheeks. "Goodness, I'm still burning up. That was mortifying. Millennia, Isabella, please forgive me for dragging you into it as well."

"It was fun," Isabella said with a shrug. "And it worked."

"For once." Millennia checked her tablet one more time and then tucked it away. "Alright, kiddos. I'm tempted to push Frenchie in since we've got him here, but I think his captain would pitch a fit if he didn't come back. So instead, Elaine and Agent Donovan need to take him back to his company. Hopefully everything will have been worked out by the time you arrive. Which reminds me—" She tapped her bud and said, "Millennia to Cat. Everything's copacetic, Captain my Captain. We had an English visitor from the same time as the Frenchmen."

"Jesus Christ, can we close that fucking rift already?" Cat asked. "Make sure you put in a call to McNab. I want clearance on this thing ASAP."

"Your wish is my command," she replied cheerfully. "Millennia out." Turning to Grunt, she said, "You should probably head back to Wagner, right?"

The tactical officer nodded. "Rottie is keeping watch, but they're down several members. And there's no senior officer."

"Alright then, get that perky tush back to Command, on the double. Make it bounce a little for me."

Isabella kissed her lover's hair. "Hush, *amore*. Leave the poor man alone."

Flashing Grunt an apologetic smile, she said, "Unless something terribly drastic happens, I'll meet you at Command in half an hour." Her hands tightened on Isabella's arm. "There's something I have to take care of."

Grunt's eyes flicked to the woman in the red dress. "Take all the time you need."

# THE EAGLE AND THE FROGS

## Cat
### (18:18)

"'"Those two are fucking miracle workers," Cat said as the twins appeared at the base of the hill, leading a wardrobe of a man who wobbled uncertainly between them. "They are officially my favorite miscreants. You know what happens if you tell them."

Beside her, Specs's teeth flashed in his dark walnut face. "I'm well aware."

Darwin waved enthusiastically and pointed to the stranger. "You meet the damnedest people on the N Train, Cat. Look who followed us home."

"Can we keep him?" Helix asked.

"You've already lost your last pet," Cat said, swaggering down to meet them. "What the hell did you do with the New Kid?"

"Couple of Jamal's pups needed some muscle, so we let them borrow him," Helix said.

Darwin cleared his throat and gently guided the hazy-eyed man forward. "Commander Fiyero, I'd like you to meet General George Washington. General, this is the woman I was telling you about."

Washington gravely stuck out his hand, which completely dwarfed Cat's own when she accepted it. "Darwin tells me that I am not mad after all," he said. He was clearly beginning to sober up, and it did not agree with him. "He claims that I am in the future, and that you are in charge." Eying Specs for a quiet moment, he offered his hand again and corrected himself. "That *both* of you are in charge."

"Yes, sir," Specs said, accepting the Founding Father's handshake.

At that instant, Washington let out a quiet but robust fart. "Beg pardon," he said. "Now, Darwin also tells me that you have a problem with which I can offer some assistance?"

Nodding, Cat pointed at the twins and said, "You two, get back on calls. We'll let you know if we need anything else."

"Hold up," Helix said, unzipping a pouch on the side of her backpack and offering Washington a pair of foil-wrapped pills. "Take these, General. They'll help the pain in your jaw and head. Just swallow them whole with some water. *Swallow*, don't chew."

"Thank you, my dear girl," he said. "I would be most grateful for any relief."

Cat began leading the way up the hilly path while Washington followed at his own careful pace. "General, we have a small force of Frenchmen from your own period at the top of this hill, and we're trying to convince them to come with us peacefully so that we can get them home," she told him. "Problem is, they're scared and upset, and they'll only talk to you."

"I see. Am I to assume then that the frogs have decided to stop sipping wine from the comfort of their swamps and lend us some real aid?" Washington sighed and put a hand to his head. "I apologize, Commander. My men have suffered and died while they continue to deliberate. It is a hard thing to forget."

"I understand, General." The image of Director Tamiko sitting calmly across from her rose up in Cat's mind, and her expression hardened. "Trust me."

"General, can I ask what year you've come from?" Specs

asked.

"The year of our Lord, one thousand seven hundred and seventy-six," Washington answered. "A glorious, bastardly year. Will I go home, when this business is done?"

"We'll make sure you get back to your time, General," Specs said.

The large man sighed. "And the eve of our destruction."

Specs drifted closer to Cat and leaned down. "In his day, General Howe is closing in on New York. Washington is losing men left and right to desertion and disease. He doesn't think he can hold the city, and he's right. In a few months, they'll fight the Battle of Long Island. It's going to be the largest battle of the war, and the first one that the Continental Army will face as part of an independent nation."

Cat wasn't as well-versed in history as her lieutenant, but she did remember how that particular fight had gone. "And they're going to lose."

"Badly."

Sneaking a glance back at the sturdy general, who was absorbed in his own thoughts, she said, "I know what you're thinking."

"What if we're supposed to?" Specs asked. "What if this is part of history?"

"We can't interfere."

"It's not interference if it's crucial to the timeline," Specs argued. "This next year is one of the most critical for him. His spirit, the *American* spirit, is going to be at an all-time low, and if he doesn't rally—" Breaking off, Specs shrugged helplessly. "They might not recover. And then what?"

Cat looked around at the park and the people enjoying it. "What kind of insane world is this, where I might have to give a pep-talk to a nearly three hundred-year-old man with the fate of a country potentially hanging in the balance?" Shaking herself, Cat put in a call to the security team from her walkie watch. "Fiyero to Captain Terrell. We're approaching your forward position now."

"Roger that, Commander," Captain Terrell's smooth voice replied. In spite of her tense hours on the forested hillside, she sounded almost obscenely at ease. "We've spotted you. Captain Renault has also been notified."

"Thank God for Google Translate," Cat muttered.

Terrell laughed. "It'll do in a pinch. Be seeing you. Terrell out."

"Fascinating," Washington said, watching her intently. "I clearly heard another woman's voice."

"The magic of technology," Cat said, slicking her sweaty hair back with both hands. "How's your jaw?"

"It's—" The general paused mid-step. "Heavenly Father. I feel nothing. No pain." He ran his hands along the bottom half of his face. "Have my teeth all fallen out?"

"Not yet."

Washington slowly lowered his hands and continued walking behind them. "This is a miracle. Half my lifetime has been spent in mortal agony, and now it is simply gone as if it were no more real than a passing night terror." He quickened his pace until he could place a hand on Cat's shoulder. "Commander. Please convey my deepest gratitude to Miss Helix."

"Sure thing."

After five more minutes of walking, a black-clad CIRIUS agent stepped out from behind a tree and acknowledged their passage with a solemn nod. "Captain Terrell's another three hundred feet straight ahead," he said.

Cat waved him off and kept going. "Could 'a figured that out for myself," she muttered to Specs, "since I can see her standing in a goddamn open meadow. My eyes aren't going quite yet."

"He must have seen the grey in your hair," the historian teased.

Cat snorted. "At least I don't look like the love child of Michael Jordan and Mr. Clean."

Specs coughed to smother the sudden laughter. He still hadn't composed himself by the time they reached Captain Terrell. The head of the security team was in her late fifties, with plenty of silver threaded throughout her French-braided auburn hair and well-earned lines on her pale, bare face. She was flipping through a sheaf of papers and listening to a juggernaut of a man whose head was twice the size of her own. His jawline alone looked like it could crush granite. He was the first to see the approaching Gamma pair and their companion. At his indication, Captain Terrell turned and watched them cover the last fifty feet or so.

"Good to see you, Commander," she said, nodding at Cat and then Specs. "Lieutenant Forrester."

"Captain," he said, returning her nod. "This is General Washington."

If Terrell had any thoughts on meeting one of the Founding Fathers, she kept them to herself. Offering her hand to shake, she simply said, "General. It's an honor to meet you. I'm Captain Theresa Terrell."

Washington returned the handshake in a more active fashion than he'd previously displayed. "Captain Terrell. The pleasure is mine."

"They tell me you're here to send our wayward friends home."

"I hope to," he said. "Where is the captain?"

"His name is Renault," she said, leading them across Tupelo Meadow. "He and his men've taken up a defensive position behind that cluster of rocks straight ahead. We should be stopped by his first scout any moment."

A few seconds later, a bored voice called out, "*Halt, s'il vous plaît.*"

"So polite," Specs remarked.

Terrell smiled. "They got tired of shouting at us hours ago. That sounds like Francois."

A swarthy man with curly black hair appeared from behind a thick bush, his musket pointed easily at the ground. Yawning, he said, "*Bon après-midi, capitaine.*"

"*Bonjour,*" Terrell called with a lazy wave. "Lieutenant, you're up."

Specs stepped a little ahead of the group and smiled at the Frenchman. "*Salut. Je m'appelle Lieutenant Forrester, et je l'ai amené le général Washington à parler avec le capitaine Renault.*"

"*D'accord,*" the scout said with a shrug. "*De cette façon, s'il vous plaît.*"

"We're supposed to follow him," Specs said, a bit unnecessarily as Francois turned away and began walking towards the rocks.

The security captain lifted a hand to her ear. "Terrell here." She listened intently, and after a moment she smiled and said, "Good job, Donovan. We're about to meet with Renault now. Return the soldier to his men, and keep the girl safe and out of the way."

"Is that about Elaine?" Specs asked. "I'd actually like her here, Captain. A second translator would be a big help."

"Belay that order and bring the girl to us," Terrell amended. She ended the transmission and said, "They're almost to the northern perimeter."

Cat nodded, too grateful for the flat ground to comment further. Her calves had been sore for twenty minutes, and there was a deep stitch somewhere in her left side. They had already passed her least favorite part of the Day: The eighteen hour mark, when all the bruises and strains that she had accumulated thus far really made their presence known. Unless she got a much-needed caffeine or adrenaline boost in the next hour, her exhausted brain would continue to inform her of how much her body disapproved of its treatment.

*I know, I know,* she told the knee that had been damaged in a fall nearly a decade earlier. *A little bit longer.* Much of the cartilage cushioning the joint had been worn away, and it creaked abominably for the last quarter of every Day.

Finally, the little group reached the French encampment. The attitude of the soldiers was markedly different from that morning. Men lounged in the shadow of the rocks, napping or scratching crude games into the dirt. Eight hours of tension had mellowed them out, though they came to attention quickly enough when they saw the party of four being led in by one of their scouts.

"*Où est le capitaine?*" Francois asked a pair of paler, bare-chested men who had both turned a scorched shade of pink.

"*Se soulager*," the chubbier one said, flicking his head back and to the left.

"*Attendez*," Francois said. He walked off towards a cluster of trees and disappeared.

There was a commotion to one side, and the soldiers came to their feet in an excited wave. Romain appeared in their midst, with Elaine behind him and Agent Donovan taking up the rear. Most of the soldiers were completely engrossed with Elaine, offering her their hands and chattering to her in French while she deflected them demurely. Only Romain seemed concerned with Donovan.

"Glad you could join the party," Cat remarked. "Miss Penrose."

"Commander Fiyero," Elaine said with a wide grin. "This has been simply the most exciting day of my life. We were accosted by one of my own countrymen! I've never been threatened with arms before."

"We think he was English," Donovan added. "He sounded almost American."

"Most of the English did, back then," Specs said. "Non-rhotic English—the accent that we think of as British, like Elaine's—was just coming into fashion. Before then, only the cultural elite spoke that way."

As introductions were completed amongst the expanded group, Francois appeared from the trees with Captain Renault in tow. The Frenchman had long ago abandoned his ridiculous wig and three-cornered hat, and his previously pristine blue surcoat was creased with dirt and sweat. He finished tucking his shirtfront into his pants and tied them closed before approaching briskly. Up close, he didn't look much older than the twins.

"*Général Washington?*" he demanded, trying to look down his pert nose at the much taller American.

Washington nodded. "Captain Renault. I'm told you needed to speak to me."

Elaine looked at Specs. "Would you like to, Leftenant, or shall I?"

"If you don't mind," Specs said.

"Oh, not at all!" Addressing Renault directly, she said, "*Le général lui demande comment il peut vous aider.*"

"*Mes hommes ont été séparés de notre régiment,*" Renault said. "*Nous sommes affamés et épuisés, et nous avons besoin de son aide pour rejoindre le Bourbonnais.*"

"They were separated from their company, the Bourbonnais," Elaine translated. "General, they'd like your help to get home."

"Bourbonnais," Specs muttered. "*That's* what he said earlier. They're one of the regiments that Rochambeau brought to help the colonists."

"Tell him that we can help him get home, but he has to trust us," Cat said. "Please."

"*Ces hommes et ces femmes peuvent vous aider,*" Elaine said, gesturing to the Dogs. "*Vous devez leur faire confiance.*"

Captain Renault regarded the group in front of him with suspicion. "*Un esclave et trois femmes? En quoi puissent-ils etre utiles?*"

"*Ils sont incroyablement aimables, des personnes compétentes,*" Elaine said. Her tone was now devoid of all its bouncy warmth. "*Et ils sont les seuls qui pouvrent vous aider, capitaine.*"

His eyes narrowed. "*Vous vous outrepassez, mademoiselle.*"

The Elaine of that morning would have blushed and backed away with an apology. That Elaine, however, had not braved a city out of the daftest science fiction. That Elaine had not negotiated a ceasefire between men who were long dead, and men and women who were yet unborn. And that Elaine did not bear a testament to courage on her thigh.

This new Elaine did the unbelievable: She took a step towards the French captain and asked, "*Dois-je? Bon. Il est temps que quelqu'un fasse.*"

"What the hell is going on?" Cat whispered to Specs.

"They're arguing about us," he said. "He's trying to shut her down, but she's not having any of it."

A tiny smile lifted the edges of Cat's mouth. "Atta girl."

Captain Renault's sunburned face had reddened further. He turned his attention to Washington and said, *"Général, ces gens sont dignes de confiance?"*

"Forgive me," Washington said, shifting uncomfortably, "my French is not what it should be."

"He's asking if we can be trusted," Specs said.

"Yes," the general answered immediately. *"Oui. Absolutement."*

Renault stared them down, and then shifted his attention slightly. "Romain!"

The handsome soldier gently pushed his way past Donovan. *"Oui, capitaine?"*

Gesturing the younger man forward, Renault began a rapid, whispered interrogation. At one point, the answer that Romain gave him was so startling that the unburned parts of his face whitened.

*"Quoi?"* he demanded.

Elaine, who had drifted closer to her side of the group, murmured, "Romain just told Captain Renault about the soldier who disappeared."

"Yeah, I could guess that," Cat said. "Theresa, what do you think?"

Terrell considered the man in front of them. "Renault is suspicious, intolerant, and arrogant," she answered, "but he's a decent leader. He'll take his own soldier's word much more seriously. With an endorsement from the boy *and* Washington, I think we can pull this off."

A few moments later, Renault and Romain finished their tense conversation with a curt nod and a smart salute, respectively. The French captain reluctantly turned his attention back to the Dogs and said, *"Très bien. Nous vous suivrons."*

Cat felt the tension leak out of Specs. "They're going to come with us."

"Thank fuck. Theresa, can you escort us?"

"That's what we're here for," Terrell said, stepping back a bit. "I'll put in the call. Miss Penrose, would you warn the captain that eight of my people are on their way?"

"Yes, of course." Both women stepped away from the group and began speaking rapidly. Donovan went to her captain's side, leaving the two members of Gamma alone with Washington.

"Specs, I need you to get the general home," Cat continued. "You can take him yourself, or you can pass him over to Alpha."

Specs snorted. "And let Allegra take him? Not likely."

Grinning, Cat turned her attention to Washington and offered her hand. "General, I just wanted to say thank you. You helped us save a lot of lives today."

"It was genuinely my pleasure, Commander," the brawny man said. His words flowed easier than they had half an hour before. "I fear that I am worse than useless in my own time. At least here, I have made a difference." He held on to Cat's hand and stared down at her, and the Gamma commander couldn't tell which contact carried more painful intensity. "Commander. I—" He swallowed and tried again. "I overheard your associate say that the English soldier from before sounded American. Not...not Colonial."

Until that moment, Cat had no idea what she was going to do. Somehow, staring up into that heavy, weary face, she found herself answering his unspoken assumption. "General, you're about to face some hard times. The hardest you've ever seen."

He closed his eyes and nodded.

"But you can't give in. I need you to remember that." Cat leaned in and said, quite ferociously, "You can *not* give up. Do you understand?"

Slowly, Washington's eyes were pushed open by relieved tears. "Yes, Commander. I understand. Thank you."

Cat's oyster shell of a heart cracked open then, and her own eyes burned like they'd been salted. "You're—*mgh*. You're welcome, General. It's been an honor."

Washington shook her hand one more time and then let go. "Take care, Commander Fiyero."

Wiping at his own eyes, Specs leaned down to Cat and whispered, "Thank you."

"He won't even remember it in an hour," Cat said crossly.

"He doesn't have to remember everything," Specs said. "Just the idea of it. Norms might forget the majority of the Day, but some part of it always lingers."

As the historian straightened, Washington nodded downhill and said, "Let's be on our way, then, Leftenant. It seems that I still have work to do."

# DREAMING OF ELECTRIC SHEEP

## Millennia
### (18:26)

illennia had done the absolutely unthinkable on a Day
Out of Time: She had switched her tablet to Silent.
The woman in front of her smiled and wiped her
eyes. "What if the world is ending?"

"The world is always ending," Millennia said, attempting a
flippant shrug. "One second at a time, we're all spinning away
into nothing. The world will keep ending for billions of years
until the sun swallows us whole like a grape." The physicist
mimed throwing something into her mouth and made a
popping sound. "I wonder if, taken as a whole, the earth is
actually grape-flavored. I've always thought of myself as a
chimichanga, and you're obviously *pasta pomodoro*, but—"

Isabella pulled her into a tight embrace, effectively cutting off
the ramble. She knotted the fingers of one hand in the other
woman's long red hair. "You can study what flavor the world is
all you like," she whispered, "as long as you do it where I can
always come to see you."

Millennia made a disgusting sound as she sniffed. "You can
stow away in the Doghouse. Be my sexy lab assistant. We'll
never get any work done. It'll be wonderful."

"*Amore*," Isabella breathed, pulling away so she could cup
Millennia's damp face in her hands. "You have to work.

Otherwise, you won't be happy."

"That's not true." Millennia wiped her face and tried for a smile. "I've always wanted to be a kept woman."

Isabella leaned down and kissed her, as tender as she knew how. "Until next year," she whispered against Millennia's lips, brushing kisses on the silent tears that fell. "I'll be here."

"You better be," Millennia choked out, almost losing her composure. "You had—you had just better be."

It was an impossible thing, but they pulled apart. Millennia lifted one trembling hand and opened a channel to the Charlie commander. "McNab, it's Millennia," she said, swallowing against the tiny crabs that were climbing up her throat. "Have we got clearance for the rift by the *Eagles and Prey* statue?"

His reply was gruff. "You're all good, Millennia."

She swallowed again, this time to keep a handle on the disappointment. "Thanks, Daniel," she murmured. "I'll lock the door behind me."

"Hold on. Everything okay?"

She wiped at her nose. "It's Isabella. The rift is hers."

"Ah, shit," he breathed, voice softening. "I'm sorry, kid. Call me if you need anything."

"Will do. Millennia out."

Isabella turned and faced the iron sculpture, inhaling deeply. Millennia stepped up behind her and laid her tattooed hands on the taller woman's back. Together they walked forward, maintaining that vital contact, until Isabella gasped and disappeared from under her touch. Millennia's empty hands clenched together. They stung from the nettle brush of cold rolling off the invisible rift.

The feeling faded as something other than Millennia used her hand to reach down and retrieve the LBD from its pocket. This moving thing was part machine, a rigid cyborg trapped in a fragile human body. The metallurgic-organic amalgamation that wore Millennia's face pointed the black rectangle at the rift and pressed the red button so hard that it creaked in protest, and the human hand that held it shook from the pressure. Long after the rift had collapsed, the malfunctioning cyborg continued to hold on, its wires corroded by prolactin and salt water.

No one noticed, and no one approached. After all, when it comes to machines—biological or otherwise—a breakdown is just a matter of time.

"Cat to all Gamma teams," the bud in the cyborg's ear chirped. "Has anybody seen the fucking New Kid?"

# NOT THE TYPE AT ALL

## The New Kid
### (Some Time Earlier)

The first thing the New Kid noticed was that his head really fucking hurt.

He struggled back to consciousness, even though the smallest movement sent a rocket of pain straight to the back of his skull. When he didn't move, it just throbbed in time to his traitorous heartbeat, which was a marginally more bearable experience.

The second thing he noticed was the thin gag in his mouth, followed immediately by the realization that he couldn't move his hands or feet. Letting his pounding head rest limply on his chest, he tentatively explored the limits of his mobility and came to the conclusion that all of his limbs had been bound to the chair that he was obviously sitting in.

There was the sound of movement across from him. "Hey Pat, the kid's awake." Something shuffled towards him and leveled a sharp smack across his face. "Wake up, you little piss."

The pain doubled and then tripled, first from the slap itself and then from the movement of his head as it swung to the side. The New Kid whimpered around the cloth, and tears leaked from the corners of his eyes.

"Stop whinin'," the unsympathetic voice said. "And look me in the eye when I'm talkin' to you."

The New Kid took a couple of deep breaths, and then lifted his head as gently as if it were resting on a stem of porcelain. The room was tiny, barely wide enough for the three chairs it held. Directly in front of him stood a pasty, heavyset bruiser in old-fashioned brown pants, a white shirt, and suspenders that did nothing to keep his flab from overflowing. Behind him, the New Kid could make out the shadowy form of a seated man in a suit and worn fedora. The only light came from a single bulb dangling above their heads.

The bruiser reached behind his head and untied the gag roughly, nearly causing the New Kid to white out as he brushed against the rising goose egg. "You a long way from Harlem, kid," he said when the gag came free. He shoved it in his pocket and cracked his doughy knuckles. "Who you workin' with?"

"I'm—" The New Kid's throat rasped and gave out. He swallowed a few times and tried again. "I'm with CIRIUS."

"Serious? That some new East Side punks or somethin'?"

"No, no—I'm sorry. I don't know where I am."

The two men exchanged a look. "Uh-huh," the bruiser said. "And Greta Garbo's waitin' for me back home, with nothin' but a bottle a' tarantula juice and a smile. How the hell'd you get in here?"

The New Kid tried to think, to remember how he'd gone from sunshine to this dusty, darkened closet, but he couldn't maneuver around the spike lodged in his brain. "Cold," he said at last. "I was really cold and—" Ice spread outward from his gut, turning his insides to slush. "Oh shit. Oh shit. What—what year is it?"

Shaking his head, the bruiser said, "Kid, that crazy act needs some work."

"Please," the New Kid begged, "this was an accident. I got lost."

"Tell it to Sweeney. Lost in—"

The bruiser was interrupted by three sharp knocks on the door behind him. It opened immediately after, admitting a white woman with short dark hair and a sleeveless black dress that shimmered with beading as she moved. She raised a silent eyebrow at the men in front of her.

The bruiser shifted so that she could get a good look at his victim. "We found him in stores. Kid says he got lost."

"'S possible," the seated man called Pat said at last, lifting his head. He was darker than his companions. "Them tunnels go pretty far."

"Could be one 'a St. Clair's new runners," Lonnie offered. "Tell you the truth, I wouldn't believe a word he said. Not even if he told me the sky was blue and Ruth's the greatest player that'll ever live."

The woman in black met the New Kid's eyes. "Lonnie," she said, taking two clicking steps forward, "if you think I can't tell when a man is lyin' to me, you ain't been here long enough." Bracing her hands on her knees, she leaned forward until she was on the same level as the New Kid.

"How did you end up in my place?" she asked. Her voice was husky and rich, like aged Scotch perfuming the air.

"It was an accident," the New Kid said again. "I swear."

"Okay, we're off to a good start. Who do you work for?"

The New Kid swallowed, knowing that his next answer was a gamble. "An agency called CIRIUS. We're not the authorities, we're—we're more like scientists."

She raised her eyebrows. "Scientists with a pistol like nothin' I've ever seen?"

"I'm just muscle. Security."

"I believe that." Straightening, she turned away and walked back to the door. "Cut him loose, and escort him out," she said over her shoulder.

"Miss Helen, he could be with anybody," Lonnie protested. "The Bonanno family, Luciano's boys, even the Gophers. You ask me though, I think he belongs to the spades."

"Lucky Luciano himself is sitting upstairs at the front table. You really think he'd be that stupid?" she asked.

Lonnie colored. "No. Guess not."

"Besides all that," the woman said, stroking the door

thoughtfully, "the families love me. They'd never start trouble in my place."

"And the Gophers?" Pat asked.

Miss Helen shrugged one beaded shoulder. "Same thing. No one likes a sad song like an Irishman." Without waiting for a response, she left the little wood-paneled room and shut the door behind her.

"I don't like it," Lonnie said, staring the New Kid down. "We should bust 'im up a little bit. You know, as a warnin'."

"Miss Helen say let 'im go," Pat said.

"Miss Helen's a tomato. A smart tomato, but still a tomato. They're all soft."

Pat adjusted the angle of his fedora. "What you think's gon' happen, you cross her? Think you gon' get fired? Nah, man. Not with that one." Nodding at the closed door, he continued, "That one'll gi' you over to the Boss hisself, for *in-sa-bor-di-nashion.*"

The red drained right out of Lonnie's face. "Why?"

"Because she right," Pat said. "Them tough ol' bimbos out there, the underbosses an' the captains—they *love* her, 'cause she make 'em cry. They do anythin' to make her happy, anythin' to hear one a' her sad songs. So. We lettin' 'im go."

Lonnie spit on the floor. "Fine. You take 'im up, I gotta finish countin'."

The bruiser wasn't gentle when untying the New Kid's bonds, but the manhandling was nothing compared to the sweet relief and instant agony of blood returning to his extremities.

"Work 'em out a bit," Pat said, demonstrating with his own hands.

The New Kid did as he recommended, and in seconds he could clench his fingers again. Lonnie shot his companion a sullen look, and then left the tiny room.

Pat stood up, lifting the New Kid's backpack with one hand and putting the other in his pocket. "Come on then. You be gettin' this back in a minute."

"Wait, wait," the New Kid said. "Where did you find me?"

"Where you def'nitely wasn't 'sposed to be," Pat said as he opened the door. "In the storeroom."

A chain of memories came back to the New Kid—his MagLite sweeping across an empty room, a bite of cold, crates stacked higher than his head. And then the pain. "Can I—can I just go back in there?" he asked. "I'll go back the way I came in."

Shaking his head, Pat said, "Miss Helen say take you upstairs. Tha's where you goin'."

"*Please*—look, I don't even know where I am."

"You in the Fox Den," Pat said, opening the door and pointing outside. "Best damn club outside a' Harlem. An' don' be thinkin' about drawin' that gun, boy. You goin' first."

The New Kid did as he was told. Outside, he recognized the shadowy columns and the smell of damp straw and wood. He had a second to consider bolting for the room, but then Lonnie's vast shape appeared between the rows. Instead, he went up the staircase on his left with Pat right behind him. There was a short landing at the top, surrounded by red brick walls and lit by a single bulb. Beyond a simple wooden door at the other end, he could hear the dim sound of a crowded room.

"Wait, wait," he said, raising his hands and half-turning. "What if I can pay?"

Pat paused. "Pay fo' what?"

"To stay. In the club," he clarified, pointing to the door.

The other man narrowed his eyes, then said, "I'd say you gone hafta show me that mazuma."

"Mazumba?"

"Mazuma. The money, kid."

"Okay. It's in my bag."

"Fair 'nuff," Pat said, handing over the backpack and shifting one hand from his pants pocket to the corresponding jacket pocket. "Slow, now."

"Yes, sir." The New Kid unzipped the backpack and dug past the black canvas and the first aid kit—from which he took a pair of pain pills for his still-throbbing head—to the plain brown wallet at the very bottom. Inside, he found American bills of all denominations and ages.

Careful to pull out only older, small bills, the New Kid stepped closer to Pat and fanned the money.

The bouncer whistled. "Boy, where you get that?"

"It's mine, I swear."

"Oo, Miss Helen'll have my balls in the next batch a' panther sweat, I turn that away. Go on, then." They were almost to the door when he put his hand on the New Kid's shoulder and leaned down to look him in the eye. "But chu start anythin', an' I won' be so friendly ag'in. Not t' mention what *they's* gone do if you innerupt. You unnerstand?"

"Yes. Yes, sir," the New Kid said, nodding.

"Knock two times fast an' three slow, an' wait for the click," Pat said, his voice hushed.

Once again, the New Kid followed his instructions to the letter. Two seconds after the last knock, he heard a key being turned in a lock. The door swung open, triggering a crescendo of light and sound. Overwhelmed, the New Kid froze in the doorway.

The room in front of him was filled with opulent tables and crystal chandeliers. He was directly behind a bar, and it seemed that the cheerful olive-skinned bartender in a white dress shirt was the one who had let him out. He was busy filling a gleaming silver cocktail shaker from an unmarked bottle, while a pair of waifish white women giggled to each other across the dark wood of the bar. Their faces were rosy from laughter and not a little illicit booze.

The rest of the room was much the same: Caucasian men and women sat at the velvet-covered tables and chatted together over crystal glasses or china teacups. They were dressed to the nines in silk pinstriped suits and short dresses. Smoke trailed up delicately from cigarette holders, adding to the dreamlike feel of the room, which somehow seemed smaller than it should have.

"Over there," Pat said, pointing to a cluster of free seats.

The New Kid stepped out from around the bar, bringing

more of the room into view. A grand piano dominated the right corner. Miss Helen sat atop it, snapping her fingers softly to the melody being plinked out by an older black man with snowy hair. She began to sing as Pat guided the New Kid around the edge of the tables, and the chatter died down immediately.

Her voice skipped lightly up and down the notes, thick with vibrato. She seemed to be singing to one man in particular, a dark-haired gentleman in his mid-thirties with light scars tugging at one corner of his mouth. He watched her with quiet intensity, his cocktail forgotten on the table.

Tapping the back of a chair, Pat murmured, "Here. You want som'en, talk t' Petey. But chu best be whisperin' when you do it, 'less you want a taste a' lead poisonin', ya hear?"

The New Kid nodded and settled down into his seat.

The club's owner finished her song less than a minute later. She let the applause wash over her, and then slid down from the piano. After exchanging a few whispered words with the scarred gentleman and accepting his kiss on her hand, she made her way over to Pat.

"He got cash, Miss Helen," the bouncer murmured. "Lot a' it."

Miss Helen turned her smoky gaze to the New Kid. "What's your name, kid?"

The Dog swallowed. "Kevin Harrison, ma'am."

"Welcome to the Fox Den, Mr. Harrison." Nodding at the bar, she turned back to her one-man band and said, "Long as you got cash to spend, you can stay."

¤    ¤    ¤    ¤    ¤    ¤

As worried as the New Kid was about getting home again, he enjoyed himself immensely in the Fox Den. He used camouflage as an excuse to order one drink before beginning to plan his escape in earnest. Then one whiskey sour turned into two—both far sweeter than he was used to, yet somehow more fiercely real. They were, frankly, the best that he'd ever had, though perhaps that was the second one talking.

And the music...the New Kid had always liked music in theory, but it wasn't something that he had ever been really passionate about until he heard Miss Helen sing live jazz.

The half-full drink sat beside his hand, sweating in the close heat of the club. In line with his camouflage idea, he'd shed his flak jacket and pack, but he needn't have bothered. No one paid him any mind, not even the two white women sharing his table. One of them was passed out, her rank teacup in danger of taking a sharp tumble, and the other was blearily absorbed in the music. She wept silently to herself.

The New Kid's fingers drifted down to the pouch with his tablet only once, but the sudden attention turned on him from all directions changed his mind about bringing it out. Instead his gaze swept around the club, catching on details and committing them to memory. There were women swaying together, men hushing their tablemates...and one patron whose attention was not on Miss Helen at all.

The young man had dark hair, olive skin, and a medium build. He could have been mistaken for almost any of the other men in the club, except that he wasn't watching the stage; his eyes were locked on the back of the scarred man's head. His chest pumped up and down, and the staccato rhythm that he tapped on one knee didn't match the pace of the song.

Quiet but intense applause filled the club as the music ended. "Thank you, thank you all," Miss Helen said, allowing herself a graceful, if wobbly, curtsy. She had been sipping from her own stores intermittently throughout the night. "I think Tom can manage alone for a while, what do you think?"

Under the sounds of protest, the young man reached out a shaking hand for his teacup and downed whatever was left in one go. He braced one hand on the table and put the other in his pocket.

Before he could come to his feet, the New Kid was standing in front of him. "Please don't," he whispered.

Up close, the young man was closer to a boy than anything.

He reached up and ran a hand through his already flattened hair. "Beat it, pal."

"Shh, shh," the wasted table behind them said, picking their heads up long enough to offer a scolding.

"Hey, didn't ya hear me, halfie?" the young man asked. "I said beat it."

Pat appeared beside the New Kid, both hands in his jacket pockets. "'Zere a pro'lem here, gennlemen?"

Sagging back in his chair, the young man muttered, "Nah, Pat, everythin's jake. This guy, he just won't take a hint."

"He a payin' customer too, Frankie. An' you watch what kinda words you tossin' around in here." He pulled a chair out for the New Kid. "You wanna sit here, Mistah Harrison, tha's fine. Jest take a seat."

The New Kid swallowed and eased himself down, directly between Frankie and the scarred man's back. He couldn't hear the music anymore over the beats that echoed from his chest and his ears and the back of his skull: *Thump-thump*, *thump-thump*, *thump-thump*. He was no stranger to hate in all its forms, and the look in the young man's eyes was the kind that got people shot.

People like him, more often than not.

"What the hell are you starin' at, you nosy coon?" Frankie demanded softly, flattening his hair even further. "God, why couldn't you mind your own damn beeswax, huh?"

The New Kid released a single long breath. "Your name's Frankie, right?"

"Not to you," he spat.

"I'm Kevin." Tilting his head back slightly, he asked, "Who's the guy behind me?"

Frankie's eyes shifted to a point over the New Kid's shoulder and narrowed. "Lucky Luciano," he whispered, the words almost lost under the music.

The Gamma agent waited for a break in the music and shifted his chair closer. "What's in your pocket?"

Frankie's nostrils flared. "Quiet. You tryin' to get me killed?"

"No. Are you trying to get yourself killed?"

Meeting the other man's eyes, Frankie swallowed and whispered, "If that's what it takes."

"Why?"

"Nah, if you don't know, you won't understand," he said, leaning back and wiping at his eyes.

"I want to."

Frankie blew out a breath and shrugged. "Hell with it. I'm a dead man anyway, soon as you go to Pat." Lifting his chin at the older man, he said, "Lucky killed my boss. Same man who took me off the streets when I was a kid. Same man who put money in my pockets and food in my belly. Same man who made *me* a man, 'stead of a scrawny little ragamuffin."

He tried to wipe his eyes, but they continued to overflow. Soon his whole face collapsed, and he buried it in his hands to cover up the weeping. The New Kid let him cry it out without moving a muscle.

When he finally dried up, Frankie looked at the Gamma agent through puffy eyes and wiped his face on the stained tablecloth. "Why?" he asked. "Why'd you do it? Why'd you stop me?"

The New Kid opened his mouth, and then closed it. "I didn't want to see anyone hurt," he replied finally. "You or him."

Lifting his chin, the young man wiped his nose again and said, "So what'm I 'sposed to do now? Act like none of it even mattered?"

"It mattered," the New Kid replied. "I think you feel useless right now, and guilty. I think you're in a lot of pain, and *you* think hurting Mr. Luciano will make you feel better. But what if it doesn't?"

"What if it does?" Frankie countered.

The New Kid leaned in and whispered, "But what if it doesn't?"

In the sudden quiet that followed his words, the New Kid felt a presence on his other side. He turned and looked up at Miss Helen, but she had eyes only for his tablemate.

"Frankie," she said, nodding down at him. "Don't you think

you've had enough for one night?"

He swallowed and broke eye contact. "Yes, Miss Helen." Without another word, he gathered up his coat and left, making a beeline for a door in the back wall.

"Poor kid," she sighed, pulling out the chair on the New Kid's other side. "It's been a hard time for everybody, but he's had it harder than most."

Within seconds of her occupancy, an orange drink in a tall crystal glass appeared at her elbow. "Thank you, Petey," she murmured to the black-and-white-clad waiter. She took a sip, sighed in satisfaction, and then turned her dark eyes on the New Kid. "I still can't figure you out, Mr. Harrison. Lonnie checked the tunnels; he said all the trips are in place. How'd ya know they were there?"

He released the breath he'd been holding for the last five minutes. "Trips?"

Miss Helen surprised him by laughing quietly. "Jesus, Mary, and Joseph. I don't know how you do it. I'd swear on my mother's grave you have no idea what I'm talking about."

"I don't," the New Kid said, leaning forward to give her his most sincere face. "Miss Helen, it was an accident. I really have *no* idea how I got in your storeroom. But I need to go back down there, just for a minute."

She smiled and sipped from her glass. "Kid, you got a bright future on Broadway. I know a guy or two, if you're interested."

"Please, Miss Helen. You can go with me."

"Why, you leave somethin' down there?" she asked.

Desperate, the New Kid said, "Yes ma'am. Something important. I can't leave without it."

Miss Helen paused with her drink halfway up to her lips. She tipped it towards the New Kid and said, "That's the first lie you've told me all night. It's the only one you get."

He sighed and dropped his face in one hand, and then popped up just as suddenly with a wince. "Okay. I'll tell you everything."

"Not the first time a man's promised me that, kid," she said, clapping as the latest song came to an end.

The New Kid waited until the pair started up a new, lively tune, and then he leaned in close to Miss Helen's ear and murmured, "I'm from the future."

She snorted into her drink and covered her mouth. "Now *that's* a new one."

Undaunted, the New Kid tried again, feeling an odd calm sweep through him. "Today's the Day Out of Time, right? Every year, portals open to different years, and you can cross between them. Time travel is real."

She turned to look him in the eye, which put them nearly nose-to-nose. After a solid ten seconds of searching his face, she whispered, "I'll be damned. You believe that."

"I do," he said. "And I'll show you, if you let me go home."

"Aw, what the hell," she said, swigging the last of her drink. "It'll cost me a walk down the stairs."

Hardly believing his luck, the New Kid grabbed his gear and followed Miss Helen as she made her slow, winding way around the edge of the room. They paused a few times to chat with suit-clad men and their glittery dates, more than one of whom reached out to give the New Kid a cheeky squeeze.

As they rounded the bar, the cheerful bartender turned to the door and pulled out a heavy key. He held the door open for the both of them, and then locked it behind them when it closed.

Miss Helen led the way down the dimly lit staircase. They were halfway to the bottom when they heard a startled yelp and the sound of a scuffle. The proprietress paused on the steps and lifted the fringed hem of her dress, revealing a tiny revolver tucked inside a thick black garter. She drew it and cocked the hammer back as a dark face appeared at the foot of the steps.

"*Shit,*" the man said, jumping back around the corner. "We got one white bitch packin' heat."

"It's okay," the New Kid tried to say, but Miss Helen drowned him out.

"Who the hell are you, and what the hell are you doing in my club?" she yelled. "Lonnie?"

"Ma'am?" a new voice called up. "My name is Jamal DuBois. I'm looking for one a' my men."

"They're talking about me," the New Kid said.

"Ay vanilla swirl," a third voice called, "zat'chu?"

"Man, shut the hell up—"

There were two short smacks, and both voices went silent. "Ma'am, I don't want any trouble," Jamal said. "I just want my boy to come home safe."

"Where's Lonnie?" Miss Helen called, taking a step down.

"The big guy? He's fine. He ain't happy, but he's fine. We're gonna back off a bit if you wanna come on down."

"You do that," she said, carefully descending with the gun braced in front of her. She paused at the bottom of the staircase, just around the corner from the storeroom. "Alright boys, I wanna see hands in the air."

"I can't do that, ma'am. I need to make sure that my boys are safe."

"Let me talk to him," the New Kid said. "I promise, everything's gonna be okay."

Miss Helen considered him for a moment, and then nodded once.

The New Kid eased his way around her and said, "Jamal? It's Kevin Harrison. I'm coming around alone, okay?"

"Okay, Kevin."

His heart kicking around uncomfortably, the New Kid eased his way around the corner, making sure that Miss Helen could still see him. He could make out the shadowy forms of three Watchdogs in tactical black standing between the rows of wooden crates. The two standing guard over the bound, thrashing figure of Lonnie the bruiser looked vaguely familiar, but in the poor light it was impossible to make out the features of the third man.

"Kevin?" he asked, shifting forward a little. "I'm Jamal. Any way I can see your badge?"

"Yeah, yeah. Um—" The New Kid reached for his pocket, and Jamal held up a hand.

"Easy, man. Let's not scare anybody."

Flushing, the New Kid muttered an apology and slowly withdrew his CIRIUS badge. He opened it and stepped back so the light shone on the black dog.

"A'ight, cool. Can you introduce us?" he asked with a nod at the concealed stairs.

"Sure. Jamal, this is Miss Helen," he said, gesturing at the woman, who was slowly lowering her gun. "Miss Helen, this is my—well, he's not my team leader. He's a coworker, I guess." Looking her right in the eye, he said, "Nobody's gonna hurt you."

She nodded and pointed the gun down, gently releasing the hammer to its original position with deft precision. "How many of 'em are there?" she asked, tucking the gun back into her garter.

"Three, plus Lonnie."

"Okay." The dark-haired singer shook herself, and then stepped cautiously around the corner.

Once Jamal saw that she was unarmed, he stepped out from behind the barrier and lifted both hands in the air, making a point of tucking the gun into its holster. He was on the tall side and made of dark, wiry muscle. His short blond-orange dreadlocks were held out of his face by a headband, and he had a black goatee topped by a sincere smile.

Offering one thin-fingered hand, Jamal said, "Nice to meet you, Miss Helen. That's Ray and Demarcus."

Another faint memory rose up in the New Kid's mind, of staring at the poorly-rendered tattoo on Ray's arm and trying to decipher it. They had been...walking somewhere.

Though she returned the handshake a bit stiffly, Miss Helen's tone was a shade more cordial now that all the weapons had been put away. "Likewise. I guess you're time travelers too?"

If he was surprised by the question, Jamal didn't show it. "Yes ma'am," he said. "I'm sorry about all of this."

She snorted. "Tell it to Lonnie. He's the one hogtied by two Negroes."

Ray took a step forward. "What did she just—"

All Jamal did was turn and look at his teammate, and the younger man backed off. "We'll get out of your hair now, Miss Helen."

"I'd appreciate that," she said, a bite to her words. "Kid, I don't care *how* much mazuma you got, you're more trouble than you're worth."

The New Kid ducked his head. "Yes ma'am."

"I guess you'll go on home now?" she asked, putting both hands on her hips.

"That's the plan," the New Kid said, following Jamal's crooked fingers obediently. Just before they reached the two Watchdogs and their charge, he looked back at the quietly fuming club owner.

"You've got a great place, Miss Helen," he said. "It was—I had a good time."

"Hope it was worth it, kid, 'cause you ain't gettin' back in."

Before he could respond, Jamal took him by the arm and pushed him into the frigid embrace of the rift. His last glimpse was the woman's shocked face as the world around him shifted.

The underground room melted around him, becoming dark and hollow. He was only alone for a few seconds before Ray, Demarcus, and Jamal appeared as well. Jamal turned back and closed the rift with the LBD.

"What happened?" the New Kid asked, reaching up to gingerly finger the top of his receding goose egg.

"The hell you mean, 'what happened'?" Demarcus asked. "Yo' stupid ass up and disappeared. We was doin' all the work, like usual—"

"An' then you was just gone," Ray finished.

Jamal put the LBD away and looked his two Watchdogs over. "Took 'em half a goddamn hour to figure out somethin' was wrong."

"It's alright," the New Kid said. "Thanks for coming after me."

"Forget it, man. It's my job." The team leader grinned and

threw his head back with a laugh. "God, I can't believe it. Helen Morgan. Man, they always said she had another club that never got busted, but nobody could prove it. Breaks my heart to shut it down like this." Tapping his bud, he said, "Jamal to Cat, I got him. Yeah, he's alright. Nah, you're never gonna believe where he was."

Jamal led the way up the rickety steps towards a faint triangle of light, still filling Cat in. The same red brick walls stood on either side, but it looked as though the doorway had been sealed up with plaster. The New Kid squeezed through the opening and found himself surrounded by wholesale destruction. Holes had been gouged in the white walls, and large chunks of plaster littered the hardwood floors. There was a lighter section of floor where the bar had been, and a thinner strip that marked the divide between the club and a second room.

"I remember this," the New Kid said, looking around. "We were...we were cleaning it, right?"

"Yeah, they had us bein' fuckin' *janitors*," Demarcus said. "Pilin' it up in one spot so them anacondas don't hafta work so hard."

Ray scratched his nose. "Lazy, freaky motherfuckers."

Ending his call to Cat, Jamal regarded the two Watchdogs and said, "You were *also* 'sposed to be doin' a final sweep."

"Yeah-yeah, cuz they had somethin' big and slimy hangin' out in here before," Demarcus said. "Hey Ray, you know where yo mama at?"

"Man, fuck you," Ray muttered.

"Shut up bitch, you know I'm playin'. I lu' yo mama. I lu' her *real* good."

"A'ight, that's enough," Jamal said to Ray and Demarcus. "You two finish up here. I'll get the kid back to Cat."

Jamal and the New Kid left the building together and headed in the direction of the park. "So," Jamal said as they strolled along the hot sidewalk, "who gave you to those two idiots?"

"I was—I think I was passing through, and they needed help."

"Man, they didn't need *help*," Jamal said. "If that job took three people, I'd a' sent three people. They just didn't wanna do all that work by themselves if they didn't have to."

The New Kid's embarrassment at being used didn't surprise him. What *did* come as a surprise was the hot flush that crept up the back of his neck like a coal-shod little spider.

Before it could really gain momentum, the cool green trees of Central Park came into view around a building. It was packed with people, many of whom had just gotten off work and were hoping to catch some of the Day Out of Time festivities.

"This is where I leave you," Jamal said, offering his knuckles for a fist bump. "Don't let nobody else pass you 'round like that again, a'ight? You're a Dog, not a hot potato." He touched two fingers to his brow and flicked them forward. "Keep it real, kid. See you around."

The New Kid watched the lanky man walk away, wondering if he'd imagined the faint trio of dots tattooed at the corner of Jamal's right eye.

◻    ◻    ◻    ◻    ◻    ◻

It was well into dinnertime when the New Kid came jogging into camp. Most of Gamma's officers had gathered back at Command with bags of takeout food and various sources of caffeine. Only Millennia and Helix were still out and about.

"Not a scratch on him," Darwin observed, toasting the New Kid with a purple can. "It's almost like you were worried for nothing."

Cat glared at the zoologist. "You let him out of your sight, and he ended up in the Prohibition era. Spin it however you want, you fucked up too."

"I told you that Jamal's team had him."

"Yes," Cat hissed, "but I assumed that you wouldn't be fucking *stupid* enough to give him to Ray and Demarcus."

"Don't ask me to obey assumptions, Cat," Darwin said, washing a grilled mac n' cheese sandwich down with the last inch of his cancerous energy drink.

"I'm okay," the New Kid said. "Is Elaine still here?"

"She's on the bridge," Specs said.

"It's time for you to take her home," Cat added. "Did you get something to eat?"

"Oh, yeah. I grabbed a couple of hot dogs on the way."

Nodding, Cat said, "Good. If you're still hungry, Darwin has another sandwich. It's all yours."

"The fuck it is," Darwin said. Under Cat's level stare, however, he became suddenly charitable. "I mean—fuck yeah, it is." He took the wrapped sandwich out of its paper bag and held it out to the New Kid. "Sorry, bro."

"It's—thanks," the New Kid said, accepting the gooey peace offering. "Hey, um—can someone show me how to look for rifts again?"

"Didn't you read the Damn Handbook?" Darwin asked.

"I—" The New Kid flushed. "I think I accidentally deleted it."

The zoologist held out his hand for the New Kid's tablet. "Alright, alright. C'mere."

After his brief lesson (and with the tracker on his tablet newly activated), the New Kid headed out along the path to the Bow Bridge. More than one couple leaned against the railing, taking pictures or staring dreamily out over the verdant water. Elaine Penrose, though alone, also stared dreamily, committing the sight of the New York City skyline to memory.

When he joined her at the rail, she turned a sunny smile on him. "Hello, there. Where on Earth have you been all day?"

He shrugged. "The Ramble. The Museum of Natural History. Downtown. The 1920s, for a while."

Elaine laughed, and the delighted sound instantly lifted the mood of anyone within ten feet of her. "You've had quite the day! I would say that I'm jealous, but then, I've had quite the day myself."

"Why don't we go for a walk, and—and you can tell me about it."

The smile turned overcast, and she looked back at the skyscrapers. "It's so strange to think that a place so marvelous exists," she remarked softly. "It's even stranger to think that I shall never see it again. I will wake up tomorrow, and so much of this will be gone."

"It'll be back," the New Kid said. "I promise."

Elaine nodded and followed him along the bridge, keeping her eyes on the view for as long as possible.

"Do you know where you're going?" the New Kid asked, dodging a group of teenagers bound for parts unknown.

"Of a sorts," she said. "Right after I felt the cold, I passed by an old wooden structure. It didn't have any walls, only a frame."

"That's probably one of the rustic shelters," the New Kid said, pausing to check a map just beyond the bridge. "So we go straight, and then take the second left. We can figure it out from there."

As they walked along paths that still bustled with people, they described the events of their respective days. "It was so romantic," Elaine said, sighing. "Romain was the last one through. He took Agent Donovan aside, and gave her a button from his coat as a token. Then he took her hands, kissed her on the cheek, and left without saying a word. Oh, I do wish they had really kissed! She thought that she was being discreet, but I saw her tuck the button in her pocket."

They reached the end of the path where the rustic shelter waited, empty and solemn. "I suppose, then, that I should go," Elaine said, straightening the lines of her dress.

Something was crawling up the back of the New Kid's throat, some awful word-vomit that he hadn't realized was coming until it was too late. "My brother remembers the Days," he blurted out. A blush filled his cheeks, and he clarified, "Earlier today, I told you it was just me. It's not. My brother Mark remembers too."

Elaine tilted her head and tucked a stray curl behind her ear. "Why would you lie to me about him?"

"Because I lie to everyone," he said. Now that the finger had left the proverbial hole, the dam was cracking all over the place and he was powerless to stop it. "When we were kids, we saw a bunch of Native Americans come through a rift at a festival back in my hometown. It was only for a few minutes, but they caused a lot of trouble." The New Kid swallowed and looked down. "Then the next day no one else remembered, and we didn't know why. But Mark—he wouldn't stop telling people, so they hospitalized him for six months. They did all these tests, and, and they were *this* close to diagnosing him with schizophrenia. So he finally stopped talking about it, and they said it was just a cry for attention and he could go home."

Elaine had drifted closer to him, her eyes round. "He was put in an asylum?"

"They called it a hospital, but yeah. We never brought it up again." A pair of tears plopped down on his flak jacket, one right after the other. "That's why I don't talk about him. I'm not used to it. I just buy supplies the week before the Day and keep to myself and I-I—"

Abandoning all propriety, Elaine pulled the New Kid into her arms. She rubbed his back in soothing circles and listened as he took deep, panicked breaths. "I've been alone," he said at last. He buried his face in the fabric of her dress, inhaling the scent of sweat and warm cotton.

"It's alright now," she said, strangely calm. "It's alright. You're safe."

Snorting, the New Kid picked his head up and stepped back. He wiped at his streaming eyes and said, "That's what got me into this mess in the first place. Being safe."

"I don't understand," Elaine said, leading him inside the rustic shelter. She sat down on one of the benches and patted the spot beside her.

"That's how the Dogs found me," he clarified, taking a seat on the bench beside her and bracing his elbows on his knees. "They noticed that I was gearing up for tornado season in the middle of New York City."

"Tornado season?"

"Tornadoes are these giant wind funnels," the New Kid said. "They're absolutely terrifying. And they're just...a force of nature. You can't stop them. All you can do is get the hell out of their way, or hole up and survive them." He laughed once, short and bitter like the end of a cigar. "I figured out pretty quick that I couldn't get out of their way, so I bought supplies and hid. Food, water, a radio, a power source. Light. My loft's in a converted warehouse, so it's pretty secure. That's the reason I picked it when I moved here almost three years ago."

"You wanted someplace where you could be safe," Elaine said quietly.

The New Kid leaned back with a sigh. "Things were good. I had a shitty job with okay prospects, and a freaking fortress for a home. I'd made friends. I thought I could make this work. Then someone showed up at my door about a week ago."

"Someone from the agency?"

He nodded. "One of their recruiters. He said they tracked me through my spending habits. I bought the same survival supplies two years in a row, and when I did it a third time they approached me."

Elaine's brow furrowed. "They can do that?"

"Yup."

"And it's...legal?"

"Probably."

"Perhaps this time is not as wonderful as I thought," she said. "Not if the government can allow something so despicable."

"They're just trying to help," the New Kid said. "They need to recruit new people somehow. Better this than pulling me out of some nuthouse."

Touching his shoulder, Elaine said, "But then your brother..."

"He was a minor. His records are sealed. But I wouldn't be surprised if they'd done it before."

"Can I..." She smoothed invisible creases in her dress. "Can I ask where your brother is now?"

"Up in Montana somewhere, on a dude ranch. He and his horse go on a camping trip during the Day." The New Kid picked at the material of his pants for a moment. "We don't talk a lot. Mostly birthdays and Christmas. He's never said anything about it, but he blames me for keeping my mouth shut. Like I should have said something and gotten myself locked up with him."

"Does the agency know about him?" Elaine asked.

"No," the New Kid said, clenching his hands. "I lied on all my intake paperwork. I couldn't—" He swallowed and tried again. "I couldn't mess up his life like that, not without checking it out myself. If I survive the next few hours, I'll go visit him this summer. We'll talk it over."

They sat in silence for a few minutes, each absorbed in their own thoughts. Finally Elaine stirred and said, "I find their methods abhorrent, but I understand why they do it. From what I've seen, there seem to be very few of you."

"Less than one percent of the world population," he confirmed. "Way, way less."

"So they do the best they can, I suppose." Leaning over slightly, she put her hand on his knee. "Don't be too hard on them, or yourself."

The New Kid managed a short chuckle. "You've been so calm this whole time, while I've been losing my mind. I wish I was as brave as you."

She looked him in the eye and said, "I think that you are very brave, Kevin. Braver than you realize, and stronger too."

"Thanks," he said, ducking his head.

"I'm being sincere," she insisted. "No one else knows what you have been through."

"I'm pretty sure they don't care. Actually, I'm pretty sure they hate me. I'm useless."

Elaine frowned. "You helped me, and guided me through the madness of this new world. Completely discounting the importance of those actions alone, you allowed me to be in the right place to help your people. I don't think that Captain

Renault would have waited much longer. You helped save more than one life today, just by being kind."

His eyes burned, and the New Kid bullied the tears back with a manly swallow. "I should be more...more assertive. Like Grunt, or Oz."

"Both wonderful men, I'm sure. But why would you want to be anything other than what you are?" she asked. "What great authority decided that assertiveness was valued above kindness? Above compassion?"

Wiping at his eyes, the New Kid said, "I guess we haven't come that far, huh."

"In some ways, yes," Elaine said, smiling faintly, "but I think there's a lot of work left to do. It seems to me that you can stay in the background, or you can speak up." She came to her feet and offered him a hand up. "I should go, before it gets dark. I'm sure Mattie has positively lost her mind with worry by now."

The New Kid took her hand and stood. "Yeah, you're right."

Taking a moment to orient herself, Elaine said, "This way," and stepped confidently off onto the grass. The New Kid followed her into the slender trees. After thirty feet or so, she turned in a circle and said, "This feels familiar."

The New Kid lifted his tablet and carefully opened the program that Darwin had shown him. "It's right there, between those two rocks." He consulted the band of his walkie watch and turned the dials. "New Kid to Commander McNab?"

"I read you, kid," McNab replied. "What's up?"

"I've got a rift, um, over in the Ramble."

"Hold on—yup, that's a new one for us. Turn your tracker on and I'll send someone your way to close it up."

"Okay. New Kid out."

He closed the connection and looked up at the young Victorian woman. Swallowing, he asked, "Can I...is it okay to hug you?"

Elaine's eyes filled with tears, and she let them spill freely down her face. "I should—I should be quite cross with you if you didn't."

They embraced, and the Victorian woman's slender body trembled as she cried. The New Kid hugged her just as tight, and he lost the battle against his own tears. They spilled out in hot streams, spotting the green and white cotton of her dress.

When they finally separated, Elaine put her hands on either side of his face. Her cheeks were blotchy, and her lungs had been replaced by a rusty motor. "I will n-*never* forget you," she promised, staring at him more intently than anyone had ever looked at him in his life. It was a heady experience, being memorized like that. "I refuse. I don't c-care if I'm not one of you. I won't forget. I promise."

On impulse, the New Kid hugged her again and whispered, "Just in case, I'll remember extra hard."

"Thank you."

They finally stepped apart, wiping their faces futilely. The New Kid checked his tablet one last time to confirm the rift's location, and Elaine paused at the edge to look back, sniffing hard. "Goodbye, Kevin. Please, have a good life."

He smiled. "Only—only if you promise to have one too."

Returning his smile, she nodded and said, "I will. It's going to be magnificent." Then Elaine Penrose stepped forward and vanished.

Turning back to the rustic shelter, the New Kid sat down to wait for Charlie. He hoped that somewhere—or rather, some *when*—there was a girl in a green and white dress who had chosen the same spot.

# DREADNOUGHT RISING

## Command
### (19:12)

"A less exhausted commander than myself might be made suspicious by all of this silence," Cat remarked, rubbing at her itchy eyes. "Has anybody heard from the twins?"

"They're working on other calls," Specs said. "And I think you need a break."

"Maybe when I'm dead." Leaning forward, Cat twisted her back until popped. "Five more hours. We can do this. Five more—"

An unholy roar shook the ground around them, and Cat instinctively shared a look with Grunt. "Well that can't be any fucking good."

"*Gear up!*" the tactical officer barked, grabbing his pack and slinging it over his shoulders. The remaining members of Rottie followed his example, and within seconds they were boiling out of the Command center like an overturned hive. As a pack they raced up to Cherry Hill, where a heavy crowd milled around the central fountain in confusion. The sound of screaming drew their eyes in the direction of Bethesda. The roar came again, full of rage, and something made of stone broke.

"*Fuck*," Cat hissed, leading the charge down the largely empty path.

Within a few minutes they came in sight of the railing above the Terrace. A veritable stampede of humanity was trying to stream up every available staircase. The crowd was so thick that it threatened to push the Dogs along with it like a current.

"Grunt, Specs, stay topside with me; we need to get a look at this thing," Cat called as they approached the horde's flank. "Everyone else, get those people out of there. *Do not engage.*"

The Watchdogs broke off to follow her orders, fighting their way in pairs through the crush of people. They did their best to protect those who fell and scoop up the ones who were injured. As Cat and her officers reached the edge of the Terrace and looked down on Bethesda Fountain, the commander lost her breath.

"Jesus Christ," she whispered, fear curling its arctic fingers around her insides. The men beside her were inclined to agree with the sentiment.

The creature currently decimating the polished granite ring of the fountain was a moving slab of blue-grey muscle on two legs. It had a round, brutish head with bulging eye sockets, a protruding lower jaw, and apelike arms that allowed its knuckles to brush the ground when it crouched. It looked most of twelve feet tall and about two tons. A white collar with a giant crack on one side gleamed around its neck. By this time, it was alone on the lower level, which didn't seem to lessen its murderous rage.

Elias slipped on one of the steps in shock, nearly colliding with Fahd. "Holy shit. *Holy shit,* is that a goddamn mountain troll?!"

"Grunt, get down there," Cat said from the terrace. "I'll back you up. Specs, I need an APB."

"Roger that." Specs opened a wide channel on his bud and said, "Priority call one, I need half of all available Gamma teams within a half-mile radius of Bethesda Fountain here *now*. Millennia, Darwin, Helix, drop what you're doing and get here. We've got a hostile unknown; it's big, it's pissed, and it's wrecking the fountain all to hell."

While the historian put in additional calls to Med Bay,

Security, and the Hive, Cat and Grunt turned and vaulted down the side stairs as fast as they could, passing a few stragglers and more than one idiot recording on a cell phone. Cat confiscated one such phone and chucked it over the railing.

"Hey!" the beer-bellied owner bawled. "Bitch, you can't just—"

Cat, who had been in the process of turning, shifted again and walloped the larger man in the eye. He reeled back and hit the stairs, all six feet of him knocked silly.

"Lindsay, Tamika, get that moron out of here," she said, gesturing over her shoulder.

The creature below seemed to be particularly upset with the Angel of the Waters statue. It lumbered through the shallow pool of water around the fountain and slammed its fist into one of her cherubs, knocking the statue off its place. Water cascaded over the creature, turning its hide slick and shiny.

"Shoot to stun," Cat said as they crept up on it, dodging the craters left behind by its fists. "Five to seven rounds. All that water should boost the output."

"Yes ma'am."

"If it charges, put it down. I'll be right behind you."

"I know you will."

She grinned and drew the Peacekeeper. "Take care of it, Grunt."

The tactical officer nodded, drew his own weapon, and started for the creature. It was busy ripping out the cherubs and throwing them into the nearby arm of the Lake. Grunt stopped short of the cracked remains of the fountain, observing the damage. Water leaked out through the shattered rim, spreading in a pool that nearly reached the much larger expanse of green water on the far side.

The Watchdog captain drew a bead on the creature's back and fired six stun rounds in quick succession. The creature barely seemed to register their presence in its thick flesh. Four seconds later the stun rounds discharged in a cascade and fell off, plopping into the water below. The creature, however, remained completely upright.

"Shit," Cat hissed. She darted sideways and took cover behind one of the short pillars on the inner railing, keeping the Peacekeeper trained on the creature. As a precaution, she dialed the power up to something that would fricassee a decent-sized rhino. Grunt fell back to his own mock shelter and loaded a new clip.

Above and behind them, Specs was updating Darwin as the zoologist and his sister frantically made their way to the Terrace in a Go-Kart stolen from one of the festivals. "Tiny eyes, slit nostrils. Three toes on each foot and three fingers. One of them looks opposable."

"Man, it'd be easier with a picture."

"I'm trying, but I can't get a good shot."

"Okay, okay. Skin color?" Darwin asked.

"Grey, I think, but the light's going. Might be bluish-grey, or green."

From behind the wheel of the Go-Kart, Helix tapped her bud and joined the conversation. "Any casualties?"

"Some broken bones, a lot of cuts and scrapes. One minor head wound." At that moment, Specs witnessed the complete failure of the stun rounds. "Oh. Oh damn, that's bad."

"What? *What?*"

"The stunners had no effect," the historian said. "Grunt just fired half a dozen into the thing, and nothing happened. It's standing in the middle of the fountain too."

"Wait. Wait-wait-wait—" After a minute of searching, Darwin came back on the open channel and asked, "It's got giant sockets but beady little eyes, right?"

"Yeah."

"Got it! It's called—aw, Jesus Christ, I think it's a Telaran storm-walker. Labor species from the Telarus cluster. They're used to mine the Telaran equivalent of lightning. Which means—"

"They're shock-proof," Specs said, widening his connection with the twins. "Specs to Cat and Grunt, that thing is immune to electricity."

"Yeah, we got that," Cat said. "Tell me something I don't know."

Less than a quarter of a mile away, Darwin was furiously reading about the lightning mines of Telarus IV. "Okay, how's this: Your Peacekeeper's just gonna piss it off more."

"*What?*"

"Cat, this thing is regularly hit with eight *billion* joules of energy. That's the Peacekeeper's highest setting, right? The one that's supposed to slice a comet in half? Storm-walkers have skin that is pretty much the least conductive thing in their solar system. It scatters incoming energy. Now, if you hit him dead on the base of the skull at the right angle, you might stun him, but that's about it."

"So brute force?" Grunt asked.

Helix snorted. "Sure. Let us know if you find a building to drop on him."

"Something sharp might work," Darwin said, "but good luck cutting through that hide and the blubber underneath. I think even bullets would just get stuck."

Cat watched the storm-walker, which was still completely involved in the demolition of the fountain. From what she had seen, its eyes were vulnerable, but only the size of a halved kiwi. That would be a hard target to hit even if it held still, and if it was roaring at you—"

"We make him swallow it," Cat murmured. Louder, she asked, "Darwin, it's just the skin that's the problem, right? The inside of him isn't shock-proof."

"Yeah, yeah. As far as I can tell. But there's no way you're getting past this stuff."

"Leave that to us. Call me if you find something else." Cat ended the transmission and opened a new one. "Grunt, it's just you and me now. We have to get that thing to open its mouth long enough to hit it with more stun rounds."

There was a pause as the Watchdog thought it through. "That should do it, Commander. How many?"

"As many as you can squeeze off," Cat said with a smile. "Oddly enough, your survival is my top priority."

"Appreciate that, Commander." After observing their target for a moment, Grunt said, "It's slow, and heavy. It'd have a hard time getting up if it fell."

Cat grinned. "Make it happen."

Grunt holstered his sidearm and calmly approached the ruined fountain, battle armor reflecting the fresh light from the street lamps. He stepped over the granite rim and into the shallow water, uprooted plant life brushing against his ankles. He noted the feel of the basin beneath his boots, slick with patches of brownish-green scum.

The storm-walker, its vendetta against the metal cherubs satisfied, turned its attention to the tiny creature crossing the water. Its great, hulking form trembled with bloodlust and territorial rage. Though sapient, the storm-walker was hardly what one would call an active thinker. It lunged for Grunt, but he simply rolled beneath its massive hand and came up slashing with his monster of a knife, scoring a long cut along the back of the storm-walker's thigh that didn't bleed.

Faint thuds shuddered through the fountain as the creature stumbled forward and regained its balance. Grunt turned to face it, shaking water from his fair hair.

On the terrace above, Darwin and Helix arrived in a screech of cheap brakes. They tumbled from the Go-Kart gracelessly and scrambled up to where the Specs kept watch.

"What's happening?" Darwin gasped, crashing into the stone railing. "Jesus *fuck*, that thing is big."

"First pass. No damage to Grunt, minimal to the storm-walker," the historian answered grimly.

The zoologist hit his bud. "Darwin to Grunt, this thing has no nerve endings or blood vessels for the first few inches of skin. You're gonna have to go deep if you wanna hurt it."

From his spot in the fountain, where he and the storm-walker stood regarding each other, Grunt tapped his own ear and said, "Acknowledged."

As if they had reached an agreement, man and alien charged each other at the same time. The storm-walker bent forward and tried to swipe its tiny opponent from the side. Grunt lunged aside and stabbed his knife into the storm-walker's foot, where it stuck. Thrown off-balance, he couldn't avoid the second arm that barreled into him with the force of a car at twenty miles an hour.

Though the armor absorbed most of the impact, Grunt flew almost ten feet before crashing into the shallow water. He cradled his head as he fell, landing instead on his arms and side. Most of the Gamma team members watching cried out, but Cat remained as silent and still as the Angel of the Waters herself.

Grunt spit slimy water out of his mouth and rolled into a crouch, taking a brief inventory. He was sore, but that was nothing new. Soreness could be ignored; broken bones usually could not. The armor was dinged but still functioning perfectly. He was down his favorite knife, which remained firmly stuck in the storm-walker's blubbery foot. If he wanted it back, he would have to go in close again.

"You okay?" Cat's voice asked in his ear.

Eying the storm-walker, which hadn't followed up on its attack, Grunt said, "Yes ma'am. I think it's hurt."

"I think you're right. You were too busy getting flung through the air to notice, but it's limping."

The daylight was fading fast, and the storm-walker continued to stare him down with its practically vestigial eyes. "Commander," he said, "I'd appreciate some light."

Immediately, Cat put out a team-wide broadcast. "Any members passing by Gamma Command, bring as many floodlights as you can carry." She got a chorus of affirmatives within seconds.

The Watchdog captain tilted his head, considering. "Permission to do something stupid, Commander."

From his position, he could see the glint of Cat's smile. "Permission granted."

Playing on a hunch, Grunt came to his feet and uprooted one

of the last surviving plants from its basin. He held the cluster of long shoots in front of himself like a shield. The storm-walker leaned back and bellowed a challenge to the darkening sky. Grunt obliged it by charging.

As he came almost within reach, Grunt suddenly threw the plant away from him. The storm-walker's beady gaze followed its movement, giving Grunt the opening he needed to dart forward and wrench the knife out of the creature's foot. He pushed off against the rim of the fountain and turned, but he wasn't quite fast enough. A vice clamped around his arm and squeezed, fracturing several panels of armor.

The storm-walker roared at him, nearly finishing the job that the thunderbird had started. Grunt swung his free hand and stabbed the knife deep into the storm-walker's arm, ripping out a chunk of flesh the size of his head when he twisted. This time he made it past the blubber and bared muscle. The storm-walker roared in pain and released him, confirming that it had nerve endings somewhere. Green and purple fluid leaked out, floating on the water like oil.

The watching Dogs cheered as Grunt retreated, putting what was left of the Angel's fountain between himself and the storm-walker. A handful of agents appeared with the requested floodlights, and within minutes the dim lower level was as well-lit as midday. At almost the same time, several of them became aware of the sound of heavy footfalls approaching quite rapidly. A giant bird broke free of the tree cover, carrying a petite rider with pepper-red hair on its back.

The ostrich came to an abrupt stop and Millennia slid off the back end, looking a bit pale. A brown cotton bag circled the bird's beak, and leather reins swung free as it twisted its serpentine neck. Its black and white feathers were tipped in royal purple, and an ornately decorated saddle was wrapped snugly around its middle.

Darwin and Specs were momentarily distracted by Millennia's shaky approach. The ostrich's throat distended as it bugled at her through the bag and immediately bolted back the way they'd come.

"Found a 19th century circus," she said, waving a hand weakly in the direction of the retreating bird. "I was all the way on the other side of the Reservoir, so I commandeered a vehicle. It is absolutely nothing like riding a horse. What's going on?"

"*That* is going on," Specs said, turning back to Grunt's standoff with the storm-walker.

"Holy mother of shit," Millennia breathed. "I'm on it." She whipped out her tablet and began scanning the storm-walker. "Jesus Christ, this thing's ion signature is off the charts. I've already got a lock on it."

"Specs to Cat," the lieutenant said, opening a channel. "Millennia's here. She's running the program."

From her post below, Cat put a hand to her ear. "Atta girl. How are we on injuries?"

"Helix is working on them now, and we've got a back-up med team on the way. They should be here in less than five minutes."

"The media blackout?"

"The Hive knocked out all video and outside communication for this entire half of the park. They've got a second team working on damage control for the witnesses."

"It's right below us," Millennia said, joining the conversation. "The rift is somewhere in the arcade."

There was a pause. "*Shit*," Cat said. "There's a good chance some norms got caught up in it. Specs, get a group of Gammas together and take them down there."

"Cat, they're not trained to be a retrieval team," Specs protested.

"Then fucking teach them, because we're running out of options. Call McNab, but I don't think we have a choice."

Specs hand tightened on the rail. "Cat..."

"I know." Had there been any action going on, the others would have missed Cat's quiet words entirely. "Listen to me: You think I would let you anywhere near civilians if I didn't think you could handle it?"

They were interrupted by the storm-walker's frustrated bellow as Grunt continued staying well out of its reach. The wound on its foot was clotting, but the pierced flesh of its arm still bled sluggishly. It blinked against the light from the flood lamps, skin speckled and ridged in the harsh radiance.

"Damani, there might be more of these things waiting on the other side of that rift," Cat said. "I need you to do this."

Specs lowered his head. "Okay. Goddammit. Okay." Turning away from the railing, he checked the Watchdogs arrayed in front of him. "*Gammas!*" he yelled, and they all came to attention. "I need Fahd, Lindsay, both Pauls, Michele, Isadora, Ren, Patrick, and Davide. Gear up for an away mission and report back to me."

The sun was just a campfire glow behind the trees by then, and full dark wouldn't be far behind. Spurred on by the dimming light—and apparently tired of waiting for its enemy to make the next move—the storm-walker took a shuffling, experimental step forward. When its foot held, it pounded its fists against the ground and attempted an awkward charge. One of the cherubs warped with the weight of its passage, and water kicked up in a wide spray.

Millennia covered her mouth to stifle a shriek. Specs yanked her around and said, "*Focus.* I need you to get me down to that rift."

"Y-yeah. Okay. Okay." Her fingers flew over the screen. "Almost there."

Below, the storm-walker reached Grunt's former position, but the Watchdog had already rolled away to relative safety. Unable to brake or turn effectively, the creature skidded past, clumsily windmilling its arms. After several seconds the storm-walker regained its balance and continued lumbering after the much quicker Watchdog, who scrambled away as carefully as he could.

"I've got it!" Millennia cried. "It's beneath us, in the arcade."

Specs ran his fingers over each of his weapons like he was

counting prayer beads. "Good work. Stay with Darwin and—"

"I'm coming with you," Millennia said.

"Like hell you are," Specs growled. "I don't know what's on the other side of that rift."

"Yeah, but if you have to go ranging, you might need me to get you home," Millennia insisted. "I'm the only one here who has the tech and the training to actively track a rift."

Specs glared down at the petite physicist, who had lifted her chin lifted to meet him. "Fine," he said. "But if anything happens, you know what to do."

"I know what you *want* me to do," she said, tapping a finger against her stun payload. "It won't come to that. But if it does…" Millennia reached out with her free hand and squeezed his arm. "I'll be with you."

By then, every member of the makeshift away team was lined up and waiting. Their eyes went to the ruins of the fountain, where Grunt was still playing keep-away with the storm-walker.

"We still have a job to do," Specs reminded them with a jerk of his head. He tapped his tragus as they jogged towards the back entrance to the arcade. "Cat, we're on the move."

"Good luck," she replied, eyes trained on Grunt. "I'm counting on you if it all goes sideways. I don't know how much longer we can hold this thing off."

For the tenth time, Grunt dodged the storm-walker's attempts to grab him, and the closed fist around Cat's gut loosened.

Then he hit a patch of slimy floor hidden by the churned-up water and slipped. Before anyone could react the storm-walker was on him. It picked him up easily and began squeezing him like a medicine ball. His face contorted with pain, and there were several sharp cracks as more of the armor broke.

The storm-walker opened its mouth to roar, only to be knocked back by an energy blast right to its misshapen face. Though uninjured, the creature was distracted enough by the new attack to let its captive fall to the ground. Grunt caught the brunt of the fall on his forearms, but the rest of him followed painfully enough. He lay on the salty-slick granite, breathing heavily, but otherwise still.

Cat came on like a thundercloud, firing with clockwork precision the moment the Peacekeeper recharged. Darwin had been right; the blasts mostly just pissed the storm-walker off, but they also succeeded in holding its attention.

"Aaron Lewis Walker, you'd better not be dead, because this is as far as my plan goes," Cat called, knocking the storm-walker's head back with a well-aimed shot. It started forward, the muscles in its arms and shoulders so thick that it had to swing them halfway around its body in order to move. "Goddammit, I will drag you in front of the council by your fucking *balls* if you don't get up right now."

She thought she caught feeble movement out of the corner of her eye, but most of her focus was on the two-ton monster following her backwards retreat. The storm-walker braced its knuckles on the ground and bellowed a challenge.

"Grunt, that's an order," Cat screamed. *"Get the fuck up."*

And Grunt—the man known as the Dreadnought, and the Golden Wind—slowly, stubbornly came to his feet. Blood dripped from his busted lip in a languid trickle, mixing with the scummy water on the side of his face and fanning out across his chin. His hair was plastered flat on one side and raised up in wild spikes on the other, and there was something sharp and new glittering in his eyes.

"Oh shit," Darwin muttered to himself. "Oh shit, he's going into Beast Mode. Now we're all fucked."

The storm-walker was almost on Cat. She had hopped the inner railing and taken shelter behind a pillar, but her defiant blasts were doing little to slow its advance. Then Grunt picked up his knife, got a running start, and flung himself at the storm-walker. He plunged the knife into the middle of its back and let go, leaving the hilt sticking out of the creature's blue-grey hide.

Roaring, the storm-walker arched its back and tried to swat away the thing that had bitten into it. It spun in pained circles, causing Grunt to scramble out of the ruined circle of the fountain. The storm-walker crashed into what was left of the statuary and sent the poor Angel of the Waters the way of her cherubs. It then stumbled over the rim of the fountain and went sprawling with a ground-shaking *thud*.

"Commander—" Grunt called, but Cat was already aiming the Peacekeeper.

She fired a blast at the knife hilt. When it connected, the blue-white beam lit up the whole terrace like lightning. The creature jerked and thrashed its muscular limbs, and then fell still. Silence settled over the Dogs, broken only by Cat and Grunt's ragged breathing. The tactical officer fell to his hands and knees on the stone, wincing in pain.

From behind the pillar, Cat said, "Talk to me, Grunt."

"I'm—I'm okay, Commander," he wheezed, putting a hand to his side. "I'm okay."

She swallowed against the roughness in her throat and approached slowly, kneeling down beside him. "You won't be after you tell Ming-Na that we broke her armor on its first day out."

He choked out a laugh. "Frankly, Commander, that—that scares me more."

"That's because you're a very smart man." Cat helped him to his feet. "Where does it hurt?"

"Everywhere, but mostly my ribs," he whispered, his skin washed out in the artificial light. "They're bruised, maybe cracked. Everything else is superficial."

"What about the blood?"

"Blood?"

Cat brushed her thumb just under his bottom lip, which was already starting to swell. He licked the spot automatically and winced.

"It's fine," he said. "Just busted."

"Here," Cat said, tucking her smaller body under his arm. "Millennia's going to be pissed at me for letting you mess up your pretty face."

Grunt wheezed out a single breathy laugh and eased his

weight down onto Cat's shoulders. "Is that...too much?"

"It's fine. I'll tell you if I'm having trouble."

Addled a bit by pain and exhaustion, Grunt snorted softly and said, "No, you won't."

Two Watchdogs from Viszla came running down the stairs to help. "I've got him," Cat said, turning aside a bit so that she was between them and Grunt. "One of you go poke that thing and see if it's dead or just stunned. The other can play backup."

The men exchanged a look and quickly mimed *One-two-three-shoot*. The taller one played rock against his opponent's scissors and slugged him lightly on the arm. "Have fun, sucker."

"Go fuck yourself, Mal."

Cat pushed her way past the bickering pair and helped Grunt up one of the side staircases. Helix met them halfway down and made a move to take Grunt the rest of the way up.

"I got it," Cat snapped again.

"Cat, give him to me," Helix said, quiet but firm. "He's hurt. The rest of the med team is busy with the civilians. And Specs and Millennia haven't come back yet."

Cat's nostrils flared as she inhaled deeply and released the breath through her mouth. "You're right. Just—just be careful," she said, handing Grunt over as gently as she could.

"I know. I'll take care of him. You go get our people."

Smothering the sudden sick ache in her gut, Cat turned and sprinted down the stairs as fast as her legs could take her.

# TERRIBLE NEWS

## Helix
(19:50)

E ven though Helix knew it must have hurt him to do it, Grunt craned his neck so he could watch Cat leap back down the stairs. "I should go with her."

"Please," Helix scoffed, "you can barely stand. And frankly, I'm a little disappointed in your performance. Last year you slayed a dragon; this year a mountain troll nearly took you down. I think you're getting rusty."

"*Slayed* isn't a word," Darwin called from the terrace. "It's *slew*. And I'm just glad that move worked this time."

"Me too," Grunt murmured.

"You're not going to make a habit out of this, are you?" Helix asked. "Right now you're at fifty percent efficacy."

"Better than my batting average," he said with a shrug.

Helix paused. "That...that was almost a joke. We'd better start praying, because I don't think you're long for this world."

Grunt hacked out a quiet chuckle. "I'm surprised she...let you take me," he said.

"I was shaking the whole time," Helix confessed. They made it to the top of the stairs, and she led him to a nearby park bench. "When she gets protective like that, it's like trying to pry open a bulldog's jaws. I thought I'd have to treat you with her hovering over me like a goddamn helicopter." She eased him down onto the bench and fetched her overstuffed backpack. "How does the chest piece come off?"

"Panel under...left armpit. Ridged."

Gently, Helix lifted his left arm and found the tiny black panel with a line of grey nubs running down its center. She pressed it, and the chest piece loosened with a soft hiss. It peeled away from him almost like a second skin, revealing a thick layer of white compression gel on the underside.

Helix whistled as grey shards clattered to the pavement. "What the hell happened down there?"

"Squeezed me," Grunt wheezed, lifting the bottom of his undershirt and hooking it over his head. The paler skin beneath was mottled black and purple in a huge stripe where the storm-walker's opposable finger had pressed in. A black and grey eagle with an anchor, a trident, and an old fashioned pistol had been tattooed over his heart.

The geneticist paused. "I didn't know you were inked."

"Just the one," Grunt said. He let his head fall back over the bench and closed his eyes. "It's the Budweiser. The SEAL trident."

Helix pulled out the yellow x-ray glove and opened a program on her tablet. "I should take pictures. For medical reasons, of course."

A smile flickered across Grunt's face. "Of course."

Once the glove warmed up, she began running it up and down Grunt's front. "I never figured you for the kind of person to get a logo tattooed on you."

Grunt took a pair of careful breaths before answering. "Do you know how long it takes to be deployable as a SEAL?"

"Mm. Two years?"

"Three. And that's if you pass the recruitment tests on the first go."

"Did you?"

Snorting softly, Grunt rolled his head so he could look up at her. "No. My swim time sucked."

"That's kind of important if you're supposed to be aquatic,"

Helix said.

"My CO said the same thing." He winced as Helix prodded the bruised streaks with soft fingers. "It took me five months and seven days to pass. I got so drunk that night I stole my CO's dress blues and put them on a dog."

"You *didn't.*"

That faint smile returned at the memory. "I did. Being a SEAL was all I wanted out of life." As quickly as it had appeared, the smile faded. "And then we went east."

The yellow glove paused on its path across his stomach. "Life doesn't really care what we want," Helix murmured. "Does it?"

"Not from what I've seen," Grunt said. "Everyone talks about the men I brought back from the ridge that Day, but no one brings up the ones I lost. I was supposed to protect them too." He closed his eyes again. "I can't even tell their families how they died."

Helix reached down for Grunt's hand and squeezed. "I don't know what to say," she admitted. "I don't think anything I say can make it better. But you know that we'd all be dead a few times over without you. So try—try to remember that, okay? When it hurts too much."

He squeezed her fingers back. "We don't deserve you."

"I'm aware," she quipped, turning her attention back to his chest. "You're lucky. Your ribs look bruised to hell and back, but I don't see any fractures. Looks like your fourth and fifth ribs are out of place on the right side—that's probably why you're having some trouble breathing—but a chiropractor can shift them back where they belong after the bruising's gone. Give it a week with the Cradle."

Peeling the glove off, Helix said, "Well, Mr. Walker, I've got some terrible news: You're going to be stuck with us for a while longer." She passed him a pair of white pills and a water bottle. "This'll tide you over until you can get down to Med Bay. No side effects, I promise."

Grunt swallowed the pills with a swig of water and dumped

the rest over his head. "No pictures after all?"

"Oh, honey," Helix said, tapping the tablet. "It's been taken care of."

"Ah. Just crop my head out if you're going to post it somewhere." Gesturing at the chest piece, he said, "Can you help me?"

"Yeah, of course." Together they rolled the armor back on, and when Helix lined up the seams under his left arm and pressed the ridged panel again, it sealed together with a hiss. Grunt winced at the pressure, but didn't complain.

"That must be the compression gel," she said, helping him to his feet. "An electric field inflates it and molds it to you, right?"

"Think so," Grunt said.

Shaking her head in admiration, Helix said, "That's one amazing piece of tech."

"Maybe," Grunt said, "but going to the bathroom in it is a little tough."

Helix's laugh was bright and unrestrained. "We need to exhaust you more often. Tilt your head down a bit."

He obeyed, and Helix pulled a Q-tip from a pouch on her backpack. Cracking it, she gave it a gentle shake and reached up. "You're not gonna like this," she warned.

Grunt winced as the alcohol-soaked tip brushed against his busted lip. "Ow."

"I know, I know. But it's better than your face rotting off. Any more open wounds?"

"I don't think so."

"Good." She dabbed antibiotic ointment on the cut and then handed him a small tube of sealant. "Wait for that to dry and then apply this. Give it ten minutes to set before you try talking; I know it'll be a challenge for you, but do your best."

He nodded at her. "Thanks for patching me up. And for listening."

"Anytime." Leaving the tactical officer to coordinate his teams, she walked over to the terrace railing and leaned against her brother. "What's the latest?"

"The storm-walker's down," Darwin said, flicking through the tablet in his hands. "Could be dead, could be in something called *ferra state*. It's like a reparative coma. If they take a lot of damage, their bodies shut down nearly every function, even respiration. They've got some organ that can keep pushing blood around for up to a hundred and twenty hours, doing repairs and re-oxygenating a few key areas. One of which is *not* the brain, by the way."

"Charming. What about Cat?"

"She disappeared under the terrace about ten minutes ago," he said. "Haven't heard from her since."

"And the away team?"

Her twin's expression darkened. "They're still gone too. I can't reach anyone on the buds or watches."

"Hey," she said, reaching over and linking her fingers with Darwin's. "They're gonna be okay."

He squeezed her hand twice. "I hope so."

# BLACKBIRD SINGING

## Specs
(Some Time Earlier)

This wasn't right.

"No, no," Specs whispered as the icy grip of the rift slid away from his flushed skin. He whipped around, a faint roar growing in his ears. "I'm not supposed to be here. I'm not—I can't be here."

But he was. The burned-out buildings of the Barrio rose up around him, their insides like rotting tree stumps softened by water and time. Piles of ash were scattered everywhere, ash that could have been the remains of cars or fire hydrants or a group of Latino school children; there was no way to tell after the Redeemers did their work. The whine of a low altitude missile streaked overhead, maybe destined for the older parts of SoHo or even across the Hudson to Jersey.

And the smoke. He could never forget the eternal smoke that hung in a pall over the entire world. It coated his lungs and throat, and the back of his teeth.

The historian's heart twisted in animal terror, and he drew his weapon, but the searing pain in his leg told him that it was too late. He looked down as his left pants leg burned away in a flash of heat. All that remained was a gleaming brown prosthesis.

The image flickered, and Specs pushed back against the sudden pain in his skull with the heels of his hands. The pain built and built, and he opened his mouth to scream.

And then there was something beautiful that didn't belong. It took Specs a long time to figure out what it was that had no place in this ugly world.

It was a voice, soft and a little off-key, singing his favorite Beatles song. The sound of it pulled gently at him, drawing him away from the hot noise and cloying smells. Then the voice said his name.

"Specs," it said. "Specs, you're right here with me. It's Millennia. We're in a forest. I don't know where you think you are, Specs, but you're safe. You're safe in this forest with me, and Fahd, and Lindsay, and the Pauls. Ren and Isadora are watching our backs. They're all here, and we're safe. It's beautiful, Specs. I want you to see it. Can you open your eyes? Please?"

Specs took a few deep breaths, trying to come the rest of the way out of the flashback, but he couldn't get past the phantom pain in his leg.

"It's okay, it's okay. Can you hold this twig for me?" Millennia asked. "Can you let go of the gun and hold the twig instead?"

Without opening his eyes, he lowered the hand that held his gun, offering it to her handle first. It was lifted gently out of his grip, and then something thin and springy took its place. With trembling hands, he felt along the edges of it and pressed it against his face, inhaling deeply. Like the beautiful song, the smell of growing things didn't belong in the world that he was remembering.

Slowly, the edges of the flashback began to fade. His heart rate slowed, and his chest didn't heave quite so hard. Specs opened his eyes a little at a time and found himself safely tucked in a green cradle. The Terrace was gone. So was the fountain, and the Lake, and everything familiar about their surroundings. Golden sunlight filtered gently down through the sparsely-wooded land. Healthy grass glittered at their feet, and all around them, songbirds swooped back and forth like winged flutes.

Against that background, Millennia was impossible to miss. Her tablet was on the ground, and her hands were raised in a placating gesture.

"Hey," she said, smiling. "Hugs that last longer than ten seconds release oxytocin and help calm the nervous system. Can I hug you?"

He wasn't quite able to speak yet, but Specs nodded and opened his arms. Millennia approached him calmly and hugged him, slowly increasing the pressure until she was squeezing him as hard as she could.

"Welcome back," she whispered.

Specs swallowed, and his dry throat clicked uncomfortably. "Thank you."

"Anytime, Papa Bear." She let him be the one to pull away, but when he did she let go without comment. "Now then," she said, surveying their surroundings, "let's get to work. Guys, fan out in your pairs and look for signs of anyone from our time passing through. You can call out, but don't get crazy."

The Watchdogs nodded and did as she said. Picking her tablet up, Millennia turned in a slow circle and surveyed the immediate area. "Hmm. Someone from our time definitely came through, but I can't tell how many someones. It's all a bit muddy."

"They were probably running from the storm-walker," Specs said, taking a water bottle from his pack. Fahd offered his gun back, and he holstered it with a nod of thanks.

"Good point. Either way, they didn't really leave much in terms of biological remains. I hope the teams turn something up, because I don't see this being much help." Glancing up, she frowned at the sky. "Why is it still daylight?"

There was a startled yelp from behind the trees. Seconds later the Pauls appeared, their weapons drawn on an androgynous figure that seemed spectacularly unimpressed. The tall humanoid was dressed in loose pants, a long split tunic made of silver-white leather, and a hooded purple cloak. Its face—if it had one—was hidden behind a smooth, featureless purple mask.

"We found him hiding in the trees," one of the Pauls said, eying the figure with naked suspicion.

Without looking around, the figure said, "I am Telaran, agent. The proper personal pronoun for my gender is *faen*. For the possessive, *faiet* will do. And I was hardly hiding. This is my assigned sector."

Specs stepped forward and signaled for the Pauls to lower their weapons. "My apologies. I'm Lieutenant Damani Forrester. We're with CIRIUS—"

"Yes, I gathered," the Telaran said. "The star dogs. You are seeking your fellow humans, I presume? They are safe."

"You know where they are?" Specs asked, relief nearly making his knees weak.

The Telaran bowed *faiet* head. "Indeed. They are just beyond these trees."

On instinct, Specs bowed deeply from the waist. "You have my thanks. Am I right in assuming that you are missing something as well?"

"My storm-walker, yes," *faen* said, putting a hand on *faiet* belt where a coil of white metal rested. "The suppression collar was damaged in an accident. Has it hurt anyone?"

"I don't know," Specs said. "My mission is to save the men and women who passed from my time to yours."

"Allow me to lead the way, then." Without waiting for confirmation, the masked Telaran turned and strode through the trees.

Jogging to keep pace with the faster alien, Specs asked, "Are you some kind of ranger?"

"In a way," the Telaran said. *Faiet* voice remained the same in spite of the brisk pace. "We look after this land and the creatures that call it home. When properly tamed, the storm-walkers make excellent beasts of burden and deterrents to poachers."

Finally settling into a rhythm, Specs said, "Can I ask how you and the storm-walker ended up here on Earth? Or is it rude to ask personal questions?"

"On the contrary," the Telaran said, "my people value personal questions. It shows interest in the affairs of something other than oneself. I came to this land—what do you call it in your time?"

"New York City, in the United States of America."

"I came to New York City one hundred and twenty-seven of your years ago, when Telarus joined the Empire. A decent span of time for a Telaran, and a pittance for a storm-walker. My beast and I traveled here to be with the other members of my mate group." Shrugging, *faen* added, "And our progeny, I suppose. Young ones are moderately amusing when they are young, at least until their wings fall out. Then there is little to recommend them."

Specs chuckled, and he felt an unseen knot of tension unwind in his chest. The beautiful forest was working its magic on him like a pair of healing hands.

"I've got a question," Millennia said, practically sprinting to keep up. "How come it's still daylight here? In our time, the sun's already gone down."

"The sunlight that you feel is artificial," the Telaran said. "It comes from special cells in the atmosphere. Look closely, and you will find no discernible source of light."

Millennia craned her head up, and frowned. "Holy crap, you're right. I don't actually see the sun."

"That is because it set approximately twenty-three minutes ago. This sector is still classified as 'recovering,' so it receives an extra hour of harvested solar energy every day. The light will begin to dim in thirty-six minutes as the cells lose their opacity, and full darkness will come soon after."

"Cool," Millennia said, looking around her with a grin. "What's it recovering from?"

The Telaran glanced back without breaking pace. "Humans."

The physicist winced. "Oh."

"Indeed. Though the Eugenics Era ended many decades before my own arrival, Telarans have long been involved in the reforestation process here on Earth. In fact, it was our idea to convert this island into a sanctuary."

"Do humans still live here?" Specs asked.

"Of course. Not on this land, currently, but this is still primarily your planet."

Specs looked around at the incredible scene around him, and he felt tears prick the backs of his eyes. "I've been to the Eugenics Era," he remarked softly. "It's—it's good to know that this comes next."

"Is that where you sustained your injury?" the Telaran asked.

"Oh yes," Specs said with a short huff. "That time definitely left its mark."

The soft rumble of conversation reached them. "Here we are," the Telaran said, leading the Dogs around a tall grass hummock.

Huddled in a clearing were a dozen humans in various states of agitation and wonder. An old man was talking quietly with three kids below the age of thirteen, each drinking in their surroundings. Five adults paced or tapped their feet anxiously, and three teenagers sat clustered together. Those sitting came to their feet when they saw the black-clad group of agents approaching.

A pair of young girls about ten years old, one a soft peach and the other like warm toast, walked up and offered the Telaran their fists.

"Wicked place, dude," the darker one said.

"Yeah," her friend added. "Wicked cool."

The Telaran accepted their fist bumps passively and allowed the old man to shake *faiet* hand. There were tears in his eyes as he said, "Thank you, my friend," in a heavy Russian accent. "It is beautiful here."

"*Pozhaluysta*, Nikolai," the Telaran said. "Racquel, how is your leg?"

The African-American teenager with beaded braids grinned and turned her leg from side to side. "Perfect, man. Thanks a ton."

"Okay everyone, gather up," Specs said. "We're going home."

The Watchdogs formed a protective bubble around the norms, with Specs and the Telaran at the head. They began trekking back through the trees, buoyed by the soft exclamations of wonder.

After a couple of minutes, the bud in his ear came to sudden life. "Specs? Specs, it's Cat."

The historian held up a hand and said, "I hear you, Cat. We've got the civilians. Everyone's safe."

"Thank fuck. Grunt and I are good too. Where are you?"

"In the trees, only about fifty feet or so away from the rift. We're on our way."

"Roger that. I'll wait here."

Specs smiled. "It's good to hear your voice, Cat."

"You too, Specs. Cat out."

Turning to the Telaran, Specs asked, "Will you come through the rift with us?"

"It should be fascinating," *faen* said as they came to the small clearing where the Dogs had crossed through. "Besides, I must retrieve my beast."

Cat was pacing the length of the clearing obsessively, and she froze at the sight of the purple and silver figure leading her team.

"It's okay," Specs said. "This is our guide. The storm-walker is *faiet.*"

"*Faiet?*" Cat asked, checking each of the Gammas one by one. Her eyes flickered over to the newcomer periodically.

"It is the personal pronoun for my gender," the Telaran explained again. "I provide the eggs for my mate group, but I neither incubate them nor provide nutrients."

Cat took the information in stride. "I'm Commander Fiyero. You said the storm-walker belongs to you?"

"Yes, the beast is mine. Is it alive?"

"I don't know," Cat said, shaking her head. "We had to go a little rough on it, since it was trying to kill us and all."

The Telaran inclined *faiet* head. "I apologize again. Normally, the suppression collar keeps it quite contained."

"Yeah, well it almost squished my tactical officer into paste."

"Almost?" the Telaran asked. "They survived?"

"He did," Cat said, stretching out a sore part of her arm. "It'll take something a lot nastier than a mountain troll to take Grunt out."

"I do not know what a *mountain troll* is, but this Grunt must be impressive indeed to subdue a storm-walker. I would like to meet him, if I may," the Telaran said, gesturing to the rift. "After you, Commander."

"Before we go," Specs said, speaking to the norms, "does anyone have any gum? The stronger, the better."

There was a chorus of no's, and three hands reached into pockets and purses. Specs accepted a stick of peppermint from the old man and started chewing it.

"Alright, everyone," Cat said, addressing the norms. "I know you've had a rough day, but it's almost over. I need you to partner up with one of the agents around you and walk with them from now on."

The most attractive Watchdogs found themselves snatched up quickly. Racquel, the pretty teenager with the braids, wasted no time in sidling up to Specs.

"*Mm-mm,*" she said, eying his physique. "What a sister gotta do to land a fine thing like you?"

"Double in age," Specs replied, moving to the back of the line.

Cat joined him. "Guess you're stuck with me."

Specs grinned and gently bumped her shoulder with his arm. "I'm glad you made it out of there alive."

"You and me both."

"May I join you?" their Telaran guide asked, standing on Specs's other side. "I believe that it would be unwise to cross the rift without sufficient authority figures to vouch for my presence."

"By all means," Cat said. "I appreciate you looking after my missing people. Do all your people remember the Days Out of Time?"

*Faen* nodded. "Oh yes, Commander. A most peculiar phenomenon. They can be quite amusing for my species, but not so for others. This is not the first group of wayward humans that I have gathered, and I imagine that it will not be my last."

"Mmm," Cat said, eying the much taller alien thoughtfully. "What's your name?"

Shifting *faiet* weight to one leg, the Telaran said, "My name is Feniris-Dul, of the Tempestoria line."

"You ever think about coming to work for the Dogs, Feniris?"

"The thought has occurred to me," *faen* said as the line ahead of them grew shorter, "but always within the confines of my own era. I was not aware that cross-temporal employment was possible, especially for an as-yet-unfamiliar species."

"It's rare, but it does happen," Specs said. "Telarans have a long lifespan, don't they?"

"Quite prodigious, compared to humans," Feniris agreed. "Far less so to something like a warp rider. A few decades spent with the star dogs would not consume a substantial part of my remaining years."

From a pocket, Cat took out one of her cards and scribbled the year on it. "Think about it," she said, passing the card to *faen*.

"Thank you, Commander, I will."

Then it was their turn to pass through the rift. As the cold rearranged his molecules again, Specs squeezed Cat's hand and sucked on the peppermint gum so hard that it burned his mouth. The sound of her quiet muttering filled his ears, and he leaned down automatically so that he could hear her better. She was repeating the opening paragraph of the Declaration of Independence under her breath, and it startled a chuckle out of him.

"Don't laugh," she said sourly. "I memorized it in college on a bet, and the damn thing's been stuck in my head for twenty years. Are you here with me?"

"Yeah." In spite of his tense muscles and rapid breathing, he had stayed firmly in the present. "I'm okay."

"Fascinating," the Telaran said, glancing around at the darkened arcade under the Terrace. Ahead, the floodlights illuminated the damaged fountain in stark detail.

"Damn, we really tore that place up," Cat muttered, eying the gouges in the arcade's pillars that marked the storm-walker's passage. "Well, us and the mountain troll." Pointing to the opposite end, where a staircase led out of the arcade, she called out, "This area's off-limits now. Shoo."

Most of the civilians took her words to heart and scampered away. Outside, Dogs were scattered across the remains of the fountain, sifting through debris and communicating through their buds or watches. Grunt himself was guarding the storm-walker. Cat's eyes took in every stripe of broken and missing panels that crossed his back.

"Grunt," she said, stepping up beside him.

He never took his eyes off the creature in front of him, though he did straighten. "Commander."

"Relax. Did Helix take care of you?"

"Nothing to take care of, Commander," he said. "The armor did its job."

"*Cat!*" a voice called from above. "Helix, they're back!"

Cat looked behind her and waved up at Darwin. A moment later his sister joined him, and they both went slack-jawed at the sight of the Telaran ranger currently kneeling by the storm-walker.

"It lives," Feniris said. "Good. Sending for a new one from my world would be...tedious." Reaching into a flat pack hidden by *faiet* cloak, the Telaran pulled out a smooth bar of white metal that matched the collar around the storm-walker's neck. *Faen* broke off a piece and used it to fill in the crack, almost like putty. With a small tool, *faen* melted the metal and smoothed it over until it was pristine again.

"You are the one who injured it, correct?" Feniris asked Grunt over *faiet* shoulder.

Grunt nodded. "Yes."

Examining the storm-walker, the Telaran said, "May I ask where you found the proper weaponry? Such a thing would be hard to come by in this time."

Cat snorted. "Grunt stabbed him, and I shot the knife with a Jakenite Peacekeeper. Went right past his skin and toasted him from the inside."

Feniris paused and turned *faiet* upper half all the way around, displaying a flexibility of the spine that humans didn't possess. "Truly? The two of you defeated a storm-walker with only a blade and a Jakenite weapon?"

"And teamwork," Cat said, reaching up to clap her tactical officer on the shoulder.

Slowly, the Telaran's head turned from Cat to Grunt and then back. "Would either of you consent to joining my mate group?"

Millennia choked on the water she had been sipping and nearly spewed it all over Fahd. Cat snorted indelicately and pressed the side of her finger against her mouth to prevent any further outbursts. Grunt's only response was to raise both eyebrows and glance at Cat.

"It may be more beneficial for both of you to join, if you wish," Feniris continued, unperturbed by their reactions. "Our mate groups are typically composed of five to six members: Three to procreate, one or two to provide extra financial stability, and one other to defend the nest, as it were."

"And that's why you want us?" Cat asked, gaining control of herself for a moment. "To defend your nest?"

"Primarily, yes. Individuals within a mate group also enjoy free sexual expression with any other member not currently engaged in nurturing activity, though our two species are sexually incompatible. Hence my suggestion that you might both like to join."

The same man who had survived a furious storm-walker only

minutes before now looked as if he wouldn't mind it getting up for round two, and his commander turned a delicate shade of pink.

"This can't be happening," Millennia whispered to Specs. "Pinch me. This can't be real."

Meanwhile, the Dogs surrounding them were either shushing their partners or trying not to violently burst into laughter themselves. Two people who succeeded at neither of these activities were the Ramachandra twins; they were currently hanging over the Terrace railing, laughing themselves sick.

"Fire those two the second the clock hits midnight," Cat muttered to Specs through her pursed lips. A quick glare around the artificially lit fountain was enough to quiet the rest of the team. To the Telaran she said, "Thank you for the offer, but we're happy where and *when* we are."

"Ah. Well, one cannot know if one does not ask." Reattaching the metal chain to the storm-walker's collar, *faen* stood up and gave it a tug. The Dogs jumped back as the gargantuan creature came to its feet obligingly and stared out at them with no trace of emotion.

"The collar bypasses most higher brain functions," Feniris explained. "As the beast is not currently using *any* functions, this becomes even easier. I will see that it gets the proper care."

Specs bowed deeply from the waist. "Thank you again for all of your help."

"Of course. I sincerely hope that we will see each other again." *Faen* led the storm-walker into the arcade and disappeared without further fanfare. Every human still on the Terrace and fountain deflated in relief.

"Lindsay, go shut that thing down," Cat said before turning to Grunt. "Why are you still standing up? Go sit down for a while. And somebody get me a fucking espresso!" This last part was yelled across the fountain.

"I'm fine, Commander," the tactical officer said.

Cat narrowed her eyes at him, and then touched her bud. "Cat to Helix, what's Grunt's condition?"

"Oh, leave him alone," she called from the Terrace, still wiping tears from her eyes. "Grunt's a big boy. If he wants to be tough and stick it out with six broken ribs and internal bleeding, let him. I mean, *I* wouldn't want to work with half my leg missing and a good case of bowel cancer to boot, but it—"

Cat cut the transmission and waved her off with an irritated huff. "Grunt, you're no good to me if you keel over."

A tiny sigh escaped him. "Honestly, Commander, I could use some coffee too."

"Fair enough. Espresso and a drip!" she bellowed to no one in particular. "Anybody seen the New Kid?"

"I'm here," a voice called. The New Kid maneuvered his way through the crowd. "I was evacuating people."

"Good job. I want the rest of them out of here A-fucking-SAP, okay? We've got the clean-up crew coming in forty minutes."

"Clean-up crew?" the New Kid asked Specs.

The historian grinned. "Trust me, you can't miss them."

# DENOUEMENT VERT

## Cat
(21:40)

C at walked to the railed edge of the Terrace and looked down at the poor Angel of the Waters, who was laying half-drowned in the murky fountain with her little cherubs scattered in pieces all across the stone. A colossal serpent was coiled in the air above them, his flat scales the same electric shade of green as the inside of a lime. When straightened, he would be the length of two football fields. He curled back and forth sinuously just as an earthbound snake would, inspecting the wreckage with a calm eye. Three pairs of tiny, vestigial legs were spaced along the length of his body at regular intervals.

The air around him began to glow a lighter shade of green than his scales, and a large metal and crystal cylinder lifted up from the ground. He turned his head, and the cylinder floating alongside him began sucking up the pieces of the ruined fountain. On his third pass, he spotted the Dog watching him from her post.

"Howdy, Cat," the giant serpent called, floating over to her as the cylinder continued vacuuming up the remains of Bethesda Fountain by itself. "How's the year treatin' you?"

"Hey, Tanolon," Cat said with a wave. Up close, his head was easily as tall as Specs, and each tooth was the length of her forearm. He had long, drooping white whiskers like a catfish. "My sister-in-law had her baby a few months ago. Ugly little monkey shit. How's your polyp?"

"Oh fine, fine." Tanolon turned slightly, revealing a bulbous sack that hung along a good portion of his length. "Should hatch in about twenty years or so. Shifty tyke though; it keeps pressing on my air bladder, so I'll just randomly head for the skies, no warning. Makes having a conversation real tough sometimes, I'll tell you."

Cat nodded sympathetically. "That's rough, buddy. It'll settle down soon."

"*Ugf.*"

She turned around and saw that the New Kid had followed her onto the Terrace. He was staring up at Tanolon with eyes like tiny moons. "What—what—"

Sighing heavily, Cat asked, "Did you even *try* to read the Damn Handbook?"

"Um—it's, it's a flying snake. And it's *really fucking big.*"

"Don't be rude," she said, popping the side of his head. "How would you like it if Tanolon looked down at you and said 'Wow, that's a really fucking tiny human'?"

"But what *is* he? And what—what—" From this vantage point, he could see more of the serpents floating over the dark park grounds. Most of them were some variation on the green color scheme. "What are they?"

Cat rubbed her temples. "They're ouros. I mean, they've got a real name, but nobody with less than six tongues can pronounce it."

"Some northern European teams call them jormunds," Specs broke in, lugging a cherub out from under the arcade, "and a few hardcore comic nerds here in the States call them middies, after the Midgard serpent. But the most common term—" With a tremendous grunt of effort, Specs flung the cherub into the cylinder's path and wiped his brow. "The most common term is ouro, plural ouros, after the Egyptian *ouroboros*, or the snake that is eternally eating its own tail."

"It's a name that I have always been fond of," Tanolon said as he sucked the last specks of stone dust into his crystal cylinder. "There, that should just about do it. Ready, Cat?"

"Go ahead. Once we take care of this sector, we can grab a late dinner if you want."

The ouro wriggled in excitement. "*Excellent.* Kaneshkil was telling me about this food called sha-war-ma and I have been *dying* to try it." Without waiting for further instructions, the ouro used the glowing cloud to aim the cylinder and pull the trigger. The fountain slowly began to fill in like an oil painting.

There was a tug on Cat's sleeve, and the New Kid's anxious face appeared in her view. "Commander, what—where did he come from?"

"Earth, in about a thousand years. We become quite the hub for this part of the galaxy, and thanks to—which ruler again, Specs?"

"Her Radiance the Fifth Cosmic Empress."

"Yeah, her. In exchange for free travel within her borders, the ouros agree to come back every year and help us clean up the mess."

"It's the least we can do," Tanolon said demurely, finishing up the base as casually as a gardener spraying his roses. "Truth be told, I rather enjoy popping in every year." He leaned his whiskered face close and said, "And don't tell the others, but Gamma has always been my favorite. Especially the years under your leadership, Cat."

"Aw, thanks, Tanolon. Can I at least tell Haverty?"

The ouro snorted and went back to work. "I'd very much like to squish him."

"I'd very much like that too. Maybe if we ask nicely."

"That doesn't promote a good work environment," Specs pointed out from below.

"Specs, if you can't say something nasty about Haverty, don't say anything at all."

The big historian sighed. "Some day, I'm going to find a less exhausting commanding officer who just wants me for my body."

"I want you for your body," Cat protested. "Look at you, lugging around cherubs and shit. I can't lift naked metal children to save my life."

"True. Heaven forbid the day when one of us is trapped beneath a pile of naked metal children."

Cat leaned on the railing and grinned at her lieutenant. "I'm going to start praying every night for it to rain metal children so I can finally be rid of all of you."

"Then you'll have to do your own dirty work."

"Darn," she said, smacking the railing. "Guess you'll have to stay."

Tanolon snaked through the air and examined his work, chuckling the whole time. "This is why you're my favorite, though I'm not sure about this new member's manners."

Cat glared at the New Kid, who flushed and ducked his head a bit. "He's not quite house trained yet, Tanolon. I apologize."

"Me too," the New Kid said, trying his best to look up at the enormous ouro. "A lot—a lot of this is new to me, and um—I'm sorry." Swallowing, he offered, "I haven't even read the Damn Handbook yet."

"He hasn't read the Damn Handbook?" Tanolon demanded. "Cat!"

"I know, I know. Tamiko's orders. They dragged him out of his little cave last week, slapped a badge on his chest, and sent him to me."

"Well, in that case—apology accepted," the glowing serpent said easily. With a flourish he restored the Angel of the Waters to her rightful place and moved on to the cracked pillars of the arcade.

"Ouros are the most easygoing species in their quadrant," Cat said. "Probably because they've never been invaded. Look at them; they're a race of giant psychic dragons. I wouldn't invade them either."

"And we've never been at war with each other," Tanolon added. "Frankly, we've never seen the point. We reproduce far too slowly to strain the resources of our home world, and any decision is made by local assembly. Easy as pie."

"Yeah." The New Kid shifted his weight. "Uh, Commander?"

Cat turned at his voice and raised an eyebrow. He ducked his head again, and then picked it back up with a deliberate motion. "Could I—could I talk to you?"

"Sure, kid," she said, patting the stone beside her. "Pop a squat. What's on your mind?"

The New Kid leaned against the railing and swallowed. "I don't—um." He took a deep breath and let it out slowly. "I don't think I want to do fieldwork anymore."

Nodding, Cat said, "Okay. Any idea what you wanna do instead?"

"That's it?" he asked. "I just say 'no' and you let me go?"

"Kid, if you don't wanna do fieldwork, you don't wanna do fieldwork. Forcing you to do it doesn't give me another agent, it gives me a time bomb that I have to watch out for." Considering him for a moment, she added, "If you're willing to stick around, though, there are other ways you can help. Have you ever thought about going into counseling?"

"I—um." The New Kid sat back and rubbed his scratchy eyes. "Honestly, I did for a little while in college. But I don't know if it's a good fit for me."

"Maybe it is, maybe it isn't," Cat said. "You pay attention to people, and you see things about them that no one else does. You ask the right questions. And you're nosy as fuck, which I guess means that people interest you."

"They do," he admitted.

Cat shrugged and leaned back. "Think about it some. I'm not gonna lie, good counselors aren't high on our priority list, but they should be. We see a lot of shit here, shit that's hard to get over. And we know more than we should about what's coming next, and a lot of it isn't very nice. We've got the highest percentage of PTSD outside of the military, not to mention what can happen to the poor assholes like Grunt who get a double helping. The commanders who give a shit do what they can, but most of the time they just stick a BandAid over the problem and hope it holds for twenty-four hours."

"I was a psych major," the New Kid admitted. "I never finished my degree though."

"Go back to school. We can either supplement your education here, or free you up to take more classes."

He looked her in the face for the first time since he'd said he didn't want to do fieldwork. "You'd support me like that?"

Sighing, Cat said, "What you and that Briar girl don't get is that you're both an investment. We're short on just about everything at the Doghouse, so when we offer to train you—or pay for your training somewhere else—we're not doing it to be nice. We need you. Hell, I'd be willing to make you Gamma's personal counselor, if that's what you want. I know my team would want it."

The New Kid was quiet again, and for once Cat Fiyero bit her tongue and didn't push. "I think—" He swallowed and tried again. "I think I need some help of my own first. I've got stuff I need to work out before I can help anyone else."

"Thought you might," Cat admitted. "We've all got bridges we need to cross. Yours just happens to come with spikes." She bumped his shoulder gently. "But we're Gammas, kid. That means we get knocked around a lot, and we get back up for more."

"Cat," Tanolon remarked from the air above the Terrace, "I thought the flying reptiles of your planet went extinct quite some time ago."

Cat's head whipped around. "Why? Do you see one?"

"Well, yeah—just over there," the ouro said, turning his large snout towards a cluster of trees.

"*Get it*," she hissed. "That's my missing pteranodon."

"Okie-dokie then." The faint glow around the ouro spread out across the water and plucked something out of a tree close to the opposite bank. It squawked and struggled in vain.

"Son of a bitch," Cat muttered, drawing her stun weapon.

"That's where you've been hiding, you sneaky little—hold her right there, would you?"

"Sure thing."

The captured pteranodon froze about thirty feet off the ground, still very much offended at her capture. With a lazy squeeze, Cat fired a stun round and pegged the pteranodon in the meat of her pale belly. The indignant squawks reached a new pitch, and then abruptly cut off.

"You want me to put her down now?" Tanolon asked.

"Yeah, here's fine," Cat said, nodding at the ground beside her. "She can go be Darwin's problem when he gets back."

Below her, Specs began climbing the right-hand staircase to the upper level. "That's not exactly a punishment."

"Well, he did a good job with Washington."

After a few more minutes, Tanolon floated closer and said, "I'm just about done here, Cat. Gosh, you guys really wrecked this place, huh? I mean, Gamma's not exactly known for doing things small, but *woooo*."

"Hey," Cat protested, "that wasn't us. That was a Telaran storm-walker."

The ouro widened its eyes in a curiously human gesture. "From Telarus Prime or Telarus II?"

"Telarus *IV*."

"No!" Tanolon said, completely turning his back on the nearly finished fountain. "That's the wildlands! They've barely inhabited that planet in my time. They say it'll take another hundred and ten Ursan years before it'll be fit for Telaran communities. The storm-walkers they breed for those mines are monsters!"

"Grunt and I took one down with a Bowie knife and a Peacekeeper," Cat said, laying a smug hand on the butt of her gun. "And its handler invited us to be security for *faiet* mate group."

Tanolon abruptly began to float upward. With a visible effort, he lowered himself again until he was floating at head level. "Sorry, sorry about that! Sometimes when I get excited, *it* gets excited, and then *whoosh*, I'm gone. Cat, the Origin of a Telaran mate group actually invited you to join them?"

"Yup. Me and Grunt."

"Do you know what kind of honor that is?" Tanolon asked. "Telarans are a proud race. I mean, for good reason, but they are very, *very* picky about their mate groups. They want the best, especially Origins. In nearly six thousand years of travel, I've only heard of two hundred and twenty-seven non-Telarans who've ever been invited." Nodding down at the edges of the fountain, where Grunt stood watch, he said, "You two are the only humans I know of."

"How do you think that'll look on a résumé?"

The ouro snorted. "Very impressive, I should say. But I guess you said no."

"Nah. It was a nice offer though."

There was a pleasant *ding* from below them, and Tanolon turned back to his crystal vacuum cleaner. "Done! What do you think?"

The Gamma commander surveyed the fountain carefully. "The angel's head is on backwards."

"Goodness gracious," Tanolon said, peering closer, "how embarrassing. One second, I'll have it fixed right up."

"Take your time. We've still got—" Cat checked her watch. "An hour and twenty minutes before you're scheduled to be back. This is the only major damage to our sector." Turning to the New Kid, she asked, "Think you can go down to one of the festivals and pick up shawarma and tacos? There are some good food trucks down at the Mall. If nothing's destroyed them, that is."

Blinking, the New Kid looked at his own watch, which read 22:11. "Are they still open?"

The strange look that Cat gave him morphed into comprehension. "I forgot that you hole up every year. The festivals don't shut down 'til midnight, and most of the trucks stay open a hell of a lot later. So four beef tacos with no lettuce, seven chicken with no veggies, and whatever Tanolon wants."

"Something that's shawarma," the ouro said easily. "I'm not picky."

"Thank God the giant glowing snake isn't picky," the New Kid muttered, but only when he was well out of Cat's reach.

◻ ◻ ◻ ◻ ◻ ◻

For once, the Universe seemed to think that the Gammas had suffered enough. They spent an easy hour guiding displaced, sane people back to their appropriate times and visiting with their clean-up crew. The members of Rottie had an especially good time launching fistfuls of food in the air for Tanolon to snap up. Because it had been evacuated anyway, Bethesda became the new Command so they could keep in easy contact with the ouro.

"The new season of *Scandal,*" Mia said, holding up a case of burned discs. "Courtesy of myself and the Hive." She set it down in the overstuffed gift basket that most of Rottie had contributed to. "Sasha had a bunch of those cookies you like, but she's still in Med Bay."

"Oh, that's alright," Tanolon said. "Tell her I hope she gets better, and she can keep the cookies all to herself."

Mia smiled and continued going through the basket. "Oz said you just wanted a look at one of these?" she asked, holding up a Rubik's Cube.

The ouro considered it from all sides, and his whiskers drooped a bit. "Oh. He was right, it isn't nearly as much fun as I thought. Can he really solve it behind his back?"

"He can. It's annoying as hell." Mia settled everything back in its place and asked, "Any requests for next year?"

"Everything that is in any way related to *Game of Thrones,*" Tanolon said eagerly. "I've read the datacores, of course, but most of the televised series was lost in...some war, I forget. Have you been following along?"

"Most of us have, but not Cat," Mia said, looking back at the commander with an impish smile. "She's not a fan."

"My entire life is a science fiction movie of the week," Cat pointed out. "In what little free time I do have, I like to read about normal people leading normal lives. Now *that's* suspension of disbelief."

"Fahd to Cat," the bud in her ear said. "I found a tribe of Tinkigees down here in the arcade. They're requesting safe passage from my leader."

Tapping her tragus, Cat said, "Roger that, Fahd, I'll be down in a minute. Specs, the Tinkigees are back."

"Right behind you."

"See what I mean?" she asked Tanolon, scooping up the pteranodon. They trotted down the stairs to where Fahd was waiting with the diminutive merchant race. They were no more than waist-high, and they communicated primarily in deep, obeisant bows. The last time they had come through, they had gifted her with a packet of carefully sealed spices, each of which Specs promised would sear every taste bud off of her tongue. Sure enough, their leader had a similar pouch in his gnarled hand. He held it out to Cat with a look of grave reverence.

"Thank you," she said, plopping the pterosaur down so that she could accept the pouch. "I officially extend safe passage to your people. Agent Kader will escort you home."

The members of the lavender-skinned race bowed, their overlarge earlobes flapping, and followed Fahd up the stairs as quickly as they could manage. Holding the spices at arm's length, Cat muttered, "Remind me to re-gift this to Haverty during Secret Santa."

"You know, one of these years he's going to catch on," Specs said.

"What, because of last year? Those fancy pens explode all the time."

"Oh sure. With designer squid ink that smells like rotting fish if released too quickly."

"And who knew that if you put a SmartBand with malfunctioning conductor wires in the same pocket as your wallet, it would literally melt everything together like rock candy?"

"Science. Science knew that."

Cat couldn't hold back her salted caramel smile anymore. "What can I say? Haverty has rotten luck with presents."

"Speaking of Rotten and Luck," Specs said, "they're on the way back from 81st. You were too busy bellowing for more coffee to hear it."

"Excellent." Cat eyed the pteranodon at her feet, which had begun to stir. "Darwin's probably going to piss himself." Checking her watch, she handed the spices off to Specs and called up, "Tanolon, it's time!"

The ouro winked at Mia and slithered through the air until his snout was hovering just in front of Cat's head. "Until next year, Cat."

"If we live that long," she said, grinning. "See you next time, big guy." She stood on tiptoes and kissed the very tip of his scaly nose.

To the sound of many goodbyes, the glowing group of ouros ascended into the sky, where they vanished. A deeper dark fell abruptly over the park, but it was still only the fey glow of twilight that always existed in New York City.

"Oh hell," Specs said suddenly, rubbing his face. "We forgot Wagner Cove."

"Wagner—ah *fuck*, the pavilion."

The historian glanced at her. "Vandals again?"

"Why not? It's worked before." Cat exhaled in a long breath. "Half an hour. We can do this. Where the hell did I put that last taco?"

"You ate it," Specs said, passing her the bag with its cold goods. "I saved one of mine for you, if you want it."

"What a sweetheart," she said, unwrapping the foil.

"*Cat!*"

The voice that snarled her name from the Terrace above was angry rather than afraid, so Cat chose to calmly take a bite of her taco instead of responding. Within seconds, Chris Haverty appeared at the top of the stairs and stormed down them like a living Michelangelo sculpture, all muscles and impressively clenched jawlines.

"You fucking bitch," he spat, brushing past the handful of exhausted Watchdogs who surged to their feet. "You fucking *bitch*, you *poisoned* one of my guys."

Speaking around a mouthful of beef and tomato, Cat said, "Things must be pretty quiet Downtown if you can come all the way up here to yell at me, Haverty. And I have no idea what you're talking about."

"You're full of shit. Jorgenson was babysitting Washington one minute, and then flat on his ass the next." Pointing a finger at her, Haverty took a step closer. "I don't know what you gave him, but he was out for hours. They dumped him on our front door like some drunk hillbilly."

"Was he a drunk hillbilly?" Cat asked.

Haverty's color worsened. "My people don't drink on the job."

"Oh, just at frat parties and keggers then?" Before he could spew more venom at her, she asked, "What makes you think it was us anyway?"

"The last thing he remembers is a hot Indian chick," Haverty spat. "Now who the fuck does that sound like to you?"

"It sounds like he saw a hot Indian chick." Cat swallowed the last of her taco and wiped her mouth delicately. "Look, I have no idea what happened to Jorgenson. My people found Washington while on assignment and they brought him in."

"Don't you *fucking* lie to me, Cat," Haverty swore. "That little whore and her psychopath of a brother stole him, and we both know it."

"For your information," Darwin said, swinging his long legs over the staircase railing and hopping down the last four feet, "I'm actually a sociopath." His face went blank, and he picked up a survey pole from the ground at his feet. Holding it across his chest, he said, "And if you ever call my sister a whore again, I'll beat you to death and feed your body to the tyracroc."

Cat felt Grunt's solid presence at her back. She hadn't even realized that he was nearby. "You should apologize to both of them, Commander," he told Haverty in his straightforward manner, "and then walk away."

Specs crossed his arms. "I've had a bad day, Chris. Don't make it worse."

Even the pteranodon put in its two cents with a groggy croak. Haverty eyed the quartet warily, his gaze catching on what was left of Grunt's dented battle armor, Darwin's improvised club, the bulge of Specs's muscles under his clothes, and Cat's unflinching gaze. The fierce glower of the surrounding Watchdogs was like a smoldering ring, and they were slowly edging closer.

"You always land on your feet, don't you?" he asked, his voice now carrying no further than their circle. "That kind of luck won't last forever."

"Hey Specs," Cat said, as if Haverty weren't there. "Did you know that cats are the only animals known to kill just because they can?"

"I did not know that," the lieutenant told his commander, keeping his eyes on the Alpha leader. "Anything special?"

"Oh, I guess it depends. Darwin, what do cats murder for fun?"

"Lizards, rodents, birds for sure," the zoologist said helpfully. "The occasional mouthy Chihuahua."

Cat gave Haverty an appraising look. Even though she had to tilt her head to finish it, the overall impression was of a predator sizing up its prey. "Hm. Maybe the Chihuahuas should keep that in mind."

Haverty's handsome face pinched inward. "I don't want to turn this into a war, Cat. But those two owe Jorgenson big time. I'll be lucky if Tamiko doesn't put him up for review."

Cat raised an eyebrow. "Why the hell would he do that? Some crazy person must have spiked Jorgenson's drink while he was on duty."

Haverty's nostrils flared. "You—"

"I mean, it's not like you were purposefully holding General

Washington hostage," Cat continued. "It's not like you were wasting agency resources for a petty feud that Tamiko told you to drop. And you *definitely* weren't preventing a fellow commander from resolving a dangerous situation with as few casualties as possible, so I don't see any motivation for Gamma to be involved. Do you?"

Flushing, the Alpha commander turned on his heel and began walking up the stairs.

"Chris," Cat called out.

Haverty froze and looked back over his shoulder at the older woman.

"I meant what I said before," she told him quietly. "I'm ready to end this when you are."

He absorbed this information, and then nodded. As he turned to go, the tension leaked out of the Gammas faster than air from an untied balloon.

"Break time's over," Cat said to the Watchdogs. "Go relieve first wave, and when your team leader clears you, go home. Report to Med Bay for final checks by tomorrow night."

The weary men and women murmured, "Yes ma'am," and departed, leaving only the four officers. Cat rucked her hair up with an impatient hand and regarded Darwin carefully.

"It's done," she told him. "No retaliation."

"But—"

"Do you like getting picked on?" Cat asked. "This might be our chance to stop it, so I'm gonna say this one more time: If I hear of any 'accidents,' especially the incendiary kind, I will bury you so far in paperwork you'll need a forklift to dig yourself out. Clear?"

Darwin scowled. "Yeah, yeah."

"Good." She pointed down at the pteranodon. "Don't you have a habitat to prep? Shoo."

The zoologist did as he was told, stalking under the arcade with all the dignity of an offended tiger, muttering to himself the whole time. After a reproachful look down at his commander, Specs followed to play peacekeeper.

Cat rubbed her forehead. "Jesus Christ, I hate people like Haverty and his bullies." She turned until she was facing Grunt and squinted up at him. "You were with Bravo for your first year, weren't you?" she asked, nervously checking her watch. Thirteen minutes to go.

Grunt nodded. "Good group."

Snorting, Cat said, "Yeah, they're goddamn boy scouts. You know, it always surprised the hell outta me that you got bumped down to Gamma. Stefano sang your praises like a fucking canary. He might've even shed a tear when he saw your new badge, heh."

"I didn't."

"Hm?" Cat asked, looking at the younger officer again. "Didn't what?"

"Get bumped."

The groggy pteranodon at her feet croaked, and Cat automatically put a hand down and scratched behind its fin. "Then how the hell did you end up with us? System error? Lose a bet? You lost a bet, didn't you."

"I asked to be put in Gamma, ma'am."

"*Ha.* So you could see how a world-class fuck-up operated?" Cat asked, gesturing around at the freshly restored fountain. "It's a miracle they didn't bump *me* over to Jersey years ago."

"Respectfully, Commander, you're wrong."

Cat's eyebrows disappeared into her hairline. "You wanna explain yourself, Captain?"

The normally compliant soldier pursed his lips. "Permission to speak freely?"

"Please," Cat said. "You never offer opinions unless they're work-related. By all means, don't clam up again on my account."

Looking her in the eyes, Grunt said, "You're the best commanding officer I've ever served under, ma'am. You really go to bat for all your people, not just the officers. And I've known generals who'd go home crying after six hours of doing your job. And frankly—" As quickly as the flood of words had started, it dried up.

"Go on," Cat prompted, crossing her arms.

Grunt pressed his lips together for a single second. "Frankly, Commander, on top of all of that—you're a hell of a woman."

Had the pteranodon at her side suddenly sat up and recited poetry, Cat couldn't have been more surprised. "Where is this coming from?" she asked. "Is it because of what that Telaran said about you and me?"

He shook his head. "No ma'am."

"Then what—" For the first time in four years, Cat stopped and looked at Grunt, really *looked* at him, and he looked back. "Grunt," she said at last, "did you ask to be in Gamma because of me?"

The soldier nodded. "Yes ma'am, I did."

Slowly, Cat let her gaze slide down and then back up. "Grunt—*Aaron*," she amended. "We should go rock climbing when this is done. Together."

A smoky grin spread languidly across his face. "Yes ma'am, I think we should."

Because he knew his sparring partner so well, Grunt saw the movement coming, but he let Cat grab the front of his flak jacket anyway. Her mouth was hot and hungry on his, and in the sudden firestorm that followed, the perfect soldier forgot himself long enough to reach behind and cup the back of her head with one hand, though the other stayed firmly on the butt of his sidearm.

One three-second supernova of a kiss, and then they pulled apart. Cat swallowed hard a few times, and the younger officer's face was flushed as he said, "So. Rock climbing."

"Oh what fresh nonsense is *this?*" Darwin demanded from the entrance to the arcade behind them. He seemed to have completely forgotten about his anger.

Cat put a hand on the pteranodon's head. "I thought you had a job to do, Darwin. Somewhere far away."

"Why? So the two of you can make out some more?" The moment the words left his mouth, Darwin's face twisted in sudden panic. "*Sorry, sorry,*" he chanted, running forward and scooping the wobbly pterosaur up into his arms. "We're going. We are going so far away that satellites won't spot us."

Cat watched him scamper away and grimaced. "Well. There goes any chance at keeping this quiet until we figure it out."

Grunt's lips twitched through his tell and settled into a real smile. "Be honest, Commander; with Gamma, is there any other way?"

"Mm." Eying the tactical officer, Cat licked her lips and said, "We could always skip rock climbing."

Grunt swallowed to cover the sudden hitch in his breath and nodded. "I'd like that." Winking at her slowly, he said, "Heights make me nervous."

"Aren't you supposed to be the hero of some mountain pass?" she teased, listening to the quieting park. Now that the "light show" that City Management put on every year—consisting solely of floating green dragons—was over, the official festivals were winding down and the after-parties were beginning.

"It was a ridge," Grunt said, "and I was distracted."

"Oh, and I guess—"

A loud beep completely drew Cat out of her banter. She looked down at her watch, relieved and not a little surprised to see what it read:

# 00:00

"I'll be damned," she said, looking up into Grunt's eyes. "We made it."

The Watchdog glanced out at the celebrating agents. "What's that toast you and the lieutenant always make?"

Cat laughed. "Here's to surviving the madness just one more time."

Shedding his pack, Grunt knelt down and pulled out two water bottles. He cracked the seals and passed one over to Cat, and then offered the side of his own.

With a grin, Cat Fiyero tapped her bottle against Grunt's and took a sip. In the false light of the flood lamps, with the sounds of her people all around her, it was the sweetest thing that she'd tasted all day.

# THE FINAL HOURS:
## An Epilogue in Five Parts

## Darwin

J ai Ramachandra had reached that level of exhaustion wherein one bypasses stupor and moves straight on to hyperactivity, and he was currently making a nuisance of himself down in the Savannah.

"Do not pass GO, do not collect $200," he said to the poor environmental control specialist named Kathy who was working the graveyard shift. "I want this beauty in one of my personal containment units. Settle her in for a while; Santa Fe'll want her, but I'm gonna stonewall them like a slab of *granite*. Get it? Stonewall, granite?"

Kathy nodded, already tired despite having been on the job for only twenty minutes. It was 12:50 in the morning, and while she was being paid quite a bit of money (plus excellent benefits), it was not half of the compensation she was owed for enduring Darwin's sleep-deprived mania. She had considered herself lucky not to have been helping the intake coordinator construct and tear down temporary enclosures all Day, but the pyromaniacal zoologist in front of her was making her reevaluate this conclusion.

"How's the Caledonian devilfish?" Darwin asked as he reluctantly handed over the pteranodon, who had succumbed to an additional dose of GH and resisted her treatment about as well as a rubber chicken.

"Fine," the older woman said. "She's settled in nicely. We flooded her with puzzles and toys until we can design a proper habitat to keep her amused. I was thinking of a shifting maze that leads to her feeding area."

"Good! Good, I like that. What else?"

She seemed a bit flustered by the question, and the limp pteranodon in her arms was sinking lower by the minute. "I don't know yet, Dr. Ramachandra. You'll have to give me time. I only just got here."

"Then what the hell are you doing with a pterosaur?" Darwin demanded, reaching for the pteranodon.

Kathy dodged his attempt with a little trouble. "Dr. Ramachandra, do you have a degree in Forestry or Marine Systems?"

"Um, no—"

"Environmental Science?" she asked. "Ecology? Do you have any experience in the delicate balance that must be achieved for even the smallest of these enclosures to function properly and guarantee maximum health for the inhabitant?"

Darwin started shrinking back into himself. "No."

"Then let me do my job," she said simply. "The devilfish is fine. The dinosaur will be fine."

"Pterosaur," he corrected softly. "And I've been calling her Batman."

Kathy the environmental control specialist took a deep breath in through her nose and let it out through her mouth. "Batman will be just fine, Dr. Ramachandra. I promise. I'm going to call Santa Fe and ask for their enclosure specifications."

"No, don't do that!" Darwin said, throwing his hands up. "The minute you admit that we have her, they'll start the transfer request!"

"Dr. Ramachandra," Kathy said, finally starting to lose the firm grip she'd had on her patience. "This is not a puppy or a turtle that you've brought home from the pet store to hoard in your room. This is an extraordinarily complex creature that we are not currently prepared to deal with, and if you do not let me request information so that I can care for her to the best of my abilities, I will put in a formal order to have you banned from her sector of the Savannah. Do we understand each other?"

Like a scolded teenager, Darwin hung his head a bit and said, "Yes, ma'am. I'm sorry."

Kathy softened. She had a fourteen-year-old back home, after all. She understood the behavior. "Go home, Jai," she told him gently. "You've had a long day. We'll take good care of her."

"Okay. Thanks, Ms. Franks."

She nodded and hitched the pteranodon a little higher in her arms. "You're welcome. Goodnight."

"Goodnight." Darwin watched the matronly woman turn and walk away with Batman cradled close to her body, and he slowly straightened up from his hunched position. A puckish gleam entered his eyes, and he whistled softly to himself as he strolled along the dim columns, sparing a single remorseful glimpse up to the open maw of number 15-23.

When he came to column eighteen, he stepped on the walkway and raised it all the way to the top enclosure. The only illumination came from the main overhead lights. True to Kathy's word, there were puzzles strewn all across the aquarium floor. More than a few had been pilfered from the sirens' former home.

The devilfish was playing quietly in one corner, two arms committed to the task of extracting a piece of lobster from an intricate box. Behind her, a simple shelter sat disguised as a pile of rocks.

"Dr. Ramachandra to Savannah control," Darwin said into his watch, "can you lighten the opacity of enclosure 18-15?"

"Roger that, lightening opacity to fifteen percent."

"Thanks, control. Darwin out."

There was no visible change from his side, but the devilfish's movements slowly came to a stop as her attention was caught. She picked her head up curiously, and then abandoned the box altogether to glide over to where Darwin stood. Watching her approach in the gloom, the zoologist felt a thrill deep in his gut.

She examined the wall with two arms, and then two more until half of her body was pressed against the glass. Her soft pink suckers adhered and came free with ease as she explored his image enthusiastically. In response, Darwin lifted both hands and placed them over the underside of her gelatinous limbs. They stood like that, human and devilfish, becoming re-acquainted in the half-light.

# Cat & Grunt

[Explicit Content]
[Explicit Content]
[*Really* Explicit Content]
[Explicit Content]

## Helix & Millennia

Helix wasn't surprised by the knock on her door, even though it was close to 2:00 in the morning. She answered it dressed only in a soft pair of shorts, an ancient "Save the Manatees" t-shirt, and her favorite black glasses. Her hair hung in tangled waves over one shoulder.

"You didn't have to get dressed for me," Millennia said from the other side of the doorway. She too was dressed for bed, but in longer checkered pants and a shirt that hung off her slender frame. Fuzzy black slippers protected her toes from the cold tile floor in the hall. "I only put clothes on to preserve the Dogs' fragile sensibilities."

Helix smiled and stepped back. "I'll remember that next time. Come on in."

"No visitors tonight?" Millennia asked, bending down to pet the delicate tortoiseshell cat currently rubbing against her legs.

Snorting, Helix nudged the cat aside and closed the door. "I'm way too tired to deal with any of them, though that didn't stop Kim or Tanisha from trying. Honestly, how could sex be on anybody's mind right now? I just want to sleep for a hundred years."

Millennia scooped the cat up and nuzzled into her neck. "Good thing she's got a guard kitty then, huh, Turtle?"

Turtle purred and rubbed her cheek against her second favorite human's head. As the main provider of food and snuggles, Helix had the honor of the top spot. Her brother was probably somewhere around seventh place.

The faint smell of incense drew Millennia's attention to the softly lit altar in the corner behind her. "Oh shit, were you still praying?"

"It's okay." Helix reached into her discarded backpack and pulled out a pair of pale blue flowers from one of the park's gardens. Offering them to Millennia, she said, "I was just thanking the *Mataji* for keeping all of your dumbasses safe."

Turtle sneezed as Millennia approached the altar and laid the flowers across Helix's own offering. Lamplight flickered across the four ornate icons, bringing the black eyes of the goddesses to life. The small silver bell to their right chimed when Turtle flicked it with an inquisitive paw.

"Bad fur baby," Millennia scolded.

"She's fine," Helix said, flicking on the electric kettle in her kitchenette. "The *Mataji* know better than to expect reverence from a cat. And if we thought the gods were going to get offended every time a pet knocked something over, we wouldn't have made the altars so low to the ground." She opened the cabinets and pulled out two mugs. "What'll it be?"

"Extreme Sleepytime please, barkeep." Still cradling the cat, Millennia flopped down on the queen-sized bed. The acoustic guitar leaning against it slid sideways until it hit the wall with a faint thrum. "My mind is going a billion miles an hour, and if I don't shut it down soon, I won't ever sleep again."

Turning away from the kettle, Helix braced her lower back against the counter and crossed her arms. "So talk."

The physicist laid her head back on the pillow and let Turtle curl up on her chest. "I've got this theory," she said, "that all the things we experience on the Days—all the little coincidences and stuff—are actually connected on some level. We know that on an atomic scale, similar things bond together. Like calls to like."

"A bit New Age-y, but I'm with you so far," Helix said, turning the beeping kettle off. She opened the cupboard and took down two boxes, one chamomile and one unmarked. Picking a teabag from each box, she dropped them in the mugs and poured scalding water over both.

"I think that it works for the Days too," the physicist said, ticking points off on her fingers. "That thunderbird ends up in a bird sanctuary. Two different species of dinosaurs from *millions* of years apart end up here on the exact same Day, and in the exact same territory. We desperately need a very specific human to step through a rift, and lo and behold, he appears. The odds of all that happening are...not just astronomical, but *galactic*."

"Yet they happened."

"Yet they happened," Millennia agreed, shifting Turtle over so she could sit up and take the offered mug. "I don't know, man, when you start getting into theoretical territory—like string theory, causal sets, and all that, things get real messy." Looking down, she murmured, "But it makes you think that maybe things and people are more connected than we know."

"So what cosmic force set you up with Isabella?" She curled one long brown leg under herself and let the other dangle off the bed, silently willing Turtle to stay tucked in the other woman's lap. "Personally, my money's on the Flying Spaghetti Monster."

"Knowing the life we lead, I wouldn't be surprised."

Helix was quiet for a minute. "The Chinese believe there's an old man who lives in the moon. He ties all predetermined couples together with red string, and once they're linked, nothing can stop them from finding each other one day."

"Maybe that's it," Millennia said, swallowing hard. "Maybe that's why she always finds me. There's this...this cosmic string tying us together. Leading her back to me. God, by now it's gotta look like a fucking cat's cradle."

"Do you think you can keep walking away like this?" Helix asked.

"I've done it every year so far, and it's always like a knife in my gut." Millennia took a healthy swig of enhanced tea and gestured down at herself. "Look at me. I've got so many holes I should be leaking tea like fucking Swiss cheese. I'm bleeding internally right now, and you can't even tell."

"*I* can."

"It's an easy choice," Millennia said, not seeming to hear her. "I'm going to hurt no matter what, so I may as well be happy for a little while. It's worth it to me. *She's* worth it. All of it; the pain, the, the heartache—she's worth every goddamn second of it." The last part was said fiercely to the cooling mug of tea clenched between her hands. The tea seemed to believe her; it trembled in fear, practically begging for mercy.

Helix rescued the intimidated tea and set it down on the bedside table next to her own untouched mug. Gently, she took the smaller woman in her arms and turned her around so that they were spooning. Millennia's unrestrained sobs burst out of her like a ruptured cell, shaking her whole body and reverberating into Helix's chest through her back. So much pain should have torn the physicist to shreds, but somehow she withstood it. She locked her own arm over the one that was pressed against her chest, like the single pressure point that held a splintering piece of glass together.

Helix stayed with her through it all, swaddling her close and speaking to her. They were nonsense things, the words that she said: Promises of fairy tale endings and a *deus ex machina*, meant to soothe and calm. The cat named Turtle climbed atop the two women and inserted her malleable body between them, adding a mellow counterpoint to her owner's cherry-wine murmurs.

Aided by friend and cat and tea enhanced with the gentlest GH available, the heartsick Dog's breathing slowed. Lamplight from the altar played across her slack face and winked out between her eyelids. Her grip on Helix's arm relaxed.

And finally—finally—she slept.

# Specs

The little house in Astoria was asleep when Specs opened the front door. His suit—clean but not too clean, with a tiny coffee stain on one cuff and a river delta of wrinkles across the shirt—whispered quietly to itself as he eased the deadbolt closed. He stepped over a skateboard, a helmet, and a minefield of Transformers strewn across the living room floor.

Pausing at a closed door covered in Black Panther and Young Justice posters (and one from Sailor Moon Crystal tacked on a corner, like a guilty afterthought), he eased it open. The bluish glow of a night-light showed him a lumpy bed and one dark arm flung outside the covers.

He let out the breath that he'd been holding and closed the door again. Down the hall he opened a second door and entered the silent room behind it. In the faint light that filtered through the curtains, he saw the shine of pale rose-colored silk against mahogany skin. The head wrap she wore looked good on her, as did his old t-shirt. She had his pillow tucked in the curve of her upper body. Loose-limbed and dreaming, she was everything he could ever want in a homecoming.

Kneeling down, Specs gently smoothed his fingers across the skin under her head wrap. "Gracie," he whispered. "Gracie."

She stirred and cracked her eyes open. "Mani?" she asked groggily, letting go of the pillow with one hand so she could rub her face.

"Go back to sleep. I just wanted you to know I'm home."

"Henry's sick," she murmured. "'S got a fever."

"He'll be better in the morning," Specs promised. "I love you."

"Love you too. Night."

He undressed quietly, electing to simply strip down to his boxers. Sitting on the edge of the bed, he removed his prosthesis and neoprene sleeve and set both within easy reach. He sank back into the comfort of their bed—sans pillow—and closed his eyes.

It seemed that only seconds passed between that moment and gradual sunlight falling across his face. Grace was gone from her side of the bed.

Stretching, Specs rubbed his eyes and sat up. He reached for the prosthesis and sleeve combo and pulled them back in place, rubbing at the sore muscles a bit as he went. His prosthesis was comfortable enough in general, but the strain of working a Day was never kind to his body. He would have to go in to Dr. Gupta soon for a check-up.

In the slender house's well-used kitchen, Grace was making breakfast. "Morning, sleepyhead," she said, grinning as he came around the island. She was just as beautiful this morning in a charcoal pantsuit and sky blue shirt as she had been the night before, and she knew it. "I think I'm making pancakes. You want any juice? For some reason, we have two cartons of apple juice and one orange."

"Mmm. Morning," Specs said, pecking a kiss first onto her crafted curls and then her upturned mouth. "You should have woken me up."

"Making breakfast every now and then won't kill me," she said, checking the inside of a sausage patty for any sign of pink. "It might kill both of *you*, though."

"Death by chocolate chip pancake," he said, leaning over to smell the brown-speckled creations on the griddle. "There are worse ways to go."

Grace snorted and put one manicured hand on her hip. "Those are the burned bits from my test batch. Megatron might've gotten the rest of them."

Specs winced. "There's a reason that guinea pig weighs four pounds."

"Don't act like it's all my fault," Grace said. "Your son is the one who fed him Reeses Pieces when he ran out of pellets."

"Where is my son, by the way? Misery loves company." Specs stole another kiss from his wife's laughing mouth and left the kitchen, padding down the carpeted hallway on one foot of skin and bone and one made of metal and polyurethane.

He knocked on the poster-covered door and cracked it open. "Henry?"

A muffled voice called back, "Hey, Dad. You can come in."

"Thanks, buddy," he said, opening the door all the way.

Henry was sitting up in bed, the covers completely flung off. He was small for a ten year-old, with his mom's deep black eyes and his old man's long-fingered hands.

Specs was careful to close the door completely behind him. He sat on the edge of the bed and ruffled Henry's fluffy hair. "How did it go?"

"Pretty good," he said with a shrug. "She almost made it out the door, but I took the pill and she came back. I got a bunch 'a juice and chicken soup the day before so she didn't even have to go out. We stayed on the couch and watched TV all day. I think an elephant might've gone by once, and then someone started yelling in some weird language, but I told her it was just Mrs. Henkelman's crazy brother who's from Iceland."

Specs pulled his son's head forward and kissed his crown. "Smart man. I'm sorry you had to use the pill."

Henry tried to shrug the compliment off, but the edge of a smile still bloomed across his face. "'S okay. It was better than last year."

"I know, buddy. Still, a fever's not nice. You did good."

Grinning, he said, "Thanks, Dad. So what'd ya see?"

"First things first," Specs said, nodding at the door. "Go say nice things about Mom's pancakes, and I'll tell you everything on the way to the park. We'll get brunch."

"Deal." Henry hopped out of bed and bolted for the kitchen with Specs not far behind him.

Grace smiled at her two boys and waved the spatula at a trio of plates covered in lopsided golden-brown pancakes and fat sausage patties. "Dig in, you animals."

"Thanks Mom!" Henry called, scooping his plate up with both hands.

"Baby, wait." When he paused obediently, Grace put the back of her hand against his forehead.

Henry looked at her like she was crazy. "Mom? What're you doing?"

"I—" Frowning, Grace pulled her hand away. "I have no idea. Sorry, baby; go eat your breakfast. You want any juice?"

"Apple!" he chirped, crashing down into his spot at the kitchen table.

"Hey, take it easy, buddy," Specs said. He grabbed both remaining plates and took them over to the table.

"How was the retreat?" Grace asked as she set an amber glass in front of Henry. Her purse buzzed twice, but she ignored it. "You got home pretty late last night."

"It was a pain in the butt," Specs answered honestly, biting into his pancakes. All things considered, they weren't half-bad. "But we got a lot of good work done. You guys do anything interesting for the Day?"

"Just the usual, I guess." Unconsciously, Grace's hand strayed over to Henry and circled the back of his head in a protective gesture. "Tell you the truth, I barely remember it. Must not have been that exciting, huh?"

Specs shared a wink with his son. "Yeah. Must not've."

## The New Kid

The New Kid was so tired that he felt like his bones were made of putty. The moment the door of his room at the Doghouse closed, he fell into his mussed sheets and immediately bid *adieu* to his consciousness. He slept the sort of deep, unrestricted sleep usually reserved for coma patients and the recently deceased, and when he woke up he couldn't have told you his own name.

A shower and shave helped this immensely. As he pulled on clean clothes, he felt less like his insides were being filtered through sand and more like there were just some lingering bits stuck in unfortunate places. Cat's warning about the consequences should he choose to skip his medical check still rang between his ears; in fact, he was pretty sure he'd had at least one nightmare about her chasing him with a thermometer.

Someone knocked at his door, and he answered it with a stifled yawn. On the other side was a willowy blond man in slacks and a crisp white shirt, holding a wooden box. "Kevin Harrison?" he asked.

Still feeling gritty in spite of his shower, the New Kid rubbed his eye and said, "Yeah, um—yeah, that's me."

"I'm Agent Jensen, from Archival Requests," he said. "We handle written missives or packages left for future agents and departments. I've got a collection of letters archived on August 15 of 1914, scheduled to be released to you today."

"For me?" the New Kid asked, dumbfounded. "They've just been—what, sitting there for a hundred years? But I didn't even—I only just—a *hundred years?*"

Agent Jensen smiled and shifted the box to one hand. With the other he pulled out a tablet and offered it to the New Kid. "I need you to sign off on it, please."

"Okay." He searched the screen for a minute and said, "So, do I just, um, sign anywhere? With my finger?"

"Oh, no," Agent Jensen said with a laugh. "Sorry, I didn't think you were *that* new. You have to hold your thumb in the middle and verify your call sign."

The implications didn't dawn on him immediately. "O-oh. Okay. Um. Could you—could you just go away for, like, ten seconds while I do it?"

"Sorry, I have to watch you verify your identity," the other agent said with an apologetic shrug. "A lot of the information that we look after is highly confidential or classified. We can't cut corners."

Swallowing, the New Kid put this thumb on the black screen and said, as quietly as he could manage, "Um, um, Kevin Harrison, call sign: Sneaks."

The screen blinked to green, and he mutely traded it for the wooden box. When he could bring himself to look up, he saw only a sunny smile on Agent Jensen's face.

"That's funny. Most people want something dramatic," he said. After a second, he held out one large, square hand. "I'm Nikolaj."

"Uh, Kevin," the New Kid said, shaking the offered hand. It was warm, and oddly comforting. Something unwound deep in him, something that he hadn't even realized was tense.

"It's nice to meet you, Kevin," Nikolaj said. "Maybe I'll see you around some time. It's a small place, you know."

"Tell that to my feet," the New Kid said without thinking.

Nikolaj snickered. "I should get back, but—welcome to CIRIUS, Agent Harrison." He licked his lips, nodded, and said, "Kevin."

His face flushing now for an entirely different reason than usual, the New Kid snuck a few looks at Nikolaj's retreating back before turning his attention to the box. It was about as long as a loaf of bread, and made of some fragrant wood that had been darkened by time. For having been locked away for a hundred years, it was in excellent condition. The iron hinges weren't even rusty.

Closing the door behind him, he undid the clasps and opened the lid, revealing a stack of about a dozen tri-folded letters tied up with purple ribbon. They were creamy with quality rather than buttery with age, and pleasant against the sensitive ridges of his fingers. He unwrapped the first of them and let his eyes fall on the graceful salutation.

*Dearest Kevin,*

*I remember everything.*

The New Kid folded the letter closed as a sudden spike of realization lodged itself in his brain. It burned and dug in, growing hooks. There was no question as to who these letters had come from, just as there was no question that she had probably been dead for half of a century.

He read them all, pausing only to get a spare roll of tissue from the bathroom. They told the story of a few rich years spent in London, of the scandal that came out when her crocus tattoo was revealed, and of the only man who would agree to marry her with such a thing hanging over her head. His name was James Bordeaux, he was a captain in Her Majesty's Royal Navy, and he was the kindest man she had ever met. He too had a tattoo: A sea serpent that curled around his leg. They sailed the world together, and made each other ludicrously happy.

They had two daughters, Charlotte and Anna. The oldest, Charlotte, was the spitting image of her gentle, serious father, and Anna was the fulfillment of every parent's wish that their difficult child would some day give birth to one just like them. She was vivacious and bright, and frogs were her favorite thing in the entire world. There was even one cupped in her hands the day that she collapsed suddenly in the family's little garden, allowing it to hop away to freedom. The town's doctor diagnosed her with tuberculosis, and in the early days of 1913 she passed away with a soft sigh. She was nine years old.

Unable to stay in the newly quiet house, the family moved to New York at the beginning of spring and stayed until the end of the following summer. Elaine Bordeaux—formerly Miss Elaine Penrose—promised to brave the madness of the Day Out of Time so that she could find the Dogs of that age and ask them to keep these letters for him. *It is strange,* she wrote, *to think that I have spent all these years missing someone whose parents are not yet born! What an odd, wonderful life we lead.*

There were thirteen letters in all. By the end of the second, the burning spike in his head had burrowed down the back of his neck and into his chest. It twisted in a friendly way, becoming intimately familiar with the contours of his breaking heart.

Not caring about the pile of spent tissue beside him, or the hot marbles behind his eyes, the New Kid picked up the first letter and read it again.

*Dearest Kevin,*

*I remember everything. That first and last glorious view of the skyline, the horseless cars, Romain the lovesick French soldier! I remember all of it. But most importantly, I remember all of you. Even when I am a hundred years old and have seen a hundred thousand things, I shall never want to forget you.*

*I wrote down as much as I could once Mattie tucked in for the night. I must have looked positively mad, scribbling away as I did! But I didn't want one single thing to fade from my memory. Imagine how it felt this morning, when I woke up and I could recall your face as if you were standing before me. It was like being born and realizing that you remembered the miracle of Heaven.*

*I want you to know what this has meant to me. When my heart is broken, and I feel as if I can't get past it, I will always know that things can get better. I will hold hope for the future deep in my soul where nothing can hurt it, and it will see me through my darkest times.*

*Soon enough I will be someone's wife, and I suppose that I will have to fade a bit so as not to overshadow my husband. But for today—for this Day—I was truly spectacular. I will never be the same, and it is all your fault.*

*Thank you.*

*Love,*
*Elaine*

# ACKNOWLEDGMENTS

A funny thing happens when you get told *no* often enough in this business: You come to accept it as inevitable. Anyone who has ever sent out query letter after query letter knows what I'm talking about. It's like a defense mechanism; you see that reply in your inbox, and you say to yourself, *Okay, here we go again.* Because it doesn't have to hurt as much if you see it coming, right?

But it does hurt, just in smaller ways. You become obsessed with the idea of traditional publishing because you need that validation. You need someone in *the biz* to tell you that you aren't just a delusional hack who couldn't string a coherent thought together if your life depended on it. You may not realize it, but what you're really looking for—maybe even more than validation—is permission. And it turns out that you really don't need it at all; you just have to channel your inner Cat Fiyero and decide to do what you damn well please.

In truth, I'm a little overwhelmed at the prospect of writing one of these pages at last. My heart is so full with love for these people that I barely know where to begin.

Except, that's a lie. I know exactly where to begin.

First and foremost, I want to raise a glass to Gay Clifton, #1 fan and mother extraordinaire. I think you knew where this path would lead way back in the third grade, when you helped a precocious eight-year-old craft a new story for the class anthology that spanned two whole pages (single-spaced), instead of the ten lines that everyone else wrote. Twenty years later, you're still helping in every way imaginable.

To Lindsay Francis, bestest friend and science sounding board. Thanks for letting me test out every harebrained hypothesis and thought process on you, and thanks for gently correcting my faulty knowledge when necessary. Who else would spend half an hour helping me figure out exactly how many gallons of water a Savannah tank might theoretically hold?

To Erin Glew, best friend and favorite speed-reader. Thanks for waking me up two days after a new draft with an anguished *HOW DARE YOU* message, and thanks for always being one of the first to encourage me to *Do itttt*. I hope that I always have you in my corner.

To all my beta readers, near and far, for telling me when I was great (but more so for telling me when I wasn't). To Kaitlyn Clifton, for filling me to the brim with sisterly support. To Mia Fairooz and Divya Padhiar, for answering every cultural question that I lobbed your way. To Manon Fourneret, for your help in correcting my subpar French. To Miranda Moorhead, for bringing my babies to gorgeous life. To Sara Stricker of New Leaf Literary, for helping me make this book what it is—and for believing in it when no one else in the publishing world would. To Jimmy Wood, for telling me one drunken night in Florence that you thought I was going to win.

And to Matt Moore, for telling me to *just make it happen, dude*. Without you I might still be sitting on my ass, waiting for permission to publish my own damn book.

# ABOUT THE AUTHOR

Kelsey Clifton is a science fiction and fantasy writer who hoards books the way dragons hoard gold (seriously, it's becoming a problem). She lives in Houston, Texas with the bossy cat from her websites and too many succulents. *A Day Out of Time* is her debut novel.

Feel free to follow her (because she's a millennial and she needs the attention):

https://kelseyclifton.com
Twitter: @kelsey_writes_
Instagram: @kelsey_writes
Facebook.com/kelseycliftonauthor

Like what she does? Consider becoming a supporter:
www.patreon.com/kelseyclifton

# APPENDICES

# Appendix A
## Cast of Characters

### Gamma Team
*Officers*
CAT: Commander. Real name Alexa Fiyero
SPECS: Lieutenant. Real name Damani Forrester.
GRUNT: Watchdog Captain. Real name Aaron Walker.
DARWIN: Zoologist. Real name Jai Ramachandra.
HELIX: Geneticist and molecular biologist. Real name Devi Ramachandra.
MILLENNIA: Physicist and temporal expert. Real name Eleadora Mendes.

*Watchdog Teams*
ROTTWEILER
—Team Leader: Sasha Conway
—Territory: Command
—Other members: Oz McAfee, Tamika Johnson, Kerry Pierce, Elias Burke, Lindsay Francis, Fahd Kader, Mia Islington, Adam O'Connor, Camilla Caffrey
MALINOIS
—Team Leader: Melanie Ramirez
—Territory: Harlem Meer
—Other members: Raj Patel, Erin Glew, Jackson Pert
VISZLA
—Team Leader: Farrah Zidane
—Territory: The Great Lawn
—Other members: Mal Beeshaw
DOBERMAN
—Team Leader: Frank Edwin
—Territory: Lennox Hill and Upper East Side
—Other members: Cole Kowalski, Heather Pips
PIT BULL
—Team Leader: Marco Cicchi
—Territory: Upper West Side
RIDGEBACK
—Team Leader: Paolo Cicchi

—Territory: Lower East Side
MASTIFF
—Team Leader: Hiroto Loss
—Territory: Umpire Rock
—Other members: Michael Argent, Ren Shibata, Patrick Barker, Paul Vickers, Paul Wilson
KOMONDOR
—Team Leader: Jamal Dubois
—Territory: Lower West Side
—Other members: Ray Branson, Demarcus Dubois, Isadora Ambrosio, Davide Fracchia
SHEPHERD
—Team Leader: Marisol Guevara
—Territory: Yorkville and the Barrio

## Other CIRIUS Members

NEW KID: Temporarily adopted by Gamma for the Day Out of Time.
MAXIMILLIAN TAMIKO: Director of the New York City Doghouse.
CHRIS HAVERTY: Commander of Alpha Team.
DANIEL MCNAB: Commander of Charlie Team.
FERGUS CALHOUN: Commander of Echo Team.
SIA HOUNSOU: Engineer with the Batcave.
SARAH DONOVAN: Member of a Doghouse security team.
DAVID KREVITZ: Former member of Gamma. Deceased.
THERESA TERRELL: Captain of a Doghouse security team.
GABE O'BRIAN: Registered nurse assigned to Med Bay A.
KATHY FRANKS: Environmental specialist with the Savannah.
NIKOLAJ JENSEN: Archivist with the Sticks.

## Time Travelers

HAROLD VANCE JR.: Serial killer from the 1950s.
ELAINE PENROSE: Young Victorian woman.
CAPTAIN JEAN-PAUL RENAULT: French captain under Rochambeau during the American Revolution.
TUBULAR TIM: Tour guide from the 22$^{nd}$ century.
ROMAIN DE COURCY: French soldier under Captain Renault.
ISABELLA PANNIA: Woman from the early half of the 20$^{th}$

century.

GEORGE WASHINGTON: American historical figure.

PRIVATE LICHBERG: English soldier from the American Revolution.

FENIRIS-DUL: Telaran Origin from Telarus IV.

TANOLON: Ouro from Wiconora.

## Civilians

CARLA GERMANOTTI: Tattoo artist.

YASMIN AGITA: Manhattan entrepreneur.

BRIAR JONES: Teenaged natural.

HELEN MORGAN: Performer and club owner from the early half of the 20th century.

LONNIE LAUGHLIN: Hitter for Helen Morgan.

PAT PIERS: Hitter for Helen Morgan.

FRANKIE MATTUCHIO: Runner for Salvatore Maranzano (deceased).

GRACE FORRESTER: Assistant district attorney. Married to Damani Forrester.

HENRY FORRESTER: Eight-year-old son of Grace and Damani Forrester.

# Appendix B
## A Translation of Elaine's Conversation With Captain Renault

"Tell him that we can help him get home, but he has to trust us," Cat said. "Please."

"*These men and women can help you,*" Elaine said in French, gesturing to the Dogs. "*You have to trust them.*"

Captain Renault regarded the group in front of him with suspicion. "*A slave and three women? What help could they possibly be?*"

"*They're incredibly kind, competent people,*" Elaine said. Her tone was now devoid of all its bouncy warmth. "*And they are the only ones who can help you, Captain.*"

His eyes narrowed. "*You overstep yourself, mademoiselle.*"

The Elaine of that morning would have blushed and backed away with an apology. That Elaine, however, had not braved a city out of the daftest science fiction. That Elaine had not negotiated a ceasefire between men who were long dead and men and women who were yet unborn. And that Elaine did not bear a testament to courage on her thigh.

This new Elaine did the unbelievable: She took a step towards the French captain and asked, "*Do I? Good. It's time that someone did.*"

"What the hell is going on?" Cat whispered to Specs.

# Appendix C
# The (Damn) Handbook

- "The Georgian calendar was the first to disregard the illogical rules required to follow a solar calendar. It turned instead to the steady, deliberate phases of the moon as a guide. Twelve months of varying lengths, almost none of which could evenly accommodate a seven-day week, became thirteen perfect months of twenty-eight days each, with only a single day left over in the exact middle...[at the time], King George II of Great Britain, for whom the calendar was named, did not have an amicable relationship with the Catholic Church. In exchange for adopting the new calendar, he offered to name the thirteenth month after the current pope, Benedict XIV. Thus the month of Benedictus was born. Between the reach of the British Empire and the Catholic Church, the reform spread quite thoroughly through Europe and much of the Americas, not to mention down into Africa and even parts of the East. Despite papal support, there was still quite a bit of turmoil over the extra day that seemed to have no place. To quiet the rumors that these 'days out of time' were dangerous, godforsaken things, King George and Pope Benedict invited the Western World to regard them as days of high spirituality. They encouraged meditation upon God and his gifts."

- "*Arcturus orbitonia* is a large spore-based plant from Arcturus Omega, in the Perseus system. Mother plants are imported as needed and stored in-house, where they release their seeds into the environment via controlled bursts 5-7 times a year. The seeds are harvested and stored away from outside influences until they are released to agents. Unlike the ear buds often used by private security, the *Arcturus* buds maintain the integrity of their transmissions across great distances, even across the span of the globe, and they are impossible to hack from the outside; the only way to listen in is to have a bud tuned to the same frequency. The average functional expectancy for a bud is approximately six months...the buds function through psychic intent, and it has been posited that nonverbal communication could be possible with a disciplined mind. Research is even being conducted into the possibility of using the buds to help hearing-impaired agents improve their communication abilities."

- "In 1852, right before that year's day out of time, a pub owner in

Richmond, Virginia named Silas Cooper found himself with a large supply of bananas by accident, and no way to get rid of them. As they were taking up space in his store room and beginning to rot, he gave one away with every pint. When people asked why, he told them that it was to celebrate the day out of time. Sales shot through the roof, to the point where Mr. Cooper was out of bananas by dinner. The next year he approached several local business owners, and they all agreed to offer strange deals on the day out of time. One candlemaker hired an artist to draw small horses on all of her candles, and a grocer gave away a spool of ribbon every time somebody bought a bunch of carrots, and Mr. Cooper himself ordered an even larger amount of bananas. Through their efforts, the cultural significance of the days out of time began to experience a shift from that of the holy to that of the secular and strange."

• "Normal episodic memories begin in the prefrontal cortex and are then transferred to the hippocampus, where they become part of our short- or long-term memory banks. For reasons which are currently being debated, the memories that are formed on a Day Out of Time are more dense than normal. Some neurologists think that an increase in serotonin production is to blame, similar to the process of waking up in the middle of the night, having a thought, and then being unable to remember it the next day. Others have suggested that it involves a chemical that we currently have no name for. Whatever the cause, there don't seem to be enough neural pathways to support the transfer of these denser memories from the prefrontal cortex to the hippocampus. While we think serotonin interferes with a norm's ability to retain the dense memories, it could be the opposite for naturals. The leading theory suggests that our extra neural pathways only activate when in the presence of high levels of serotonin, such as during REM sleep. A high percentage of naturals report being able to accurately recall all of their dreams...Current thinking suggests that the mutation for retaining these memories is actually tens of thousands of years old. As it was neither beneficial nor detrimental up to a certain point in history, it was quietly passed on without really making an impact, but recent speculation from our associates at the New Delhi Doghouse suggests that the increase in Day activity is going to have a direct impact on global survival rates. Within two or three thousand years, the saturation level of the mutation could reach up to fifteen percent of the population."

• "Rifts require a power source, so they take energy from the ambient dimensions, which creates an endothermic reaction and results in a spooky 'cold spot' feeling. It also disturbs the atoms of anything that passes through and creates a unique ion signature that is trackable with the correct technology.

The adventure continues in *After/Effects*, out March 24, 2019.